WINGS OF A DOVE

The first volume of
The Zoë Journals Series

by

BEVERLY BUSH

WORD PUBLISHING
Dallas·London·Vancouver·Melbourne

PUBLISHED BY WORD PUBLISHING, DALLAS, TEXAS

This novel is a work of fiction. Names, characters, places, and incidents are either the product of the author's imagination or are used fictitiously. Any resemblance to actual events, locales, organizations, or persons, living or dead, is entirely coincidental and beyond the intent of either the author or the publisher.

Unless otherwise indicated, Scripture quotations used in this book are from the Holy Bible, New International Version (NIV). Copyright © 1973, 1978, 1984 International Bible Society. Used by permission of Zondervan Bible Publishers.

Chapter 35 includes lyrics from "Arms of Love" by Craig Musseau © 1991 Mercy Publishing (administered by Music Services). All rights reserved. Used by permission.

LIBRARY OF CONGRESS CATALOGING-IN-PUBLICATION DATA:

Bush, Beverly.
   Wings of a dove / Beverly Bush
     p. cm.
   ISBN 0-8499-3887-2
   I. Title.
Ps3569.M5114W5 1996
813'.54—DC20

95-36079
CIP

678901234   987654321

PRINTED IN THE UNITED STATES OF AMERICA

To Carol and Diane,

my "Aaron and Hur"

Acknowledgments

My warmest thanks to:

Ernie Owen, who shepherded this book from proposal to publishing . . .

Jane Helmeczi for graciously sharing her expertise in physical therapy . . .

My exacting but encouraging critique group: Elaine, Hank, Dick, and Martha.

1

⁊

From Zoë's Prayer Journal:

August 24: Dear heavenly Father, here I am, coming to You again about Leslie. You gave my daughter her life, Lord, but she's not alive. Not anymore. I look at her pictures from these past eleven years of her marriage to Charles, and with each photo, I see her diminishing: the loss of her spunk, her liveliness, her life. She hides those splendid green eyes under bangs that are much too long. When she's with Charles, she looks like a frightened doe. And she is afraid. Of him. Please work in both their lives, help them communicate and listen, and, bottom line, Lord, heal their marriage. I love You and I trust You and I thank You! In Jesus' name, amen.

LESLIE DIDN'T HEAR CHARLES COME INTO THE KITCHEN, but she sensed his presence. She always did. A silent alarm seemed to go off. Warning: Proceed with caution.

He leaned over her shoulder as she finished spreading margarine on three slices of bread and reached for the peanut butter.

"*Les*-lie." He accented the *Les*. "Is one of those—for me?" He measured out each word so it echoed like an accusation.

She grimaced. *I wasn't concentrating,* she berated herself. *I was too busy thinking about my new patient at work.*

Without looking at Charles, she reached in the bread sack for another slice. Grabbing her shoulders, he turned her around. She glanced past him to the kids, who were beginning to tease each other at the breakfast table.

Charles seemed not to hear them. "How many times do I have to tell you?" he asked. "I do not *like* margarine on a peanut-butter sandwich. I cannot imagine how you ever got such a ridiculous idea. My mother never—" He broke off and shrugged, clearly deeming her hopeless.

She turned back to the sandwiches.

His hand on her shoulder again. "Would you give me the courtesy of looking at me when I talk to you?"

"I thought you were finished." She turned and tried to focus on the knife-straight part in his meticulously combed, tobacco-colored hair.

"Not yet. How did you manage to put twenty-two miles on the car yesterday?" He emphasized the first syllable of twenty. "It's only six miles to the physical therapy center."

Oh, Lord, the odometer again. She never knew when he'd check it. She felt her face flush as she tried desperately to remember. "I, uh . . ." she stalled. "After I left work, I went to pick up your suit at the cleaners."

"And?"

"I picked up your suit . . ." She stalled again, voice barely audible, knowing he'd already figured that was no more than three miles extra.

"And what else?"

The harder she tried, the less she remembered. "I—I had to get some bread." She hated lying, but she hated his inquisitions even more.

"Mmm." He stared at her, the set of his mouth accented by his close-trimmed moustache that formed two yellow-brown slashes angling down at the outer edges. At last he turned to the breakfast area.

As he approached, Michelle and Scott's playfulness ended abruptly.

"What is that on your face, Michelle?" Charles demanded. "Your eyes—your cheeks—you look like a trollop! What are you trying to do? Imitate your mother?" He laughed a mirthless laugh. "You are not going to day camp like that! You're twelve years old, in case you have forgotten. Go wipe it off."

Leslie turned to look at her daughter. She'd been busy fixing lunches when Michelle came in. But now she saw the black eyeliner, green eyeshadow, the exaggerated bloom on her cheeks. Charles didn't like makeup on women, period, and this *was* a bit much. But after all, Michelle could easily pass for a fifteen-year-old. A well-developed fifteen-year-old. No wonder she wanted to . . .

"But Dad," Michelle protested.

He pulled her out of her chair. "Go—take—it—off!"

She wrested her arm free from his grip and tossed her copper-colored hair over one shoulder as she flounced out of the room, muttering under her breath. She wasn't wearing a bra, Leslie noted, and definitely needed one. She'd better get to Michelle before Charles saw *that*.

"She came in while I was fixing the lunches. I hadn't seen . . ." She heard the rustle of the newspaper and let her voice trail off, hoping he'd become absorbed in the morning headlines. As she popped the sandwiches in their sacks, the phone rang. Leslie picked it up.

"It's Mother," a cheery voice announced. "Just picked the most gorgeous tomatoes. Okay if I run some by to you now?"

"Oh, Mom. Not now."

"Problems?" Leslie heard the concern in her mother's voice.

"You've got it."

"I'll let you go and bring them over after work. Love you, darlin'."

"Thanks, Mom. Me too, you."

She picked up her cereal bowl, headed to the table, and tried to relax in the still-cool breeze coming through the sliding glass door. Already, the sun glared off the water of the tiny lake outside. Another hot one in store.

Charles peered over the newspaper at Scott. "Scott, you're eating like a baby. Certainly making as much mess." He raised his right hand, spreading out the fingers, then tucked them into a fist. "Even though you have no fingers on your right hand, Scott, you can still use that hand to anchor the toast while you butter it." He demonstrated, placing his fist on top of the toast.

Leslie pressed her lips together. *There he goes again, rubbing it in with Scott,* she thought. *If I'd buttered the toast for the poor kid, this wouldn't have happened.* She looked at her son. With his head bowed, she couldn't see his face—only the tousle of dark, straight hair. He seemed to grow smaller in his chair as he moved his right hand under his napkin. In a moment he asked to be excused.

Two minutes, Leslie thought, *and Charles has everyone upset.* She sighed. She'd triggered it. She knew about the peanut-butter sandwiches; why hadn't she remembered? She tried so hard to conform to all his likes and dislikes, to second-guess him, but she blew it again and again.

She stared at his impeccably manicured nails, the starched cuffs of his white shirt. *Perfect.* The whole shirt was perfect. He saw to that. The one "domestic chore" he'd undertaken when she went back to work was ironing his own shirts. The laundry couldn't get them right.

4

She cleared her throat. "You have a busy day today?"

He nodded. "Yes. Starting to get some data on that Midwest flood. Lots of material to process. That is really going to cost the company; I guarantee you. Also, I need to get the books up to date after work on the Hope for the Children Fund." He smiled for the first time that morning. "Did I tell you I had a letter from Raoul? What a kid!"

Raoul again. Sometimes she thought Charles cared more for the "adopted son" he contributed to in Guatemala than . . . No sense in dwelling on that. "I have a full schedule too," she said. "And a new patient. Body-surfing accident. Twenty-two."

Charles shook his head. "I suppose he will try to sue? These surfer egocentrics. Think they are immortal and then want to cash in when something goes wrong. Just as well Scott can't get into that subculture."

"Can't?"

"Well, how in the world can he hang on to a surfboard to get out there? With his teeth?"

"Charles," she said quietly. "This fellow doesn't use a board. He's a *body* surfer. His body rides the wave. He—"

Charles continued as though she hadn't spoken. "Honestly, Leslie, you are so unrealistic about your son. When you have no bloody fingers on your right hand, how do you hang on? Face it. The child is defective!"

"Shhhh!" She frowned, not wanting Scott to hear.

"A defect!" he shouted. Standing, he shoved back his chair and left the room.

ॐ

With Charles's stinging label of Scott still echoing in her mind, Leslie slammed the car door, jammed the key into the ignition, and twisted it so hard it broke away from her key ring. *How can he do that to his own son?* she fumed as she backed out of the garage. *He's had ten years to accept this "defect" and still can't bear the idea that he could have fathered a child that's not absolutely perfect.* As she turned into the street, she replayed the scene in her head.

She groaned. "Well, I started it this morning," she admitted aloud. "I see that. I got him into that hypercritical mode. I should have known better."

Turning onto Lake Forest Drive, she stuffed a tape of praise songs into the cassette deck. "Got to detach from all that," she told herself. "Got to focus on something good."

The music washed over her like a balm. By the time she turned into the parking lot, she'd joined the chorus. "I will call upon the Lord . . ." She waited for the number to finish before she left the car and pushed through the glass doors that read "Saddleback Valley Physical Therapy Center."

"Hi, Terry," she greeted the office manager. "How was your dinner out last night?"

Terry frowned and pointed a thumb down.

"Uh-oh. Sorry 'bout that." Leslie moved through the reception room with its fresh flowers and green plants and turned down the hallway, waving to her associate. "You got an early start, huh Kelly?"

On the wall just outside her office, a World War II poster of a Rosie the Riveter defense worker read, "We can do it!"

And that, for her, neatly summarized the positive spirit of the center and her work there. *Good things happen here,* she thought. *We work together, and people get better. Different— really different—from home.*

At her desk she reviewed her schedule and the charts for each patient. First a young woman, improving from an auto accident, able to drive again without a neck brace. Then Mrs. Jackson—Myrtle. Stroke patient. Walking again with a walker but still discouraged. Leslie's eyes swept the posted schedule on the cork board by her desk. Fifteen patients—they'd keep her mind off home.

She read the doctor's report on her new patient, David Matthews. Paralyzed two months ago and just out of the hospital. She wondered about his mental state. It had to be tough for anybody to wonder if he'd walk again, but especially for an athletic, active young man.

Outside the office she saw Jan, a physical therapy aide, working with Harry, age eighty-seven, patiently walking him up and down the corridor as he leaned on a four-pronged cane.

"Good, Harry!" Jan encouraged. "You're walking so much better than when you came in today!"

A note on Leslie's memo pad reminded her of Jan's anniversary. She reached into her desk and pulled out a bottle of soap-bubble solution and a wand. Standing in the doorway, she blew bubbles and hummed the tune to "Here Comes the Bride." The aide laughed, and for the first time, Harry cracked a smile.

Midmorning, as she finished with a man struggling to regain use of his hand after surgery, she found her thoughts shifting to her son, remembering how he had hidden his hand that morning at the breakfast table. *Poor kid, he—* She looked up to see a wheelchair pushed by a youthful man wearing baggy shorts, thongs, and one of the deepest tans she'd ever seen on a blond.

But her gaze gravitated immediately to the young man in the chair. Sandy hair, cut short, possibly growing out from a crew cut, an angular face with a strong jaw accented by a deep dimple, and eyes that matched his turquoise, open-necked shirt. A well-toned upper body contrasted with much thinner legs that angled out from his khaki shorts.

She caught her breath and realized she was staring. *All the girls must be lined up for this one,* she thought.

She approached his wheelchair and said, "Hi, David. I'm Leslie." She stooped down to his eye level.

He grinned, revealing slightly overlapping eye teeth, and his eyes crinkled at the corners as he sized her up. "Okay if I call you 'Les'?" he asked.

Charles's accusatory "*Les*-lie" echoed through her mind, and she clenched her fists.

David didn't miss it. "Was that a 'no'?"

"Sorry, it's a definite 'no,'" she said firmly.

He thought a moment. "Sounds like 'less'? That it? As in 'less than'?"

She looked away from him.

"No. Not you." He shook his head. "Besides, don't you believe that less can be more?"

She relaxed. "Yes, but if it's all the same to you, I'll be Leslie. Do you want to be Dave or David?"

"David. A man after God's own heart."

A Christian, was he? "And are you?" she asked.

"A man after . . . ?" He shrugged. "I want to be. Want to be all that He wants me to be."

His face was so earnest she felt herself melt. If he were to walk, what a privilege it would be for her to be a part of his rehab. And if he didn't walk, well, she'd help him do the most he could. A vision of him in wheelchair sports played across her mind, but she blinked it away.

"I want that for you too," she said softly. "We'll both pray that He'll use me to help."

"Good. Because if it's His will I wanna . . ." David's voice broke and he bent his head down. She heard him swallow and knew it hurt.

"Okay, David." Her voice was gentle. "What's on your mind? You can level with me."

"Deal," he said at last. He cleared his throat and looked up at her. "Bottom line: I wanna swim, wanna bike, wanna run, wanna ski, wanna dance. Who'm I kiddin'? I'd even settle for walking. But I'm petrified. Maybe I won't. And it—it—"

"It really bums you out," she finished his sentence.

"I was going to use a more graphic term. But yeah. You've got it."

"I don't blame you. I would be ranting and raving if I were you."

"Well, I've done that." He showed her his bruised knuckles.

"Hole in the wall?" she asked.

He nodded.

"You animal!" She smiled.

"Yeah, some animal. Look at me. You've read Dr. Scanlon's report?"

She nodded.

"He's not sure about walking. My MRI shows lumbar compression fractures. Man, I can't do diddly-squat with my legs. Hard to believe how quickly I lost muscle." He looked down at his legs with their fading tan and dry, flaking skin. "It's like, from the waist down I'm something out of Somalia. Wasted."

"Well, I've seen worse." She stood and picked up a clipboard. "Lots worse."

"Yeah. Bet you have. Didn't mean to have a pity party."

She pulled a chair over and sat down beside him. "Let's review your medical records. Fortunately, you're in good physical condition as far as heart, lungs, liver, all the vital stuff. You have bowel and bladder control. That's a biggie." She smiled at him. "Listen. You're in better shape than you realize. So! I'd like to hear from you just what happened. Then we'll talk about where you are now and where you're going."

"Okay. What happened." He leaned forward, obviously

eager to tell his story. "I don't want to brag, but I'm not a novice. I love body-surfing. People say, why don't you board? Well, it's like somebody said: This is the chamber music of surfing. Refined, intimate. Just you and the wave. Sometimes you can look right through the tube. And then there's God's power in that wave. Awesome." His eyes shone. "Well, this wave was really epic. It was right after that hurricane in Mexico, and we were getting double overheads."

"Meaning?"

"Twice as tall as a guy standing at the bottom of the wave. So—I was swimming back out and tried to dive under a wave. It turned out to be huge—and hollow. Broke on top of me, whiplashed me."

She winced inwardly as he continued. "Basically I got drilled down into the sand. Fortunately, ol' Clyde, the guy who brought me here, saw I was in trouble."

She made notes. "So you went to the hospital."

"Yup. For eight l-o-o-ong weeks."

"And did you have inpatient rehab?"

"Yeah. At first it was as basic as being able to roll from side to side. Then both occupational and physical therapy. Couple, three times a day. You know, so I could dress, shower, get in and out of my chair in the therapy gym."

"Good. So what did you do before the accident, David, besides body-surf?"

"Well, I had another year to finish at Cal State Long Beach when I decided to take some time off. I'd been on the ski team, so last winter I got a job teaching skiing in the Sierras. At Mammoth. That seemed to work pretty well with the summer job I've had all through college. I coach a community swim team. While I was on staff at the ski school, I trained to be on the ski patrol. So I was planning to do that this winter." He gave a short, ironic laugh. "I *don't* think so."

"Maybe next year." She gave him a confident nod. "Tell me what you can do for yourself. Manage the wheelchair just inside, or how about parking lots? The car?"

"Yeah. But doors and stuff are hard. That's why Clyde helped me in."

"Bathe?"

He nodded. "I have a shower bench. But I need some help in and out."

"Dress?"

"With a little help from friends. The pants, y'know."

"Transfer in and out of the wheelchair?"

He wobbled his hand back and forth. "Need a little help. I lose my balance, fall backward sometimes."

"Pain?"

"Yeah. Back. Mainly some achiness, tightness."

"Did you learn pressure releases? You're strong enough to use your arms to lift yourself up, so you don't get sores?"

He nodded.

"Can you roll over, change positions at night?"

"Tough, but it's getting easier."

"How about sensation? How much do you feel in your legs?"

"I can feel my toes and the outside and back of this leg." He pointed to his left foot, and Leslie saw his Teva sandals. "My right thigh. Sometimes there's a little tingling down that leg."

"Those are good signs." Leslie stood, feeling a stirring of hope. "Okay. Let's get you out of the chair and onto the low treatment mat. I'll get Brynne, my aide, to help. Then we'll check the range of motion of your trunk and legs, strength, sensation, all those good things. And we'll start working on getting your arms, trunk, back, and stomach stronger."

In case . . . she thought. *In case he doesn't get his legs back.*

꒰

As she left the center late that afternoon, Leslie felt an inner elation, a certainty that there was no other work in the world she'd rather do. *At least,* she thought, *this part of my life holds hope, promise. There's such an intimacy during those thirty or sixty minutes I spend with each person. They tell you where they hurt, open up, aren't afraid to be honest. Sometimes I feel I'm looking into their very souls. And I—with some help from the Lord—I can make them feel better. What a high! Sometimes, watching a patient improve, it's like—like what?* She tried to think of a simile. *Like watching a flower unfold. And they appreciate me. Look forward to coming in. For some, it's the highlight of their day.*

Today she'd made Carrie, her last patient, recovering from shoulder surgery, cry. But she'd at last stretched Carrie's arm high above her head so her surgeon wouldn't have to manipulate her under anesthesia to regain motion. And even that crotchety Mrs. Anderson had worked hard on her hip-strengthening exercises for a change and said thank you when she left.

But David—would he walk again? That was the thrill, the challenge of her work. "Lord, help me. Help him. Heal him, please Lord," she murmured as she unlocked her car.

The steering wheel was so hot she wondered if her flesh would sizzle as she drove home.

Home. Charles was likely to be too hot to touch too. And how would she find the kids after he'd picked them up from day camp? Michelle petulant and demanding, she'd bet. And Scott retreating further and further into himself. Just thinking of them made her feel powerless, defeated. How could she help them when she couldn't help herself? She looked at the therapy center and longed to go back in and stay. *My home is not a home,* she thought. *Just a house. A house full of discord and pain. If Charles is still in his hypercritical mode where the smallest thing's a trigger point, it's not going to be pretty. Better get myself together, see if I can humor him, distract him, placate him— somehow, some way, buy a little peace.*

2

LESLIE PAUSED, HAND ON THE FRONT-DOOR HANDLE. HOW she dreaded opening the door and facing Charles and his accusations, sarcasm, contentiousness. *Don't have a choice,* she told herself, taking a deep breath before she stepped into the house. *Walking on eggs,* she thought; *coming home is always walking on eggs.*

As she closed the door, she heard Charles call out, "That you?" The voice was light, cheerful.

She shook her head. Was this the same man who'd lit into her and the kids this morning? Exhaling slowly, she felt a wash of relief but quickly wondered how long his good humor would last. She tried to match his tone. "Nobody else!"

"Good," he said, coming around the corner from the kitchen. His kiss was warm, lingering. She glanced into the kitchen. Flowers on the table. Places set. "Charles!" she exclaimed. "Did you do that?"

He grinned and nodded. "I cannot tell a lie."

"What a great guy!"

"Come on. Let's have a drink." She saw that he'd already switched his white shirt and suit pants for a casual plaid top and shorts.

"Be right with you," she said. "Where are the kids?"

"Watching TV. Want your usual?"

"Yes," she called, heading upstairs to change into shorts.

When she came back down, she opened the oven to check the pot roast. The rich, meaty aroma filled the kitchen. Thank goodness she'd programmed the timer correctly that morning.

Charles took a sip from a glass of wine and handed a soda to her. "When will you start being companionable?" he asked, pointing at his glass.

She shrugged. Better not get into that. Charles drank enough for both of them, and she needed to keep her wits when she was around him.

They went to the patio, and Charles gave her a blow-by-blow of his day. Amiably. No rancor. He ran his thumb and forefinger up the stem of his glass. "I've been thinking. I ought to get to work and begin studying for another actuarial exam."

She groaned inwardly and stared past the patio at the ripples on the lake. It was never easy to live with Charles, but even more difficult when he was under pressure for two or more months, studying for an exam. But she nodded. "Think it's time, do you?"

"More than time, maybe. I've passed four. And if I want to get on with my career, or look like I want to get on with it, it is undoubtedly the politic thing to do. To be candid, I am perfectly happy with what I am doing. Nobody bugs me much, and it is mostly me and the computer, figuring, figuring some more, getting the answers, putting it all together. But if I want to take another step up, yes, I need to start on the next exam."

"And that would be?" she asked.

"Economics and theory of risk insurance." He scowled. "I admit I've dragged my feet."

"Because it's so tough?"

"Mmm." He nodded. "The prospect is somewhat like scheduling the surgical removal of a little finger without anesthesia."

"I know you've said the exams make a college final look like kindergarten. Still, the idea seems to have put you in a good mood. You must be—" She stopped as she saw him frown.

"What do you mean, 'a good mood'?" he asked as though he was always a beaming ray of sunshine.

"Oh, I don't know," she hedged. "You just seem especially up tonight." Even as she said the words, she realized the truth: It isn't deciding about the exam. It's that he vented this morning, let off the pressure that was building, especially, she suddenly realized, after another of his nightmares last night. So she said quickly, "So I say you should go for it."

He stroked his moustache. "Yes. I believe I shall." He sat without speaking for a moment. Then, "So. Your day? How did you get along with the surfer?"

She waited for the sarcasm, but it didn't come. She described David. "I was really quite taken with—well, it's quite a combination of what I'd almost call sweetness—plus determination."

"Mmm," Charles nodded. "I expect you will be able to help him a lot."

Mr. Congenial, she thought. It was as though this morning had never happened, and she wondered for a moment if it had been a dream.

But later when she checked on the kids, she knew it was real. Scott lay on the floor, curled into a fetal position as he watched TV. He remembered, all right. Tears stung her eyes.

How could anyone mitigate the stab of the word *defect* coming from a boy's own father? She looked at him helplessly and started toward him when the doorbell rang, and she heard Charles say, "Hello, there, Mother Lang. Good to see you. Come in."

"I'm in the family room, Mom," she called. Her mother paused at the doorway. "I'll be right back. I'll just put these tomatoes in the kitch."

In a moment she returned. Leslie hugged her mother. "Your hair's wet," she said.

Zoë nodded. "Just got out of the pool. Did my laps, A to Z."

Leslie smiled, remembering that her mother prayed her way through the alphabet, rather than counting the laps she swam. "Your twenty-five-yard prayer closet." She pushed a tendril of Zoë's damp hair into place. "Why didn't you pass along the genes for that wonderful, wavy, wash-and-wear hair to me, huh?"

Zoë touched Leslie's auburn hair. "Honey, women would kill for this color. Don't knock that gift from the Lord." They turned together to look at the kids, still absorbed in the TV program. Zoë's keen blue eyes took in the scene, resting on Scott. She raised a questioning eyebrow at Leslie. "Charles been on the warpath again?" she whispered.

"Called him 'a defect' again."

Zoë pressed her lips together. "I could . . . " She formed a threatening fist. She saw the alarm in Leslie's eyes. "You know I won't." She sighed. "But honey, I worry about what this does to Scott. Please, love, try to define some limits."

Leslie felt the familiar sting in her eyes again. "I know. It's just so *hard*."

Zoë gave her a reassuring pat and turned toward the kids. "Hi, you two! Who has a hug for your poor ol' Gram?"

"I do!" Michelle turned away from the TV and came to her grandmother for a long embrace. "Love ya, Gram."

At last Scott rose slowly, and Zoë came to meet him. She put her arm around him and drew him onto the couch beside her. "How's my favorite grandson in all of Lake Forest?" she asked.

He shrugged. "Okay, I guess."

"This looks interesting," Zoë said, nodding toward the screen. Together they watched, the glow of the TV highlighting the silver of Zoë's hair. She took Scott's right hand between hers and caressed it lightly.

Leslie saw Scott relax against his grandmother. She'd held that hand in an unspoken affirmation since the day he was born. Her touch seemed to spread a balm over it, over him, and Leslie loved her enormously for it. She leaned over the couch. "I'm going to get dinner on. Will you stay, Mom?"

"No thanks, dear. I'll just slip out when you serve."

~

It was Michelle's turn to say grace before dinner that evening. Leslie was grateful that Charles condescended to any form of prayer. Her appeal, "So the kids won't take everything for granted," had won him over, and she found it often helped set a softer tone for dinner. Tonight she could sense the effort Charles made to be a "good father." He never apologized or, indeed, acknowledged his outbursts. But often she felt his struggle to balance them. *He isn't all bad,* she thought. *There's a lot that's kind and decent about him.*

"How about those Angels, Scott?" he asked. "Can you believe they let the Blue Jays walk all over them?"

"Yeah, but the Dodgers won." Baseball was one safe topic for Scott with his dad, and the boy made a point of keeping up with the majors. "A shutout for Astacio. How 'bout that?"

"Outstanding. What does that make his ERA now? Must be—" Charles thought a moment. "A little less than three, hmm?" Charles's enunciation was as precise as his math.

As the stats flowed, Michelle rolled her eyes and mouthed the word, "Boring!" Baseball was not her thing. "May I be excused?"

Glancing at Michelle's plate, still half-full of food, Leslie started to protest. "Honey . . . "

"Honest, Mom, I'm full."

Leslie knew Michelle thought herself too fat and worried that her willowy daughter wasn't eating enough—or that she was trying to compensate for junk food consumed during the day. Charles looked across at Michelle. "Yes, you may be excused."

He turned back eagerly to continue the analysis of the ball season with Scott. "Maybe I can get some tickets for you and me to see the Angels," Charles said thoughtfully.

Scott's face brightened. "Yeah!" he exclaimed.

As they finished dinner and Scott excused himself, Charles moved to the patio for his coffee, and Leslie cleared the table. Michelle slipped back into the kitchen. "Mom, I think Stacey's brother—Jason's his name—likes me."

She stared at her daughter. "But isn't he—"

"Yeah. In high school."

"But well along in high school, isn't he?"

"So he's a junior." Michelle's voice was defensive.

Leslie tried to take it slow and easy. "I guess I'm a little surprised that there wouldn't be a lot of attractive girls more his age."

"Well, see, redheads turn him on."

Leslie grinned.

"What's so funny, Mom?"

"Oh, I was just remembering a guy I knew who would only

date girls with red hair. He finally married one. I got a Christmas card last year with a picture of him with his wife, a red-haired baby boy—and an Irish setter."

Michelle didn't see the humor. "So is it okay if he comes over?"

"When?"

"Tonight."

Sheesh! A high school junior with her twelve-year-old. Well, maybe better to have him here than to force her to try to meet him away from home.

"Okay, but you're to be in the family room. And he leaves no later than nine."

"Nine!" she shrieked.

"Nine," Leslie kept her voice firm.

And she's not even a teenager yet, Leslie thought as she watched Michelle leave the kitchen. *I hope I make it through these next years—keep the communication flowing—keep up with her. I'll really have to set limits and stick to them . . . Limits.* She thought of her mother's statement about setting limits with Charles. It was so hard when she never knew what reaction to expect. She couldn't approach him when he was angry. But now, when he was being so sweet, she hated to say anything. Still, when he was mellow . . . maybe this *was* the time.

She took a deep breath, poured their coffee, and brought it to the patio.

"Scott loves to talk baseball with you," she said. "And you use it well to stimulate him to use his head, figure out averages."

Charles nodded. "He's a bright kid."

"Right." She touched his hand lightly. "And Charles, it's so good when you accent the positive with him instead of emphasizing his 'defect.' I mean, after all, is it a 'defect' in a pitcher like Jim Abbott not to have a hand?"

Charles straightened in his chair. "Of course it is a defect." His voice had a tone of exaggerated patience, as though he were explaining a simple truth to a dull child. "Remember, Abbott is not able to bat. He cannot conceal his pitching hand like a two-handed pitcher. He is handicapped."

Not perfect, heaven forbid, she thought. She remembered the definition of a optimist as one who sees a glass half-full and a pessimist as one who sees the same glass half-empty. Charles couldn't see any water at all, she decided.

She couldn't resist. "Interesting that a handicapped man can bring in a few million bucks a year, isn't it?"

"What is the point here, *Les*-lie?"

She heard the accented syllable and back-pedaled. "I just thought playing up what Abbott *can* do, what he's accomplished, could be an encouragement to a kid, who—who—" She wanted to say, "whose dad keeps telling him he's no good." But she couldn't. She felt the tears about to gather. "Oh, Charles, if only home could be a safe, pleasant, building-up place for Scott."

Charles gave her a crooked smile. "I had this strange perception that I provide well for him. Is he hungry?"

She shook her head.

"Wearing rags?"

"Of course not." *He doesn't get it at all—or doesn't want to,* she thought.

"Have a rather nice roof over his head? His own room? Good school?"

Yes . . . yes . . . yes! her mind screamed.

Charles set his coffee cup down with a clang. "What is it you want from me, *Leslie*?"

She couldn't outstare his penetrating brown eyes, and when she finally spoke, she could barely hear her own voice. "To love him the way he is."

He stared at her silently, his mouth a straight, thin line.

What was the use, she wondered.

He looked at his watch. "Ball game tonight. The Phillies are only two games out of first place."

The Phillies—ball game—family room. She'd better tell him. "Oh, that reminds me, Michelle has somebody coming over tonight."

"So?"

"A boy." She decided not to mention his age. "I told her they'd have to be in the family room."

Charles stood. "Fine. Hope he likes baseball."

Well, she thought, *maybe that's one way to cool this budding romance.*

He peered at his watch again. "Today is the twenty-fourth. Did you start your period?"

"Not yet. Why?" she asked, surprised.

"Late, aren't you?"

He keeps track of everything, she thought. "Yes, but that happens."

"Later than usual, wouldn't you say?" he persisted.

She tried to meet his gaze, knowing he now had her on the defensive once again. "No more than a day or two."

He glared down at her. "Well, you'd better not be pregnant. Do you hear me? You had jolly well better not!"

3

WITH CHARLES'S WORDS JANGLING THROUGH HER HEAD, Leslie watched him stride toward the family room and the ball game. She'd been so busy she hadn't paid much attention to the calendar. The idea of another pregnancy had never entered her mind. She was so acutely aware that another child was not an option for Charles, she'd taken extreme care to guard against conception. But now Charles's admonition filled her with apprehension. She remembered how distraught he'd been when she became pregnant with Scott so soon after their marriage.

"This is not in my timetable!" Charles had exploded. "It is not the plan. Much too soon. You're always in a hurry, always want your way."

Then, the very day Scott was born and Charles saw his son's malformed hand, he'd made it clear. No more children, period. "This child is a mistake," he'd said as they looked into the hospital bassinet at the baby that to her was so beautiful, with his wavy, dark hair, his faint shadow of eyebrows, the pink-and-white perfection of his skin. "We will not take a chance on another," Charles decreed.

Now the very idea of a second pregnancy opened a long and twisted path of "what-thens?" in her mind. She immediately explored them. First, Charles's inevitable anger and accusations. Then his certain insistence upon abortion. The thought made her feel queasy. What would she do? Comply? She couldn't. Run away? How? Where? She tried to push the thoughts away. Her cycle wasn't always regular. It certainly wasn't cause for worry. Or was it? The melody of the doorbell broke into her contemplation. Michelle's young man.

She reached the front door just in time to hear Michelle say, "Hi. C'mon in, Jason."

With a puff of exhaled cigarette smoke, Jason stepped into the hallway. Looking at his cigarette, he thought better of it and tossed it outside. He stood a full head taller than Michelle. The jet black of his hair was definitely from a bottle, and it hung in clumps down to his shoulder. The crown, however, had been shaved, except for a closely mown two-inch strip of bristle that stood straight up, like a horse's clipped mane, arcing back from his forehead.

Leslie swallowed. This was a joke, right?

"Whassup?" the boy said to Michelle, and Leslie saw two gold earrings glistening in one ear, and—she took a closer look to be sure—another earring, pierced through his eyebrow.

Michelle saw Leslie. "Uh, Jason, this is my mom."

"Unh," Jason grunted, avoiding eye contact, his arms swinging awkwardly at his sides. The short sleeves of his extra-extra-large black shirt covered his elbows, but not the tattoo of a snake on his forearm.

"Happy to meet you," Leslie said, extending her hand. He ignored it and said to Michelle, "So?"

"Uh, how about we go in the family room?" Michelle said. "My dad's watching the ball game."

Turning, Leslie saw that the crotch of his over-sized black shorts reached half-way down to his knees, and a gold-colored chain dangled from one pocket. She quickly opened the door and went outside, located the cigarette, stamped it out. Charles would have a fit. She tucked it under a potted plant.

She caught up with Michelle and Jason just as Charles glanced away from the TV screen, then back to the game and quickly back to Jason. "What, pray tell, is this?" he demanded.

"Uh, Dad, this is Jason," Michelle said. "We'll just sit over here." She indicated the sofa.

Charles nodded, his eyes drawn back to the ball game. In just a few seconds, a commercial broke into the action. Charles turned to Leslie, speaking loud enough that Jason and Michelle couldn't miss it. "What *is* this, Leslie? You tell me a boy is coming over. I thought we were expecting a twelve-year-old, for heaven's sake, not someone going on twenty, looking like something out of a bad movie, and on the make!"

"Daddy . . . " Michelle pleaded.

"Leslie, have you taken complete leave of your senses?" Charles demanded.

"No, Charles, I—" Leslie began, but Charles had decided to turn his attention to Jason.

"What grade are you?"

"Junior."

Charles sneered. "High school, then. Where do you go? Over on Toledo?"

Jason nodded.

"So what in the world are you doing here?"

Jason squirmed on the sofa. "Came t'see Michelle."

Charles nodded wisely, staring relentlessly at Jason. "Ah. To see Michelle. Why in the world would a high school junior want to spend time with a twelve-year-old? You having trouble catching the eyes of girls your own age?"

The roar of the stadium crowd drew Charles back to the game. He swore vehemently. "Missed the best play of the blasted night."

As Charles concentrated on the screen, Leslie gestured to Michelle and Jason to follow her into the kitchen. "C'mon, I'll get you some Cokes."

She pulled two cans from the refrigerator, and Michelle and Jason perched on the kitchen stools. "Hey, what's with him, tryin' to dis me, anyway?" Jason whispered to Michelle. "You didn't tell me your old man's an ogre."

They were just beginning to relax when the higher volume of the TV heralded a commercial. Charles came in, reached into the refrigerator for a beer, and turned toward Jason and Michelle, frowning. "You still here?" he said. "Listen, boy, you *go*. Now! And I do not want you back again." Then he headed back to the family room.

"O-k-a-y!" Jason headed for the door, Michelle trailing behind. Leslie heard the front door open and close. She walked toward the hallway just in time to see Michelle lean against the door and break into tears.

"Well," her daughter wept, "so much for me ever gettin' to have a boyfriend. So much for me ever havin' a guy over again. I might as well be a n-n-n-nun!" Her wail followed her up the stairway till her bedroom door banged shut.

Leslie blinked hard. She wasn't sure whether to laugh or cry. Certainly Charles had overreacted; so what else was new?

But she had to admit, the boy was like something out of central casting. Even so, she felt Michelle's pain. "Oh, Lord," she whispered, "help me keep my sense of humor."

"*Les*-lie," came Charles's commanding tone from the family room.

She moved to the doorway. "Yes?"

"Are you out of your mind letting that creature into the house?"

"I—I—"

"Let us not have a repeat of that unfortunate experience."

"I understand what . . . "

Already he was absorbed in the ball game again.

My fault again, she thought. Sighing, she glanced at her watch. Eight-thirty. Time for Scott to be getting to bed. She climbed the stairs and knocked on his door.

"Come in."

She opened the door as Scott pulled on his pajama top.

"Want to read?" she asked. "We haven't done that for a while."

"Nah. That's all right."

She sat on the edge of his bed. "How're you liking the day camp at church. Still okay?"

"Yeah. We've had some good soccer games."

"You like that?"

"It's okay."

"That might be something you'd like to continue in the fall. There are some teams right here, you know. Mr. Stern down the street coaches one."

"Yeah, maybe." He sat down on the floor in front of her and gave her a quick look. "Better than football or baseball. That's for sure."

"Had you thought any more about Scouting?"

"Huh-uh. I'm not really that interested."

"Well, then, maybe the soccer." They sat quietly for a moment. "Tell me some more about day camp."

"We've had a good Bible study about God's love. Not the icky lovey-dovey kind of love, y'know."

She smiled and nodded. "Unconditional love."

"Yeah. It's cool. You don't earn it."

"In fact, can't earn it. *Very* cool."

Scott grinned. "Think God loves Jason unconditionally?"

"Jason was something else, wasn't he?" She laughed. "But seriously, yes; God does love him, though I suspect Jason doesn't realize it. I'll tell you a young man who *does* know God's love though."

"Who?"

"David, the paralyzed body-surfer."

"Good. Bet that helps."

"I'm sure it does." She smiled. "So what else is happening at day camp?"

"Well, we're makin' some stuff for a play we're doing. Turns out I'm pretty good at painting big stuff."

She smiled. "I'll bet you are."

"I've brushed my teeth," he volunteered.

"Good. You ready to be tucked in, then?"

"Guess so."

She stood so he could slip into bed then pulled up the sheet and sat on the edge of the bed. "This is probably all the cover you need right now. Want to pray?"

"Yeah." He closed his eyes and thanked God for loving him and watching over him. Then, "And God, I'd sure like to do some of the painting on that big piece of scenery, if that seems cool to You." He paused a moment. "And God, please help me not to make Dad get so mad. Help me be the kind of kid he wants me to be. Bless him and 'Chelle and Mom. In Jesus' name, amen."

She leaned over to kiss him. How could she phrase a response without undermining Charles? "Honey," she began, "it isn't always your fault that Dad gets mad. You don't have to try to be—or pretend to be—something you're not."

Scott exhaled in a long sigh. "At least God loves me just the way I am."

She let out an inward sigh. "He definitely does that. It's that unconditional love. No conditions attached." She smiled. "And Scott, *I* love you that way, too."

"I know. G'night."

"G'night, love."

She closed the door and stood outside for a moment.

Easy for me to say, she thought. *Easy for me to tell him he doesn't have to base his whole life on trying to be what his dad wants him to be. But I base* my *life on what Charles wants. It's easier that way.*

She started down the steps and stopped midway. *No, wait,* she realized, *there's more. I did that with my own dad. I'd have stood on my head, hung by my thumbs, whatever it took to please him, to be what I thought he wanted me to be.*

4

~

From Zoë's Prayer Journal

August 29: Dear Lord, You are El Roi, the God who sees, and I know You see how Charles is hounding Leslie—so hot and bothered, thinking she might be pregnant. Does this bug You as much as it does me? Father, he's probably all riled up about nothing. But if my daughter should be pregnant—well, You and I know there really isn't such a thing as an unplanned pregnancy. So if she is, then I ask You to strengthen her. And oh, dear Lord, please change Charles's heart and help him accept Your will. For that's my bottom-line prayer: Your will be done. In Your Son's name, amen.

CHARLES LOOKED UP FROM THE OPINION SECTION OF THE Sunday *Times* as Leslie came into the living room wearing a green-print summer dress the color of her eyes. She kissed him lightly. "We're off. Be back about eleven."

Charles glanced at the Bible in her hand. "Ah, yes." He nodded wisely. "Church." She marveled how he could give one word such a mocking tone. But he had agreed when they married that she and Michelle and any children they might have could go to church. So even when he made sarcastic remarks about religion as her "crutch" and protested the mileage to church, she never wavered.

"It's probably a good thing you're going," he said.

Surprised, she asked, "Why is that, Charles?"

"If you truly believe in the power of prayer, you had better pray that you are not pregnant." His smile was a straight line across his face, his eyes burning without even a glimmer of a twinkle.

He couldn't let go of it, couldn't stop pressuring her. She decided to say nothing.

But Charles wasn't finished. "Look, Leslie, I have been extremely patient, waiting these three days since we first discussed this matter. Now it is time. On your way home, you will pick up a pregnancy-test kit."

Her shoulders sagged. "Oh, Charles, that's way premature. I don't have any symptoms. I've been late before."

"Not this late." He stressed each word.

"Whatever you think," she said, her heart racing as she left the room. *What if the test was positive? But no, surely not.* "Michelle? Scott?" she called up the stairway.

In a moment they clambered down toward the door.

As they drove to church, Leslie tried not to think about Charles. "Thanks, Lord," she said, "for getting us all together and making it possible to go to church to learn and to worship."

"Yeah," Scott said, obviously looking forward to Sunday school.

"Yeah, sure," echoed Michelle, sarcasm dripping from her words.

Leslie tried to tease her. "What's the matter? No cute guys in your class?"

"Babies!" Michelle exclaimed.

Yeah, sure. Leslie's thoughts echoed Michelle's sarcasm. *Babies, meaning no mature hunks like the irresistible Jason. Thank God for that!*

She dropped the kids off at Sunday school and parked near the sanctuary. As she walked in, the specter of a pregnancy test cast a heaviness in the pit of her stomach. Why couldn't Charles just wait and see? Why did he have to be so darned precise, so on top of everything?

During the service, a young woman sang a solo, her soprano voice so true and clear it brought tears to Leslie's eyes. Or was it the text that stirred her so? "Oh, for the wings—the wings of a dove. Far away—far away would I flee!" Afterward the pastor addressed "those of you with heavy hearts, weighty concerns, those of you who wish for the wings of a dove. Won't you please have the courage to stand and come forward for prayer?" he invited.

That's me, she thought. *Heavy heart, weighty concern. Yes, I'd love the wings of a dove. But I can't go up. Can't share with anyone. My whole situation is just so—so embarrassing. So stupid!* She closed her eyes and tried to pray, but there was no way she could pray as Charles had asked her.

On the way out of church she met her friend Norma, and soon another friend, Sandra, joined them.

"What's happened to our support group?" Sandra asked. It was true—the threesome who had met every other week for a couple of months had missed gathering twice now. "Can't we get together this week and pray for each other?" Norma suggested.

"I'll be out of town. How about next week?" said Sandra. "Can you make it at seven a week from Thursday, Leslie?"

"Yes, sure," Leslie said, thinking how much she might be needing their support by then.

On the way home she pulled into a neighborhood shopping center. "I'll just be a minute," she told the kids.

She heard Michelle groan.

"Can I come in with you?" Scott asked.

She certainly didn't want Scott peering over her shoulder. "No, honey—tell you what. We need milk too. Would you be an angel and run into the supermarket while I grab one thing in the drugstore?"

"Yech—no—I won't be an angel. But yeah, I'll get it," Scott grinned.

She gave him the money and headed into the drugstore. Where to look? She scanned the shelves in the aisle marked "feminine needs." No luck. Then she spied the sign, "testing kits" in front of the pharmacy. *Let's see: diabetes—no. Oh, here they are, pregnancy tests.* She stared at the shelf. She'd had no idea there were so many choices. But she did learn one thing from the packages. It wasn't too soon. "Accurate one day after a missed period," several of them proclaimed.

Charles's words, "You'd better not be pregnant. Do you hear me?" sounded in her mind again.

I hate this, she thought, finally grabbing one labeled "one-step." She headed for the checkout, thinking, *If this were a movie, there'd be some ominous music right now.*

At home Charles had found a ball game to watch. She stood at the door of the family room till he looked up. "Get it?" he said.

She nodded.

"Get what?" came Scott's voice behind her.

"Foot powder your Dad needed," she lied, hating the untruth, hating the whole sordid business.

33

ॐ

When the kids decided to go to the neighborhood pool that afternoon, Leslie reluctantly watched them leave.

The door had no sooner closed than Charles declared, "All right, let's go upstairs and see what is going on here."

In their bedroom he fished the kit out of the bag and read the instructions. "You understand what to do?"

"Of course I do, Charles. I dip the little stick, and . . . "

"No," said Charles. "*I* dip the little stick. Bring the little cup out of the bathroom."

It's as though I'm some little child, she thought. *A child who can't follow direc— No, that's not it. He doesn't trust me. That's the problem.* But a few moments later, she dutifully brought the cup of urine out of the bathroom.

"All right. Let's see now," said Charles, carefully dipping the stick. He glanced at his watch. "We have to wait five minutes."

"I know." The silence seemed to weight the passage of time, put it into slow motion. Outside she heard the clip-clip of hedge shears, the roar of a motorcycle. Charles said nothing, simply drummed his fingers on the table every now and then. She couldn't think of a thing to say.

One dot, please, Lord, she prayed silently, knowing that one pink dot on the stick would mean negative.

At last color began to appear. "Here we go," Charles announced.

She watched in disbelief as the pair of dots grew darker, deuces staring at her. "Gotcha!" they seemed to say.

She swallowed hard. "Maybe we should try it again. There's another test there," she hedged. "These tests aren't always ac—"

The stream of profanity made her want to clap her hands

over her ears. He pressed his index finger against her chest, his face crimson. "I knew it! I knew it! You bitch! From the moment I married you, it's been like carrying an albatross around my neck. Sometimes I think you're some sort of curse laid upon me." He prodded her with his finger. "*You're* the one with the responsibility to take precautions, young lady. You *know* how I feel about another child." He began to pace back and forth across the bedroom. "You and all your Christian values. Doesn't the Bible tell you to be submissive to me? Well, then, why did you not submit in this? Why can you not learn from the past? You had to go and get yourself pregnant right after we got married, just when I was trying to study for an actuary exam. Missed the exam, and why? Because of you and a so-called emergency in your pregnancy with Scott."

She didn't know where to look, what to say. The pressure on her chest was so heavy it was difficult to breathe. All she could do was stand and feel the sting of his words blazing down on her.

He turned on her. "You are an educated woman. You know all about muscles and body mechanics. Why can't you get birth control right? Are you stupid?" As he stared at her his eyes slowly grew bright and hard. "Or, was this your plan all along?"

"No, no, Charles, of course not," she managed to interject.

"Yes, now I remember," he said slowly. "You said you loved being pregnant, felt—What was the word? Ah, yes—fulfilled—with a nursing babe in your arms. That is it, is it not?" He was screaming now. "You made this happen! Planned it! *Didn't you?*" He grabbed her throat, his eyes wide and glittering.

He's going to kill me, she thought, and she heard herself scream.

He relaxed his grip, released her. A quick look of panic

flashed across his face, but just as quickly, he spat out, "You are pathetic. Just pathetic. I cannot imagine how I ever saddled myself with you."

She gasped for breath, rubbed her throat, still feeling the terrible strength of his fingers tightening around her neck.

"But I promise you one thing. This child will never be." He shook his head. "Nice try, *Les*-lie. But you will have an abortion. At your earliest possible convenience *or* inconvenience."

There it was. Her worst fear. "Oh, no, Charles, no. I can't do that."

He raised his hands as though to grab her again. "Oh, yes, you can. *Yes—you—will*!"

She ran from the room then, sobbing, and stumbled down the stairs. In the kitchen, she grabbed her purse, glancing over her shoulder, afraid Charles would follow her. *Have to calm down, have to think*, she told herself as she got in the car, backed it out. *Mustn't hurt anyone*. The song of the morning, "Oh, for the wings of a dove," reverberated in her mind. "Far away would I fly!" *Oh,* she thought, *if I could just fly far, far away from all of this!*

In a blur, she drove to her mother's. Knees and hands shaking, tears coursing down her cheeks, she climbed the steps to her mother's condominium and rang the bell and leaned against the rough cedar of the walls. No answer. Maybe Zoë was in the pool. She turned to walk back down—and collided with her mother, droplets of water still glistening on her cheeks.

"What a nice sur—" Zoë started to embrace her but stopped abruptly as she saw Leslie's face. "Uh-oh. Let's get inside."

Zoë led Leslie into the fresh country ambiance of the living room and settled her in a chair. She drew a footstool in front of Leslie, sitting on her beach towel, still wearing her Speedo swimsuit.

Leslie poured out her story, finishing, "I c-can't m-murder this baby."

"Of course you can't!" Zoë held her daughter's hands, sending up a quick prayer for wisdom. "And I am here for you, darling, to help you in any way I can." She looked at Leslie carefully. "Tell me what you're thinking."

Leslie dabbed at her eyes. "I'm thinking I wish I could fly away, go to Hawaii, anything! But Mom, if he's adamant about the abortion, what can I do? Leave him?" The tears began again. "That terrifies me, Mom. How? With or without the children? If Charles tears them down all the time when I'm there, what might he do if I leave them with him? And where? Where do I go? What would become of us?" She hugged herself, rubbing her arms, looking small and helpless. "I can't support three kids on my salary, can I? Not and live here, where I work. Oh, Mom, you know I'd have to fight Charles every inch of the way for any help. What if I get sick and can't work? I just have this picture of us all pushing a grocery cart full of all our belongings and me with a sign, 'Will work for food.'"

Zoë laughed. "Honey, not you! You're far too capable and resourceful. And you have family to help you: me, Tracy nearby. But please, darlin', don't sell yourself short."

"No, no, I'm not. Don't you see? Without Charles, I'm—I . . . why, I've never gotten along without a man since school. I married Tom right out of college. And right after he died, Charles was there for me."

It's true, Zoë thought. *She's never really been on her own.*

"Mom," Leslie wailed, "I don't think I can make it alone." She lifted her head. "Oh, God, what shall I do?"

5

CHARLES STROLLED DOWN THE SUBURBAN STREET, ORDERLY
and neat, noting the freshly painted houses, precisely manicured grounds and plantings. The rain began to fall. It pelted
off his face, and he was surprised at the color: a pale pink. He
could see the color in the drops absorbing into his white shirt.
Gradually, the color darkened. Red. Blood red. Blood flowing
all over him. Blood in his hair, on his hands, splashing beneath
his feet as he walked. Charles opened his mouth to scream, but
no sound would come.

Thrashing, gasping, he struggled till at last he woke,
drenched with sweat. "The blood! Always blood!" he muttered.

Beside him, Leslie murmured but didn't wake. He fumbled
for his robe, hands shaking, and groped for his slippers.
Shivering in the night air, he stood and tugged the robe on,

hurriedly tying the belt and thrusting his feet into his slippers. He bumped into the wall in the hallway and had to grab the railing to steady himself as he descended the stairs.

"Always the blood," he repeated as he made his way to the kitchen. "Isn't this ever going to go away?"

Flicking on the light, he opened the cabinet door and pulled out the bottle of bourbon. He found a glass and poured, hearing the clank of glass upon glass in his tremulous hands. He drank till it was gone and stood, waiting for his heart to stop racing. He shook himself like a dog coming in from the rain and refilled his glass, taking it into the living room. The moonlight from outside was sufficient for him to find the couch. He sat down and pounded his fist on the coffee table. Gradually the vividness of the dream subsided, replaced by an anger that began as a small flicker within, then built till it seared through his gut.

"Leslie, damn you, woman!" he growled.

Everything she did seemed to thwart him. Why wouldn't she listen to him? Why wouldn't she do the few simple things he asked of her? She had to have everything her way. Oh, it was subtle sometimes. But she'd do anything to get her way. Just like his mother: manipulating, plotting, at war with him every inch of the way.

A snapshot of his mother flipped into his mind. Smiling so sweetly, promising him the world, professing boundless love—and never being there for him. Not when she ran off with that hot-shot entrepreneur who wouldn't have anything to do with him. Not when she came back, remarried, and his stepfather abused him. She was always looking away, always refusing to see the truth. He ground his teeth together, feeling once again the physical pain, the helpless anger, the powerlessness.

Gradually the image of his mother dissolved into the likeness of Leslie. Why hadn't he seen it in the beginning? Sometimes she even talked like his mother. How could he have been so deluded, so deceived, so stupid? How much there was to despise about her! Her silly little smile, her walk, her talk, her carelessness, her vagueness. Letting water boil and boil needlessly . . . destroying his system of alphabetizing the canned goods . . . folding his clean T-shirts in half instead of with the sleeves neatly turned back . . . using green ink in the checkbook instead of black . . . making peanut-butter sandwiches with margarine, for God's sake! One thing alone wouldn't be so bad, but it was an infinite series, like some mathematical nightmare that increased exponentially. Why couldn't she get things *right*?

Then, too, she was always wanting to have her way with the children, so afraid that what he did or said would damage their tender little psyches that she made them into spoiled brats. He longed for the day they were gone from the home. But in the meantime, what they needed, both of them, was a strap— applied frequently.

He shuddered at the idea of another child, the expense, the mess of diapers and spit-up, the interrupted sleep, the lack of order to his life. "It will not be! It will not be!" he muttered.

Leslie, the romantic, he knew, never thought of such things. She was so unrealistic, so *unconcerned*.

He had actually felt like killing her this afternoon. He squeezed the glass between his two hands. It would have been so easy. But no, he would never do that. He was more controlled than that. Yes, *he* was in control.

One thing I will not do is hurt her, he promised himself for the hundredth time. *No,* that *I will not do.*

∿

Leslie wasn't sure how she muddled through the next day—or the next. Somehow she went through the motions at work: "Philip, you're doing great!" . . . "Now, Helen, it's your choice. You can do another set of bicep curls, or you can stop now. Can you keep going? Good!" . . . "You can wiggle your toes, David? Great! Okay, Brynne's going to start you on some work with dumbbells for your upper body. And some crunches. You've been working hard. I'm proud of you."

But beneath it all lay the terrible truth: She'd seen her husband's hatred for her.

She watched an aide take ice into a treatment room. *My heart feels as though it's had an ice massage, with the ice rubbed directly on it, leaving it numb—anesthetized, deadened,* she realized.

And each day when Charles urged her to call the abortion clinic, she realized that something within her had already aborted. Love—that's what it was. Love, brutally scraped away.

"If you don't call, I will," he threatened, and she knew he meant it. When she refused—and refuse, she would—he'd tell her to leave. She was sure of it.

That terrible Sunday afternoon after the pregnancy test, her mother had suggested that Leslie ask her sister in the neighboring city of Mission Viejo if she could move in. Tracy had a house with a bonus area—a large room with a sleeping loft and a bath—unused, now that her boys were in college. It was a possibility. But Michelle and Scott too? Sure, she could drive them to school on her way to work. But they'd miss their own rooms so much. And besides, she wasn't sure she could put her sister on the spot like that—even if she paid rent. But a place of their own was out of the question financially. She had no available funds. Oh, why, why, had she let Charles talk her into the "better return" of putting all of her earnings in *his* company's credit union? All she could pray was, "Oh, Lord, help me; show me what to do."

She'd never suffered morning sickness in her pregnancies with Michelle and Scott. But now huge waves of nausea washed over her as she struggled to decide what to do.

⁓

Early Wednesday morning she began spotting and cramping. David, doing pull-downs with a weighted bar to strengthen his back, studied her face. "What is it? You look terrible."

"Hey," she protested, trying to keep her voice light, "you talk about me being mean to you in our sessions. What is this? Retribution? You really know how to get to a gal."

His turquoise eyes continued to assess her. "It's just that— well, you don't look yourself."

"Oh, well, maybe I have a touch of the flu," she said and changed the subject.

By noon the flow grew copious. She rested her face against the sink in the bathroom at work and wept, flooded with conflicting emotions. A part of her mourned. *Dear babe that might have been,* she grieved, picturing a newborn with its flattened features and ruddy coloring.

Then she wondered: *Was it a false positive on the pregnancy test? Did we get all wrought up for nothing? I'll probably never know.*

Well, Charles would be ecstatic. Imagining his exaltation filled her with anger and despair. Now she had no reason to leave him, and she wasn't sure if she felt relieved—or disappointed. To love him again seemed as impossible as—as Scott growing fingers on his right hand.

"Lord," she wept, "You've given me an answer, I guess. And I accept Your will. But I still don't know what to do."

She struggled to her feet and washed her face. Lunch had no appeal, but she felt weak, knew she needed to eat something.

She was surprised to see her mother waiting in the reception area. "I was in the neighborhood. I'll treat for a deli sandwich," Zoë offered.

It would be good to get out for a few moments, pull herself together, she thought. "I'll grab my purse," she replied.

At the deli counter Zoë asked her, "Split a turkey-breast sandwich?"

"Sure."

"Squaw bread?"

"Fine."

Zoë gave the order to the dark-eyed young woman behind the counter. "Hold the mayo, but give us everything else, including avocado." She turned to Leslie. "You look like you could use some cheese in this."

She didn't care. "Whatever."

They took the sandwich to the shaded patio, where a pleasant breeze blew.

After she asked a blessing, Zoë glanced at her daughter's pale, puffy face, the smudge of mascara. *Now what?* She'd wait.

Leslie nibbled gingerly at the sandwich and put it down. Tears welled in her eyes, and Zoë reached across the table to squeeze her hand. "Darling—"

"Well, I'm un-pregnant. If I ever was," Leslie blurted out, grabbing a paper napkin to stem the tears.

So that was it. "You must be a wreck." Zoë's voice was soft and tender.

Leslie nodded. "But I'm sure I've made my husband a very happy man."

"I'd assume so." Zoë waited quietly till Leslie stopped crying, trying to assess her own emotions, realizing she'd almost welcomed a pregnancy as a catalyst for her daughter to make wholesome changes in her marriage, her life. Perhaps if she'd leave Charles, he'd see their need for counseling. One thing she knew: She did *not* want Leslie to live any longer with this insufferable man. *Forgive me, Lord,* she prayed silently, *but I want her out, away from this—this jerk!*

Leslie blew her nose. "Sorry, I'm just—well—I'm a mess, that's what. I didn't know what to do if I was pregnant. And I don't know what to do now. How do you go back to square one? That's what Charles would do, I know."

"Pretend the positive pregnancy test and his cruel words never happened?"

Leslie nodded. "That's the way he always does."

"Yes," Zoë said. "That seems to be his pattern." She looked at her daughter and added gently, "You do see that?"

"Of course."

"Maybe there's a way to break that pattern," Zoë suggested. "I keep wondering if you'd leave, maybe he'd see the need for counseling."

"If I'd leave, he'd say good riddance."

"I don't think so. He needs you." *Needs you to pound on verbally,* Zoë wanted to add but didn't.

"He'd let me go before he'd consent to counseling. His mother had years and years of therapy, and it didn't help. No, Mom, if I left, it would be a disaster. I know it."

"Then what do you think you should do?"

Leslie took a deep breath. "I think I have to go back and pick up the pieces."

Zoë could feel her daughter's resistance building. Time to pull back. "Then Leslie, please don't go back to square one.

Please try to make your marriage a partnership, not a tyrant-slave relationship."

"Sure." Leslie pursed her lips in doubt. "How?"

"It won't be easy," Zoë warned. "But it's called setting limits and sticking to them." She took Leslie's hand and squeezed it. "Oh, darling, I pray for your strength and courage to do it. You're not being your husband's helper if you allow him to behave in this way. Why do you listen to his lies, buy into them, accept the way he walks all over you? You don't deserve that. And he doesn't deserve it either."

"Because . . ." Leslie's eyes filled again with tears. "There's always a grain of truth in what he says."

"But sweetheart, 5 percent right and 95 percent wrong doesn't make it all right."

Leslie sighed. "I guess not." She ran her fingers up and down the water glass. "I guess, bottom line, I don't really want to leave him."

Zoë groaned inwardly. "No," she said softly, "because deep down, you still love him. But honey, because you *do* love him, I'll be asking God to strengthen you and help you to take a stand for what's right and real and true and good."

As they stood to leave, Zoë glanced at her daughter's eyes, already furtive and fearful beneath her bangs. *Well, Lord,* she thought, *all things are possible. But somehow fixing this marriage looks more complicated than parting the Red Sea.*

꒰

Leslie returned to work feeling wretched. The cramps grew intense, and the quarter sandwich she'd managed to swallow seemed to lie, uneasy and tentative, just beneath her throat.

Glancing at her watch, she saw she had five minutes till her one o'clock patient. *I suppose I should call Charles,* she thought, *though I'm tempted to leave him in suspense, just for spite. No, that's childish. Besides, if I don't, he'll be furious. I'd better,* she decided, picking up the phone and punching in the numbers.

"Harper," the familiar voice came.

"Charles . . . "

"*Les*-lie." He sounded distracted.

"I got my period."

Silence. Then, "Lucky you."

That's it? she thought. *Yup. That's it.* She felt compelled to fill the silence. "I, uh, thought you'd want to know."

"Thanks."

She hung up. "Lucky me!" she muttered, gritting her teeth, feeling her anger surge. His tone of self-satisfaction. His complete lack of compassion. No, it was more than that. She felt, somehow, it was his fault, that he had willed his desires into existence. *One way or the other,* she thought, *he always, always gets his way.* She could picture his smug satisfaction. Why, he was probably doing a little dance around his desk. She smiled in spite of herself at the unlikely image of Charles doing a dance around anything or about anything.

Then the anger swelled again. *When I get home,* she told herself, *I'm going to tell him I'm tired of always taking the blame. If he's so blasted determined that we not have another child, then he can take the responsibility. I'll say to him,* "Charles, go have a vasectomy." *That's what I'll say.*

By the time she left work, she'd practiced her pronouncement repeatedly.

But when she got home and checked to see if the table was set, she found a flat, oblong box at her place. She could see the See's Candy insignia through the wrapping paper.

"Charles?" she called.

He appeared from the family room.

"What's this?"

"Why don't you open it?" She saw warmth in his smile.

She tore off the wrapper and raised the lid. The heady aroma of dark chocolate wafted toward her. She lifted the rectangle of waxed paper to reveal identical squares of glossy candy arranged in such meticulous alignment they reminded her of paving tiles.

"I knew you liked the dark-chocolate-covered caramels the best," he said. "So I got you a whole box full."

She turned and shook her head. "Charles, I don't know what to do with you!"

Somehow the speech she'd rehearsed seemed entirely out of place.

6

AS SHE STEPPED OUT OF A TREATMENT ROOM TWO DAYS later, Leslie saw David lying on the mat with Brynne holding his knees bent as he worked on his abdominal crunches. His eyes were closed, face flushed and shining with perspiration. "Hey, Brynne," she called to the aide, "this man is *sweating!* You threatening him with worse punishment—or promising him a giant Snickers, or what?" She stopped in front of David, who opened one eye and, without missing a crunch, managed, "She's a killer."

"Hey, don't blame me." Brynne looked up at Leslie. "You tell this guy to do ten reps and he does thirty. Ask him to use thirty-five pounds for his pec flies, and he complains they aren't heavy enough."

Leslie smiled. *Grit,* she thought. *Incredible grit.* "David is getting ready to meet Goliath," she said.

"Darned right." David winked and did five more crunches.

"Show-off!" Leslie grinned, then held up a warning finger. "But David, there *is* such a thing as too much of a good thing. It's great to push yourself, but if you overdo, especially with the abdominal exercises or by lifting too much weight, you could get overfatigued and strain your back."

"O-*kay*." David shot her a reluctant but resigned if-you-say-so glance.

A few moments later, as she worked with him on the mat, Leslie said, "Wish all my patients wanted to get better as much as you do. You listen, and you work. And you're doing much more than I expected in such a short time. I admire your determination."

"Yeah, me too," he said. "And look how I'm improving. Watch this." He wiggled his left foot back and forth. "I'm even getting so I can feel the muscles in my thighs twitch a little. But I can't pick up my leg without using my arms to help—yet. When do you think . . ."

She held up her hand. "Whoa, there. Let's not get too far ahead of ourselves. And let's keep working on the upper body."

"Hey, you're supposed to encourage me," he protested.

"Yeah. And be realistic too."

"Killjoy!" He pulled the outer corners of his lips down in a grotesque tragic mask, and they both laughed. He looked at her earnestly. "You're lookin' a *little* better these days. But I was thinking, in a month, you know more about me than most anyone—except my mother. I'd like to know a little about you. Tell me about your family."

She smiled as she motioned him to lie on his back on the mat. "Well, Michelle is the oldest, and she's twelve going on twenty-one and much too pretty and shapely for her own good." She knelt at his feet and lifted his left leg straight up, stretching the back of his thigh. The leg was dead weight, heavy for her to lift. "Gorgeous, copper-red hair, huge, green eyes—" she continued.

David raised an eyebrow. "Uh-oh."

"Uh-oh is right." She stretched his leg a little higher, resting the calf on her shoulder. "You should have seen the dude who came to see her the other night. A junior in high school. Tattoos, chain, earring through his eyebrow, the works." She shook her head at the memory.

"Whoa! Must've been hard for you."

She nodded. "And for my husband. He's ver-ree straight. And Michelle's got a real attitude—wants to look like an explosion of a Maybelline truck. Moody, dramatic—stuff I thought wouldn't come up for a couple of years. Not sure I'm ready for that." She paused to lower David's leg and begin stretching the other.

"This leg's tighter," he said. "I feel it more than the other in my back."

"I noticed." She eased off a little before adding, "Then there's Scott. He's ten. I love that age. Old enough to have some smarts and start to be a little independent. Young enough to still be pretty rooted in home and mom." She paused. "Maybe a speck too rooted."

She lowered the leg and said, "Now we'll work on your left foot strength. See if you can pull the toes toward your face. I'll help you." She pressed her palm against the sole of his foot. "Good. Relax. Good. Again."

"Too rooted? Scott, I mean?"

"I'd like to see him have more friends. I'm trying to get him more involved in activities."

David cocked his head. "That a problem?"

Leslie placed her palm against his other foot. "Now with the right foot. Scott was born without fingers on his right hand.

We're not sure what happened, though I suspect it's a medication I took before I realized I was pregnant. Anyway, of course other kids can be really mean." *And so can his father,* she thought.

"Bummer." David thought a moment. "Can he swim?"

"Yes, he's had lessons. Why?"

David pursed his lips. "Oh, I have an idea that might work for him."

"He's pretty easily discouraged." She concentrated on his foot a moment. "I tell him a lot about you. You know, to try to show him what it is to work against difficulties." Her tone grew apologetic. "Guess I've made you a kind of role model. Now sit up. Let's see if you can move that left thigh muscle. Press your leg into the table."

He pushed himself upright. "Hey, I'm flattered. If you think it would help, why don't you bring Scott in so we can meet and he can see I'm real?"

"That's really thoughtful, David!" She touched his thigh. "Tighten the muscles on the top of your thigh. Good. I see your quads working a little." She thought about his suggestion. "But I wouldn't want to bother you with a little twerp. And generally I make it a point not to mix family with business."

"But what if it could be therapeutic for your patient?"

"How so?"

"Well, I love kids. And if I could help one even a little bit, it'd give me a big lift."

"Ah. When you put it like that—" Her mind calculated how she might get Scott here to meet David. Was he old enough to ride his bike over? No. She'd figure something out.

"We could set my appointment at a time that would work for Scott. What do you say?" David's voice was eager, enthusiastic.

He really wants to meet this kid, she thought.

"I mean, of course, if he'd like to," David added.

"I suspect he would. I'll talk to him."

"Good. Good." David smiled.

Leslie thought eagerly of how this brave, determined young man might motivate her son. "Maybe," she said, "we can work it out for late in the afternoon—um, let's see—let's try for next Wednesday."

"Sure. Tell me what time to come."

After they finished, they set the appointment time. "Great!" David said. "That gives me something to look forward to."

"Me too," she said, realizing there wasn't a lot in her own life to look forward to right now.

⁓

She was a little late leaving home after dinner and hurried to her meeting with Sandra and Norma. They were waiting in a tiny private room in the back of a natural foods cafe.

"I ordered Great Earth herbal tea for you," Norma said, easing out of her mustard-colored linen jacket.

"Thanks." She slipped into a chair. "Good to see you, ladies. How're you doin'?"

"God is faithful." Norma smiled, brown eyes sparkling. "I've just been seeing how true His Word is for my life. For so long now I've been praying that verse from Jeremiah. 'Heal me, and I will be healed. Save me, and I will be saved. For You are my praise.' And Leslie, it seems as though my rheumatoid arthritis is in remission. I'm having less pain every day!" Indeed, Norma's very countenance seemed to have a much healthier glow than the last time they'd met.

"Isn't that fabulous?" Sandra asked.

"It is. Wonderful news!" Leslie exclaimed. "And you, Sandra?"

"Pretty good, except the same problem with my grandfather." She rolled her eyes. "He's eighty-eight, and his judgment is poor; but he insists on driving. My folks got him to give up his keys, and then he went out and had a new set made. Unbelievable! I'm so afraid he's going to have an accident."

"And hurt someone else," Leslie added.

"We definitely need to pray about that," Norma said. "What about you, Leslie? If you'll forgive me, I've, ah, seen you looking better."

Leslie hesitated. In the months they'd been meeting, she'd simply asked for prayer for "a difficult marriage." No more. It wasn't that she didn't trust the others. But she didn't want to expose Charles, even for prayer. God knew the specifics, she figured, and the other women didn't need to. But now, as she looked around the table and saw the concern in the other two women's eyes, she decided to be honest. Briefly she spilled the story of the "pregnancy." Already, in her own mind, she put the word in quotation marks, not sure if it had been real or not.

Norma put her hand on Leslie's. "Oh, my dear Leslie. I had no idea. This obviously has been going on—this verbal abuse—for years. Why, you're just a saint to bear with all that."

"A saint—or an idiot?" She asked the question of herself as much as of the women.

"Why, of course a saint! You've turned the other cheek, as Jesus would have you do. You've suffered for your faith."

"But how long am I supposed to do that? And am I to continue even when it's harming my children? I have to be honest—sometimes I just want to pray, 'God, get me *out* of here!'" *Give me the wings of a dove,* she thought.

"No, no, no, my darling," Norma protested, her voice rising. "God designed marriage to be forever, and He's called you to stay and to be a gentle and quiet spirit and to submit to your husband."

"Yes, but He's called my husband to love me as Christ loved the church. Charles doesn't even know what that means."

"No, he can't right now," Norma said. "But he will when he comes to believe. Oh, we have to pray more than ever for his salvation now, don't we?"

"Now, Leslie," Sandra said, her mouth firming into almost a straight line. "I want to talk to you like a Dutch uncle—or maybe a Dutch aunt, if you prefer. You *are* called to submit to your husband, and you vowed to love him for better or worse. You simply must be obedient to what God called you to be. God will give you the strength, the staying power. I just know He will!"

"Then what you're basically saying is that I'm condemned to a living hell," she said, feeling a profound weight in her abdomen.

"No, no. I'm telling you to hang in there and trust God," Sandra insisted.

"Maybe," Norma said slowly, her elongated face thoughtful, "this is the crux of the matter: If your faith was a little stronger, if your trust was what God asks it to be, perhaps you wouldn't be struggling so."

Leslie blinked, astonished at what she was hearing. "So my problem is that I haven't enough faith? How do I *get* that, Norma? Huh?"

Norma's pitying glance seemed to say, If you have to ask, you're hopeless. Leslie sank back in her chair. She'd come hoping for comfort, understanding. Some comfort! She mentally reviewed what they'd said and felt her skin prickle. It was tough stuff. But maybe she needed to be chastised. Maybe she didn't have enough faith. *It's true,* she thought, *that God's Word tells me to submit to my husband—and that he may be won over without a word. I guess maybe I just have to grin and bear it.*

They talked a little longer about their prayer needs then spent half an hour in conversational prayer.

Why, Leslie wondered when she left, *don't I feel better? Am I feeling convicted by what my friends said and prayed? Maybe they're right. Maybe God's mad at me. Or maybe there's something intrinsically wrong with me.*

Pondering all this, she missed a street and started to backtrack when she realized she'd turned toward her mother's home. Well, why not? Charles would be working upstairs on the finances for the Hope for the Children Fund tonight.

She found Zoë balancing a sack of groceries and unlocking her front door.

"How nice!" her mother exclaimed. "I just came from your grandmother, and she sends her love."

"Good. Thanks." She followed Zoë into her condo and perched on a kitchen stool while her mother put away the groceries."

"Feeling better?" Zoë asked.

"Physically, yes. Emotionally—spiritually—" She shrugged.

Zoë shut the refrigerator door and turned toward her.

"Want to talk about it?" She smiled. "Or did you come to discuss world trade?"

"It's a thought. But not exactly." She picked up a paper napkin on the counter and folded it, creasing it carefully. "Just came from my prayer group."

Her mother listened thoughtfully while Leslie described Norma's and Sandra's exhortations. "Sounds like Job's friends," Zoë said at last.

She gave her mother a quizzical look.

"Remember, here's Job, everything taken from him, covered with boils. And his friends tell him everything he's done wrong and is doing that's wrong. Some friends. I've heard these

55

kinds of people called Christian crazy-makers. Good description. They're terribly sincere. But they pick up on a part of the Word and use it so it comes across as a kind of accusation. Honey, that's not using the whole counsel of God. You've got to look at the whole package."

"For instance?"

"Okay. In Ephesians, 'Wives, be submissive to your husbands.' First of all, *submissive* is not the same word as *obey*—a word that *is* used in the same passage for the children-parent and slave-master relationships. So you need to remember that *submit* doesn't mean lying down and playing dead, and it doesn't mean always saying, 'Yes, dear; whatever you say, dear.'"

She pursed her lips. *Is that what I do?* she wondered.

"Then, remember," Zoë continued, "God also tells wives they're to be their husbands' helpers. So let's think about that a minute. Does helper just mean waiting on him, serving him?"

"Well, it does mean that, doesn't it?"

"It means much more, I think. I think it means helping him to be the best he can be." Zoë paused a moment. "Okay now, does standing by and allowing your husband's anger to escalate as he rants and raves and degrades and tears down—does that help him to be the best person he can be? Leslie, his behavior is sinful, not what God wants for him."

Her head ached. Yes, it sounded logical, but— "Mom, okay. I shouldn't let him keep doing that. That's easy for you to say."

Zoë sighed. "I know it. Hard for you to do." She put her arm around her daughter. "But important, my darling. The key— you've heard this before—is to hate the sin, not the sinner."

"Mom," She pulled back and saw her mother through a mist of tears. "I don't know which is which anymore."

7

❧

From Zoë's Prayer Journal

September 20: Lord, You are so good! You're giving my grandson a chance to meet a brave young man who's working like crazy to overcome a huge handicap. Thank You that I get to be a part of it by taking Scott to get acquainted with David. How I pray that this will be an encouragement! You know how much this little boy needs a godly male role model. Thanks, Lord, that as much as I love my grandson, You love him even more. And Lord, I pray that You in Your mercy will heal David and allow him to walk and run once again. We'll give You all the praise and glory. In Jesus' name, amen.

"I DUNNO, GRANDMA," SCOTT WHISPERED AS THEY PUSHED through the glass doors of the physical therapy center. "What'm I gonna say to this dude? I feel kinda dumb being here."

"I have the feeling he's going to be easy to talk to." Zoë gave her grandson an encouraging smile. "Oh, here's your mom."

She looks better, Zoë thought as Leslie came toward them

wearing neatly pressed beige slacks, a green blouse that precisely matched her eyes—or what you could see of them beneath the auburn bangs.

"Hi, Scott," Leslie said, bending to hug her son. She looked up at Zoë. "Thanks so much for bringing him, Mom. Want to stay for a minute to meet David?"

"Why do you think I came?" Zoë heard the door open and looked around to see David easing himself through with just a little help from his surfer friend.

David's face lit up. "Ah! This must be Scott!" He held up his hand, and Scott came toward him to exchange a high five. Scott grinned but said nothing.

"And David, this is my mom, Zoë Lang," Leslie said.

"Zoë," David said thoughtfully, holding out his hand. "Isn't that the Greek word for life?"

"I knew I was going to like you!" Zoë shook his hand. "Not too many people know that."

"Well, life is what my mom is all about," Leslie said.

"I can see that," David said, giving her his knock-'em-dead smile.

"She has life in the Lord, and she's a swimmer and—" Leslie stopped as Zoë held up her hand. "Don't bore the poor fellow, darling. I'm on my way, anyway. It was wonderful meeting you, David. I'm praying for you."

"You are?" David seemed surprised.

"I am," she said firmly. "Now, what are you all doing just standing there? Get to work!" And with a wave, she slipped out the door.

"What a together lady," David said. "I envy you, Scott, having a grandmother like that."

"Yeah, she's old, but she's cool. We're buddies." Scott grinned. *David's cool too,* he thought. *Man, look at the muscles in his arms and chest. Awesome!* He carefully avoided looking at David's legs. He didn't want to seem like he was staring.

"Okay now, first David is going to work with Brynne. You remember, the PT aide who works with me, Scott?"

"She's my drill sergeant. You'll see, Scott. Man, she is *tough.* C'mon." David wheeled his chair down the hall to the exercise equipment.

Scott followed, greeting Brynne and perching on a stool to watch.

"Okay. Let's start with some bicep curls." She removed the arms from his wheelchair. "We're using twenty-five pounds, aren't we? Okay, I'll count, so you two can talk."

"You want to know how this happened?" David asked.

Scott nodded.

As David lifted the weights, he recounted the details of his accident. "So when I woke up in the hospital and couldn't move, man, it blew me away. I thought, if I can't get better, I'd just like to check out, thank you very much."

"I bet."

"I mean, I couldn't even sit in a wheelchair. That's how bad I was. And then when I could finally get into a wheelchair and sit in it without falling over, I hated having to look up at everyone. Like being a kid all over again, you know?"

"Yeah." Scott hadn't thought about being "short" again when you were used to being big.

"But it'll help when I can drive myself. Your Mom's arranging for hand controls in my car, and I'll start driver's ed next week."

"Okay, guys," Brynne interjected, "we're going to transfer to the exercise mat."

David wheeled his chair beside the exercise mat. With his hands, he lifted his legs off his footrests and placed his feet on the floor. Then he pushed with his arms, lifting his bottom off the wheelchair seat and onto the mat. Using his arms and upper-body strength, he scooted his body into the center of his mat. But with each move he made, he had to reposition his legs, using his arms to drag them along the broad vinyl mat.

"Awesome," Scott breathed.

David grinned and gave him a thumbs-up.

"We're working on balance here," Brynne explained, bringing out a ball. "This is called a medicine ball, and it weighs about five pounds." She began throwing the ball to David, first to one side, then the other. "The idea here," she explained, "is to challenge David's ability to keep his balance as he leans from side to side to throw and catch."

As he caught the ball and returned it, David talked to Scott. "I was really wiped out mentally when I realized what a mess I was. In shock awhile. Then really furious! I think if you've never been into sports, or if you've always been this way—well, of course, that's terribly tough—"

"But you weren't, and everything changed for you that day," Scott volunteered.

"Yeah. Good. You got it." David looked pleased.

"But you're gonna get better," he nodded.

"Well, we're not sure how much. Last week I was really on a roll. This week I feel bummed. I mean, I don't see any improvement at all."

"Okay now, David," Brynne interrupted. "Some body-lifts."

He concentrated on pushing with his arms, lifting his buttocks from the mat, then slowly lowering his weight back down. His words came in short bursts. "But," he continued, "I'm gonna work my rear end off . . . to do as much as I can . . . and the ultimate is to get back on my feet—literally." He stopped and thought a moment. "But the Lord knows the beginning and the end of all this . . . and He has a purpose in it. It's just up to me to try to . . . learn what it is. And I've gotta face up to it . . . what'm I going to do with what's left? For sure, I could still go on with my artwork. Keep on coaching kids. I can make my upper body like Arnold's. Maybe do some wheelchair athletics. Bottom line is . . . you want to do the best you can . . . with what you've got."

He repeated the exercise until Scott could see the muscles in the back of David's arms begin to tremble. That had happened to Scott once riding his bike a long distance, when his thigh muscles got so tired they quivered. He couldn't believe how hard David worked once he was warmed up. His face grew red, and perspiration rolled down his face as he pushed, pulled, and lifted while Brynne counted.

"What do *you* like to do, Scott?" David asked between exercises.

Scott shrugged. "Soccer's pretty good. I'm a pretty good runner. Baseball and football are—" he hesitated. "Hard."

"That's what I mean about doing the best you can with what you've got. You like swimming?"

"Yeah, Gram taught me. She even figured out a way to fasten a little paddle on my hand, y'know? To make up for not having fingers."

"Smart grandma."

"Uh-huh."

"You ever think about a swim team?"

"Nah."

"Why not? I started age-group swimming when I was ten. Man, I looked like somebody who needed a CARE package. Skinny. You could count my ribs. Even my backbone stuck out."

Scott grinned. David could have been describing him.

"Swimming's how you got a bod like that?"

"Yeah, that and weights—part of the swim and water polo program in high school and college. The best part about swimming is that you've got a real measure of your improvement: your time. So you're not just racing against the other guy but against yourself. Sure, you don't win or even place all the time. But you see that when you work hard, you get better."

"That's what you're doin' now, aren't you?"

David glanced at him. "You got it."

They continued their conversation in the gym with Leslie. "Now what we're trying to do here, Scott, is to try to help David with the spasms he gets in his legs. They really hurt." With David lying on the mat, she knelt at his feet and lifted one leg straight up. "This stretches the back of his thigh. David has come a really long way for such a short time, but we hope one of these days we can get him up taking a step or two between the parallel bars."

"Yeah," Scott breathed.

"Yeah!" David grinned.

After David left, Scott waited to go home with his mother; he thought about David and the huge handicap he battled. He looked at his own right hand and thought, *This is nothin', compared to his. Man, it makes me realize how I've never thanked God that I can walk and run and do all that good stuff. I'd better thank Him in my prayers tonight for making my legs strong!*

Scott's encounter with David injected an energy into Leslie's day that surprised her. Their meeting had gone even better than she'd prayed, and for the first time in many months, she felt hope for her son. *Hope. That's a novel emotion for me,* she thought wryly.

That evening, at the dinner table, Scott told his father about his meeting with David.

"So you met the jock, did you?" Charles said.

"Yeah."

"And?"

"He's awesome. Man, he works hard. He really wants to get better. And he sure looks like he's in great shape—from the waist up anyway. He said he used to be skinny and bony like me—till he started swimming."

"Competitively, you mean?" Charles asked.

"Yeah."

"Well, don't get any ideas about that, boy," Charles warned.

"You mean because—"

"Well, yes, of course, your defect. Come, now, how many Olympic swimmers have you seen with—"

Leslie saw Scott's head bend down. "Charles," she interrupted, "we're not talking Olympics. Why couldn't he work out with a swim team, maybe use the hand paddle Mother fixed up for him?"

Charles let out a disgusted "Pffft," and shot her a warning look. "There you go again, always protecting him, always trying to fix things up for him."

Scott pushed the food on his plate into tidy clumps but didn't eat another bite.

Michelle took over the conversation, and Leslie turned toward her, grateful for any distraction that would draw Charles's attention away from Scott.

"Well!" Michelle exclaimed to Charles. "I didn't know you were such a big expert on swimming as well as baseball. Wonder how many laps you could swim without passing out."

Leslie blinked. Unlike Scott and herself, Michelle could dare to deliberately confront Charles. Leslie cringed, anticipating his eruption, but before Charles could react, almost in the same breath, Michelle continued, "We're gonna go on a field trip to the LaBrea tar pits." She looked at the ceiling. "Bo-o-ring! Did I tell you there's a new guy in my history class? He wears a necktie, wouldya believe? A total spank."

The tone signaled a new word for "dork" or "jerk." Sometimes Leslie thought she needed an interpreter for her daughter. But Michelle went on. "And we had this assembly with a guy talking about not drinking and driving. He'd wrapped his car around a light pole when he'd been drinking, and he looks kinda, y'know, a little bit of a re-tard from his head injuries. And he goes, 'I just made this one bad decision, and look how it changed my life.' Kinda made you think, y'know. Oh, did I tell you Beth got this outfit at an outlet in L.A.? She goes, 'How much d'ya think this cost?' And I said, 'A bunch.' And she goes, 'W'dya believe $14.99?' And it's sweet—totally great. Oh, and I got an A on our math quiz today."

Charles beamed, and Michelle glanced at her mother as though to say, "How's this for a high-wire act, huh?" Her monologue continued till dinner was over.

After the kids had excused themselves from the table and Leslie poured their coffee, she said, "Charles, maybe you didn't even realize it, but you did it again."

"What?" He seemed genuinely puzzled.

"Used the word *defect* talking to Scott." She leaned across the table. "Charles, I'm not trying to shield him from the facts of life. I just think the word *defect* is loaded. Please. I don't want you to say that anymore." She hadn't even rehearsed the speech and was so surprised at her boldness that she leaned back and held her breath, afraid to look at him.

"All right, Leslie," Charles said, his voice calm and matter of fact. "If this is so important to you, I will not use that word anymore."

She blinked in disbelief, swallowed, and managed, "Thank you, Charles. I really appreciate it."

His compatibility continued through the evening. *Maybe Mom's right,* she thought. *She always says if you don't ask for it, you don't get it. I asked, and he said yes. It was so incredibly easy. Maybe, if I keep at it, things really could get better.*

But doubt edged in as she flossed her teeth that night. *Will he actually stop using that word? And how long will his good humor hold?*

The next evening she saw her answer in Charles's resolute walk, the set of his jaw, the squint of his eyes. She heard it in his monosyllabic answers to her questions. "Yes" . . . "Very" . . . "Not really."

She braced herself. Maybe she could at least defer a confrontation till after dinner. She grabbed the conversational ball, much as Michelle had the previous night. Desperately she kept it bouncing, asking the kids questions, commenting on the news, anything to keep Charles from grabbing hold and letting loose.

"Leslie," he said at last, "I'd like to go over some paperwork with you after dinner."

She recognized the tone of voice. Inquisition time.

8

LESLIE STARED OUT THE WINDOW AT THE ELONGATED SHADOWS
of the chairs on the patio and remembered late-summer
evenings as a child when she had laughed at her shadow and
how very, very tall it made her seem.

End of September, and the days were growing shorter. She
watched the white swan, the lake's year-round resident, glide
past, realizing that soon other birds would migrate south to
winter with him. Normally, she loved fall and the sense of new-
ness and adventure it engendered—a holdover from school
days, no doubt. However, this year, with Charles homing in on
the November actuary exam and Michelle growing up much
too fast, she wasn't so sure.

But here she was, once again looking way down the pike,
when she faced a much more immediate challenge: Charles and
his "paperwork," which always meant expenses. Every month

they went through this, and it always evolved into an inquisition time as she accounted for—no, defended her expenditures.

She delayed the inevitable as long as possible, wiping fingerprints off cabinet doors, polishing a copper bowl, stopping by the family room to chat with Scott and Michelle. Then Charles's voice boomed from upstairs. "You coming, *Les*-lie?"

Sighing, she mounted the steps to his tiny study. Sure enough, he had spreadsheet printouts arranged on the desk in front of him.

"You're way over budget for last month," he announced without turning to look at her. "What, pray tell, is this twenty-nine-dollar cosmetics item from the Broadway?"

She leaned over his desk to look. "Oh, um, that's my makeup."

"Twenty-nine dollars?" he asked, his voice incredulous. "Don't I see bottles of makeup for around five dollars in the drugstore?"

"Well, yes, Charles, but you see, my skin—"

"Ah," he nodded wisely. "Yes, now I remember, your sensitive skin. Expensive skin, I'd say." He stared at her analytically for a moment, and she sat down, feeling an almost physical weight to his gaze. "Why don't you go for a natural look? If you saved money on makeup, maybe you could do something about your hair."

She winced. "My hair?"

"Yes. I've been thinking," he said. "I think I'd like your hair blonde."

"What?" She recoiled. People stopped her in the supermarket to remark on the glory of her burnished auburn hair. Bleach it? Surely he was joking.

"Yes, blonde. I think that would be a pleasant change." He

reached over and picked up a strand of her hair, nodding and smiling to himself.

"I, uh," she managed, "I'll think about it." And then an inspiration. "But you know it's much more expensive having your hair colored than buying makeup. I mean, once you start, you have to keep at it every few weeks. And it's quite time-consuming too."

"Yes. Well, you *would* find the time. Make some calls and see how much it costs. I think—yes, a nice tawny shade." He stared at her a moment longer before returning to the spread sheets. "Now. This $51.65 at Miller's Outpost?"

She cleared her throat. "That would be jeans. For Michelle."

"Fifty-one dollars and sixty-five cents for *jeans*?" he shouted. "Have you taken leave of your senses?"

"Charles, they were on sale. We bought two pairs. She's out-grown all her others."

"Oh, so they were *only* $25.85 apiece. What an incredible bargain! Yes, of course, now it's perfectly clear. You certainly couldn't let that slip by." He let his breath out in a long, low "Whoo."

She waited, feeling the tension spread down her neck and spine. "Relax, let those muscles go slack," she'd tell her patients. *Come on,* she told herself. *Let go, neck. Let go, back.*

"Forty-two ninety-three. Swoboda's." His voice grew louder.

She sat, rigid, in her chair. "Yes, that would be shoes."

"For?"

"Michelle."

"And I suppose this is for Michelle. And this?" He pointed to the bills.

"Charles, as I mentioned, she is growing. She needs—"

"She needs a mother who doesn't indulge her every whim.

That is what she needs." He jabbed his pencil toward her. "May I remind you, woman, that I took on this girl out of the kindness of my heart, that she is not my flesh and blood, that my mission in life is not to make her happy, that she is an immensely fortunate young lady to have the home I provide for her?"

"Yes, I know, Charles. And I appreciate what you've done." It was true. He'd been kind enough to take on the two of them when he married her. Many men, she knew, wouldn't even date a woman with a child, much less consider marriage.

"Well, then, is this the kind of thanks I get? This mad spending spree?"

"Charles, I hardly think these few items constitute—"

"Come, come, now Leslie. This is not the first time. Do you not see? Do you not know how you take advantage of me?"

She looked down and picked at her cuticle. "I'll try to be more careful."

She stood, and he immediately reached for her arm and yanked her back into her chair. "I am not finished. Food bills. Much too high."

"But Charles, you do at least half of the grocery shopping."

"Well, *I* buy store brands and look for the specials. You seem compelled to plan a menu and then shop instead of noting the specials in the various stores and then building your menus." He shook his head. "But obviously, that is typical of you. Do what *you* want to do and let good old Charles pay for it. Take— take—take. That's all you do, Leslie. That's all you do."

Me? she thought. *What about him taking my salary and salting it away? Insisting that we not live on it because we may need it and because, after all, he is capable of providing.*

His eyes began to glitter as he warmed to the subject. "I would say that your extravagance costs me—" he pursed his lips then pulled out his calculator and punched in several numbers. "Yes, at least two thousand unnecessary dollars a year." He broke the pencil in two. "Think what two thousand dollars could do for my retirement."

She blinked. "Retirement?"

"Yes. Of course. Why do you think I work?" He laughed in a condescending tone. "So someday I will not have to work. You knew that."

"Well," she said, "I guess I didn't realize that's such a concern right now. Charles, you're only thirty-nine."

"Aha! You thought I enjoyed going to work, punching computer keys, crunching numbers."

"Well, yes, I guess I did."

"Wrong! It is a means to an end."

And the end, she thought, *is not providing for his family. In fact, that's something that impedes his goal. Why in the world did he ever get married?*

It was as though he'd heard her thoughts. "In fact, sometimes I wonder whatever possessed me to get married. Why, if I hadn't, look where I would be!"

"Where is that, Charles?"

"Why, way ahead in business. Earning much more. *Saving* much more!" He shook his head. "So here I am with a floozy money trap of a stepdaughter, a defective son who can never be the man I want him to be, and a wife who—"

His moustache formed an inverted vee. "—thwarts me at every turn, sabotages all my efforts to meet my goals. What I have is—let me see—on a scale of one to ten—I would say you are about a three as a nanny, maybe a four as a cook, and . . ." He snickered. ". . . a one as a housekeeper. Then, as a mistress, oh, I would say about a two." The outer corners of his eyes drooped as he scrutinized her as though examining some pathetic lower species.

She looked away and shivered, feeling naked, stripped, not just externally, but inwardly. All that she was or thought she was—and that hadn't been a whole lot to begin with—had been peeled away in a few devastating sentences. If she dared to look inside herself, she knew she would find—nothing.

She wasn't sure how long she sat there before she spoke. "Then what would you like to do, Charles?"

"Do?" He seemed surprised.

"Yes. What are we going to do about our marriage, if I've failed you so completely?"

"Why, nothing."

She managed to look at him. "You mean we just rock along?"

"Certainly."

"I'm not sure I can do that."

He let out a sharp, "Pfft. Of course you can."

"But Charles, if you're so miserable, if you've made—I mean, if our marriage is such a mistake, why don't you bail out?"

"No, I could not do that to you."

"But look what you *are* doing. Do you have any idea how much your words hurt me?"

"Oh, Leslie! You are so sensitive!" he exclaimed.

She blinked back tears. "Charles, please. We don't have to just rock along. Please let's get some help. Please say you'll go to counseling with me." There was no holding back the tears now.

"That," Charles said with finality, "is not an option."

"But why, Charles?" she pleaded, dropping to her knees beside his chair. "You're suffering, and so am I. Just one meeting? Just one? I know there's hope for us. But the way it is now . . ."

"I believe this conversation is over." Charles rose from his desk and left the room.

She struggled to her feet, ran to their bedroom, and threw herself on the bed, pulling a pillow over her head.

I feel ravaged. There's nothing left, she thought. *Whatever, whoever I thought I was—it's all gone.* The pain was too deep for further tears, and she heard herself groan again and again.

Gradually the desire to get out of that house—Charles's house—seeped into her mind, and she found enough strength to rise and wash her face. Grabbing her purse, she headed downstairs. Charles was watching the ball game, and Scott and Michelle had started a game of Monopoly.

"I'm going out," she said, praying Charles wouldn't stop her.

He nodded, without looking at her.

⟿

Zoë had thought Leslie looked ghastly the day of her miscarriage. But when she answered the doorbell and saw her daughter's thin, taut face, she gasped inwardly. "Come in, darlin'." She moved to give her a hug, but Leslie stumbled past her into the living room, flinging herself into a chair. Zoë drew up a footstool and sat before her, waiting.

Finally Leslie took a deep, shuddering breath and, in a flat monotone, spilled out the story of the conversation with Charles. "And," she finished, "he absolutely refuses to consider counseling."

Zoë shook her head, leaning toward her. "He is such an angry man, isn't he? Remember, darlin', he did have a nightmare childhood—that mother who left him during his earliest years then just stood by and let his stepfather abuse him."

"I know," Leslie said, impatience finally coloring her words. "But why do *I* have to keep paying for it?"

"Why, indeed?" Zoë settled back on the stool.

They sat without speaking while the clock on the mantle ticked off the minutes. From time to time, Zoë glanced at Leslie's face. *Oh, Lord,* she prayed silently, *I can't give her strength. But You can. Help her, Father.*

Gradually Zoë thought she saw a flicker of resolution, of determination, in Leslie's countenance. When she finally looked at her mother, Leslie's eyes looked brighter, surer. "I can't go on this way."

"All right."

"Will I go to hell if I leave Charles?"

"Of course not! Didn't I teach you any better than that, for heaven's sake?"

Leslie closed her eyes. "'God hates divorce,'" she quoted. "But," she looked at her mother. "He doesn't hate you."

"Certainly not."

"But, Mom, it was dad who left you, wasn't it? He was the one who filed. Right?"

Zoë took her hand. "But Leslie, we're not talking about divorce for you right now, are we? You're thinking separation, aren't you?"

Leslie nodded.

"Darlin', maybe this could be a means of a real reconciliation. If Charles sees that you're serious, that you can't go on like this, then perhaps he'll be willing to do something."

"Do you think?" Leslie looked at her mother like an eight-year-old, asking for reassurance.

"It's possible. Time-out will give you both a chance to think and to get your heads together. You know, I've always suspected that Charles is like a lot of people who will do as much as they can get away with—until somebody blows the whistle."

Leslie's eyes brightened. "Get me that whistle, Mom."

Zoë laughed. "Gladly."

"I think I'll go to Tracy's house. If she'll have me. With the kids, of course. I'm not going to leave them to cope with Charles's reaction."

"I agree. I think all it would take would be a phone call to your sister. She's more than willing, and that bonus area of her house is just sitting there."

"May I use your phone?"

Zoë grinned. "You have to ask?" As they stood, she grabbed Leslie's arms and turned her around. "Let me look at you. There's something different about your anatomy."

Leslie looked over her shoulder, surprised. "What?"

Zoë ran her fingers down her daughter's back. "Why, sure enough. I think it's called a backbone!"

9

❧

From Zoë's Prayer Journal

September 23: Dear heavenly Father, I can scarcely believe my daughter's decided to leave Charles. May this be a wake-up call for him so he'll seek You as his Lord and also seek help with his anger. Thank You for giving Leslie the courage to take this enormous step. I ask You to strengthen her and stiffen that backbone so she will not waffle or weaken. I look forward to Your doing a mighty work and someday reuniting them in a marriage that is truly a marriage. And I praise You and thank You! In Jesus' name, amen.

LESLIE SLIPPED INTO BED HALF AN HOUR AFTER CHARLES that night.

Good. He didn't stir, and his breathing was regular, with that familiar little wheeze as he inhaled. She stretched out on the far edge of the bed, turned away from him, eyes wide open.

Oh, Charles, she thought, *if you'd only come to your senses, see things as they are, and as they could be!*

All night the list of to-do's paraded in a circular course

through her mind: call the office, rearrange schedules, clue in the kids, do laundry, pack, take this, take that. But over all that agenda, the anxious awareness that she must write and explain to Charles hovered relentlessly.

I never seem to be able to communicate with him face-to-face, she thought, *and a letter gives me time to think it through. But writing it down is such a permanent thing. It's there, on the paper, in black and white—or maybe blue and white—not to be erased or rephrased. And Charles would be good at misinterpreting. How do I make myself clear? How do I make him understand?*

Phrases drifted through her mind: "I'm up to here, and I'm not going to take it anymore." . . . "Find someone else to degrade." . . . "Here's a diagram on how to find the stove and turn it on."

No, no. Be serious, Leslie, she told herself. *You can't be sarcastic or inflame him. Be kind. Don't accuse. Tell him how you feel.*

She turned over, turned back again, trying to find a cool spot on the sheet without drawing closer to Charles.

Then the "what-if's" closed ranks. *What if the kids refuse to go? What if Scott thinks it's his fault? Oh, what if they take sides? Is that inevitable? I don't want to bad-mouth their father to them. And what if they want to stick with Charles? What if he becomes violent with them? What if he tries to hurt them?*

She tried to focus on a sense of release, relieved to soon be away from Charles, tried to feel confident about her decision. *This is good,* she told herself. *I'm finally taking a step. I won't have to walk on eggs now.* But then she wondered if she was being fair to Charles, and the anxieties returned, deep and shadowy as the night outside.

It seemed she hadn't slept at all, so she was surprised to rouse to the sound of water running in the shower. Had she missed the alarm? She glanced at the clock. Only six. Then she remembered: Charles had an early meeting of the Hope for the Children Fund this morning. How convenient! She'd have a chance to explain her plans to Scott and Michelle before they left for school.

As she went into the bathroom to wash her face, Charles emerged from the shower. "Oh," he said, "I didn't set the alarm for earlier. Thought you could catch a few extra winks."

Thoughtful, congenial. As though nothing had happened the night before. *It's enough to drive me crazy,* she thought, *like that husband in the movie* Gaslight *or the one in* Midnight Lace, *playing with his wife's mind till she was sure she was insane.*

"Thanks," she said, "but it's time I'm up and moving."

She dressed and hurried downstairs, where she picked up the list she'd begun the night before and hidden on top of the refrigerator. She jotted down "heating pad" for the shin splints Scott sometimes had at night.

That note to Charles, she thought once again, feeling her stomach tense. *I have to do it. But where to begin? What to say? What should the tone be? Not angry, but what? Conciliatory? Apologetic? Or . . .* she didn't know.

She put the sandwiches together, cut carrot sticks and wrapped them, rinsed and dried apples. *There. Three neat brown lunch bags.* Then she realized. *It's Wednesday. Charles likes eggs on Wednesday mornings.* She hurried to heat the skillet.

Charles glanced at the stove as he came through the kitchen. "Eggs not ready yet? I'll skip 'em."

No criticism.

Maybe I am crazy to leave, she thought. Then she remembered the piercing stab of his words the night before. "An albatross around my neck . . . on a scale of one to ten, a three as a nanny . . . a one as a housekeeper . . ." She put her hands over her ears to mute the echo. *You have to do it,* she told herself. *Now, before you forget those words.*

Yet when Charles left, kissing her on the cheek and saying, "See you this evening," guilt dripped over her like glue, rooting her to the spot till she had to will herself to move on.

When Scott and Michelle were seated at the breakfast table and well into their cereal, she joined them. Michelle stared off into space, a faint smile on her lips, caught up in some private reverie. Scott crunched his Grape-Nuts with determination.

"I, uh—" she began, and neither of them paid the least attention. She tried again. "Scott, Michelle, I have something to tell you, and it's important."

"Yeah?" said Michelle in her prove-it-to-me tone. "We're going to Hawaii on vacation, right?"

She raised an eyebrow. "Close," she said. "The 'we're going' part is correct."

"Going where?" Scott asked.

"We—you, Michelle, and you, Scott, and I—are going to go and live at your Aunt Tracy's. For a while." She looked at their questioning faces and continued, "You remember, she has that bonus area where the boys used to live—really nice—with that living room and the kitchenette downstairs and the sleeping balcony and the bath, and the pool right outside and—"

"Just us three, right?" Michelle pointed her spoon at Leslie.
"Yes."

"You getting a divorce?" Michelle persisted.

"Heavens, no. No, it's not like that." She felt her face flush.

"Well, practically everybody I know has parents who're divorced. Stepmoms, stepdads, that kinda thing."

"Yes, well, it's not like that. You could think of it as—" Leslie struggled to phrase it just right and remembered Zoë's words, "time-out." Yes, that was it.

"As a time-out," Leslie said. "Your dad and I need time to think, to be apart from each other."

Neither of the children spoke for what seemed an eternity. She couldn't read their faces. She took a deep breath to try to fill the silence, but Michelle nodded. "Okay. Yeah. I'll be closer to where Jason lives. Is there a TV? How 'bout a phone?"

She'd expected an emotional outpouring, not such practical questions. "Yes," Leslie said. "There's a TV. And people can use Aunt Tracy and Uncle Greg's phone number to reach us."

Michelle curled her mouth into her most petulant pout. "No phone! I thought my cousins used to have their own phone in their pad."

"We'll see," she hedged.

Scott looked up at last from his cereal bowl, and she saw half-relief, half-terror on his face. *He's a mirror of me,* she thought. *That's exactly the way I feel.* "You okay, Scott?" she asked.

"Yeah."

"Okay, I want you to come straight home from school, both of you, and you'll have an hour to decide on clothes and stuff to take." Was she talking too fast? She tried to slow down. "I'll do the wash so everything's ready. But it's all going to have to fit in one load in the car."

Michelle groaned.

"It'll be fine, honey," she assured her daughter. "It's not like we're going to darkest Africa. You can come back and pick up stuff you might need."

"Does Dad know?" Scott spoke at last.

"Not yet. I'm going to leave him a letter." She looked from one to the other. "It's best that way."

And it's the only way I can pull it off, she added to herself.

After the children left for school, she realized she'd been

holding her breath during most of their conversation. She breathed out a long sigh. First hurdle accomplished. And not as hard as she expected. She called work and asked Terry to rearrange her appointments so she could get away at 2:30, then she sorted the wash and started a load.

Hurrying up the stairs, she stood at the door of her closet and turned indecisive again. What would she need? She couldn't remember how much closet space there was for three of them. At last she grabbed randomly from the slacks and tops and carried them down to the car. She glanced at the clock. 7:45. Time to write the note before she showered and dressed.

She kept it short, trying to avoid accusations. "Send 'I' messages," she remembered reading somewhere. So she concentrated on phrases like, "I feel a lot of pain from our conversation last night . . . I need some time to think . . . I'm convinced it's best that we be apart for a while." No closed doors. Then she tackled the practical points: where they would be, that she wanted him to see the kids whenever he wished.

She left the note on her dresser while she showered in case she had additional thoughts, but nothing came. After she dressed, she reread the note, wondering how Charles would react, what he would do. Would he simply say, "Oh," and tuck the note back in the envelope? Would he be glad for time alone for ball games and studying for the actuary exam? Or would he explode and throw things? Would he come and try to drag them back? She thought of newspaper stories about angry husbands following their wives and shooting the whole family, and she remembered the revolver Charles kept by the bed. Maybe she should take it. No, that would really enrage him.

She added to the note, "I hope you will respect and honor my need to be away from you for a bit." Now how should she sign it? "Sincerely?" Too much like a business letter. "Yours truly?" No, I'm not even sure I want to be his, especially truly his. "Love?" She sighed. Down deep, she knew she still loved him. She wrote the word quickly, signed her name, and folded the note into the envelope, placing it on Charles's dresser.

"Oh, Lord, help him understand," she prayed. "Help him want to change."

✌

That afternoon Michelle stood at the door of her closet and shrieked, "I need *every*-thing!"

"Michelle, you *can't* bring everything. Tell you what, pick six outfits for starters and whatever you need to go with them," Leslie suggested. "You can leave stuff on hangers, but pack the shoes and things from your dresser in this bag."

"Why are you *doing* this to me?" Michelle wailed, grabbing pants, tops, and dresses from her closet and heaving them onto her bed.

Leslie left Michelle and headed for Scott's bedroom, recalling that decisions tended to come hard for him. She was surprised to see him methodically layering clothes, including his swimsuit, together with a beloved stuffed cat, in his suitcase. "Good for you, Scott!" she exclaimed. "You're really organized. I appreciate that."

Without looking at her, he asked, "How do I get to school? When do I get to see Dad?"

"I'll drop you off on my way to work and leave in time to get you. Your grandmother might pick you up once in a while. And Scott, I told your dad he could see you anytime he wanted to. But you could always call him and tell him you want to get together too."

He nodded, keeping his focus intent upon the project at hand. Ten minutes later he announced he was ready.

Leslie went to check on Michelle. "It's easier for Scott," Michelle said. "He doesn't need as much."

"That may be, Michelle. But please be ready by four-thirty," she said.

By the time they loaded the car, Leslie couldn't see through the rear window. *Thank goodness for side mirrors,* she thought as she backed out of the garage. She took a last look at the house she loved. It had taken her six years to make it pretty because Charles never wanted anything but bare bones rooms. He'd kept reminding her it was the location, with the little stretch of lake for a backyard, that "made" the house. And in many ways, it did. She would miss the light of the sun dancing on the water, the winter birds that would soon return. While still in the driveway, she felt a pang of homesickness. *It's hard,* she thought. *Hard not knowing what's ahead—when I'll be back—if I'll be back. Hard to leave a place I love.* She bit her lip and put her foot on the accelerator.

The drive took only twelve minutes, and her sister came out to the car to greet them. Tracy, whose slightly Roman nose reminded her so much of Zoë, was graying becomingly, with little glistening streaks in her dark, short hair. Leslie thought Tracy felt a little softer around the middle than the last time she'd hugged her.

"It's about time," Tracy whispered. Then, to the children, "I'm *so* excited about you being here! This place has been like a morgue since number-three son finally moved out. Guess I've been in an empty-nest funk. Anyway, you guys are great to come here, and Greg and I hope you'll be comfortable. Here, let me show you what's where, though I think you know the bonus area pretty well."

She led them toward a breezeway that separated the main part of the house from the garage and the bonus area behind it. A wrought-iron gate stretched across the breezeway from the bonus structure, joining the house just past the entry. Behind it, a Siberian husky stood, blue-eyed, with a mask of white accented by wolf-gray fur, his tail swishing the air.

They stepped through the gate. "Hi, Boris," Scott said, reaching down to pet the dog, who promptly rolled onto his back, legs in the air, an obvious invitation for attention. "Oh, o-*kay*," Scott condescended, kneeling to scratch the dog's belly.

"You found a live one, Boris." Tracy laughed and stepped around them, pulling open the sliding door to the bonus area. "Okay, here you are. Beds are made, and I stocked a few things in the fridge."

"Oh, Trace, you didn't have to do that," Leslie protested.

"I know. I wanted to." Tracy turned to Scott and Michelle. "Okay, you guys start bringing stuff in. I'll show your mom a couple of things about the kitchenette." She hustled them out the gate.

"This is so good of you, Trace," Leslie said. She laughed nervously. "I can't even believe I'm here. I'm not sure if I've taken leave of my senses or not."

"More like you just found them, I'd say," Tracy said. "I'm sorry, but I hope you'll tie a can to that jerk, Leslie. This marriage hasn't been good from the beginning, and you know it. It's not you. God knows you've tried. Charles is just not built for marriage. Face it, the man should have been a hermit out in a hut somewhere."

Leslie didn't know what to say, and she glanced nervously to see if the kids were coming.

Tracy took her by the shoulders. "You are doing the right thing," she said firmly. "You're as abused as the woman who's had her teeth knocked out. Your wounds just aren't visible. Stick to your guns. Stop being a doormat. Stop making your kids doormats for Charles to wipe his feet on. You don't have to take it, and neither do Michelle and Scott."

Glancing outside, Tracy saw the kids coming. "And," she added pleasantly, "you're all invited for a welcome dinner with Greg and me." She held up her hand as Leslie took a breath to protest. "After that, you're on your own, folks."

They carried clothes to the loft, and Michelle immediately complained about not having her own closet. She eyed the bunks. "Dibs on the lower—unless you wanta give me the double bed, Mom."

Leslie ignored her, and Scott said, "I wanted the top bunk anyway."

"Oh, then I changed my mind." Michelle gave a wicked smile.

"Huh-uh. Too late," Scott said.

Tracy had prepared a lamb roast with browned potatoes and carrots, and Greg put the finishing touches on the salad as Leslie and the kids arrived. Greg managed to captivate Scott immediately with tales of coaching high-schoolers in football and wrestling. It was hard not to respond to his enthusiasm, his round-faced boyishness, which Scott had once described as "like a little kid—with wrinkles." Michelle, however, resisted his good spirits and sat, sullen-faced, throughout the meal, eating the salad and ignoring the meat and vegetables.

The food had smelled irresistible to Leslie when they entered, but now her throat felt so constricted, she had trouble swallowing. Taking small bites, she tried to relax. As she watched the good-natured exchanges between her sister and brother-in-law, she hoped both kids were taking it in. Maybe they'd learn from them that all marriages weren't like hers and Charles's.

Each time the phone rang, she tensed, sure it would be Charles. But he didn't call. After the kids went to bed, she tried to read her Bible in the downstairs living area. She hadn't read more than two verses when Michelle's voice came from above. "Mo-om! How can we sleep with that light glaring up at us?"

Leslie sighed and switched off the lamp. So many adjustments for them all. Their new home might be considered cozy—or cramped. She missed her privacy and wished she'd brought her own blanket.

She brushed her teeth and washed her face and climbed into bed. *What is Charles thinking, planning?* she wondered. *Is he glad I'm gone? Have I managed to kill our marriage by leaving? Will he simply say, "That's it"? Will I be tossed out with no more feeling than getting rid of yesterday's newspaper?* An overwhelming sense of aloneness, of abandonment, flooded over her.

She looked around her bed. Unlike the bedroom at home, no light at all seeped into the loft. Black as that huge, deep pit she'd dug for herself, the pit she could never climb out of. She wept silently into her pillow. "Oh, Lord, that isn't what I meant to do. Oh, help me. I've made a terrible mistake!"

10

CHARLES WILL CALL ME AT THE OFFICE TODAY, Leslie thought as she drove Scott and Michelle to school. *That's what he'll do. He wouldn't want to talk with Tracy or Greg. Never even liked them much. That's why he didn't call last night. But oh, when he calls, what will his reaction be? Angry? Cold? Will he hate me? Have I blown it? And if I have, can I have a life? What will all this do to the kids?*

"I kinda like door-to-door delivery, instead of the ol' yellow school bus." Scott grinned as she dropped him by the playground.

"No problem," Leslie answered. "It's on my way. And I'll pick you up as usual following your after-school enrichment classes."

"I hate having to stay after regular classes till you come to get us. What a drag," Michelle grumbled as they drove the mile to her school. "How come we can't be latchkey kids?"

"Well, first of all, because there's no way to get you to Tracy's after school. You know the school bus doesn't go to Mission Viejo. And second, my darling, because I prefer you to do something constructive—and supervised." Leslie smiled. "Really, it isn't exactly cruel and unusual punishment."

"Sure, sure," Michelle muttered as she unfastened her seat belt. "See ya."

"Right. Have a good one." Leslie waited for her to slam the door then pushed a cassette of praise songs into the tape player as she drove away. "Lord of all," came the words.

"Lord even of this mess. Got to remember that," she murmured to herself. "You are in control, and I *will* praise You, Lord." She let the music bathe her, washing away all thoughts of Charles.

But as her day progressed, those thoughts crowded back. Would he indeed call her at work? Would he barge into her workplace?

By the time David arrived for his appointment, she found it difficult to concentrate. He picked up on it immediately. "Hello?" he said as he worked on getting back into the wheelchair from a fallen position. "Anybody home?"

She shook the intruding thoughts away. "Sorry, David. You're right; I'm distracted."

"Is it related in any way to moving my appointment to later in the day?" He looked at her intently.

"Oh, that's because I get in a little later now that I'm taking the kids to school."

"Thought they took the bus."

"Yes, well, we're staying at my sister's in Mission Viejo for a while." She tried to smile. "You did that nicely, David. Try it again."

"Sounds serious," he persisted.

She nodded, determined not to bring her personal life into their relationship. "See you in the treatment room after you

87

finish in the gym," she said. She turned, talking firmly to herself. "You don't bring your problems to work, lady. Be professional."

When she came into the treatment room, David held up a hand, palm toward her. "I don't know if this is permitted or not, but ma'am, my gut feeling is that you need prayer."

She felt tears begin to rise and said quickly, "I'm okay." A glance at his blue-green eyes told her he wasn't buying it. "Okay," she said. "I just, uh, had to have some space from my husband."

"Okay. You don't have to explain. Let's pray." He closed his eyes, and she bowed over the treatment table. "Father, we bring Leslie before You, and we know that You know everything, including all about what's bugging her marriage and her. Lord, take away her fears, help her trust in You. I ask You to keep her safe and give her strength for whatever's ahead. In Jesus' name, amen."

She wiped the corners of her eyes, moved by his caring, his sensitivity. "Thanks. I needed that."

As her strong hands massaged a tight cord in his neck, she admitted, "I've been half-afraid Charles would walk in the door—and, I guess, half-afraid he wouldn't."

"If you moved out on him, sounds like you needed some distance. So why would you want him to come?"

She blinked. "I don't. I, mean, well . . ."

"I mean, do you want to be away from him, or don't you?" She hesitated, realizing the ambivalence of her feelings. David twisted his head to look at her. "He beating on you?"

"No. He hasn't hit me."

He settled his head back on the treatment table. "But with his mouth?"

"You've got it. Now, turn over on your left side, David, and we'll work on strength. I'll help you move your right leg backward and forward."

"Ahhh. I always wondered why you hide a nice face under those long bangs. I keep wanting to bring in some scissors. Kept thinking you were hiding something. Now I understand. It's yourself."

His candor was beginning to rankle. What was this kid doing, analyzing her? "What is this, psych 201?" she asked.

"Nope," he said. "Real life 201."

She stopped moving his leg. "You're not serious."

"My dad had a temper and a mouth like you wouldn't believe. He could reduce my mother to a quivering pulp with a few quick strokes of his tongue. She got so she couldn't look anyone straight in the eye, and on a scale of one to ten, her self-esteem was about a minus five."

David's scale of one to ten reminded her of Charles, and she winced. "Now, sit up," she said, "and we'll work on your transfer." She waited and finally dared to ask, "And what about you kids?"

"We got it, too, but not as bad." He smiled to himself as he sat up. "Now I know why I felt so drawn to Scott. We have more in common than I realized. Or should I call it a common handicap?"

"*Has* it been a handicap?"

"It's been—" He hesitated. "—something to overcome. But I want you to know, it has a profound effect on kids. I kinda withdrew. But my older brother acted out. Basically imitated my dad. Got so he did the same thing to my mom as dad."

She swallowed hard. The tendency was definitely there in Michelle. "Verbal abuse?"

"A real attitude problem. Zero respect. He learned the technique well. Now I see him doing it to his wife."

"And then *his* children will learn . . ." Her voice trailed off.

"The sins of the fathers," he said. "So—you getting any help? A group of other women in a situation like yours, maybe?"

She shook her head. "I haven't had time . . ."

"Leslie, do yourself a favor. Take the time. You don't need to gnash your teeth waiting for your husband to call. You need to relearn that you're smart and capable and that God loves you big time. And it's really hard to do all by yourself."

She smiled, marveling at his discernment. "David, is there something you haven't told me? Are you really an eighty-year-old wise man in a twenty-one-year-old body?"

"Shh." He held his finger to his lips and whispered, "Let that be our little secret."

⌇

David's right, bless him, she thought as she left work. *I know there's a support group at my church. I'll call and check it out.*

After she picked up the kids and they were splashing in the pool just outside the sliding doors of what Scott called their "pad," she made her phone call and learned that the group would meet that night. She glanced across the breezeway. Tracy and Greg had gone out for the evening, leaving their portable phone with her. She just didn't feel right leaving the kids alone their second night here. Besides, Charles might call.

"There I go again," she muttered to herself, trying to concentrate on fixing a dinner of veggie-and-cheese pizza. Thank goodness for ready-made crust.

The phone rang three times during the evening, each time with a message for Tracy or Greg. Still, it was only at bedtime that her imagination kicked in. *Charles has left. Disappeared. Dropped off the face of the earth. No clues. No one knows. We'll never hear from him again. It's déjà vu, like—yes, like when Tom literally dropped off the face of the earth in that ski accident and left me a widow.* She shuddered. *Eleven years, Charles has been an integral part of my life—ever since he came into therapy for carpal tunnel syndrome. Oh, how he came on to me then—so witty, so charming, so polished. Will he turn that charm on for someone else now? Someone at his office? Someone on the Hope for the Children Foundation board? Why, he could be busy right now filing for divorce, getting all the paperwork going, figuring out how to get around the joint-property laws.*

She shook her head. *What does the Bible say about "vain imaginations?" That's what I'm doing.*

"Stop it," she told herself firmly.

ॐ

By the third day they were all beginning to adjust to their new surroundings. With their own phone installed, Michelle could curl up and chatter endlessly with friends. Scott swam each day before dinner and before bed, practicing again and again, trying to master a flip turn.

Her mother called at dinnertime. "How's my favorite trio?" she asked.

"We're really doing pretty well," Leslie said. "It's cozy, you know, but we're learning how not to step on each other. I, uh, haven't heard one word from Charles."

"That's all right."

"Yup. That's what I decided. I guess I'm just used to holding my breath to see what he'll do next."

"And that's one pattern I'd be delighted to see you break."

"I thought I might go to a support group for—you know—people like me."

"I think the word is *abused*." Zoë's voice was soft, gentle. "I know that's hard for you to say, honey."

"I guess since I don't have any teeth missing . . ."

"No, all that's missing is your natural laughter and playfulness, your spunk, your . . . Don't you see how that's been knocked out of you?"

"I guess I've forgotten how I was before."

"Yes. And, oh, Leslie, how I pray you'll find it again. Please, dear one, hang in there. Don't give in to loneliness or fear of the future, or any of the jillion things that must be running through your head. Use this time to get in touch with you, as God created you, to be true to that person instead of always trying to be what Charles wants you to be. You can't make Charles change. But you can change." She paused before she asked, "Now, how can I help? When's the next meeting?"

"Wednesday."

"Okay. Why don't I pick up Scott and Michelle, and we'll have dinner together that night?"

"Oh, Mom, that would be great. They love being with you, and it would give me a little time."

"That's a date, then. Love you, darlin'."

"Me too, you."

I am so blessed, Leslie thought as she went back to dinner, *to have a supportive family. How can other women do anything without a mother and a sister to encourage them? Hopefully, they have a David to keep them on track. I really need to count my blessings. What I should do is journal my prayers the way Mom does.*

She started that evening. But just as she began writing out her thanks, Tracy knocked on their door. "Phone. For you."

"Is it—?" Leslie felt her heart begin to thud, adrenaline rushing. *Fight or flight,* she thought. *Think I'd prefer flight.*

Tracy nodded. "Thought maybe you'd rather take it in our study."

She followed Tracy into the house and to the study and gingerly picked up the phone as she heard the door close. *Oh, no,* she thought instinctively. *Now I'm alone with Charles.*

"H-hello?" She heard her voice crack.

"Les-lie. I really thought you'd come to your senses by now, stop playing games and come back like a reasonable person." He waited for her reply, but when she said nothing, his voice grew louder. "What *do* you think you're doing, young lady? Have you taken leave of your faculties? Do you have any idea the embarrassment you have caused me? The neighbors saw you loading the car and could not wait to ask me where you are. You were supposed to pick up my suit at the cleaners for a meeting today, and there I was, without it."

As he paused, she could hear the thud of her own heart. "For God's sake, *say* something, Leslie!"

"What do you want me to say, Charles?"

"Well, tell me what this is all about."

"I did. In my note."

"Leslie, that note made no sense at all. Listen, Leslie, there are dozens of women who want *me*. Do you want a divorce?"

"No, Charles."

"I want you to know, Leslie, that if you intend to separate, I will fight you tooth and nail for the children. And I *will* win. It won't be difficult to prove your incompetence." His voice was so loud she held the receiver away from her ear.

She twisted the telephone cord. "Charles, I told you what I'm after here is a time-out. Time for us both to think about our relationship. Better yet, time for us to get some counseling. I definitely need it."

"Well, I don't. That is not an option."

"Then I guess I'd better go on my own."

"And you'd better pay for it on your own. Look. This conversation is going nowhere. Let me know when you come to your senses." She expected him to hang up, but almost as an afterthought, he added, "Oh, and what about our dinner engagement tomorrow evening? With my boss."

"You'll have to explain to him, I guess." She wound the spiral phone cord around her finger.

"There! You see what I mean?" he shouted. "The embarrassment you're causing me. Well, I shall think of something to—"

His voice broke off and she felt the telephone cord snap against her hand. She looked with dismay at the plastic plug, cleanly uprooted from the phone. *He thinks I hung up on him. He must be livid,* she thought. *Shall I call him back? I don't want him to think—*

Quickly she dialed their number.

"Yes," snapped Charles's voice.

"I didn't mean to hang up, Charles. I pulled the cord out of the phone."

"Typical," he said, and she heard the phone slam down.

11

CHARLES SLAMMED THE RECEIVER DOWN SO HARD, THE phone rang once from the impact. "Selfish shrew," he muttered. "Never thinks of anything or anyone but herself. We shall see how long she can make it on her own. She will be back. If I hadn't taken pity on her and Michelle, where would they be today? She can never get along without me."

He stood, shoving the chair back. "But if she thinks she can be so 'liberated,' she jolly well better take me seriously when I promise to fight her for the kids. Of course, I have no real need for them, but that would *really* get to her!"

He paced back and forth across the family room. "The problem is her pushy family. She has no backbone. So easily influenced and swayed. Especially by that intrusive mother." He pounded a fist into the palm of his other hand. "There is the biggest problem. Zoë. Always quoting Bible verses. 'The Lord

95

this, the Lord that.' Never can leave well enough alone; has to bombard me with her ceaseless attempts to 'save' me. What do I need saving from, eh, old lady?"

At last he headed for the kitchen. Another beer. That's what he needed. And some peanuts. He opened the refrigerator and slipped a can of Bud out of the twelve-pack. Shoving the door shut with his foot, he reached up into the cabinet. The can of peanuts felt light. He swore vehemently and pulled off the lid. Five—no, six nuts nestled midst a dusting of crumbs in the bottom of the can. He threw it to the floor, scattering the contents. *Stupid broad! Can't even keep the pantry stocked.*

Michelle, no doubt, was the peanut-eater. What had he done to deserve *her*? Argumentative, rebellious, she seemed to dedicate her life to getting his goat. Not many stepfathers would put up with her.

He sucked on the beer for a while, staring at the sky, still glowing from the sunset. At last he returned to the dining-room table and the study materials for his actuary exam. *Let's see now*. Where had he stopped when he phoned Leslie?

He spent another hour studying, pausing midway for another beer. So much to cover, so much still to learn. He yawned and stretched. Should he go to bed or put in another hour? Maybe if he didn't sleep so long, he wouldn't dream as much. He shuddered, recalling the horror of the previous night. He could see the woman again, sitting in a pool of blood so deep she was beginning to float. And the sound—oh, the chilling, soul-searing wail, repeated again and again.

He tried to shake the sight and the sound from his head and turned the page. He'd work a little longer. Better take advantage of the stillness in the house while he could.

꒰

Leslie felt her face flame as she hung up the phone. What did Charles mean, he'd fight her tooth and nail for the kids? She'd thought he didn't even like them, that the last thing he'd want would be to saddle himself with two kids as a single parent.

No, no, single parenthood wasn't what this was all about. Was it? She felt confused, frustrated. It was as though he hadn't really read her carefully composed note. She tried to remember what she'd written. *I must not have explained it properly,* she thought. *Charles always says I don't make myself clear, don't express myself well. That must be what happened. And he gets me so discombobulated when we talk. Maybe I need to write him another letter. Maybe if I think it out a little better, phrase it better, I can get him to see what's bugging me.*

Unlatching the door to the study, she walked slowly down the hall to the family room. Tracy was pulling brownies out of the oven in the adjoining kitchen. "Want one? Nice and hot and gooey?"

She shook her head.

"How'd it go?"

"Well . . ." She leaned against the counter, feeling a wave of nausea as the rich sugar and chocolate aroma filled the room. "It began something like this: 'Young lady, what do you think you're doing?'"

"Young lady!" Tracy exclaimed. "What are you, some little eight-year-old? Give me a break! So that set the tone, I guess?"

"Pretty much. I'm causing him terrific embarrassment. My note to him made no sense whatsoever. And if I plan to leave permanently, he'll fight me tooth and nail for the children. Oh, and he won't go for counseling."

Tracy raised her eyebrows till her forehead crinkled in three horizontal folds. "Okay, so in a few minutes, he managed to place the blame on you, say you can't express yourself clearly, threaten you, and refuse to take any responsibility to change. And it's all framed in terms of 'I, Charles.' Did he even ask how you are?"

She shook her head. "No." She sighed. "And your analysis is right on." She looked down at the countertop. "Oh, Trace, I don't see any hope." Her chin quivered. "I don't know what I'm going to do."

"Nothing." Tracy wiped her hands on a towel. "Time's on your side."

"You think so?" Her voice sounded tight, pinched.

"I do. He can't get along without you."

"Oh, sure." She gave a sarcastic laugh. "How—" She hesitated. "How did Charles sound to you when you answered the phone?"

"Oh, like always. By the way, have you noticed he almost never uses contractions? 'I am happy to hear that you are doing well.' That's the way he always sounds. But he was affable to me, as usual. 'How are you and Greg? Boys doing well? Team seems to be off to a fine start.'"

"See, that's one of the things that makes it so hard. He *is* affable and even witty—with other people. Trace, it makes me feel like there's something intrinsically wrong with me. I seem to bring out the worst in him." She rubbed her forehead. "I get so muddled."

"Maybe—maybe it's part of his plan. Ever think of that?"

"What?"

"To keep you muddled." Tracy lifted Leslie's chin to look into her eyes for a moment.

"But why would he do that?" Leslie blinked.

Tracy tilted her head to one side. "Seven-letter word: Control."

"He wants to—"

"Maybe needs to," Tracy interrupted.

"—to control me? But why? I don't try to control him. I do my best to do things the way he wants them. Why would he feel he needed to . . ."

"I'm no shrink, honey. But that's how it looks to your big sister. You know, it wouldn't hurt if you'd try writing down some of the hard things he's said to you. You might see a pattern."

Her head hurt, and she needed a Tums. "I'll think about it. Thanks, Trace." She hugged her sister, who held her close for a moment.

"Hang on, Leslie. Hang on," Tracy whispered.

As she stepped out into the breezeway, Leslie saw Michelle watching her from the bonus area. Leslie took a deep breath and slid the screen door open.

"That Dad?" Michelle asked.

"Yes."

"Is he pi—"

Leslie interrupted before she could say the word. "Yes. He's not exactly happy."

"What'd he say? What'd you say?"

"Michelle," she sighed, suddenly feeling bone weary, "cool it."

"Okay, Mom, I get it. You keep wanting me to confide in you, be honest with you, and now you can't even tell me what my own father said."

Leslie sighed. "I'm sorry. I'm not trying to shut you out, honey. It's just that I'm exhausted and need to—well, process all this before I can talk about it."

Michelle tossed her hair so it shimmered in the overhead

light. "Okay. Fine. Sure. Then don't expect me to tell you what Jason and I are planning."

Leslie let herself drop on the couch, her body feeling at least two hundred pounds. "You had better not be planning anything illegal or immoral, my darling."

"He can come over here, then?"

"You know what your dad said."

"Aha!" Michelle said, her tone gloating, triumphant. "But Dad's not here. The rules have changed. So, he can come over then?"

She couldn't think, much less make a decision she'd have to live with. "Honey, I am so tired, I don't want to make a decision on this right now."

"Is that the same as 'We'll see'?"

Scott's voice interrupted from the balcony. "Ready for bed, Mom."

Saved from the inquisition, she thought. Sometimes Michelle could be as persistent as—as Charles, it suddenly occurred to her. Had to be a learned behavior, not heredity, she decided as she headed up the stairs.

She reached up to the top bunk and pulled back the spread. "Probably a sheet is all you need for covering for starters."

"Right." Scott clambered up the ladder and into bed. Standing next to the bunks, she could just see him eye-to-eye. "Prayer time?"

He nodded and closed his eyes. "Lord, thanks for this place to stay and the pool and everything. I pray that You're taking good care of Dad and that he isn't too mad at us. Uh, I kinda miss talking about the pennant races with him. Uh, well, bless him and Aunt Tracy and Uncle Greg and Mom and 'Chelle. I love you, Jesus. Amen."

Kissing him, she started down the stairs as the phone rang.

"I'll get it," came Michelle's eager voice. "Hello?" she said. Her voice grew soft and seductive. "Hi." She curled on the end of the couch, her face and the phone muffled into the corner and spoke very quietly. Now and then she laughed, her voice low and throaty. Definitely not a giggle-with-a-girlfriend conversation, Leslie concluded. She went upstairs to shower, and when she came out, she heard Michelle say, "Tomorrow?" She moved downstairs, towel in hand, and, tapping Michelle on the shoulder, pointed to the clock. Michelle gave a defiant shake of her head, then listened and interrupted her caller, "Hang on just a sec. That's call waiting." She clicked the hang-up button. "Hello? Oh, hi, Gram. Yeah. Can she call you back?"

"No, Michelle," Leslie said with firmness. "You finish your other call." She knew her mother wouldn't be calling again unless it was important.

Michelle connected back with her call. "Hey, I'm really bummed, but I gotta hang up. My gram's on the other line. Yes. Sure. Okay, don't forget." Michelle listened intently.

Leslie made wind-it-up motions with her hand. At last Michelle released the phone to her. It felt hot in her hand. "Hi, Mom. What's up?"

"Leslie, I just heard from your Uncle Martin—in Chicago. It's not good news."

She felt her heart quicken. "Dad?"

"Yes, he's in the hospital. A stroke." Zoë's voice broke on the last word.

Even in the panic that filled her, Leslie realized, Mom still loves the old boy. She swallowed. "How bad?"

"Left side paralyzed."

"Oh, Mom!" she cried, tears springing to her eyes. "Of all people. How can he c-conduct? How can he . . . "

"I know."

"Is—does Uncle Martin think he's in danger? I mean, might he . . . "

"He's not sure of the amount of damage yet. Promised to call tomorrow. It's after eleven there, you know."

"Oh, Mom, this is so hard. How're *you* doing?"

"I—" Zoë hesitated. "It *is* hard. I'd like to be with him. But Martin didn't think so. Best thing we can do is pray."

"Oh, I am. I will." She tried for a light touch. "Listen, Mom, he's such a stubborn ol' coot, he'll fight this with all he's got. I work with a lot of stroke people in therapy, you know. He can recover most—even all of what he's lost."

"Thanks, honey. I'll hang on to that. I'm going to call all the kids. I love you, darlin'."

"Me, too, you, Mom. I'll be praying. Keep me posted."

A few moments later she looked across the breezeway to see Tracy beckoning her. "You get yourself into bed by nine-thirty, Michelle," Leslie said. "And next time you're on the line and I get an important call, you please give me the phone immediately!" She started toward the door. "I'll be over at Tracy's." She slid open the screen and closed it behind her, meeting Tracy in the breezeway.

"Let's sit outside," Tracy said. As they started back to the patio chairs, Leslie's tears flooded. Tracy held her while she cried and cried. When at last they loosened their embrace, Tracy said, "It's harder for you. I was married by the time Dad left. You were only eighteen."

Leslie nodded, snuffling. "It's strange. It's like losing him all over again. This could be the end of the dad I knew: energetic, creative, physically strong but oh, the music he could make. More times than not, it moved me to tears." She thought a moment. "I guess he could still conduct from a wheelchair. With one hand, if he had to. But would he?"

Tracy shook her head. "He's pretty—well, he sees himself as all of the things you just listed. I don't know if he could. But, Leslie, it may not be that bad."

"Right. It may not be that bad."

"Let's pray for him," Tracy said.

"Right. You start, and I'll finish."

Tracy took Leslie's hand and began, "Oh, heavenly Father, we do bring our dad before You and trust him to Your loving care. Put Your arms around him. Take away all fear. Be his strong tower. Help him trust in You completely."

In a moment Leslie began, "Lord, to be real honest, what I want to say to You is, please, either take him or heal him. But Father, you know what's best. You see the big picture. So I, too, want to trust him to You and Your perfect will for him. And Lord, will you comfort our mother? It seems so clear how much she still cares for him and how completely she's forgiven him."

She swallowed hard. "I just realized when I said that, that there's some forgiving of him I still need to do. Help me with that, Lord. And if any of us are to go out to him, please make that clear too. Thank You that we can turn to You and You always hear us—no busy signals or being put on hold. And we praise You in Jesus' name. Amen."

They were quiet for a moment, and Leslie could smell the honeysuckle in the still night air.

Then Tracy spoke. "Remember the time—I think I was about twelve, so you were really little—the time he sat down at the piano and played a set of variations on 'Row, Row Your Boat,' for us?"

"Kind of." Leslie tried to recall.

"It was really cute. He was so creative. And spontaneous. And how about the times he took all four of us kids to the circus? That was our special time just with him. Mom never went."

"Oh, yes," Leslie recalled. "The first time I got scared by something, I think."

"It was a cannon firing. It surprised you."

"And I had to sit on his lap. And remember all the clowns getting out of the car? We never could figure out how they got so many in."

Tracy laughed. "And just when you thought that was the last one, another squeezed out. Remember how Dad would laugh? He was starting to get what we called his bay window, and that tummy would jiggle when he laughed."

"Yes." Leslie thought a moment. "But it wasn't all fun. He could be tyrannical, unfair. He scared me sometimes."

"He did?" Tracy seemed surprised. She thought a moment. "Well, I do agree that he's a powerful man."

Leslie nodded. "Yup. I guess I felt like I never lived up to his expectations, and part of me always thought it was my fault when he left Mom."

"But that's not so!" Tracy protested. "It was that woman from Northwestern. And then she changed her mind about marrying him." She laughed as though to say, "Served him right."

"Yes, but Dad had a way of making us—well, me—feel nothing I did was good enough." She thought a moment. "I remember one time I was practicing a piano piece. I loved playing his big Steinway. I played this number through several times, and finally Dad stormed into the room, and shouted, 'No, *no,* NO, *Les*-lie. It's a B-flat, not a B. Can't you *hear* it?'

She swallowed. "I was absolutely devastated. Never practiced again when he was around. As an adult, I can see how frustrated he was with my making the same mistake over and over. But I still remember the pain."

"I never knew about that. That was hard. But Leslie," Tracy looked intently at her sister, "who does that remind you of?"

"I don't know." Then Leslie sat up straight as she saw it. "Charles. Dad's 'Can't you *hear* it?' sounds exactly like something Charles would say."

"Ah." Tracy nodded.

"But there were so many good times with Dad, too."

They sat without speaking. In the hills a coyote howled. "Do you know what we're doing?" Leslie said. "We're talking like we're at a wake."

"No, we're not. We're just remembering. It's okay." Tracy put her hand on Leslie's. "Even in this dim light, I can see you're exhausted. Let's hit the sack."

"You're right. Thanks, Trace."

"I'm glad you're here, Leslie."

As she climbed the stairs to the loft, Leslie realized how grateful she was to receive the news here, where she and her sister could comfort one another and pray together. Charles would have—what would he have done? Probably minimized the impact for her in some way, told her she was too sensitive. Undressing, she thought, *it's a relief not to have to contend with that, or to try to figure out how to respond to him without precipitating still more flack from him.*

The wings of a dove—to fly far away from all that—that's what she'd prayed for, wasn't it?

In the bathroom, while brushing her teeth, she studied her face in the mirror. She stopped, toothbrush still in her mouth, dampened her hand and brushed her bangs to one side. I'm not going to hide anymore, she told her reflection.

12

⁑

From Zoë's Prayer Journal

September 26: Dear Lord, a stroke is so tough. Watch over my husband—for I know in Your eyes Benjamin still is my husband. Comfort him, give him hope in You, patience, and if it's Your will, complete healing. Most of all, help him focus on You as his rock. And Lord, please don't let this situation with her dad weaken Leslie's resolve. This has to be so unbalancing for her, because I don't think she's ever come to terms with her relationship with her dad. She only knows that he was the first man in her life to leave her, and then Tom left her when he died, and I think maybe she takes all that garbage from Charles because she's afraid of being left again. Oh, Lord, make her strong and courageous. In Jesus' name, amen.

WHEN THE ALARM JARRED HER AWAKE THE NEXT MORNING, Leslie thought immediately of her dad. How was he? Did he make it okay through the night? Should she try to go see him, give professional input? No, he'd certainly have good care at the medical center. Should she phone her mom? No, her mother had promised to call whenever there was news.

Got to get in the shower so Michelle has time for hers, she told herself. A moment later, standing under the hot water, she noted that somehow her concern for her dad had lessened the impact of her conversation with Charles the night before. In fact, in a strange way, it made her feel stronger.

Out of the shower, she dabbed mousse on her bangs and blew them dry, lifting them off her face toward the left. "You *do* look better," she told her reflection. "No more hiding under the bangs."

"Hey, Mom, cool," Michelle said on her way into the shower.

"Your face looks—uh—kinda bare," Scott said when he rolled out of bed and took a sleepy-eyed look at her.

"Well, better get used to it—even if I do run the risk of catching cold." Leslie gave her son a playful swat.

At breakfast she told the kids, "I got some bad news last night—too late to tell you. Granddad's had a stroke, and he's in really serious condition."

Scott frowned. "What's a stroke anyway?"

"It's like a heart attack," Michelle declared.

"No," Leslie said, "a stroke is caused by the rupture or obstruction of an artery in the brain. It can affect movement, thinking, speech. It's complicated, and sometimes we don't know how much damage has been done for days or even weeks or months." She tried to smile. "But many people make remarkable recoveries. I see it often at work. So let's pray it'll be God's will to heal him."

"Yeah. We want him to be able to conduct his big Christmas program. Could we fly out for that this year?" Scott asked.

"Maybe. We'll see how it goes."

She pictured her father in his black tails, standing before the orchestra and chorus, tall and erect, his strong arms and expressive face urging, cautioning, emphasizing every nuance of the sacred music of Christmas. "Worship through beauty," he called it.

Tears filled her eyes, and she wiped them away hastily, forcing herself to focus on the day's agenda.

⌇

The next day, when David came in for therapy, he took one look at her hair and flashed his Crest-toothpaste smile. "Hey! You look great," he said. "I always wondered if you had any eyebrows. And look—you have gorgeous eyebrows."

She laughed. "Well, this smart-talkin' kid I know has been after me to make a change. Thought I'd give it a try."

"Where do I get the feeling it's more than a change of hairstyle?"

"Well, this same smart kid wondered what I was hiding from. I've decided I'm not hiding anymore."

He gave her a high five. "Way to go!"

After David did strengthening exercises with Brynne, Leslie took over. "I watched your work today, and you're really doing well. I think it's time to have the orthotist come to fit you with leg braces."

His eyes grew enormous. "You serious? Then that must mean—"

"It means we hope to get you on your feet."

He slapped the exercise mat. "Did You hear that, Lord?" he yelled. "Hallelujah! Amen!" He looked at her. "Then you think I'm gonna walk?"

"I would say it's likely, with support. Then we'll see."

"That's good enough for me. How long do I have to wear the braces?" He frowned. "Forever?"

She hesitated. "I don't know, David. I sure hope not. What I'm praying is that it'll just be till you build up your thigh muscles and your knees get strong enough."

"That just blows me away!" he exulted. "Thank You, Lord! And thank you, Leslie."

"Okay now, before you get too euphoric, let's work on those legs." She pushed against one foot. "Push against my hand. Release. Now again."

"How're the kids doing?" he asked.

"Pretty good, so far. I'm praying a lot."

"You bet. Hey, I didn't tell you." He lifted his head to look at her. "I'm taking over coaching the Y swim team. It's age-group swimming, elementary and junior-high age. Think Scott would like to join?"

"I think he might. You are absolutely the greatest—in his eyes. He's been talking a lot about you. And he's been practicing in my sister's pool. He's almost figured out a flip turn."

"Cool. Why don't you bring him in again, and we'll talk?"

༄

As soon as Scott jumped into her car that afternoon, Leslie told him about the swim team.

"I dunno if I'm good enough," he hesitated.

"Why don't you let David be the judge? I'm sure he works with all different ability levels."

"Well . . ." She could feel his tension mount.

"I'd sorta like to," Scott continued, "but I just, uh, y'know, don't wanna be the worst one."

"Oh, honey, I know you wouldn't be. David would be glad

to talk to you, answer any questions. He suggested you come in to therapy and talk. Or do you want to call him?"

"Yeah, well, maybe. I'll think about it."

He's afraid to try anything new, afraid of being put down, she thought. Reaching over, she patted his shoulder. "Good."

They drove on to her daughter's school. Michelle climbed into the back without a word. Was it Leslie's imagination, or did Michelle seem unusually fidgety?

"Got all my homework done," her daughter announced.

"Good." Leslie couldn't resist. "Maybe staying after regular classes isn't all bad."

Michelle made gagging sounds.

After they reached their "pad," Leslie changed into shorts and started dinner. "I'm doing that stir-fry you like," she told Michelle.

No response. Michelle went upstairs, and a few moments later emerged wearing shocking pink lipstick. "Going for a walk," she announced.

"Oh? Where?"

"Just down the greenbelt a ways." Michelle avoided eye contact.

What's up? Leslie wondered. "Okay," she said cautiously. "Be back by five-thirty."

"Five-thirty?" Michelle protested.

"Yes. It's your night to fix the salad. And we need to eat early tonight so I can get to a meeting at church."

I am going to get to that recovery ministry orientation meeting I read about in the church bulletin, she promised herself. *Mom's right. I need to meet some people with problems like mine. I need a network to keep me on track.*

Michelle slid the screen door open and shut it with a bang. Leslie heard the metallic clang of the breezeway gate and the swish of Boris's tail as he stood, watching her depart.

She turned to see Scott looking at Boris. "Do Aunt Tracy and Uncle Greg have a harness for Boris?" he asked. "I was thinkin' how huskies are bred to pull sleds and stuff. Maybe he could pull me on my skateboard."

"I don't know. Why don't you ask?"

"Yeah, I will. After I swim. Would you watch me and tell me what you think of my flip turn?"

"Sure."

Scott changed into his swimsuit, and a moment later, she heard him dive into the pool. When she went out to watch him, she saw that he'd figured out on his own how to do the flip. "That's terrific, honey. Now, can you get a little closer to the edge of the pool, so you get a good push-off?"

He grinned, treading water, then swam away from the end of the pool. Turning back, he took a few quick strokes, tucked his head down and flipped over, but his feet missed the wall of the pool.

He surfaced, shook his head, and swam out to try again. The next time, he came closer to the wall, but his turn was more a roll than a flip. "I just can't seem to get it," he fussed. He tried again and again, and she could see his frustration escalating.

"Tell you what. Why don't you take a break and just swim some laps? I saw you doing the backstroke the other day, and it looked pretty good."

He nodded, and as he began swimming, she saw how much his stroke had improved.

"Scott, you're a lot better than you think you are," she told him when he paused at one end of the pool.

"Yeah, but that danged turn."

"I know. It's really hard to learn. But that's one reason for having a coach. David wouldn't expect you to come already knowing everything."

"Yeah, but . . ." He let his voice trail away.

She thought a moment. "You know who else could help you?"

"Who?" He broke into a grin as he understood. "Gram, right?"

"She'd love it. I'll call her, okay?"

"Sure."

When she went inside, she was surprised to see that it was 5:40 already. Where *was* Michelle? They needed to eat by 6:00 or a little after so she could get to the seven o'clock meeting.

At five of six, Scott came in. "I'm starving."

She sighed. "The rice is ready. Go get dressed and I'll start the stir-fry."

Six o'clock. Still no Michelle. "I *told* her to be back to make the salad," she muttered aloud. Shaking her head, she tore some lettuce into a bowl and cut a tomato into eighths.

Five after six. "Where's Michelle?" Scott asked, as he came downstairs pulling on a T-shirt. Then he gave her a sly grin. "Maybe we could have a peaceful meal for a change. Without her big mouth."

She turned with a stern stare. "Well, maybe you can. I think I'm going to go look around outside. You can go ahead with dinner."

"Want me to come?"

"No, that's okay. It may not be a pretty sight when I find her."

He grimaced. "I hate bloodshed."

She nodded, trying to pick up on his humor. "Better stay put then." She gestured toward the stove. "Help yourself."

She slipped sandals on her bare feet. *Maybe I'd better talk to Tracy first,* she decided. She crossed the breezeway and saw her sister in the kitchen at the sink.

"Hi, Trace."

"Hi." Tracy turned toward her. "Just talked with Mom. Word is that Dad's doing a little better."

"Oh, good. Thanks, Lord."

"Like we both said, a tough old goat." Tracy came toward the door. "What's up with you tonight?"

"Well, I was going to a recovery ministry meeting at the church. But right now I'm very ticked off with my daughter. Went out 'for a walk,' at about four forty-five. Warned to be back at five-thirty. Haven't seen her, have you?"

"Sorry. No." Tracy shook her head. "Maybe she's playing volleyball on the greenbelt and lost track of time."

"Maybe. I'll go have a look." She stopped to pat Boris, who rewarded her by offering his paw. "I'll be back, Boris," she promised, slipping through the gate.

Oh, Lord, please, she prayed silently, *bring Michelle back with me.*

She hurried down the street to the greenbelt, a long stretch of grassy knolls punctuated with tall eucalyptus trees. Two young boys and a bare-chested man with love handles above his shorts bounced a ball on the basketball court. A lone figure rode down the curving path on a bike. "'Scuse me," she said to the man. "Did you by any chance see a red-haired girl, twelve years old, wearing green cotton-knit tights and a striped tunic?"

He wiped sweat from his forehead. "Sorry." He shook his head.

"Thanks." She followed the path to the sandy volleyball area. No one there except a cat digging by one of the posts. Exasperated, she walked a little farther. Not a sign of Michelle. She wasn't sure if she was angrier with her daughter or with herself.

A picture of Jason with his earrings popped into her mind. *Oh, no! Why didn't I pay more attention to that furtive phone conversation a few nights ago? Stupid of me! Why didn't I pin her down to exactly where she was going? Dumb, dumb! I'm not handling her well at all. If we were home, Charles would never have let this happen.*

She glanced anxiously at her watch as she started back toward the house. Quarter of seven. *Forget the meeting. What did that matter, if something had happened to Michelle? What if someone had grabbed her and forced her into a car? No, no. Mustn't let my imagination go haywire. Maybe I'll find her at home when I get back.*

Scott heard her come through the gate. "Find her?"

"No. Guess you didn't hear anything?"

Scott shook his head. "Whatcha think?"

"I think I'll get in the car and cruise the neighborhood."

"Can I come?"

She smiled, grateful for his company. "Sure."

They drove all through the tract, glancing across the green-belt as each U-shaped street curved up against it. Each time they started into a new street, she felt a little lift of hope as she anticipated a glimpse of Michelle's red hair. And she could feel her spirits plummet each time she found—nothing.

At last, as they headed down the street toward Tracy's house, Scott turned toward her. "Man, it's like she fell off the earth."

Leslie bit her lip as she braked in front of the house.

"So what d'ya think?" Scott asked.

"I think I'm very angry. And a little bit scared." *A lot scared,* she admitted to herself.

"Yeah."

As she saw Scott's brown eyes widen, her fear escalated. "Twelve-year-old abducted from own home," a headline had read in the paper just yesterday. She slammed the car door. If a girl could be taken from her own home, how easy it would be for someone, or a couple of someones, to snatch Michelle from a greenbelt—if that's where she'd actually gone. She stood jingling the car keys from her finger and looked at her watch. Too soon to call the police.

As they walked into the breezeway, Scott said suddenly, "I know! Bet she went back to our house."

"No-o-o." She frowned. Surely Michelle wouldn't go back to her dad, who was always so imperious and severe in his dealings with her. Unless . . .

"She mighta wanted some clothes or makeup or somethin'." Scott seemed to read her mind. Then he added, "Yeah, but how would she get there?"

"Jason," she said.

"Yeah," Scott nodded. "Why don't you call Dad?"

She grimaced. The last thing she wanted to do was face Charles, even on the telephone. Last night had been bad enough.

Scott was watching her. "Want me to call?" he asked.

She smiled. Her rescuer. "Thanks, honey. But no, thanks." She stalled. "I'll give it a few more minutes."

"Okay, I'll be out here with Boris."

"Good idea." As she walked into their apartment, she looked at the pans on the stove. She knew she should eat something, but . . .

Tracy appeared at the door. "Any luck?"

"Not a bit. Come on in."

"There's probably a simple explanation." Tracy glanced at Leslie's face as she stepped through the door. "Try not to panic."

"Yeah, stay calm, Leslie." Leslie heard the sarcasm in her own voice. "You've left your husband, who thinks you're an idiot. Your dad, who you feel pretty ambivalent about, has had a stroke. You're sponging off your sister, shoehorned into tiny quarters. Now your daughter's missing. But golly, don't get upset." She stopped as she saw the hurt in Tracy's face. "Oh, Trace, I'm sorry. I'm grateful for all you're doing. I *am* panicking. I'm scared stiff."

13

TRACY GAVE LESLIE A HUG. "OF COURSE, YOU'RE SCARED. I understand." She thought a moment. "Is there a friend Michelle might be with?"

"There's this high school boy. Brother of a friend." She paused. "Oh! Why didn't I think of it? I could call their house." She found the phone book, looked up the number and called. "Please, Lord," she said aloud as she waited.

A girl answered the phone.

"Hello? Is Jason in, please?" Leslie asked.

"No, he's not."

"Do you expect him soon?"

The girl hesitated. "I hope so."

Time to be candid. "Is this Stacey?"

"Yes."

"This is Mrs. Harper, Michelle's mother."

"Oh, hi."

"I wondered if Michelle might be with Jason."

"Gee, I don't know. I really don't know where he is, and my folks aren't in."

Leslie sighed. "Okay. If he should come in, would you ask him to call me, please?" She gave Stacey the number.

"Okay."

"Thanks." Leslie set down the receiver and glanced at Tracy.

"Could she be at Mom's?" Tracy suggested.

Leslie raised her eyebrows. "There's a thought." She punched the numbers and waited.

"Praise the Lord. Give thanks to the Lord, for He is good; His love endures forever," came her mother's voice.

"Answering machine," Leslie whispered. "If she's out, Michelle's probably not with her."

She waited for the beep. "Mom," she said, "Leslie. Michelle's late—real late getting home from a walk. Wondered if she was with you, but guess since you're not there, she's probably not. Give me a call, will you?"

She hung up and drummed her fingers on the table.

"This is maybe a little off the wall, but could she have gone back to your house?" Tracy asked.

"I was thinking that."

Tracy gave her a close look. "You hate to call." It was a statement, not a question.

"You've got it."

"Would Charles call you—if Michelle was there?"

Leslie thought about it. "Probably not."

"What a prince." Tracy wrinkled her nose. "Can I do anything?"

"I can't think what. I'll give it ten more minutes."

"Keep me posted." Tracy let herself out the sliding door.

"Right." Leslie scooped the rice and vegetables into plastic containers. Eating cold food would serve Michelle right. Well, she *could* rewarm them when Michelle got there. *If* Michelle . . . No, she wouldn't even think it.

Like a rubber exercise band from the therapy gym, her ten minutes seemed to stretch out to twice—no, triple their normal length. She twice checked her watch to be sure it was running. At last, she picked up the receiver and punched in the familiar numbers.

"Yes." Charles's inflection seemed to ask, "Why are you bothering me?" How could he make one word sound so stuffy?

"Charles, it's Leslie."

"Yes?"

"Charles, I, uh, I'm sorry to bother you. Is, well, is Michelle there by any chance?"

"Michelle?" The voice was cool, detached. "No."

"Oh, well, I just wondered . . ."

"The only person I have laid eyes on this evening is your mother."

"Mother?" she asked, surprised.

"Correct. She came by with tomatoes and—gawd-ly wisdom." He gave the last two words a lofty, pontifical tone.

She shook her head. How like her mom never to give up, still trying to witness to Charles even in the midst of their separation.

"Your question," Charles continued, "seems to indicate that Michelle is not with you."

"That's right."

"And that you do not have the faintest idea where she is."

"Yes." The words tumbled out as she tried to make him understand. "Charles, she just said she was going out for a walk at about quarter of five. I told her to be back at five-thirty. I've looked all through the neighborhood."

"Well, I cannot say I'm surprised you are not able to handle her, Leslie. She needs a very firm hand. Let us be realistic. It's genetics, pure and simple. Her father was a rapscallion."

And I? she thought. *I've given her bad genes too; that's what he's saying.*

"She's a loser, Leslie."

She felt her jaw clench. "I don't think I'm willing to accept that, Charles."

"No." She could visualize his sarcastic smile. "Of course not."

Leslie tightened her grip on the phone and blinked away the tears. *What I could use right now,* she thought, *is a little compassion. Instead, I'm having it all rubbed in. And darn it, Charles is right; he's always right. I'm not able to handle her.* "Well—" She didn't know what else to say.

"Well," he repeated. "What do you plan to do now, Leslie?"

"I've called the people she might be with." She didn't want to antagonize him further with Jason's name.

"That vile young man?"

"Yes. I called him. He wasn't in."

Silence from Charles.

"I, ah, I figure it's still too early to call the police."

"Mmm." A pause, a sigh. "Well, you do have yourself a problem, Leslie, now that you are away from me. Let me know when you come to your senses. Meanwhile, I shall not keep you from your quest."

"But Charles, what shall I—"

He'd already hung up. She slammed the phone down, tears searing her eyes. Not a shred of help. Charles's unspoken message came loud and clear: "You wanted to leave, to be on your own, Leslie. Now you *can handle this.*"

She saw Scott watching her and shook her head. "Not there."

He looked down at his shoes. "I—I think I'll go over and ask Aunt Tracy if they have a harness for Boris. If they don't, maybe I'll throw a ball for him."

"Good idea."

"Boris likes it when I throw a ball onto the roof and it bounces down on the breezeway for him to catch."

"Fine," she heard herself say, her mind still filled with Charles's words.

She stared at the phone, and its image clouded. When it rang, it startled her so, she almost knocked it over. She grabbed the receiver. "Hello?" Her voice sounded hoarse.

"Darling." Her mother's voice, a little breathless, concerned. "Sorry, I stopped to see Charles on my way back from your grandmother's. What is this with Michelle?"

She explained the situation. "Mom, she is really getting out of control, and I'm feeling very inept—as well as just plain terrified."

"Darling, you are not inept. Michelle is a handful. She probably bumped into some kids, got involved, lost track of the time. You know how she can be," Zoë said.

"Yup. Clueless, at times."

"Is Scott upset?"

"Hard to tell. He's been helpful. I just called Charles, and Scott knew *I* was upset. He just went out to play with Boris. Overall he's very quiet about this whole change. Hard to know what's going on behind those big brown eyes."

"Anything I can do?"

"Nothing I can think of as far as Michelle—" Looking through the sliding door, she saw Scott's wet towel by the pool. "Well, there is one thing. For Scott. Maybe help him with his flip turns?"

"Of course!"

"He's almost figured it out. I'm encouraging him to join the swim team that David's coaching."

"I think that would be good for him." Zoë hesitated. "Darling, I shouldn't keep the phone tied up, but let's have a quick prayer."

"Oh, yes!"

"Lord, You are our all-seeing, all-knowing God. You know exactly where Michelle is. Shield her, watch over her, bring her safely home. If she's done anything foolish, put Your guardian angels around her. Protect her from herself and deliver her from evil. And Father, please don't allow Leslie to be too hard on herself. I ask—"

Leslie heard the gate open outside and saw Scott run toward it. "Michelle!" he yelled.

"She's here, Mom." Leslie said.

"Thank You, Lord. Amen."

"Yes, and thank you, Mom." She replaced the receiver and hurried toward her daughter, relief and anger warring within. "Michelle, where have you been? I've been worried silly."

Even before Michelle could answer, Leslie smelled the tell-tale herbal, sticky-sweet aroma that clung to her daughter's knit shirt and tights. Then she saw her dilated pupils.

"Smokin'." *So there!* sang her tone. Michelle lounged on the sofa, her smile insolent, defiant.

Scott, Leslie suddenly realized, stood looking first at her, then at Michelle, like an observer at a ping-pong match. "Scott," she said, "why don't you go back out with Boris?"

"O-*kay*." He ambled reluctantly back out the door.

She turned back to Michelle. "Smoking pot." She'd known immediately.

"Pot, bud, whatever you wanna call it." Michelle swung her arm, letting her hand flop to one side.

"Jason?"

"Yeah, Jason has sources." She giggled.

My daughter's going to be an addict before she ever gets to high school, Leslie thought, battling to keep her voice calm. "Oh?" she said.

"He had 'shrooms, too. But I didn't try that."

"I think that was a good decision."

"Yeah. One thing at a time."

Keep cool. Be understanding, Leslie told herself. "So what did you think?"

Michelle's eyes narrowed. "So what did you think?" She mocked her mother's tone. "I thought it was relaxin'. Well, maybe I got a little high. No big deal."

Leslie made an effort to keep her voice quiet, reasonable. "Okay, Michelle. I appreciate your being honest with me. I can understand your wanting to try it."

"Yeah. Bet you never did." *You wouldn't have the guts,* her voice implied.

"Matter of fact, I did."

"No foolin'?" Michelle stared at Leslie with interest. "You smoked?"

"No, in a brownie."

"No foolin'! What happened?"

"I ate half a brownie, and nothing happened at all. So I ate the other half, went to a movie, felt sick all through it, threw up on the way home."

"Smokin's better," Michelle replied with confidence.

"None at all is best, Michelle." She forced firmness into her voice. "I had friends who got hooked and had to quit school. Couldn't focus, couldn't concentrate."

"Yeah." A yawn. "I've seen the movies at school. What a laugh."

"Michelle, it is also against the law."

"So turn me in."

Leslie forced herself to stop and take a breath. *I'm half a step away from absolutely losing it,* she realized. *Mustn't let her take control.* "If there is a next time, I will." She gave Michelle what she hoped was a strong, firm gaze.

Michelle laughed. "Yeah, and I'm scared to death."

"There's another issue here, Michelle. You were due back at five-thirty. It's now seven forty-five."

Michelle shrugged.

"All right, Michelle. For the next two weeks, you will go to school and you will come back here, and you are not to leave this place."

Michelle cocked her head to one side and, lips pursed in supreme assurance, said, "You can't control me, y'know? Unless you lock me up all day, you can't control my whole life. Not anymore."

"My darling, I am still the parent, and you are the child, and until you are eighteen, I am responsible for you. And there are rules, and there are common courtesies, and you *will* follow them. We'll discuss this further, but right now, I am telling you, after these two weeks are up, you are to be home when you're supposed to be, and you are not to go anyplace whatsoever without discussing it with me first."

"How're you gonna stop me, huh, *Les*-lie? How you gonna stop me?"

The effrontery in her face, the intonation, so like Charles . . . For a moment Leslie's anger flashed with such intensity she couldn't even see her daughter. It took all her will power not to slap her. Then Michelle came into focus again, and Leslie wondered how, indeed, she was going to stop her. She didn't dare let this twelve-year-old know that she had no idea, that she felt shattered into a zillion fragments. She turned away from that rebellious face and tried to bring some cohesion to all the pieces.

"I'm ravenous," Michelle complained.

"Tough," Leslie retorted, then added, "there's cold stir-fry, cold rice, salad. You're on your own."

"Okay," Michelle said agreeably.

It was then that Leslie saw Scott standing just outside the screen door. "Scott!" she cried. "I told you to go play with Boris. How long have you been standing there gaping?" She opened the door, and his body seemed to fold in on itself.

"Oh, honey, I'm sorry," she whispered, stepping outside. "This really has upset me. Didn't mean to take it out on you." She looked over her shoulder at Michelle, standing, meditating before the open refrigerator door. Come in and let's go upstairs, Scott. We could maybe read a little."

"Okay." His voice sounded flat, lifeless.

She followed him up the stairs, grasping the railing to support her trembling legs.

"We're almost finished with *Call of the Wild*," she said as he got ready for bed. He didn't respond. "Does that make you think a little of Boris?"

"Yeah."

As they read, Leslie heard Michelle rummage around in the kitchen. Glancing downstairs from the balcony, Leslie could see her scarf down leftovers and a huge dish of frozen yogurt.

When they finished reading, Scott prayed, thanking God for his sister's safe return and adding a gruff, "I guess," and asking Him to bless his dad. Leslie kissed him and was surprised to see a tear rolling down the side of his face. "What—?" she asked, wondering if the episode with Michelle had upset him as much as it had her. Or was he smarting from her outburst at him? Guilt, shame, incompetency washed over her. *Oh, Lord,* she prayed silently, *I'm not handling either of these kids well. Help me.*

He squeezed his eyes shut, and two more tears came.

"I miss Dad," he said.

His words hit her like a football player butting into her stomach. She stared at him. How could he miss all Charles's put-downs, sarcasm, pointed remarks about his defect? She'd thought she was taking him away from all that emotional abuse and that he'd welcome the relief. And after all, she'd never said they wouldn't see each other.

"You can go be with him again this weekend," she said. "Aren't the pennant races narrowing down?"

"Weekends aren't the same. I—just—really miss him." He turned away and cried into his pillow.

14

LESLIE STARED AT SCOTT, FEELING A DEEP, DULL ACHE IN her stomach. "Scott, I can understand that a part of your life feels like it's missing. But honey, you can be with Dad again this weekend," she repeated.

He turned his head away from her. "I know."

She waited.

"But it's not the same as being with him, watching ball games with him," Scott said at last.

"But Scott, you don't . . ." She caught herself. In fact, Scott seldom watched the games with Charles, but that wasn't the point. Despite Charles's verbal abuse, he *was* Scott's dad, and her son missed being with him. She patted his shoulder. "I know it's hard for you, honey. Change is hard for everybody. And I'm sure you're feeling a lot of mixed-up things about not knowing where Michelle was and all. But try to think of the things that are good in your life. Tomorrow, why don't you call David and talk to him about the swim team?"

"Yeah." His voice sounded lifeless, hollow. "Maybe."

She kissed his forehead and saw the tears glinting on his eyelashes. "I love you, Scott, and I was glad to have you with me in the car this evening. You're a big help to me. Thanks."

"You're welcome. G'night." He kissed her cheek and turned over on his side, facing away from her.

Her feet felt encased in concrete as she moved down the stairs. What right did she have to make her son so miserable? And would Michelle have dared to stay out, smoking pot, if they'd been home with Charles? Her chest felt tight, irritated, as though reacting to smog. But through the window she could see the moon, pure silver in the clear sky.

Michelle had managed to make a disaster area of the kitchen, and now she turned on the TV.

"I don't think so," Leslie said. "Let Scott have some peace upstairs. He's a little upset."

Michelle shrugged as though to say, "That's his problem."

Leslie turned off the TV. "Please clean up the kitchen before you go to bed, Michelle."

Muttering to herself, her daughter rinsed her dishes and put the milk away. Leslie was too exhausted to press for more.

~

The next morning Leslie awoke to an even more pronounced tightness in the chest. "Hope I'm not getting sick," she muttered. "No time for that."

Watching Michelle's brooding face and evasive eyes renewed Leslie's sense of despair. She'd missed the recovery group orientation last night, but would tomorrow's regular support group meeting give her any help, any hope for her life? Did God want her there?

An hour later, when she tried to start the car, the engine coughed and sputtered but wouldn't take hold. She tried again. And again.

"Oh, sweet, now I'm gonna be late for school," Michelle grumbled.

At last Leslie went back to the house and knocked on Tracy's door.

It was a moment before she came, still in her robe. "Sorry. I was lying down. Have a dilly of a migraine."

"Oh, bummer."

Tracy closed her eyes and leaned against the doorframe. "Glad to hear about Michelle."

Leslie rolled her eyes. "I'll tell you about it later. But right now, do you have a jumper cable?"

"Not here. It's in Greg's car."

Leslie frowned. Now what? Charles would know what to do.

"My car won't start, and the kids are going to be late to school." She hesitated. "Any chance of my borrowing yours."

Tracy squinted at her. "No. Sorry. I'll need it."

Need it if she was laid up with a migraine? Leslie decided not to pursue it. "Okay, I'll call a cab."

"By the way," Tracy's voice held an edge of irritation. "Would you please ask Scott to bring in his towel, not leave it by the pool? And Leslie, you parked in front of half the driveway last night. Greg had a dickens of a time getting out of the garage."

Leslie stifled the impulse to defend herself and tried to quell the I-do-everything-wrong feelings that surfaced immediately. *But Tracy's right,* she told herself. *I shouldn't be so distracted, so thoughtless. Maybe it's too much, us being here at Tracy's.* "Oh, Trace," she said, "I'm sorry. We'll watch it. Now, go lie down. Hope you feel better." She gave her sister a peck on the cheek and hurried into their pad to phone for a cab.

By the time it arrived and she dropped off Scott and Michelle at their schools, Leslie was almost half an hour late for work.

"You're okay," Brynne reassured her when she arrived at the care center. "Charlie Wilson isn't coming in."

"Oh? How come?"

"He fell last night. His wife's going to call back—" She looked at her watch. "—any minute now."

Leslie felt her face flush and her gut tighten. Charlie had been doing so well, recovering from a hip fracture. She'd felt confident he was ready to walk with a cane, and he'd done well practicing with her. Had she misjudged? She let herself drop into a chair. "I feel terrible. I told him he was strong enough."

"I thought so too."

"I should have been more conservative. He was just so eager to get rid of the walker, and I . . ."

"Don't blame yourself." Brynne put her hand on Leslie's shoulder.

The phone rang. "Might as well face the music," Leslie said, picking it up. "Saddleback Valley Physical Therapy; this is Leslie," she said.

She recognized Mrs. Wilson's strident voice. "You know Charlie fell," she said, her tone accusing. "We're waiting for x-rays. They think he may have refractured his hip. You *said* he was ready for the cane. You *said* he was doing so well."

"I'm so, so sorry, Mrs. Wilson." Leslie's voice was sympathetic, gentle.

"Yes," snapped Mrs. Wilson, "so are we. I'll let you know what the x-rays show."

Leslie heard the receiver slam down and saw Terry watching her. "I do feel responsible. Rats! *Rats!*"

"Not a great way to start the day." Terry's voice was sympathetic.

"R-r-right!" Leslie felt like turning around and going home again, crawling into bed, and waiting till—till what? She sighed and tried to concentrate on her schedule. Surely the day would get better.

But at 10:30, Terry called her to the phone. "This is Sarah Burke, Beulah Ainsleigh's daughter."

Leslie gripped the phone. A daughter; it couldn't be good news. "Yes?"

"I wanted you to know—" The voice cracked, and Leslie already knew the rest. "—that my mother died day before yesterday."

"Oh, Sarah!" Leslie cried.

"Another stroke."

"Oh, no. Just when she was walking again. Oh, she worked so hard and was doing so well. I am so, so sorry."

"I know you are," Sarah said. "She really loved you."

"I loved her too. She was a beautiful lady."

"Well, I just wanted you to know."

"Thanks, Sarah. May God comfort you."

"Thanks."

Wiping the tears from her eyes, Leslie muttered. "It isn't fair, Lord. Sweet Beulah. I know she was eighty-eight, but she was rarin' to go, so pleased with her rehab." She sat for a moment, trying to regroup. Usually she could depend on her professional life to lift her up. But today . . . "What's going on here, Lord?" she asked. "One thing piled on top of another. Help me not to fall into a pit."

She felt better after the next two appointments. Then Harriet came in.

"Hi, Harriet. How's the back?" she asked.

Harriet's eyes flashed. "Worse. Much worse. I thought I was going to get better here. Your treatment's made me worse."

Why am I doing this? Leslie wondered. *I must not be any good at this—either.*

Her mother called at 11:45. "Split a deli sandwich?"

"Thanks, Mom. But I brought my own lunch from home." She thought about it. "Oh, what the heck, I'll stash it in the fridge here for tomorrow. You ready for an earful about Michelle?"

Half an hour later, as they split a honey-maple ham sandwich with everything but mayo, Zoë listened to Leslie detail the events of the previous evening. "And she was so *defiant,* Mom. Like, 'What do you think you can do about it, huh?'" Tears shone in Leslie's eyes as she added, "I think it's me. I'm not doing a good job with her at all. I don't think I can handle her by myself."

Always her fault, Zoë thought. *Whatever happens, she always turns it back on herself. Oh, why hadn't Leslie gone for help at that support group?* She shook her head. "Why are you always so ready to take the blame, Leslie? Michelle sounds like a typical early-blooming adolescent to me. She's testing her limits. The age-old struggle for independence."

"Independence? Boris is more capable of independence than Michelle."

Zoë smiled. "Probably true. But capable or not, ready or not, that's what kids want."

"But I didn't go out at that age and smoke pot and thumb my nose at you, Mom."

"No, and sometimes I wished you had." Zoë said it half to herself but saw Leslie's expression of surprise.

"Honey," Zoë explained, "most of the time you were too good to be true. Now Tracy was a different story."

"Oh, yes, I think I heard. Climbed out her window and broke a rose trellis climbing down to meet some guy."

"Scratched herself up real well on the roses too." Zoë remembered treating the swollen red scrape marks afterward. "Let's see. She was—yes, I'm sure, not quite thirteen."

"Well, Tracy always had a lot of spunk," Leslie said.

"Yes, and so has Michelle. I'm not at all surprised at this."

"But Mom, I just don't think I can deal with her."

"Of course you can." Zoë nodded encouragement. "You have good common sense, and you have God."

"Yes, but Charles is such a strong presence," Leslie said. "I think she needs his firmness."

Zoë took a deep breath. "Oh, *firmness*. Is that what we're calling it now? Haven't you told me again and again that Charles was—let me remember the words—way out of line, mean-spirited, unfeeling, inhumane, vindictive?"

Leslie brushed crumbs off the table. "Oh, well, Mom, he didn't do that kind of thing every day."

How many times does it take, Leslie? Zoë wanted to say. Instead, she raised both eyebrows. "And he didn't call you stupid or senseless or crazy or a spendthrift, and he didn't blame you for everything that went wrong or—"

"Well, no. He didn't do that every day." Leslie's eyes were large and earnest. "Really, he can be quite sweet."

"Leslie!" Zoë tried not to shout. "Do you hear yourself? You're rationalizing away years of verbal abuse. And didn't you just tell me a few minutes ago that Charles basically went, 'Nyah, nyah, look what a mess you're in,' on the phone just last night?"

Desperation washed over her.

Oh, God, Zoë prayed silently, *I know she didn't have a good role model of a marriage as she grew up. She doesn't even know how dysfunctional her relationship with Charles is or how good it could be. And she's slipping away again. I can feel it—smell it. And there's not a thing I can do about it.*

Leslie didn't seem to hear her. "The other thing is, Scott was in tears last night. He misses his dad so much."

Puh-leez! Zoë thought. But she kept her voice soft. "Of course he does. And yes, this is hard for everyone. But you have to look at the big picture, darlin'. Scott was upset over the thing with Michelle last night, and he has a hard time adjusting to change. But think a moment. Do you want your son back home, curled up in a fetal position after one of Charles's rampages?"

Leslie rubbed her forehead. "Do I have a right to separate a son from his father? I mean, a boy needs a man to—"

"Be a role model for the kind of man he'll grow up to be?" Zoë asked.

Leslie pushed the remainder of her sandwich aside. "I think I'm getting sick. My chest, my throat—"

Zoë sighed. "I think I'm getting sick too," she muttered to herself. Then she saw Leslie's flushed face. *You never stop being a mother,* she thought as she reached across the table to touch her forehead. "You do feel a little feverish." She patted Leslie's cheek. "No wonder you feel depressed. This, too, will pass, honey. Please. Don't give up."

৵

By day's end Leslie's throat hurt each time she swallowed, and the sharp bark of a cough began.

"You sound terrible." Terry looked up from her desk. "If you need to stay home tomorrow, it's a light day. We can cover."

"Thanks. I'll see how I feel in the morning."

She went through the motions of calling a cab, picking up

the kids, arranging for a new battery for the car, fixing dinner, then fell asleep watching TV. When she awoke, Scott and Michelle were in bed, and someone—Scott, no doubt, had covered her with a blanket. She drew it around her, feeling chills migrate from one part of her body to another. Without washing her face or brushing her teeth, she crawled into bed.

It seemed she moved from one dream to another. At first they focused on Charles. Charles when she first met him, coming into the care center with carpal tunnel syndrome. Suave, charming, clever. Flowers . . . concerts . . . dinners out . . . kindnesses to Michelle.

She roused at one point, wondering if all that had been a dream in the first place. Had there been any warning signs before they were married? She really couldn't think of any. She only knew that he seemed sensible, reliable, steady. So different from Tom . . .

Thoughts melted into dreams and dreams into thoughts, till they all blurred together. She saw Tom with his cocky smile on that first college ski trip. Tom at the top of Cornice in the Mammoth ski area, skating on his skis past all the others who stood trembling and cogitating at the edge of the precipitous drop. He took lots of air over the lip and scarcely seemed to touch the snow as he flew almost straight down. Then she could see him executing jump turns through narrow, almost-vertical, rock-studded passages. The guy was fearless, fun—and fascinating. She was smitten.

Then her vision switched to bills—bills as big as bed sheets, piling one upon the other, filling the room. A baby crying. Michelle. *Leslie* crying. Tom's broken body on the gurney. Voices: "Misread the terrain" . . . "That drop was impossible." . . . "Anything to be in a Warren Miller film." . . . Bills piling up over his body.

She shook with chills, wanting to get up, wanting not to dream again, but too weak to move, feeling utterly and completely alone.

"Charles," she murmured softly. "Charles."

15

⁓

From Zoë's Prayer Journal

September 29: Oh, God, You are Lord of all, and You know the beginning and the end of this whole situation with Leslie. Oh, please don't let her go back to square one—or square zero—before she's even begun to get a handle on the sick way her family functions—or fails to function. I confess I'm full of fear and apprehension about what may happen if she does. (Do You hear my big sigh, Lord?) Nevertheless, I will trust You. I give You my daughter, my grandchildren—and Charles. Yes, Charles. I wanted to smack him yesterday, I confess—his smug attitude that Leslie will come back. But I've promised You I'll love him, even if I don't love what he does. It isn't easy! Help me not to give up on him. I know You haven't. Thank You that I can come to You in the name of Your Son, Jesus, amen.

LESLIE AWAKENED THE NEXT MORNING WITH A RACKING cough, a voice that sounded like a three-packs-a-day smoker, and a head that went into orbit when she stood up. "You guys get yourselves some juice and cereal and toast," she whispered as she went back to bed. Somehow she'd get them to school.

She watched them dress and then heard them tramp down the stairs to open and close the refrigerator at least twenty times. The phone rang.

"I'll get it," Michelle called. Then, "Oh, hi, Gram." A pause. "Not so hot. She's still in bed." Another pause. "Yeah, that might be cool." She called up to the balcony. "Gram says she'll take us to school and pick us up if you want."

"Wonderful," Leslie croaked. She called the therapy center and left a message on Terry's voice mail, then settled back in bed enormously relieved.

Half an hour later she heard her mother at the door. "Y'all ready? You look great. Leslie," she called out, "anything I can bring you? Juice? Chicken soup?" She didn't wait for an answer. "Tell you what. I'll be back around eleven."

Car doors banged. An engine started. Leslie lay there, luxuriating in the quiet, and dozed off. At ten she awakened, went downstairs, and found a piece of ginger root left from the stir-fry. She cut off a slice, dropped it in a cup with water, and heated it in the microwave. She let it steep while she wrapped up in an afghan and curled up on the sofa. At last she lifted the cup, inhaling the pungent ginger bouquet. Sipping carefully, she let the liquid trickle down her throat, soothing the sandpaper roughness.

She reached for her Bible on the side table, murmuring, "Oh, Lord, I don't even know where to begin. Do You have something You want to show me?" She slipped her finger into the place where she had inserted the program from last Sunday's service and opened the Bible: 1 Peter 4.

Her eyes focused on the twelfth verse. "Dear friends, do not be surprised at the painful trial you are suffering, as though something strange were happening to you."

"Painful trial is right," she muttered.

She continued reading. "But rejoice that you participate in the sufferings of Christ, so that you may be overjoyed when his glory is revealed. If you are insulted because of the name of Christ, you are blessed, for the Spirit of glory and of God rests on you."

She reread the passage, frowning. "I know You didn't promise us a rose garden, Lord," she said.

As she took a sip of tea, she noted the cross-references in the margin and thumbed back to chapter 1. Verses 6 and 7 cautioned, ". . . though now for a little while you may have had to suffer grief in all kinds of trials. These have come so that your faith—of greater worth than gold, which perishes even though refined by fire—may be proved genuine and may result in praise, glory and honor when Jesus Christ is revealed."

"Okay," Leslie murmured, "so this is a test. Like in the book of James, I'm supposed to count my trials all joy." She coughed and sighed. "Only through You, Lord. Definitely not in my own strength."

She closed her eyes, "But the question is, Lord, am I to endure *here*—or back with Charles? You know my heart is saying I belong back with him, trying again, not being so selfish, focusing more on him, being his helper." She looked again at her Bible and skimmed the rest of the page. Turning it, she stopped short at verse 12 of chapter 2. "Live such good lives among the pagans that, though they accuse you of doing wrong, they may see your good deeds and glorify God on the day he visits us."

She felt cold and sweaty at the same time. "Do You mean Charles? He's definitely a pagan—and I sure can relate to accusations of wrongdoing."

She picked at her cuticle. But would he take her back? That was the question. What was it he'd said when they last talked?

"Let me know when you come to your senses." That seemed to leave a door open—at least a little.

She shut the Bible and stretched out on the sofa. A war of words seemed to rage in her mind. "Evil men will go from bad to worse," a deep voice warned. "Win your husbands without a word," cried another. "Don't even eat lunch with such a person," came a distant call. "Wives, submit to your husbands as unto the Lord," sang another voice.

She heard the door slide open and shut and soon saw Zoë in the kitchen ladling soup from a plastic container into a bowl. "Get some sleep?" she asked. Then, without waiting for an answer, "Good."

She felt spacey. "Oh, hi, Mom," she managed. "Chicken soup?"

Zoë nodded wisely. "It has natural antibiotics in it, you know."

"You're a good Jewish mother," she smiled. "Are there matzo balls in it?"

Zoë laughed. "What could my little Scottish mother teach me about matzo balls?" The bell of the microwave dinged and she retrieved the bowl, setting it on a plate. "Here you go."

Leslie sat up and took the soup, looking up at Zoë. "You're going to watch and be sure I eat it."

"Definitely. When you were little, I'd bring you a tray upstairs when you were sick then hear you flushing perfectly good food down the toilet."

Leslie shook her head. "I never knew you were onto me. That's funny." She thought a moment. "Guess I wanted you to think I was being a good kid, doing what you wanted me to, even when I wasn't hungry."

"Mmmm." Zoë looked at her closely, started to say something but reconsidered.

Leslie sipped from the soup spoon. "It's good. Really good."

"Well, don't sound so surprised. You get that rich flavor from cooking one chicken, then a second one in the broth of the first. I brought a vat."

"Thanks, Mom. I really appreciate it."

Zoë perched on the arm of the sofa. "You needed this time, Leslie. You've been on overdrive."

She cocked her head to one side. "Maybe. I certainly don't feel like doing much right now."

"Don't." She looked intently at her daughter. "And honey, don't give up when you've only just begun."

Here we go again, Leslie thought. *Pep talk number 232.*

But Zoë seemed to sense her resistance. "Would you like some grape juice? Lots of ice?"

"You never forget, do you? I always thought that was so refreshing when I was sick."

Zoë fixed the juice and brought it, glancing at the Bible beside Leslie. "Good. You've been in the Word."

For a moment Leslie thought of asking her about the 1 Peter passages. But something made her hesitate.

"The whole counsel of God," Zoë murmured. "It's so important not to snatch a verse or two out of context."

Is that what I'm doing? she wondered, thinking back to what she'd read that day. She mentally pressed the delete button on the idea, realizing she already knew what she would do.

Zoë bustled around the kitchen, tidying up, and as quickly as she had arrived, she was out the door, promising, "I'll be back with the kids."

"Thanks a bundle, Mom," Leslie called after her.

She stared out at the blue water of the pool, which seemed to dance with lights as the sun reflected off the ripples. She looked at her watch. Quarter of twelve. At noon, precisely, Charles would be at his desk, eating his sandwich. Had he fixed his own? Probably. "Why in the world should I buy a skimpy sandwich for four times what it costs to make it at home?" he'd say.

She spent the time rehearsing what she would say.

Be up-front, she told herself. *Admit you made a mistake. Be positive. Assume success.*

She gave him an extra five minutes, then pressed the phone buttons.

"Harper," came his voice.

"Is it peanut butter today?"

"Oh, Leslie." He seemed surprised. "Um, actually, I studied late last night and picked up a ham on rye from the damsel who parades around the office every day with her big basket of sandwiches."

"Really?"

"When we last spoke, Leslie—"

Her heart sank as she realized she hadn't phoned him the night of Michelle's absence to say she was back. She smacked her hand against her head. *Dumb!*

"I presume," Charles continued, "since I have not seen Michelle's picture on milk cartons, that she returned."

"Oh, Charles, I'm so sorry. I should have called you. Yes, she came back. I'll, uh, I'll tell you about that later." No point in getting him upset right now. "Um, am I interrupting something? Can you talk a minute?"

"Yes, I can talk. What happened to your voice?"

He actually noticed. "I'm home with a fever, cough." She hurried into her speech. "Well, Charles, to get to the point, if you're willing, I'd like to try again. Come back, I mean. I think we can still have a good marriage. I really want to work at it." She held her breath during the pause.

Finally, "Well, Leslie, I am very grateful to hear that." She was touched by the sincerity in his voice.

Then he added, "It sounds like you intend to be—" He hesitated. "—cooperative."

She wondered vaguely what he meant, but, beguiled by his tone, she said softly, "I really love you, and I miss you."

"I miss you too," he said. "And I have a plan for dealing with Michelle."

"Oh, Charles, I need help with her." She paused. "I'm really not up to packing stuff today, but I think by tomorrow—"

"Tomorrow would be fine."

"Oh, thank you, Charles. Thank you so much!" She hung up the phone and wept, repeating over and over to herself, "This is the right thing to do. This is the right thing to do."

Feeling giddy and detached, she made her way upstairs and fell into a deep sleep.

When she heard Zoë and the kids' voices, she awakened, pajamas soaked and clinging to her body. *Fever's broken. I'm better,* she realized.

She cleared her throat. "Hi, you guys," she called, and even her voice sounded better. "How was your day?"

"Gross," Michelle said.

"Okay," Scott said. "Gram's gonna help me with my flip turns."

"Good, Scott. Michelle, come on up and tell me about it," she invited.

"No thanks," Michelle said.

So much for keeping the lines of communication open.

"I'm having some grape juice," Michelle announced. Not "May I . . ."

"That's for your mother," Zoë said.

"No, it's okay," Leslie said, "but you could pour me some too? With ice, please."

A grudging "O-*kay*."

Scott came up to change into his swimsuit, but it was some

time before Michelle appeared with the juice. With head-phones clamped to her head, she made it obvious that there was to be no communication.

"Thanks," Leslie said, lifting one earpiece from Michelle's head. "I'll be in the shower for a bit."

Michelle nodded.

After she'd showered and dressed in a loose-flowing caftan, she brushed her hair and put on a dab of lipstick. Downstairs, she found Michelle sitting on the couch with Boris leaning against her legs, looking up at her as her head bobbed the beat and her mouth formed the words.

Outside she could hear Zoë. "Stroke . . . stroke . . . stroke . . . *now!*"

She saw the splash and Scott's feet pushing off.

"Better. Much better! You don't have to be afraid of getting closer to the wall. Did you feel the nice push you got? After you've done a few thousand, you won't even have to think about it." Zoë turned and saw Leslie at the door. "Leslie! You look better. This son of yours is a natural, you know that? Just a few tips, and he's doing so well!"

As she came through the door, Scott grinned. "Gram's a good coach."

"I know," Leslie said. "Want to show me?"

"Sure." Scott swam back to the center of the pool, then faced the end. A few quick strokes and he ducked his head down. His rangy legs flipped over, feet making solid contact with the wall for a strong thrust away. Leslie applauded. "Great!"

As Scott continued practicing, Leslie said to her mother, "You're so good with him. I remember how you first coaxed him into the water. Before long he was diving for rings on the bottom."

"I think the age-group swim team would be good for him," Zoë said.

"I do too."

Zoë glanced at her watch. "You okay for stuff for dinner?"

Leslie nodded. "I'll have soup. There's ham and potato salad from last night for the kids."

"Good. Now, how about tomorrow?" Zoë asked.

"No problem. I feel a lot better."

"Well, don't try to do too much too soon."

"Yes, Mother!" Leslie used her dutiful-daughter tone.

Zoë laughed and waved good-bye to Scott. She waggled her hand to get Michelle's attention through the screen door and her granddaughter waved back. "Oh," she turned toward Leslie, "you're surely not going to try to go tonight, but if you need me to stay with the kids next Wednesday, to be sure Michelle stays grounded, I can."

"Wednesday?" She hadn't a clue.

"Yes, the support group at church."

"Oh. Yes. Thanks, Mom."

I should tell her, Leslie thought. *No, not yet. But I won't be needing the support group now. Everything's going to be okay.*

16

HOME. THE WORD ECHOED THROUGH LESLIE'S MIND THE
moment she awakened the next morning, and she hurried out
of bed, filled with a joyous sense of anticipation. She pictured
the gray stucco structure she loved so much, with its white
trim, shake roof, the roses blooming by the entry, the lake
sparkling behind. Today she'd be home. Home with her own
blanket, her own kitchen, her own herbs growing outside the
door. How good it would be. Home with Charles. He'd missed
them. He really wanted them back. Now Scott would have a
dad again, and she'd have help with Michelle. They could start
afresh. It was going to be all right.

Terry called from the therapy center as Leslie cleaned up the
kitchen after breakfast. "How ya feeling?"

"Better. I'll come in for half a day."

"You sure you shouldn't lie low another day?"

"No. This will work out fine." *And,* Leslie added to herself, *give me time to get us moved.* But she didn't want to get into that with Terry yet.

As she left to drive the kids to school, she found Tracy watering the potted plants in the breezeway. "You're up early," Leslie said.

Tracy nodded. "This is my day to work at the women's shelter, so I need to be out of here by eight-thirty. Sorry you got a bug. Feel better today?"

"Much. Thanks. I—" She started to explain that she and the kids would be moving back home this afternoon but reconsidered. Tracy would try to talk her out of it, and she needed to be off with the kids. Time enough to tell *everyone* in the afternoon.

Leslie felt a little wobbly when she began working. *The bug, and maybe nerves,* she thought. *But I'm doing the right thing. Even though Mom is going to have a fit, and so is Tracy.* She pictured their reactions and felt her gut tighten. *But I have to do what's right for me, for us,* she told herself for the twentieth time.

Her mother called just before noon. "Honey, I thought you'd be sensible and take another day off."

"No, Mom, I'm fine. Really. I'm so grateful for all you did yesterday." She could hear the formality in her own voice, distancing herself from any depth of communication.

"I could pick the kids up . . ."

"No, I'm fine." She pretended to be busy, calling out, "Be with you in a minute," then added to her mother, "gotta go. Thanks for calling."

At noon she hurried back to the little apartment, did a quick cleanup, and loaded their belongings into the car. It took longer than she expected. "Guess the kids actually were a help getting everything over here," she muttered as she checked the apartment to be sure she had everything. She should write Tracy a note, but it was time to leave to get the kids. She'd write her, call her, do something later.

She picked up Michelle first. "What's all this?" Her daughter pointed into the backseat as she climbed into the car.

"We're going back home," Leslie said, keeping her tone bright and positive.

"Sheeshe!" Michelle gave her a look that mingled disgust and pity. "You really are gutless."

She felt her face flush."Thanks for your vote of confidence, Michelle."

"Am I gonna be grounded at home too?"

"Certainly."

"Oh, great, cool, mah-ve-lous!" She turned and stared at her mother at the wheel. "Man, you don't have any more guts than the amoeba we were studying in bio today."

Leslie felt her jaw tense. "Thank you, Michelle, but when I need your advice, I'll ask for it."

She glanced at her daughter, slumped in the seat beside her. *Should have expected this from Michelle,* she thought. *For her everything's a negative. But Scott will be glad. He's missed his dad.*

Scott was waiting at the curb by his school.

She rolled down the window and pointed behind her. "I think there's enough room for one boy in the back on this side."

He stood staring into the car, and his eyes grew larger. "We going back with Dad?" he asked, his voice tense, anxious.

She put her hand on his shoulder. "Honey, you told me how much you missed him. I thought you'd be glad."

"But won't he be furious at all of us? Won't he be yelling and screaming?" He made no move to get into the car. "I was just getting used to our pad there. And now I won't have the pool to practice in."

"And Boris. Don't forget Boris. We'll both miss him," Michelle added.

Scott looked near tears, and for a moment, Leslie thought she might cry too. Was she making a mistake going back? Another mistake, the story of her life? No, she'd made her decision, and it was right.

"Scott, listen to me. Your dad missed us. He really wants us back. You'll have your road-racing set and all the things you've been missing. It's going to be good."

"Yeah, sure . . . yeah, sure," came Michelle's backup lyrics.

"Get in the car, Scott," she said firmly.

⁓

She caught her breath as she saw their house. How good it looked! How she'd missed it.

She unlocked the front door and stepped inside. A musty, stale aroma assaulted her. It smelled like—oh, yes, a little like the bar her first husband liked at Aspen. That, and something sour she couldn't identify.

"Phew!" Michelle exclaimed. "Smells like somethin' died! Let's go back to Aunt Tracy's!"

"Yeah!" echoed Scott.

"It just needs airing out," she assured them. "Now please finish unloading the car and put your stuff away." She hurried to open the windows and sliding doors, making a mental note that the spent rose blossoms needed to be removed. In fact, the yard definitely needed work.

The kitchen was immaculate—so much so, she wondered if Charles had ever prepared a meal. Books and papers stood in neat piles on the dining-room table. Ah, yes, the actuary materials.

Upstairs the bed was made, with the spread hanging so evenly on all sides she wondered if Charles had used a ruler. She stroked his pillow—carefully tucked into its sham—and felt eager to see him, to be held and loved, profoundly relieved to be home.

She wondered if she needed to do some laundry. Better check the wicker hamper. Empty. He must have run the washer. Amazing.

Scott appeared with a load of her clothes, dropping a few on his way into her room. "Thanks, honey." She turned toward him, wanting so much for him to be glad to be home. "Bet you're happy to have all your games and toys again."

He nodded. "Yeah," and disappeared down the hallway.

She sighed and hung her clothes carefully, looking at the outfits she'd left, happy to have access to them again. As she put her cosmetics away, she saw the clock on the dresser. Four already. She should call Tracy—and Zoë. But first she'd see if there was anything in the pantry or freezer that might work for dinner.

In the hallway she met Michelle. "Mom, I just have to have this dress for school tomorrow, and it has these gross spots on it."

"Okay, let's get a load of wash going."

"Can't. There's yucky stuff in the washer."

Leslie hurried down to the laundry room and opened the washer. A tangle of mildewed clothes greeted her. "Oh, Charles . . ." she said, shaking her head. "You do need me." She twisted the dial and filled the washer with hot water, adding detergent and bleach, hoping for the best.

"Mom?" Michelle stood in the doorway. "I have this dumb assignment. Supposed to write this thing that describes something that shows all our senses. You know—smell, sight, hearing, and stuff."

"I've got an idea." Scott was halfway down the stairs. "Tell 'em about that time you had the flu and barfed all over the car."

"Oh, Scott, gross!" Michelle waved him away, and he departed with a pleased-with-himself chortle.

"Well, how about describing a meal?" Leslie suggested, delighted to have any sort of communication with her daughter.

"Like what?"

"Well, you could do Thanksgiving: the smell of the turkey in the oven, the sound of the potatoes being whipped, the tart taste of the cranberries."

"Yeah," Michelle didn't seem convinced.

"Or, how about telling how to make a root beer float? The vanilla smell of the ice cream. The 'psst' sound of the can opening, the feel of the cold glass, the tingle of the bubbles on your tongue . . ."

"Nah."

Leslie gave her several suggestions, rich in detail. By the time her daughter sighed her way into the family room, Leslie realized it was almost five o'clock.

Where did the time go? she wondered. *And why wasn't I bright enough to stop after the second idea? Obviously nothing I thought of would please Michelle.*

The phone rang twice, then stopped mid-ring. Michelle must have picked it up.

Jason? she thought, hurrying down the hall.

"It's Dad," Michelle called to her. "Wants to know if he can pick up pizza."

Leslie blinked. Charles barely tolerated pizza. *He's trying to please us,* she realized. She took the phone from Michelle. "Charles, that's a lovely idea, but I didn't think you liked—"

"I can handle it. This is an occasion, is it not? Want me to get anything else?"

"No. Well, yes, some salad stuff if we need it. I haven't looked yet."

"We do," he assured her.

"You might be able to get salad at the pizza place." But Charles hated to spend extra money, she remembered, so she added, "It'll cost more than lettuce from the grocery store."

"Ah, so. See you in half an hour or so."

"Wonderful." She hung up and saw Michelle watching her.

"Pizza!" It was the first positive word she'd heard from her in four days.

"What a guy, huh? Will you set the table, please, Michelle?"

Leslie headed for the kitchen. Better call Tracy. Then she remembered the wash. The cycle was finished, but as she lifted a T-shirt, she saw the mildew remained. She looked for the pamphlet that told how to remove stains. *Let's see: ink, lipstick, meat juice—ah, mildew. Wash in hottest water. Did that. Soak in bleach or treat with salt and lemon juice and dry in direct sunlight. Oh, wonderful. Guess I'll try the bleach again and let it soak. Good thing Charles likes white dress shirts.*

She decided to cut some roses for the table, adding a few leatherleaf fern fronds from the sideyard. "Nice," she said as she placed the arrangement on the table.

"Mom, I forgot," came Scott's voice from the hallway. "I need to bring a sheet of poster board to school tomorrow."

"Hon-ey!" she protested. "Couldn't you have told me when we were out in the car?"

"I have some," Michelle volunteered.

Leslie stared at her, astonished. "Why, that's really nice, Michelle. Could you get it for Scott?"

"Sure." She grinned and handed the silverware to her brother.

Maybe, Leslie thought, *she's really glad to be home, too, even though she can't admit it.*

Two phone calls interrupted her, and just when she was about to call Tracy, Charles bustled in, pizza box balanced in one arm, a grocery bag in the other. He set the bag on the counter.

"Shall I put this in the stove to hold?" he asked.

"Good idea." She opened the oven door and turned the dial.

He slipped the pizza in and reached out for her. His embrace was close and warm.

"I missed you," she said, lifting her head for his kiss.

"Good," he said, turning as he heard Scott's voice. "Scott!" He clapped him on the back and pumped his hand. She shook her head inwardly. Scott was only ten. Couldn't Charles have put his arms around him? Did this "guy stuff" have to start so early? Evidently, because when Michelle appeared, Charles gave her a quick hug.

"This calls for a celebration," Charles said, extricating a six-pack of Coke and another of beer from the sack. He gave the Cokes to Michelle and pulled out two cans of beer. Popping the top of one, he offered it to Leslie.

"Uh, no thanks, Charles. I'll go with the Coke."

He raised an eyebrow but didn't comment. "Cheers, then!"

Conversation flowed at dinner with virtually no negatives from Charles, not even a reference to Michelle's escapade. They laughed over the mildewed clothes, and Michelle regaled them with a blow-by-blow account of a film she'd seen in English class. Charles listened, responded.

This is good; this is the way it's supposed to be, she thought as she watched Charles's eyes twinkle and Scott bask in his dad's congratulations on mastering the flip turn. And after the kids are in bed tonight . . . yes, honeymoon time.

⁓

Zoë could hear the phone ringing even as she turned the key in the lock of her front door. She hurried to catch it before the answering machine picked up the call. "Hello?"

"Mom? This is Tracy. She's gone."

"What?" What in the world was Tracy talking about?

"Leslie's gone. All her stuff. All the kids' clothes. They've cleared out, run away."

Zoë closed her eyes and leaned against the counter. "Back to square zero! Oh, Tracy, I am discouraged. I somehow felt it building up, but I hoped against hope—"

"Okay, you're discouraged. I'm mad as a hosed-down hen. How can she just vanish without saying a word? I mean, am I her sister or what? Did we let her stay with us or what? I'm really miffed!"

"She didn't tell me, either, if that makes you feel any better. Don't you see, Trace? She knew what we'd say. She didn't want us to talk her out of it. She'd made up her mind."

"Then she's a bigger mess than I realized."

"She's not thinking straight; that's obvious. But change isn't easy. You should know that. When you work at the women's shelter, you see woman who run away from even worse situations. They come in all beat up, some of them, don't they?"

"Yes, but . . ."

"And how many of them go back to their husbands?"

Tracy let out a long sigh. "A lot."

"So why are we surprised? Leslie may need to do this again—and even again."

Tracy's voice softened. "I really marvel at your patience, Mom. When it seems so clear what Leslie needs to do, I just hate it when she backs down. And Mom, she's not like the destitute women I work with. She has a job. She can take care of herself and the kids. And she has a family to give her emotional support."

"Yes, but she doesn't really get it yet. And she is still emotionally dependent on Charles. Besides, if we pressure her, she has a tendency to dig in her heels."

"Yup. I recall."

Then Zoë remembered. "But you know what really irks me?"

"What, Mom?"

"Charles told me the other night that when—not if—Leslie came back, she'd better stay."

"Whew! We really need to pray for her."

"I do pray for her," Zoë said.

"I know you do, Mom. And for all of us. You never give up."

17

LESLIE WAS AMAZED HOW QUICKLY SHE SLIPPED INTO THE familiar routine the next morning: the quick waking-up hug (actually it was a little longer this morning) when the clock radio sounded . . . off to the shower while Charles lingered in bed . . . blow-drying her hair while he showered . . .

Holding the dryer with one hand, flipping her bangs back with the other, she saw Charles slide the door to the tub enclosure open. Reaching out for a towel, he said something. She turned off the dryer so she could hear. Charles smiled, but his voice was emphatic. "I said I like the bangs down better."

"You do? That's interesting. A lot of people like the change." *And so do I*, she thought. *Besides, it's my hair, isn't it?*

The smile faded, and he shook his head slowly.

Was it worth fighting for? If it pleased Charles, wasn't this a small thing to do for him? Don't sweat the little things, she'd read somewhere recently. And what was the word Charles had used on the phone? "Cooperative." She shrugged. "Okay." Rewetting the bangs, she brushed them down over her forehead.

Downstairs, there was just enough bread to make sandwiches, and as she surveyed the interior of the refrigerator, there was but one option: peanut butter. *No butter, no jelly on Charles's,* she reminded herself. He walked past her on his way into the breakfast area. "Do we have any pickles?" he asked.

"Last time I looked, yes. Bread-and-butter type. Want some in a zipper bag?"

"No, in the sandwich."

She turned toward him. "*In* the peanut butter sandwich?"

"Yes, my mother used to do that. Gives a nice crunch."

"Okay." She winced as she dug out the jar of pickles from the back of the refrigerator. "Do you want this all the time? In your peanut-butter sandwich, I mean?"

"Mmm. Until further notice." He sat down at the breakfast table as Scott came into the room. "Ah, Scott. Baseball playoffs tonight. Perhaps we could strike an agreement. I need to study for at least two hours every evening. But you could watch the game—and, well, call me if it gets close and tense."

"Like a tie in the ninth, bases loaded?" Scott asked eagerly.

"Exactly."

Michelle sauntered in and slouched into her chair. "Ah, Michelle," Charles said. "Good. Now, I can simply say this once. Please listen carefully, everyone. I am preparing for the actuary exam. The principal reason I am doing so, is to support you better, prepare for college expenses. So I shall expect your full cooperation. I need quiet when I am studying, and no interruptions—with the possible exception of baseball news. Is that understood?"

"Yes," Scott said.

"Yeah." Michelle stifled a yawn.

"Leslie?" Charles asked.

She joined them at the table. "Yes, sir, that is understood."

He gave her a sharp look. Perhaps her light tone struck him as flippant. But he simply said, "Good." He flicked a microscopic bit of something from his cuff. "Of course, I am budgeting time to watch the series."

ↈ

It was good to have the children taking the school bus once again so Leslie didn't have to drive them to school. That gave her time to write a note to Tracy. After three false starts, at last she expressed that she was "deeply grateful" for her sister's and brother-in-law's help. Glancing at her watch as she left the house, she realized there was time to drop it by Tracy's house. Oh, and she must call Zoë, though by this time, undoubtedly Tracy and her mother had talked. She felt the muscles along her spine tense as she imagined the criticism, the head-shaking. Oh, they surely were disappointed with her. How hard it was to please everyone in her life!

At Tracy's house she reached out the car window and slipped the note in the mailbox at the edge of the street. No time to go in. Besides, it was better to put it in writing. Okay, be honest: better not to have to face her. She felt a prickle of perspiration beginning under her arms and flicked on the air conditioning.

At work David was her second appointment, but she had a moment before he arrived to call her mother. *I'll go on the offensive,* she decided as she waited for Zoë to answer.

"This is the day—" Zoë began.

"The Lord has made," Leslie broke in.

"I will be glad and rejoice in it. And I do rejoice to hear your voice, Leslie."

"I wasn't sure you would, Mom. I know you're disappointed in me. Let's be honest. I know you, um, basically don't really want this marriage to continue."

"That's not true, honey," Zoë countered. "I've always wanted reconciliation. That's my bottom line. I just wanted you to stand back and recognize some patterns and see ways you could make the marriage more healthy, better. My concern is you, your future, your happiness."

"Well, I think it is better, Mom. Charles really wanted us back. He had a little celebration last night. He's getting Scott to watch the playoff games for him and report to him. He's really been quite dear."

"I see," Zoë said. It was a phrase she often used when she didn't agree with Leslie.

Tapping the eraser end of a pencil on the desk, Leslie waited. At last her mother changed the subject. "I talked to your dad. He's doing better. Doing a little work with a walker now. Morale's improved too."

"Oh, Mom, I'm so glad. Thanks, Lord!"

"Yes, I agree. Your dad asked about you."

"Me, in particular?" She was surprised.

"You in particular."

She glanced up as David wheeled past her door. "Oh, sorry, Mom, David's here. We'll talk more later, hm?"

"Give him my love. And tell him about Scott's flip turn."

"Right. Bye, Mom."

"Love you, dear."

As soon as she approached David, she could sense his depression. Usually he sat so erect in the chair, gave her his sunny grin. Today his shoulders rounded over, and he didn't even look up at her.

"What's up?" she asked.

"I maybe shouldn't have come. A down day."

"Then you definitely *should* be here. Something in particular get to you?"

"Just thought I'd be doing better by now."

She bent down to look him in the face.

"Okay, I met this girl. A triathlete. Gorgeous. She's not gonna give a crip like me the time of day."

"Well, if she doesn't, she's not a person of much substance. And also not much discernment. She'd be missing something very special."

"Yeah, sure. A real prize." He looked down at his legs.

"Listen to your therapist, David," she said, grabbing his chin and forcing him to look at her. "You are making remarkable progress. When you first came in, your legs were totally useless. You had to drag yourself in and out of the wheelchair. Now look at all the muscles that are working. As soon as your leg braces come in, we're going to get you up. I really think you'll be able to do it!"

"Yeah, but—"

She released her grip and softened her voice. "But it's slow. I know. Hang tough. There's a light at the end of the tunnel."

"Yeah, it's the Lord coming." He grinned for the first time.

"No, I mean before that."

"Okay, coach." He sat up straight in the chair. "But not if I don't work, right? So—what torture have you stayed awake creating for me today?" Before she could answer, he did a double take, looking at her closely. "What happened?"

It's my hair, she realized, suddenly unable to meet his gaze.

"You go back to your husband?" he asked gently.

She nodded. "You're not surprised."

"No, I'm not. Want to talk about it?"

"Only to say that, for many reasons, I decided it's the right thing to do." She wondered if she sounded defensive and decided to say no more.

"I see," he said.

She flinched inwardly at the same words her mother had used a few minutes ago but said, "Shall we get at it?"

"Right."

She started him with leg raises on the mat then moved into arm-strengthening exercises.

"I do have some good news," she told him.

"I could use that."

"Scott got his flip turn down pretty well. I think he needed that—to give him a little confidence before he felt ready to join you and the team."

"Figure it out all by himself?"

"Partly. Then my mom helped."

He grinned. "What a great lady. Maybe she'd like to be my assistant."

"Better not ask unless you really mean it."

"Maybe when the team grows a little." He worked on his pec flies. "Want to bring Scott over to work out next week? We go four-thirty to five-thirty, Monday, Wednesday, and Friday."

"I'll tell him. Now, let's try the recumbent bike. Here, let me strap you in. Start slow and easy." She watched him. "Good! You really are getting a lot stronger, David."

❧

On Saturday Charles gave himself time off to watch the play-offs. "I deserve this," he said. Besides, Leslie realized, he couldn't bear to miss the stronger division champions having to fight for their lives against an underdog coming on strong under pressure. "Tomorrow," he said to Scott, "you'll have to start watching at eleven, because the National League game's on the East Coast."

"But Charles," she protested. "We go to ten-thirty church."

He exhaled impatiently.

"I guess we could go to the eight-thirty," she offered.

"Okay by me." Scott's voice was eager.

"Don't expect me to get up that early on a weekend," Michelle interjected.

Leslie smiled. "I think you can handle it just this one time."

"Oh, sure, and then there'll be next Sunday, and then maybe World Series games on the East Coast. I'm a growing adolescent. I need my sleep."

"You could go to bed a little earlier," Leslie suggested.

"Sheeshe!" Michelle breathed.

⁓

Scott rose immediately when Leslie called him on Sunday morning. But when she opened Michelle's door, her daughter rolled over and plopped the pillow over her head. "In a minute," came her muffled voice.

"Two minutes, max."

But five minutes later, she realized Michelle still wasn't up. "Go give a bang on Michelle's door, will you please, Scott?" she asked.

When Michelle didn't appear as the rest of the family sat down to breakfast, Leslie began to fret. *If she refuses to go, there's no way I can make her,* she thought. *It's so important for her. A bribe? Sorry, Lord, but I'm not above holding a carrot out to her. But I can't think what.*

At last Michelle shuffled into the breakfast area, still in her robe. "Honey," Leslie protested, "you're not even dressed. What did you plan to wear this morning?"

"Not going. Too much hassle." Michelle replied.

Feeling desperate, Leslie said, "I thought there was a guy you kind of liked."

"What an admirable reason for going to church," Charles interjected.

Thanks, Charles, Leslie said to herself.

Then he turned to Leslie. "Why not simply lay off the kid? Surely you see she does not want to go. Frankly I cannot blame her." He reached over and patted Michelle's hand. "Perhaps she is getting some common sense and realizing that much of what she hears there is pure nonsense. Just because her mother wants to spend her time with hypocrites . . ."

Leslie shot him a warning look.

"Come now, Leslie," he said, "what harm will it do if she misses one Sunday?"

Because then it could so easily become one more Sunday, and one more, she wanted to say—especially with your encouragement.

From the beginning Charles had always tolerated her going to church and conceded that children need at least to learn some values. Now he was undermining her, her faith, and her children's training. *Is he punishing me for leaving? Getting back at me?* she wondered. *How dare he call church nonsense? Why can't he see that if anyone needs to look beyond herself and focus on God, it's Michelle.* She saw Michelle give Charles a wink. *Collusion,* she thought angrily. *A house divided.* She looked at their two unyielding faces and knew she was licked.

She was grateful at least that Charles didn't encourage Scott to stay home too. As though to reassure her, as they drove to church he said, "I like Sunday school. I like learning about Jesus."

She patted his knee. "I'm glad. I do too."

The sermon that Sunday was titled, "A Sound Family." The pastor detailed ten different hallmarks of family health and invited worshipers to rate their own families. He spoke first about unconditional love for one another—a love not based on performance. Then he specified communicating with each other in truth and love. As he continued, Leslie realized she could rate her family as fair, sometimes even poor, but never good on any of the points.

She looked at all the splendid families around her. Undoubtedly they had it all together. She didn't belong here at all.

Then her eye traveled to the next point on the printed outline: "We don't shame, belittle, intimidate, or control each other." She winced. This very morning at the breakfast table, in a few sentences, Charles had managed all four. She'd felt shamed, belittled—all of the above. The Bible reference was the thirteenth chapter of 1 Corinthians, beginning, "Love is patient, love is kind."

Patient? Kind? she thought. *Does Charles know the meaning of these words?* She felt her throat constrict and worried that she might cry.

She scanned the remaining points and closed her eyes. If only she could stop her ears. She glanced around her, wanting to flee. But what would people think? Verging on panic, she thought, *I don't want to hear another word—not another word.*

18

October 3: Dear Lord, I confess I'm still feel-
ing down about Leslie going back to Charles.
She thinks it will be different. I don't. Oh, Lord,
is there ever going to be any peace, any happi-
ness, in her life? When will she stop feeling so
dependent on Charles? I long for the day she'll
see You as her comfort, her Rock — You and You
alone. Watch over her, protect her. Thank You
that You care for her even more than I do. I
praise You! In Jesus' name, amen.

AFTER THE CONCLUDING PRAISE SONG, LESLIE PLUNGED
down the aisle of the church, head down, wanting only to
escape and to erase all she'd heard. But the director of the
church's recovery ministry tapped her on the arm just outside
the door.

A man in his sixties, with laugh-lines around his eyes and a
wealth of snowy hair, he asked, "Aren't you the Leslie who
inquired about the Wednesday night women's support group?"

"Ah . . . yes," she mumbled, not wanting to talk to anyone yet intrigued by his timing—her moment of panic. "We
have a really excellent woman moderating the group now.
She's had a great deal of experience working with women who

are struggling with emotional abuse. A warm, godly person, and the women really seem comfortable with her."

She heard the words but felt so shaken she could only murmur, "Yes. Well, I was asking for a friend. I'll tell her. Thank you." She knew he knew she was lying, and she made a point of pushing her sleeve back to reveal her watch. "Now I'm sorry, but I really have to meet my son. Thank you."

She almost collided with Scott as she headed toward his Sunday school room. "Mom!" he exclaimed. "Mr. McCartney wants to know if I could help him with the kindergartners on Sundays. I did today when they were short-handed. C'mon!" She allowed him to lead her back toward the school area and into a room with a wooden slide and playhouse, where a young man in his twenties stood before a supply closet. He turned toward them. "Ah, Mrs. Harper?" He held out his hand. "Larry McCartney." They shook hands, and he went on. "Scott did such an excellent job helping this morning. He's gentle and friendly with these little tykes—a natural." He put his hand on Scott's shoulder. "Would you be willing for him to help? He'd miss part of his own class, but I'd be sure he was there for the Bible-study portion."

Leslie looked at Scott. "Would you like to, Scott?"

Her son nodded vigorously.

"Looks like you have a helper." Leslie smiled.

"Good. See you next Sunday, Scott."

"Yeah," Scott beamed.

On the way home, he said, "Sunday school is really neat. We're working on some memory verses, and I'm pretty good at that."

"That's terrific, Scott. It's so good to have the Word tucked away, to draw on when you need it. David tells me he recited verses to himself when he was on the way to the hospital after his accident and during those early days when he thought he might be paralyzed."

"Yeah, that's really good. Practical."

"Uh-huh. And you know, verses you learn when you're young really stick with you. Your great-grandmother can remember Scripture she memorized as a girl. It's really a blessing for her now that her eyesight is failing and she can't read very well." She braked to a stop as a traffic signal changed. "We seem to be hitting all the red lights," she fretted. "So. Tell me, what was your verse for today?"

"Jeremiah 29:11," he said. "It goes, '"For I know the plans I have for you,' declares the LORD, 'plans to prosper you and not to harm you, plans to give you hope and a future.' That's Jeremiah 29:11. It's good to repeat the reference."

"It is. And you really grabbed hold of that one, Scott!" she enthused. "Isn't that a great verse to remember?" She glanced at the car clock: 10:40 already. Good thing they'd be home on time for the ball game, or neither of them would have much of a future!

But when they came in the front door, Charles shouted, "Where have you been? How long does church take, huh? The pregame show has already begun."

"But Charles," she protested. "You told us the game started at eleven. I thought we were home in plenty of time."

"Well, anyone knows that when the *game* starts at eleven, there's a lot of pertinent information that comes on before. Scott, get your butt in there!" He pointed to the television in the family room.

"Charles," she whispered, "be fair."

"*Me* be fair? Look at yourself, lady. Bet you stood around chitchatting, made Scott late. You never think of anyone but yourself. What an incredibly selfish person." He stamped up the stairs to his study as Leslie blinked back the tears. *Where do I go to resign?* she wondered. *What happened to that happy family that gathered around the table last Thursday?*

When she went upstairs to change, she found Michelle's bedroom door closed. But she could hear Michelle's voice. Either she had a friend visiting or had managed a no-no: taking the portable phone into her room. Leslie knocked. The voice continued. She knocked louder.

"Who is it?" Michelle asked.

"Your mother," she said with firmness.

"Just a sec," came Michelle's voice. She opened the door, phone in hand.

"Michelle—"

"I'm just talking with Amy."

"That's fine, but you know you're not to have that phone in your room. It's to remain downstairs. You may continue your conversation, but please go downstairs."

Michelle muttered something unintelligible and started toward the stairs. "I—am—now—re—locating—thanks—to—my—adorable—mom," she proclaimed in ringing tones.

From Charles's study at the head of the stairs came an anguished plea. "Qui-et, puh-leeze!"

Leslie shook her head and changed into jeans. Charles wouldn't be so testy when his exam was over. She thought about her day, knowing she didn't dare make noise vacuuming. Better get out and do some yard work for a while. As she passed by the kitchen, she saw Michelle still on the phone. How could her daughter have so much to say to a girlfriend and so little to share, other than complaint and protest, with her mother?

Half an hour later Leslie came into the house for a glass of water when she heard Charles's angry voice. "No, no, no, Scott!

Bases loaded and no score is not sufficient reason to call me. Use a little discernment. I only want to see pivotal points as the game progresses."

She winced as she saw Scott coming down the stairs, head down, shoulders slumped. Now he'd probably be afraid to bother his father and err the other way, failing to call a "pivotal point." Wondering if she should sit with him and help him, she watched for a few moments, then went outside to move the hose.

At 12:30, Charles appeared in the garden. "I believe I shall watch the game during lunch," he said.

"Are you ready now? We usually have lunch around one on Sundays."

"I expect to reach a stopping point at twelve forty-five," he said.

"Fine." She finished deep-watering the pine tree, coiled the hose, and went into the kitchen.

Michelle was still on the phone. "Enough!" Leslie declared. "I need your help with lunch." She'd planned to set out sandwich fixings for a do-it-yourself lunch but decided it would be easier for TV viewing if she made up sandwiches. She split a long baguette, spread it with mustard and piled on the cold cuts and cheese. Noting that Michelle had at last put down the phone, she said, "You slice the tomatoes and put some on top. Some lettuce, too, will you please, Michelle?"

"Why me?" Michelle wondered.

"Because Scott has an assignment to watch the game for your dad."

At precisely 12:45, Charles descended the stairs, took a beer from the refrigerator, and settled down before the TV. "Bottom of the fourth." Scott explained. "No score."

Michelle gave her dad a plate and a napkin and brought in

a tray of sandwiches, each secured by a frilly toothpick. Charles raised a critical eyebrow but quickly became absorbed in the game. Leslie ate quietly, listening to the father-son interplay. "Are you kidding? Anybody could see he was out!" . . . "It's going into the stands. Foul ball." . . . "Bunt, bunt, darn you!" . . . "O-o-o-h, that ball is out of there!"

Michelle gave her mother a this-is-a-complete-drag look and retreated from the family room, but Leslie felt an obligation to stay and demonstrate some interest. At 1:20, Charles eyed his watch and said, "I'll stay just until the next commercial."

A few moments later a beer commercial began and, glancing at Scott and Leslie, Charles departed with the sigh of a martyr. "See the sacrifice I'm making for you," it seemed to say.

During the afternoon, as she cleaned the bathrooms, Leslie heard Scott call his dad twice. Each time she held her breath and waited. Good. No explosions from Charles. Scott must have done it right.

At the conclusion of the game, Scott came in to her. "I think I did okay. In fact, Dad even complimented me. And he seems in a real good mood 'cause his team won." He paused. "Mom?"

"Yes?"

"I miss Boris a lot. I've been thinking about it and kinda waiting for a good time to ask Dad for a dog, and I'm gonna go for it tonight while he's feelin' good."

"Wooo, Scott!" She tried to control her voice, but fear gripped her immediately. She could imagine what Charles's objections would be. The barking, the scratching, the fleas, the food and vet bills, the mess . . . And he might not be gentle.

"It could be from the animal shelter," Scott said eagerly, "so it wouldn't cost much."

"Honey, I don't think cost is the only problem," Leslie said. She wanted to put him off, yet she hated to always be trying to protect her son. Charles said she babied him too much.

"But Dad had a dog when he was a kid. He ought to understand."

It was hard for Leslie to imagine Charles as a child. Did he ever dig in the dirt, make engine noises as he pushed toy trucks around, get his hands dirty, tear holes in the knees of his pants? Somehow it was impossible to picture. And she certainly couldn't imagine Charles playing with a dog. Did he have to wash the saliva off his hands every time the dog brought a stick or a ball back to him?

"Honey, I hate to discourage you," she said slowly, "but I think it's a long shot."

"Well, if I don't ask, I sure won't get it," Scott pointed out. She couldn't refute his logic. Looking at his earnest face, she thought how good for Scott it would be to have a dog to love and to love him. *He needs me to support him,* she decided. *But, oh, it will take a miracle for Charles to agree.*

At five, as Leslie emptied the dishwasher, Charles came downstairs, stretching. "My brain cannot absorb one more iota. I believe I shall declare it a day." Opening the refrigerator, he pulled out a jug of wine, poured himself a glass, and took it out on the patio.

Scott, sitting on a kitchen stool having a glass of milk, watched his father and whispered to his mother, "Maybe this is a good time." He bit his lip. "Oh, man, if I can work up the nerve. Wish me luck."

"I do," she said fervently.

Putting the silverware away, she could hear Scott. "Dad, um, see, I have something to ask you."

"Yes?"

"I wonder if . . . I mean, do you think it would be possible . . . I, uh . . . I was thinkin' . . . Oh, well, never mind."

"Come, come, come, Scott! What is it? Spit it out. Don't stutter around it! What's on your mind?"

Leslie looked out and saw Scott swallow hard, and she wanted to run out and interrupt. But before she could move, Scott blurted out, "Dad? Could I have a dog?" He plunged ahead. "It wouldn't have to be a big dog and it could come from the animal shelter and I'd take care of it and—"

She could see the rigid line of Charles's moustache, the set of his mouth. "No," he said.

"But, Dad, I'd take care of him. I'd walk him and feed him and clean up after him. I'd—"

"Scott, stop babbling. The answer is no," Charles interrupted, turning away from his son to stare at the lake. She could see the quiver of Scott's chin as he came through the doorway. She longed to hug him, comfort him. "Maybe try for a cat another time," she wanted to suggest. But he rushed past her and up the stairs.

She poured herself an iced tea and joined Charles outside.

"Of all the cockeyed notions!" He turned to her. "Was this your idea?"

"No, Charles. It was Scott's. He really enjoyed playing with Boris when we were at Tracy's."

"Then let him go over to Tracy's and play with Boris." He drained his glass.

"Charles, that's not the same. I wish you'd at least think about it. It seems to me taking the responsibility for a dog would be good for Scott."

His eyes grew as hard as two deep amber marbles. "Les-lie . . ."

She heard the warning in his voice but determined to persist. "Charles, you had a dog when you were a child."

"Yes. And it died."

"I know how painful that must have been. My family lost cats and dogs too. But is that a reason not to—"

"Do I have to spell it out for you, woman?" he shouted. "Are you stupid? The answer is N-O. That, in case you cannot comprehend it, spells NO."

She sat, stroking long stripes in the moisture on her glass with her fingertips.

At last Charles said, "Now. There is something we must get straight. I have permitted you and the children to come back. It was peaceful when you were gone. My life was simpler, without all the petty annoyances. I hoped—no, expected—you would be cooperative upon your return. That includes not distracting me and upsetting me with unreasonable and impossible matters like this dog drivel. Please take note of that. In addition, I want one thing to be perfectly clear." He paused. "Look at me, Leslie."

She couldn't bear to gaze into the coldness of his eyes, so she concentrated instead on the brown hairs between his eyebrows.

His words came with equal staccato emphasis on each syllable. "You had better not ever even *think* of leaving again." He stared at her with a chilling intensity then stood and moved into the kitchen. She could hear him open the refrigerator and pull the cork from the bottle of wine. *Nothing has changed,* she thought miserably. *I thought it would be better. Now I'm trapped. I can never have the wings of a dove, never fly away again. As far as family health and those points that were made at church this morning are concerned, we flunk.*

The pain of the realization pressed around her rib cage and spread up her throat and gripped her mind with the certainty that she was a condemned woman with no future, no hope.

"I can't stand it!" she wanted to scream.

She looked up to see Charles with two glasses of wine. He placed one in front of her. "Here," he said. "This will do you good."

19

LESLIE STARED AT THE WINE, THE PALEST IMAGINABLE
yellow, as it swirled against the sides of the stemmed glass,
beading here and there. She glanced at Charles, watching her.
He wants me to, she knew. *And perhaps—perhaps sipping wine
together would at least give us* one *thing in common. I could treat
it as a sedative,* she thought. *It could ease the pain, relax this
terrible spasm clutching at my throat and chest.* She fingered the
cool stem.

"Cheers." Charles's voice was amiable as he clinked his glass
against hers.

"Cheers," she murmured, lifting her glass. Her throat felt so
tight and constricted, she dared take only a tiny sip. Somehow,
she managed to swallow it. It tasted sour and sweet all at the
same time. Did he actually enjoy this stuff? Maybe it anesthetized your taste buds after a while. Charles stroked his

moustache, eyes on her, waiting for a reaction. "There, now, that's not so bad, is it?" he asked.

"No," she lied. Maybe if she had something to nibble, it would help. She went into the kitchen and shook a few Cheez-Its from the package into a dish and brought it onto the patio. "Hors d'oeuvres?"

"Why, thank you. Thank you very much. This is a very classy establishment." He gave her a quick smile.

Was this the same man who had addressed her in such a dictatorial, threatening tone a few moments before? Had he really said, "You had better not even *think* of leaving again"? How could he change so quickly? Was she going 'round the bend?

She took another sip. The crackers helped, distracting from the taste of the wine and creating a thirst.

"In fact," Charles continued, "there's probably nowhere I'd rather be right now than sharing a glass of wine with you. You really look quite pretty."

"Pretty?" She felt herself blush. "After working in the yard? I'm sure my lipstick is all gone."

"You will recall I have always preferred the natural look. And that T-shirt matches your eyes."

She was afraid for a moment he'd bring up the matter of blonde hair again, but instead he gazed out toward the lake. "You know, I was thinking of buying a little sailboat. Scott and I might get out together."

She stared at him. "Ye-es," she said carefully, surprised that he would even consider such a "frivolous" expenditure.

"Well, it might be possible. I should get a raise once I pass this exam. It's something to think about."

"Yes, Charles. A very nice idea."

She saw that his glass was empty while hers was still two-thirds full. They really were rather large glasses. He stood and went into the kitchen, bringing the jug of wine back out. "Let me just freshen that for you," he said, refilling her glass.

Halfway through it, she marveled at how attentive and kind Charles had become and how much better she felt. The spasm was gone, replaced by a warmth that was a welcome release. So that was why people spoke of the "happy hour."

But when at last she rose to begin fixing dinner, the flush of well-being dissipated as an inner alarm sounded and she realized how easily she could be caught up in Charles's drinking.

꒣

The next morning Leslie did a double take as Michelle came to the breakfast table wearing a skintight skirt made of a stretch material cut well above mid-thigh. Where in the world had that come from? Perhaps Charles wouldn't notice.

He glanced up at Michelle as she came into the room, looked down at his newspaper, then back at Michelle. "What is that you are wearing, Michelle?"

Her eyes flashed defiance. "A skirt and a blouse."

"Correction. That is not a skirt. It is an obscenity." He turned to Leslie. "You bought that for her?"

"I did not," Leslie defended herself.

"I, uh, borrowed it from a friend, y'know," Michelle said.

Charles pounded his fist on the table and the plates jumped. "Well, I think you will unborrow it. What are you trying to do, Michelle? With a come-on like that, you will be pregnant before you are thirteen. The way you are flaunting yourself, I think I should get you a chastity belt and throw away the key." His voice crescendoed with each sentence. "And you had better get this through your head right now. If you ever turn up pregnant, you will be out of this house—" He snapped his fingers.

"—just like that!" He gave a disgusted shake of his head. "Sometimes I cannot wait until you are eighteen and I no longer have the *joy*—" He coated the word with sarcasm. "—of having to be financially responsible for you. Now *that* will be a happy day."

Leslie glanced at Michelle's stolid face. She'd never let Charles know if his words hurt. But how could they not? "Can't wait to get rid of you," he seemed to be telling her. Eyes narrowed, mouth set, Charles turned to Scott. "And as for you, young man, if you ever get a girl pregnant, I will personally castrate you!"

"Charles!" Leslie recoiled at the malevolence of his words and his tone. *This man is truly hopeless,* she thought. How could he say that to a ten-year-old? She wasn't even sure if Scott knew the meaning of the word, but he would surely look it up.

"Yes?" Charles stared across the table at her with such vehemence, she knew she dared not say more.

She shook her head and tried to shift the conversation. "Scott's decided to go to swim team workout this afternoon," she announced. "After school we'll drop Michelle off at home and go straight to the pool. That should be plenty of time. Okay?"

Scott, lips parted, still staring at his father, could only nod.

I'll have to smooth this out later with him—and Michelle, she thought.

⁂

"I don't know," Scott whispered, as they walked toward the YMCA pool. "My stomach feels sort of fluttery. Hope I'm good enough."

Red, white, and blue lane-lines marked off the six practice lanes, and, toward each end, rows of brightly colored pennants fluttered on wires stretched across the pool. Kids of all shapes and sizes, wearing blue-and-green-striped Speedos, milled around the pool deck. "Hey," Scott noted, "some of those guys are even littler than me. Peanuts." He glanced over toward the end of the pool at a boy with an adolescent's splotchy complexion and a man's upper-body development. "And then . . ." His voice trailed off.

David wheeled up to them and held up his hand to Scott. "The very guy I've been waiting for. Welcome, Scott."

Scott gave David a high five and looked nervously at the pool. "Do I have to try out?"

Leslie moved away from the pool to the bleachers at the side as David laughed. "Naah! Everybody's welcome. The great part about swimming is that you don't have to be the very best to be an important part of the team. Everybody earns points at meets, and it all adds up, you see. And even when you don't win, you get to see your improvement." He held out his stopwatch. "We measure that in minutes, seconds, and fractions of seconds."

He lifted the whistle that hung around his neck and blew it. "Gather 'round, guys. Hey, hey, no shoving. Okay, I want you all to meet Scott. He's ten, and he's joining the team today. Scott and I have a lot in common. We're both disabled. With me it's big time: my legs. With Scott, well, I hardly notice it: his hand. I'm telling you this because I've cleared it with the league, and he's going to swim with a small hand paddle, just enough to bring his right hand up to the same size as his left hand. Okay? That's it.

"Now, lane one, five- and six-year-olds. Lane two, seven and eight. Lanes three and four, nine and ten. Scott, you take lane three for starters. Lane five, eleven-twelve, and lane six, thirteen-fourteen. We'll start with a warm-up of six laps freestyle. Nice and easy."

Leslie watched anxiously. *Oh, Lord, make this a good time for Scott,* she prayed. *May he not be discouraged or intimidated.*

She was relieved when she saw that he had no trouble keeping up with the slower lane group. But as they practiced different strokes and worked with kickboards and leg buoys, she began to realize this was far more continuous swimming than Scott had ever done. *He's going to be one tired fish by the end of this hour,* she said to herself.

But Scott emerged from the pool grinning. "That was the funnest," he said.

David followed him over to where Leslie stood. "Hey, lady," he beamed, "thanks for giving me a great addition to the team. Did he do good or what?"

"He did. Thanks so much, David. I'll see *you* at therapy tomorrow. Dum-de-dum-dum." She sang the ominous "Dragnet" tune.

David turned to Scott. "In case you didn't know it, your mom is a sadist. That means she finds great pleasure in causing people pain."

"I know," Scott grinned.

David gave him a swat on his backside. "See you Wednesday."

⁓

With the baseball league championships over, Charles had two days to give his full concentration to studying for the exam before the World Series began. But somehow the Saturday of the opening game he came to the family room equipped with statistics on each player. He had them all: pitching records,

ERAs, batting averages, home runs, RBIs, stolen bases, strike-outs for each player. Didn't the papers and television commentators give all that information? Leslie wondered. Evidently it was important to Charles to keep his own records.

"One rule," Charles warned Scott just before the national anthem. "Today and tomorrow we'll see the games live. But on weekdays some of them will be too early for me to catch live, especially East Coast games, because of work and studying. So we'll tape those. Scott, you will be in charge. Can you do that?"

"Sure." Scott seemed pleased with the responsibility.

"All right. Now this is important. On those days neither of us is going to listen to the news. That way we will not know what has happened and will both see the game fresh, just as it unfolds. Agreed?"

"Agreed," Scott said. "Yeah, that'll make watching a lot more exciting."

"Michelle? Leslie?" he yelled.

Leslie came in from the kitchen, and after two more sum-mons, Michelle appeared.

"Did you hear?" Charles said. "When we have to watch a tape of a series game played earlier in the day, under *no* cir-cumstances do we want to hear the outcome of a game before we watch it. Is that clear?"

"Of course," Leslie said.

"Sure, okay," Michelle mumbled as she filed a fingernail.

All through the series game time was to be sacred time: no interruptions, no matter what. Charles was in his element, and the fervor spread to Scott. Leslie saw her son referring to Charles's records, so each time a batter came up he could make knowing comments like, "This guy's batting three-ten."

The World Series was tied two-two the day Charles exploded through the front door at five o'clock bellowing, "Where are you, woman?"

"Upstairs," she called, tensing as she heard him swearing his way up the stairs.

What had she done now? Not put something away? Driven too far? She waited nervously.

"What is it, Charles?" she asked as he stalked into the bedroom.

His face was flushed, pupils dilated. "They're sending me to New York next week. Five days."

"Your company? But you—"

"Right. I almost never travel. But my boss is on vacation, and *his* boss is on a tight deadline with another project. I'm it." He pounded his fist against the wall. "You realize what this means, don't you?"

"No-o-o. I guess I don't—"

"I miss a week of studying, you simpleton! A whole bloody week," he bellowed as though she was somehow to blame.

"But honey, surely you could study on the plane—and during the evening."

He grabbed her by the jaw. "Please spare me from simplistic solutions about what I can do. First I got behind on my study schedule when you were gone and I had to do laundry and shopping and—" He released her and waved one hand in circles. "—those things. Now, this. It's a disaster, a bloody disaster." He whipped off his necktie and headed for the closet.

"I'm sorry, Charles. Is there anything I can do—"

"No, no, no!" he shouted. Then he turned back toward her and his voice diminished a few decibels. "Yes." He held up one finger. "One, keep the kids out of my hair. Two . . ." He raised another finger. "Iron my shirts. And do it right. No creases on the sleeves and a little spray starch on the collars and cuffs. Three, get my suits to the cleaners. Four, be cooperative. Five, keep wine and beer in the refrigerator. And six, don't bring any of your complaints about work to me."

She squinted at him. Complaints about work? When had she complained? She loved her work and enjoyed telling him about her patients' progress. No point in asking. "Whatever you say, dear," she murmured.

They finished changing out of their work clothes and started downstairs.

Michelle brushed past them. "Hey, Dad, great that your team's winnin'."

Charles let out a cry so anguished, Scott came running. "Michelle!" Charles screamed. A stream of profanities followed, and he slapped her so hard, she fell against the wall.

"Charles!" Leslie shouted and managed to grab his arm before he struck again. She pressed in front of him and stroked Michelle's hair. "Oh, honey, are you all right?"

Charles pulled her away. "There you go again, always babying them, Leslie."

She looked at the heightened color of his face, then at Michelle. *I'd better get him out of here,* she thought. "Let's go have a glass of wine, Charles," she said quietly.

Tears streamed down Michelle's face as she huddled on the stairs, holding her jaw. "I'm sorry, Daddy. I forgot," she sobbed.

"Well, you won't forget again, now, will you?" Charles turned away from her. "Because if you do, I will beat the you-know-what out of you!"

"I'll get some ice for your face," Scott whispered to Michelle.

"Come, Leslie," Charles commanded, leading her downstairs. Afraid to cross him when he was so angry, she looked anxiously over her shoulder at Michelle, still wailing.

In the kitchen Charles pulled the jug of wine from the refrigerator, reaching for two glasses. Although she'd promised herself not to drink with him again, Leslie told herself she'd better not refuse it while he was so riled up. After they were seated on the patio, on a pretext of getting crackers, she went in to check on Michelle and to try to explain. "I hated to leave you, honey, but I thought it was best to try to help your dad cool down."

Michelle, holding ice to her face, stared at her and didn't reply.

I'm not handling this well, she told herself as she rejoined Charles and he gulped three glasses to her one, gradually cooling down. It was late when she served dinner, and Charles and Scott took their desserts into the family room to watch the game. From the kitchen Leslie could hear Charles's martyred remarks about watching "even though we know how it comes out, thanks to Michelle."

The phone rang, and Leslie dried her hands to reach for it.

"Hi, darlin', it's your mother."

"Oh, Mom. Hi." She felt too fragmented to focus on anything but Charles and his path of devastation, but she forced herself to make the effort. "How was your day?"

"Good." Her mother hesitated. "Honey, are you all right? Your voice sounds—"

"Fine," she said. "Just wonderful. Never better."

20

From Zoë's Journal

October 12: Heavenly Father, did You hear how Leslie sounded on the phone last night? Silly question. Of course You did. The flatness of her voice. Charles must be dishing it out again. Oh, Father, what now? Please, put a hedge around her. Protect her from evil. Put Your whole armor on her. Help her to find refuge under the shadow of Your wings. I pray all this in the name of Your Son, amen.

"DID YOU IRON MY YELLOW BROADCLOTH SHIRT WITH THE button-down collar?" Charles stood by his carry-on bag, which lay open on the bed like a hinged clamshell.

"Why, no, honey. I didn't see it. Are you sure it's not on your rack?" Leslie started toward the closet.

"No, no! It's not in there. I looked." He grabbed her wrist. "Leslie, I told you I need that shirt."

"Charles," She looked up at his face, saw the color mounting. "You didn't even mention . . ."

"Liar! Oh, Leslie, how you lie!"

Lord, You know he didn't say a word about that shirt. Or did I forget? Where is that shirt anyway? Leslie pulled away from him and searched though the laundry hamper. "It's here, Charles." She looked at her watch: 11:00. The evening wine, which she'd again rationalized, left her bone-weary and longing only for the escape of sleep. "You're wearing your brown suit?" she asked. "How about the beige shirt with the brown stripes?"

"Leslie, do not try to wiggle out of what you should have done in the first place. Go wash it. I *told* you I need it."

"Yes, dear." She grabbed the shirt, searching for the other light colors amongst the dirty clothes. Now she'd have to stay up to get it into the dryer. She'd iron it in the morning.

"And be sure it's completely dry before I pack it. Better iron tonight, so it can hang overnight."

We're talking an hour here, maybe more, she realized. She sighed and went downstairs to start the wash. Might as well watch the late news, she decided. She switched on the TV. Riots, drive-by shootings, earthquake in Japan.

Lord, there is so much pain in Your world, she sighed, feeling tears pool in her eyes.

"Leslie!"

She jumped. Charles stood in the doorway, head thrust forward, jaw jutting. "How do you expect me to sleep with this thing blaring away? You are so selfish! Now turn that thing off and come to bed."

She gazed at him in disbelief. "Charles, you wanted that yellow shirt."

He exhaled with a seal-like bark and, reaching for the remote control, flicked the TV off. He ran his fingers through his hair, and she felt the very air of the room grow heavy, oppressive.

"Well, now you've done it," he fumed. "Got me too riled up to go to sleep, and I have this horrendous day ahead of me." He paced as he spoke, gesturing angrily. "Into the office for an hour, then off to LAX. Four-hour flight with a three-hour time change, so I do not arrive till seven in the evening. Reach the hotel maybe by eight. Then I try to go to sleep because I know I must get up at three our time to get to an eight o'clock meeting their time tomorrow. And do you realize, I'm going to *miss* the last World Series game? While I am on the bloody airplane! What sort of imbecile would schedule me to fly during the game?"

"Maybe they'll show it on the plane," she offered.

"Oh, *certainly*, and maybe they have scheduled Placido Domingo to entertain us while we dine." He gave a short, sarcastic "ha-ha," and strode to the liquor cabinet. Selecting a bottle, he poured half a glass. For a moment she was afraid he'd offer it to her. Instead he downed it in a few gulps. He took a deep breath, licked his lips, and scrutinized her as though she were a sideshow curiosity. "Try very hard to keep control while I am gone," he said. "I know this is difficult for you. You seem to think you can accomplish all things through Christian love. What Michelle needs is to have the belt taken to her. And it wouldn't hurt Scott either. He is beginning to get a large mouth, and it is not attractive. Fear, Leslie. Fear accomplishes a great deal more than love."

She looked at the rigid, unyielding lines of his mouth, the smoldering sheen of his eyes. *He is so repugnant, I can barely stand him. And the way he looks at me. It's almost—yes, almost diabolic. I see—there is only one word for it—hatred—in his eyes.*

At last he went upstairs to bed. By the time she finished the shirt and joined him, at midnight, he was snoring. Turning away from his alcohol breath, she tried to relax.

She didn't sleep well. Though the room was cool, twice she wakened feeling too warm, agitated.

She awoke tired and feeling as bleak as the dark sky of the morning. The reality of the days growing shorter added to her despair and sense of foreboding.

She tried not to make any waves and to keep the children out of Charles's path as he cursed the cloudy weather, his travel bag for being difficult to zip, and the taste of the new margarine she'd bought.

At last he came downstairs with his bag and briefcase. "Scott? Oh, there you are." He gave him a quick slap on the back. "Try to use some common sense while I am gone." He looked around. "Oh, here's Michelle." He hugged her. "Behave yourself, or you will get it when I return!" He gave Leslie a quick kiss, followed by one of his penetrating stares. "Make an effort to keep some semblance of order while I am gone, Leslie, and spare me any frivolous phone calls."

As he slammed the front door, Leslie exhaled, for, it seemed, the first time that morning. Life would be so much more peaceful for a few days.

As Scott and Michelle started out the door for the school bus, she said, "What would you think of going to Marie Callender's for soup and pie tonight?" Why not take advantage of Charles's absence to do something they'd all enjoy?

"Sure," Scott said.

Michelle was silent.

As they shut the door, the thought flashed into her mind, *Maybe something will happen and Charles won't come back. Maybe the plane will crash and I'll finally have the wings of a dove.* She stood still, shocked at her own thoughts. "I'm sorry, Lord," she said aloud.

꒰

"Okay, David, this is the day," Leslie announced when he arrived for his appointment.

He groaned, but his turquoise eyes twinkled. "Some new torture, is it? Hanging by my fingernails? The rack?"

"You'll see!" she promised. "We'll start with a little warm-up. Let's just get on the mat and stretch your hamstrings and calf muscles. We don't want to wear you out with too many exercises."

He eyed her quizzically. "How come the sudden mercy?"

"You'll see!" She watched him stretch. "Good. I'll be right back." Leslie went into her office and brought out a pair of leg braces.

"They're here!" he shouted. "My ticket to getting upright!"

"Now, don't expect too much," Leslie cautioned. But in her heart and mind she prayed, *Oh, Lord, help him, strengthen him, help him get on his feet!*

"Okay, now, off with your tennies."

"You betcha!" David leaned over in his wheelchair and took his shoes off.

She put the first plastic brace in place and fastened the self-stick straps. "Okay, now the next."

With the braces in place Leslie helped him put his shoes back on. "We'll need a shoehorn to squeeze this molded plastic that supports your feet into your tennies," she explained. "Good. Now, lean forward so I can fasten the gait belt around your waist."

When she'd fastened the belt, she said, "This way, please," and led the way to the parallel bars. Stepping between them, she faced David as he wheeled up to one end. "We're going to surround you with women, David. You know Kelly's aide, Pam. She's going to help Brynne. One on each side of you. Now your balance is going to feel a little weird. And your ankles won't bend because the braces don't allow ankle motion. Sort of like being in ski boots. And your knees may feel wobbly. Okay, you ready?"

"Am I ever!"

"Wheels on your chair locked? Good. Now, what you're going to do is lean forward and push on the bars, and on the count of three I want you to stand up. Okay. One . . . two . . . *three!*"

David gave a mighty push and, with the aides steadying him and Leslie grasping the gait belt, he rose upright.

"Good!"

Oh, thank You, Lord, she said silently.

"Now, David, look straight ahead. Stand up straight," Leslie said. "Try to find your balance on your feet." She looked at his hands and saw their death grip on the bars. "Do you feel dizzy?"

"No, not at all! Oh, man, to be upright. But—whoa, I feel way out of balance."

"You're doing fine. Now, hold it. Here comes Terry."

Terry hurried in with the Polaroid camera. "Say 'Cheers!'"

"Cheers!" David's grin spread from sideburn to sideburn as the light flashed.

"How you doing?" Leslie looked at the sweat running down his face and neck and saw his quad muscles quiver.

"Shakin'."

"All right, lean forward and we'll help you down." Together, she, Rosie, and Brynne settled him back in his wheelchair.

The gym erupted with applause, and David looked around, bowed elaborately, then held up his arms. "Why, thank you, thank you very much. You're very kind. But I owe it all to my therapist—and—" He jabbed his thumb upward. "The Lord. Thanks, Father!"

"Okay, we'll let you rest a minute. Then we'll try it again."

David waited impatiently. "Now?"

"Okay."

He stood and sat three more times.

"That's so good, David!" Leslie exclaimed.

He gave a sigh of exhaustion and leaned back in the chair. When Brynne handed him a towel, it was a moment before he wiped his face and neck. "Man, I can't believe how pooped I am." He shook his head. "I feel like I've been skiing moguls all day." Then he brightened. "But this is the start of great things! Right? Right!"

Later, as she watched David wheel out the door, Leslie pictured the day he'd walk out. "Oh, Lord, I believe You will complete the work You've begun," she said.

Her phone rang, and she hurried to grab it. "This is Leslie."

"It's Mother."

"Oh, Mom, I'm so glad you called. Listen to this! David stood up today. At the parallel bars. I am so excited. And he is—stoked!"

"Oh, why that's nice, dear."

Nice? "Anything wrong, Mom?" She felt a surge of anxiety. "Dad?"

"Dad is fine. Leslie, I'm just back from some shopping at the mall. When I came out of Penney's . . ." She paused, then said, "I saw a girl run away when she caught a glimpse of me, and it was definitely Michelle. With a fellow that sounds like your description of Jason."

Leslie's balloon of excitement popped. She glanced at her watch: 10:35. "Uh-oh. I'll call the school, and—" She dropped wearily into her chair. "Oh, help. What do I do now?"

"She just finished being confined to quarters, didn't she?" Zoë asked.

"Yup. I guess more of the same is in order."

"Mm. I'm sorry to bring bad news, honey."

"No, I'm glad you saw her. I might not have known." She thought a moment. "Why now, do you suppose? Because

Charles is gone? Thinks she can get away with it with me? Whew, she's a handful."

"She is that. And yes, the timing is—interesting, to say the least. Let me know if there's anything I can do."

"Thanks, Mom." Leslie wanted to add, "Sure, there's something you can do. Just take her off my hands till she's twenty-one." But she hung up and dialed the school. The attendance office confirmed that Michelle had attended her first class, but not her second.

"She was seen in the mall," Leslie said. "Do you have any suggestions—?"

"If she has an unexcused absence, she will get a detention. She'll need to come in on Saturday morning. The rest is up to you."

Leslie sat staring at the phone long after she'd hung up. *Up to me—and whatever I do probably won't be "enough" for Charles,* she thought. *And what might those two be up to now? More pot? Something worse? How shall I play this?* she asked herself. She looked at her schedule and frowned. Solid till 4:15, when she'd leave to pick the kids up at school. Would Michelle be there? *I'll just have to go and see,* she decided.

After she stopped at school for Scott, Leslie held her breath, driving on to the junior high. Michelle stood on the curb, looking cool and nonchalant.

"Hi," Leslie said.

"Hi." Michelle climbed into the back seat, humming to herself.

They drove on in silence, as Leslie pondered how to handle her errant daughter.

At home Scott spotted the neighbor's dog and stopped to pet him through a gap in the fence. When he came inside, he said wistfully, "I wish Dad would let me have a dog."

She gave him a hug. "I know. But it's not going to happen, Scott. Besides, with swim team three afternoons a week, you wouldn't have a lot of time to take care of a dog."

"I suppose."

"After a while—like maybe after your dad's big exam—maybe you could try for a rabbit, or even a cat."

"Yeah." *Not the same,* his tone told her. He looked up at her. "We going out to Marie's for dinner?"

In her concern about Michelle she'd forgotten about promising dinner out. Now what? Michelle certainly didn't deserve a treat, but was it fair to penalize Scott—and herself? She sighed. "I'll get back to you on that," she said. "I need to talk to Michelle."

"Oh, yeah? *Now* what's she done?"

"I'll get back to you," she repeated.

Upstairs Leslie found Michelle, math book open, headset clamped over her ears, bouncing to the beat Leslie could hear from across the room. *That child will be deaf before she's twenty,* Leslie thought. She lifted the headset from Michelle's ears.

"Hey! Don't sneak up on me like that!" Michelle yelled.

"Excuse me," she said. "We need to talk."

Michelle groaned. "Gram squealed."

"You didn't really think she wouldn't, did you?"

"So?" The belligerent tone.

"I think you know cutting school is not acceptable, Michelle. How did you get to the mall—and back?"

"Walked." Lower lip out. So put-upon.

"That's quite a walk. At least you got some exercise. So you got back to school just in time for me to pick you up?"

"Yup. Played chicken with the Amtrak on the way." She cocked her head, obviously proud of it.

Leslie felt goose bumps rise on her arms. "Michelle! That is not smart! One misstep or misjudgment . . . Come *on!*"

She could feel Michelle exulting. *Got to ya, didn't I?* her whole body seemed to say.

Oh, Lord, help, Leslie prayed silently. *I don't know what to do with her.* She stood and walked across the room and back, stopping in front of Michelle. "All right, Michelle, you're grounded for a month. And no TV during that time."

"A *month!*" Michelle shouted. "Julie's party is in two weeks."

"Well, Michelle, you should have thought about that before you ditched school today."

Leslie left the room as her daughter screamed, "You're so unfair! Man, you're never this hard on Scott, 'cause he's your favorite."

She met Scott on his way from the kitchen. "What's she yellin' about?"

"She's grounded again. Cut school, went to the mall, played chicken with the Amtrak." *Might as well tell it like it is.*

Scott's eyes opened wide. "Wow. Heavy-duty." He thought about it. "So I guess we don't go out tonight, huh?"

Leslie shook her head.

"How come *I* get punished too?"

Good question. It isn't fair, she thought. "Tell you what we'll do, Scott. We'll order in. There's Hank's Diner, with the great shakes. They deliver."

"All *right!*" Scott brightened.

When their order arrived, Michelle refused to leave her room for dinner. *Punishing me,* Leslie decided.

"Good!" Scott said. "Pig-out time for us. This kid told me if you stop eating and walk around and chew gum awhile you can eat more. Let's try that."

Leslie laughed in spite of herself.

After dinner Scott watched the final game of the series. "Oh, I hope Dad's getting to see this," he said as the score tied.

"What a game! I bet it'll go into extra innings." Leslie struggled to stay awake till it ended and both kids were in bed. *Maybe I can catch up on the sleep I missed last night,* she thought as she climbed under the covers. *Sleep is a surrender, I read somewhere. Okay, I surrender. Willingly.*

She slept so soundly she wasn't sure what wakened her. She lay in bed listening. Nothing. She wasn't too warm or too cold. But she could feel her pulse quicken. "I don't like being alone at night," she muttered, immediately countering the statement with, "Oh, grow up, Leslie. There's nothing to be nervous about."

She glanced at the clock. Midnight. It felt so much later. Maybe she should check on the kids. She reached for her robe and slipped it on as she moved into the hallway. Scott's door stood open, and she could see him spread-eagled, half-under, half-out of the covers. She tiptoed in and pulled the blanket over his shoulders, planted a kiss on her fingertips, and then touched her fingers to his cheek. Thank God for good kids, she thought as she walked toward Michelle's room. Her door was closed. She turned the knob carefully and eased the door open. Moonlight shone through the open window. How in the world had Michelle managed to get herself completely under the blanket? As Leslie made her way toward the bed, she stumbled on a backpack and fell against the bed. Not a sound from Michelle. She reached up. Pillows. Nothing more.

Stifling a scream, she struggled to her feet and ran down the stairs and out the front door. Under a streetlight a few houses away, a dog labored over a plastic trash bag set out for tomorrow's pickup. Otherwise the street stood empty, a silent study in black and white.

21

CHARLES TOLD HIMSELF HE WASN'T CLAUSTROPHOBIC, BUT he hated being sardined into an airplane, packed tight against so many people. On his flight to New York the plane was full, and he found himself squeezed into a middle seat in the center section of a wide-body plane. He felt suffocated, trapped. If only he could have been seated along the side, preferably next to an emergency exit.

The woman on his left wore perfume but reeked more of mothballs than roses, and the man on his right exhaled garlic fumes that were almost visible. Charles turned on the vent above him, but he still smelled mothballs and garlic. They didn't exchange the air properly in these planes, he was certain.

If he could only fly the plane himself, get behind those controls, it would be all right. Then he wouldn't feel so powerless, so vulnerable.

He knew he wouldn't be able to concentrate on his studying during the flight. And he couldn't even read as he waited
for takeoff. He glanced at his watch. Four minutes and forty-
five seconds late already. At last the door slammed shut and the
plane taxied away from the terminal. As it started down the
runway, Charles braced himself. *Got to get ready for the Orange
County rocket blastoff,* he told himself.

"Ladies and gentlemen," the pilot explained, "as part of our
noise-abatement program, we gain altitude very quickly in
departing Orange County."

"Blasted rich bitches in Newport Beach, even controlling
how the planes fly out of here," he muttered to himself as he
felt himself thrust hard against his seat back.

Only when the plane had safely banked back toward the
east and gained altitude could he relax a little. He looked
toward the back of the plane. When would the attendants get
around to serving drinks? That was the only way to fly.

He reached for the in-flight magazine and instead found
himself reading a catalog of useless and extravagant indul-
gences for the rich and foolish. *Just right for the Newport Beach
crowd,* he reflected. A necklace with a jade pendant caught his
eye. The jade appeared exactly the color of Leslie's eyes. He
looked at the price. $200. Ridiculous! But it would be very
becoming. He tore out the page and folded it carefully, tucking
it into a pocket. Maybe he could find something similar,
smaller perhaps, and for less in New York. Leslie really was
quite a good-looking woman, though she could stand to lose a
few pounds. If he didn't watch what she ate, who knew how
much she might weigh? And he did prefer blonde hair. He'd
have to mention that to her again. He looked toward the back
of the plane again and noticed the flight attendants pushing
carts forward. Would they serve from the front or the back?

Let's see, he was—yes, two rows closer to the front than the back. He wondered how long it would take. He made a rough estimate of the number of people in the rows ahead. Allow, say, forty seconds to serve each person. No, maybe they could do it in thirty. He sighed. It could easily take twenty minutes to get to him. He leaned back, willing himself to release his grip on the armrest, and focused again on Leslie.

It was good to have her back home. He looked forward to the day the kids would be gone and he could have her all to himself. He wasn't at all sure, knowing what he did today, that he'd have married a woman with an offspring and then have another of their own.

The child behind him kicked the back of his seat, and he turned and glared.

Children were much more trouble than pleasure, he noted. Michelle's mouth was a real problem. He thought about the episode on the stairs. Had he overreacted? Certainly she had it coming, but he hadn't intended to hit that hard. He'd have to watch it.

The problem, he noted, *is that I discipline the children, while Leslie coddles them, tries to hide them behind her skirts. They're probably out of control right this minute. I'm a peaceable man. If only Leslie would stop fighting me, see that I'm right, knuckle under, everything would be fine.*

He was glad Leslie brought in some income, though, and that she was good at what she did. He remembered how cheerful and helpful and appealing she'd seemed when they first met and he was in such pain with carpal tunnel syndrome. Was that the way this surfer dude saw her? Almost like an angel? He felt a tingle of jealousy. She did seem particularly interested in him.

Maybe I'd better check him out, go to a swim workout or meet or something, he thought.

The man next to him settled into his seat, spreading his knees and planting his arm on the armrest so his elbow invaded Charles's space. Charles turned and stared at him, but the man's eyes were closed. He gave him a nudge and the elbow moved, but not the knee. Glancing at the second hand on his watch, Charles timed the flight attendants' serving of the next beverage. Yes, thirty seconds was about right. As he stared at his watch, the idea came. Timing was what swimming was all about, wasn't it? He'd get a stopwatch and go to see Scott swim. Hadn't Leslie suggested just the other day that he should show more interest in Scott's swimming?

He tilted his seat back. *This confounded trip. I am behind in my studying already,* he thought. *I must not fail this test. I must not! That would be so—visible. Humiliating. I will pass.*

He brought his chair upright again and checked the drink cart's progress. It wouldn't be long now. He turned to the woman next to him, who responded with a dimpled smile. "So," he said. "Is home on the East Coast for you—or the West Coast?"

ॐ

Leslie shivered in the damp night air as she scuffed up the sidewalk and back into the house. She closed the door quietly and latched it. No point in going back to bed. She stood in the hallway, hating the emptiness, the aloneness. If only someone else was here. She was tempted to wake Scott, but of course that was stupid. If only she could call someone. Zoë? It wouldn't be fair to wake her. No, wait. Of course. She had Someone.

She felt her way into the living room and knelt by the couch. "Lord, I feel so alone. Thank You that You're here with me, in this very room, and that You've promised *never* to leave me or forsake me. Watch over Michelle. You know where she is. Help her not to do anything foolish. I confess this business of playing chicken with the Amtrak makes my blood run cold. Give her good judgment and a mind of her own, no matter what others may want to do. Bring her safely home and help me not to imagine the worst. Thanks for being here, for being You. Thanks for Your Son. It's in His name I pray, amen."

Even as she prayed, she felt the panic lift a little. She rose slowly, feeling her way to the kitchen light switch. Tea. A mug of tea would help. Soothing, warming to drink, comforting to wrap her hands around.

She filled a mug that bore the words, "Love never fails," with water and put it in the microwave, hoping the ding when it finished wouldn't waken Scott. She smiled at the irony as she selected a packet of "Sweet Dreams" tea from the drawer. "Stay Awake" would be more like it.

As she dunked the tea bag in the steaming water, the wind began to blow. The water in the lake, lit by the streetlights on the other side, whipped into jagged peaks. A tree branch scratched against the house, unnerving as fingernails on a blackboard. The roof creaked. *Creepy,* she thought. She went to the patio door and flicked on the outside lights.

While she sipped the tea, she tried to read some Psalms, but it was so hard to concentrate. Perhaps TV would help. She'd keep the volume low. But the choices, which included a rehash of the ten o'clock news, two Westerns, and a talk show, seemed inane. Maybe the radio. She settled for the classical music station. Orderly choral music flowed into the room. Bach. A cantata, probably. Then the stately chorale began, and she recognized the tune of the hymn, "Oh, Sacred Head Now Wounded." The choir sang in German, but she remembered the English words describing Christ's passion. To her surprise she found herself singing aloud the final phrase, "O make me Thine forever; and, should I fainting be, Lord, let me never, never outlive my love for Thee."

She felt tears on her cheeks. *That's where my focus needs to be,* she thought. She switched off the radio and opened her Bible once again. Turning to Isaiah, she read the prophet's incredibly accurate description of the crucifixion in chapter 53. "He was pierced for our transgressions. . . ." What an amazing plan God had for the universe some six hundred years before Christ was born!

Glancing up as the clock struck two, she willed herself to read on, meditating on the words. She must have dozed for a moment, for the next time she looked at the clock, it was 2:48. "I know, Lord," she whispered, "You tell me not to be anxious about anything but to bring everything to You. And You promise then that Your peace will guard my heart and mind. Oh, please, Lord, it's my mind that needs guarding. It is so easy to think about rapes and shootings and car accidents and . . .

What was that? A shuffling sound in front. The wind? She hurried to the dark kitchen to look out the window. Someone carrying—Michelle! She blocked her scream with her hand and ran to the door.

Outside Jason tried to put Michelle down, but obviously she was unconscious.

"Is she hurt?" Leslie cried.

"Nope. Wasted."

Then she smelled the alcohol. "She's drunk." She turned to Jason. "*You're* drunk."

Jason smiled. "You bet your sweet—"

"Jason," Leslie interrupted. "Help me get her upstairs. And be quiet about it, do you hear me?"

Michelle was dead weight. They thumped and bumped and

stumbled their way up the stairs, at last depositing her on her bed.

Leslie couldn't believe Scott hadn't wakened, but there wasn't a sound from his room. She prodded Jason downstairs and grabbed the front of his shirt. "What has she been drinking, Jason?" she demanded.

He gave her a blank stare.

"Try to remember. And how much?"

"Coupla beers. Coupla shots."

"Must have been more than 'coupla,'" she persisted.

"Yeah, maybe."

"Anything else? Any drugs."

"Nah."

"Okay." She released him. "Thanks for taking the responsibility for getting Michelle back here. How will you get home?"

"See, m' buddy's arounna corner in his car."

"Is he in as bad shape as you?"

"Naw. He's cool. He's a strai—a straiger . . . " He laughed and tried again. "A st-raight-edger. Honest."

She eyed him dubiously. He crossed his heart.

"Okay. One other thing, Jason." She gripped his shoulders and put her face close to his. "You are not to see Michelle again. Not anywhere. You are not to talk to her, and that means no telephone calls. I will make life very miserable for you if you do." She turned him around and thrust him out the door, glad he was too drunk to question just what she'd do, for she had no idea, and hoping he wasn't too drunk to forget what she'd said.

Upstairs she pulled off Michelle's shoes and decided to leave her in the baggy T-shirt and slacks. Checking her pulse, she watched her breathing. Vitals okay. Better turn her on her side in case she gets sick. She propped a pillow behind Michelle, covered her, and left the door open.

In her own bed Leslie felt the muscles in her legs twitch from the tension of the evening. *Alcohol,* she thought. *My drinking with Charles is wrong. I use it to ease the stress and pain, to humor Charles—and neither is right. I must not do it anymore. Good thing I hadn't had wine tonight; I could smell the booze on them instantly.* She sighed. *Oh, Lord,* she prayed silently, *thanks that Michelle's okay. But what is going on here? She is certainly piling it on. If this is a bid for attention, she's got it. If this is a struggle for independence, she's definitely not ready. Help me understand. Show me what to do. I'm exhausted. I'm angry. I'm hurt. And I'm baffled.*

She didn't know how she'd ever go back to sleep, but if she didn't, how would she function at work? Twice, she got up to check on Michelle. Sometime around 5:00, she fell asleep. The alarm sounded at 6:30. Simultaneously she heard Michelle retching.

Scott came to her door. "Michelle's barfing."

"I know." She grabbed her robe and hurried to the kids' bathroom, where Michelle hung over the toilet. Leslie pulled her hair back from her face and held her head.

When it was over, Michelle went limp against the wall, her face pale and gleaming with perspiration. "I'm so sick," she managed. "What can I do?"

"You can decide not to be such an idiot next time someone tries to get you to drink."

"Big help, Mom." And she was sick again.

Leslie left her stretched on the floor of the bathroom.

"Better use my bathroom to get ready for school," she told Scott.

"Man, she's a mega-mess," Scott said.

"She is that."

"Hope I don't get it. Yuck."

"I wouldn't worry, honey," she assured him. "You didn't have what she had."

❧

By the time Scott left for school, Michelle was asleep. Leslie called in to work at 7:30. "Michelle's sick. I'm going to try for coming in at noon. Can you juggle? I'll stay late if I need to."

"It's tight," Terry said. "We'll just make do." She did not sound pleased.

Darn that kid! Leslie fumed.

At eleven Michelle wakened and stumbled down the stairs. Leslie looked up from the sauce she was making for dinner. "Hi."

"Hi. I'm starving."

Some recovery, Leslie thought. *Guess it helps to be young.*

"Fix yourself some tea and toast then."

"No. I said I'm starving."

"Okay, a couple of burritos with onions and extra hot salsa?" She was joking, but Michelle nodded eagerly.

I should let her just dig something out of the refrigerator, she thought. *But maybe this is a good chance to talk with her.* "Would you settle for some scrambled eggs, Michelle?'" she asked.

"Yeah, with salsa."

As Leslie put the skillet on the burner and cracked the eggs, Michelle perched on a kitchen stool. "I don't remember getting home."

"No, you wouldn't. You were out cold."

"No foolin'?" Michelle seemed to regard it as an accomplishment.

"No foolin'. Jason brought you in. He wasn't in such great shape himself."

When the eggs were ready, Leslie poured herself a cup of coffee and sat opposite Michelle. She'd thought all morning about what to say. Now it was time.

"Michelle, I know life isn't easy for you right now. You're growing up so fast, and I heard your parting shot the other day about Scott being my favorite. I want you to know that's not true at all. You're my firstborn, and you are unique and you are very precious to me. Please believe that. It's true."

Michelle devoured two forkfuls of eggs. "I'd like to."

"It's true," Leslie repeated. "And honey, I know it's hard for you to understand, but the rules we have for you are not just so we can lord it over you. They're a part of loving you, wanting you to grow up in a good, safe way and to have what God calls 'a future and a hope.' I know you're dying for freedom and to be your own person, and you will have that, but you have to earn our trust, show us you are ready. And you will. I know that." She reached over and patted Michelle's hand.

Michelle glanced at her, then away again.

"I also want to remind you that there is a difference between love and approval. I love you very much, and I love you no matter what you do. But I do *not* approve of your behavior these last two days. And I'd like you to level with me about that. Okay?"

"Okay."

"Honey . . ." Her voice was gentle. "Why do you always get into trouble when Dad's not around? It makes me think you must hate me or at least be very angry at me. I'm puzzled. Why?"

"Because," Michelle said, and she paused a moment, looking directly at her, "because you're such a wimp."

It was all Leslie could do not to recoil from the physical impact of the statement. It was as though she'd been struck in the chest. As their discussion began, she'd thought she was handling the situation so well. Now she couldn't even speak as Michelle's words resonated in her mind.

"Well, you are!" Michelle shot out. "You start to take a stand with Dad and we move out and how long do we stay away? Hardly any time at all. Before anything gets taken care of, you move us back home again. Why did we bother to leave at all?" She paused, and Leslie's mind whirled as she tried to think how to respond.

But Michelle continued, "You wonder why I don't listen to you? Well, you don't listen to *your* mother, y'know? 'Cause I know she wanted you out of here. And you wonder why I got drunk? Well, it seems to make Dad feel better. And I saw *you* drinkin' with him. And *you* got mellow."

Leslie wanted to stop her ears, stop Michelle's mouth. *It's true,* she thought, *and coming from my own daughter, it's like knives. I feel cut into shreds.* But she could only sit and listen.

Michelle took a breath. "And okay, you want to know the biggie in wimping it? You just stand there while Dad digs into Scott and chews him up and spits him out in little pieces, and you just stood there when he *hit* me. You just let it happen."

Leslie swallowed painfully. "Michelle," she managed, "I did stop your dad from hitting you again."

"Big deal."

She tried a different tack. "Honey, you don't understand about marriage. You aren't mature enough yet to grasp all that's involved in a husband-wife relationship. The Bible tells us a husband is to be the head of the house, and the wife is to—"

"Just let him walk all over her and wipe his feet on her? That's what Dad does, y'know."

"Michelle, listen to—"

"So you're sayin' a wife is supposed to be scum? A lowlife? Is that the way it is? Well, if it is, I don't want any part of marriage. You better believe that."

"No, Michelle, a woman's not scum."

"Well, lady, in case you haven't noticed, *you are.*"

22

AS THE WORD *scum* HUNG IN THE AIR, LESLIE SHOOK HER head as though emerging from a trance. *Wait a minute,* she said to herself, *I don't have to sit and take it like I do when Charles dumps on me. This is my child, not my husband.* And as her anger ignited, she understood how Charles could slap Michelle.

"Enough, Michelle!" she shouted. "Where do you get off telling me how to be a wife—how to be a mother? What do you know about life? You want to be treated like an adult, and you're a baby. You're a terrible two-year-old walking around in a body that looks eighteen." She took a breath and went for retaliation. "And talk about scum. What do you think *you* were last night? Hmm?"

Michelle stared at her hard, and Leslie thought she saw a fleeting break in the unyielding mask of her daughter's face. Then her chin began to tremble.

What am I doing? Leslie thought. *No matter how much her words hurt, how could I stoop to calling my daughter scum?* She felt her anger drain away, and in its place, tears of despair welled. She turned away and buried her face in her hands. She wasn't sure how long it was before she felt Michelle's hand on her shoulder. Looking up, she saw tears streaming down her daughter's face.

They reached out for each other and, cheek to cheek, they wept, their tears merging into a unity, a oneness they hadn't shared in months.

When at last they both quieted, Leslie grabbed the Kleenex box on the counter. They each took a tissue—and laughed when they blew in unison. Leslie spoke first. "I'm sorry, Michelle. I lost it. I really love you."

"I'm sorry, too, Mom. I—I can't say I didn't mean to hurt you. I did. But I'm sorry. Maybe it's hormones."

Leslie smiled. "Maybe. But I have to be honest. I know in my heart why your words hurt so much. Of course it's terrible to have your own daughter turn against you. But worse, I know what you said is true."

"Dad's not easy," Michelle offered.

"No, but I'm sorry if I've let you and Scott down. I've never meant to do that." She put her hand on Michelle's arm. "You've given me a lot to think about, though it's tough to admit it."

"Oh, Mom," Michelle said softly.

Letting her hand rest on Michelle's arm, Leslie said quietly, "Now. I want to promise you I'll go to the support group and try very hard to learn how not to be scum. Do you think you could promise me, please, to observe the rules I lay down, to honor your grounding—"

"And not be scum?" Michelle interrupted.

Leslie smiled. "Yes. Deal?"

"Deal." Michelle started to take her mother's hand, then hugged her instead.

As she embraced her daughter, Leslie prayed silently, *Oh, Lord, even in the midst of the pain of Michelle's words, I thank You for bringing her back to me. May this be the beginning of a new understanding between us. And oh, Father, show me what to do with what she's said.*

❧

Later, as Leslie drove to work, Michelle's statements played once again in her mind. *Yes, I can see why she thinks I've been a wimp. I did bring us back to Charles pretty quickly. But I thought things would be different. I really did. He seemed to want us. But face it, nothing is different. In fact, it's more intense. And Michelle is right. My attempts to stand up for her and for Scott are on the feeble side.*

Her head hurt. *Oh, where is the balance? Can I be a Christian wife without being scum? I said I'll go to the support group, but that doesn't meet till next Wednesday. Meantime . . . I need to talk with someone now. Someone to pray for me.* She bobbed her head in "of course!" realization. *Why am I avoiding Mom? She has wisdom. I just haven't wanted to hear it.*

At her first break at work she called her mother. The answering machine. "Mom, it's Leslie. Could you possibly give your dumb daughter some counsel? I could throw an extra chop on the grill tonight if you could join us for dinner. Or let me know what's good for you. Charles is gone till next Tuesday. Love ya."

Later that afternoon, as she worked with a new patient with sciatic pain, Terry gave her a note. "Your Mom says throw another chop on. And trim the fat."

Laughing aloud, Leslie stuffed the note in her pocket.

What a mom! And no wonder she was so physically fit.

~

During dinner, Leslie looked around the table, struck by how much more relaxed the children were with Zoë than when Charles presided over dinner. *Presided is right*, she thought. *Or maybe ruled?* It was good to hear Scott's enthusiastic description of swim team and Zoë's encouraging responses.

"And how is David doing with his therapy?" Zoë asked. "Do you see an improvement, Scott?"

"Yeah. He's getting a lot stronger, don't you think, Mom?"

Leslie nodded. "Definitely. He's standing in the parallel bars for five minutes at a time. Balance is good. Knees not too shaky, and he has more feeling in his feet. I'm really getting hopeful."

"That's wonderful. I'll keep him in my prayers."

During dinner, Michelle avoided references to being caught ditching school, but she teased her grandmother and laughed with her. The kids even lingered at the table instead of rushing off as soon as they finished as they did when Charles was there.

At last Leslie said, "You may be excused, guys."

"Tryin' to get rid of us?" Scott asked.

"As a matter of fact . . ." Leslie nodded.

"O-*kay*." Michelle said. "We can take a hint."

"I'll come see you before I leave," Zoë promised as they headed for the family room.

Leslie poured more coffee for her mother and herself.

"Y-e-e-s?" Zoë leaned forward, expectancy in her raised eyebrows.

"Mmm. Where to begin. Okay, Michelle was waiting for me at school, right on time yesterday when she cut school, but I called her on it and grounded her. So last night I woke up just after midnight, and she was gone."

"No!" Zoë exclaimed. "Why didn't you call me?"

"Oh, Mom, why would I wake you and upset you?"

"So we could pray! Honey, never hesitate on something like that! Promise?"

Leslie smiled. "Promise. Anyway, Jason carried her into the house at about three."

Zoë pressed her hand to her mouth. "Drugs again?"

"Alcohol. Passed-out drunk. Oh, and I forgot to tell you she'd been playing chicken with the Amtrak that afternoon."

Zoë gasped.

"Mom, it struck me that she must be very angry at me to do all this stuff while Charles is gone. So-o-o, this morning I asked her. And did she ever let it fly! Called me a wimp for not standing up to Charles. Scum for letting him walk all over me—and for not defending her and Scott."

"Scum? Oh dear!" Zoë moved beside Leslie, put her arm around her. "How did you handle that?"

"Well, of course I was in total control." She gave a sheepish laugh. "First I got mad and said nasty things. Then I cried."

Zoë gave her a hug. "So you're human."

"But she did too. Cried, I mean." Tears brimmed in Leslie's eyes at the memory. "And we embraced and both felt better—certainly closer. It was a lovely coming-together after all our battling. And I really think we've established a loving bond, a new understanding. But Mom," Leslie looked at her mother through her tears, "the thing is, she's right—the things she said about me."

"That's tough to admit, dear."

"Well," Leslie bit her lip. "She is. And so," she swallowed, "my question for you is, how do I balance being a submissive Christian wife with being so compliant I do everything but stand at attention and salute Charles?"

"Interesting you should ask." Zoë took a sip of coffee. "It's so beautiful the way God gives us insight even before we need it. Just a week ago I heard an excellent sermon on 1 Peter 3:1 and 2. You know what a red-flag passage that is to women: 'Wives, in the same way be submissive to your husbands so that, if any of them do not believe the word, they may be won over without words by the behavior of their wives, when they see the purity and reverence of your lives.'"

Ah, yes, Leslie thought, *one of the passages that sent me back home to Charles.*

"Our pastor said *submit* means 'yield.' Just like those traffic signs shaped like yellow upside-down triangles. And I thought, Aha! When I yield to an oncoming car, it isn't that I let it rule over me or that I say it's better than me or that I have to obey it. It's a matter of order—and avoiding a collision. It doesn't mean inviting the other car to run all over me or to bang me up."

Leslie pulled away from Zoë and stared at her. "I never thought of it that way."

"And another thing, Leslie. He pointed out that submission is something you give—not something to be demanded."

"Well, in my house, it's demanded, all right." Leslie stared out at the lights from the houses, mirrored in the lake. "I'm going to have to think about this."

"Sounds like a plan." Zoë smiled and touched Leslie's hand.

"But I *am* going to go to that support group at church. I promised Michelle. And she promised to stick to the house rules." Leslie looked heavenward and steepled her hands. "Please, Lord, may she mean it!"

᠅

Just after nine that evening, after Zoë had left, the phone rang. *Charles, probably,* she thought, but immediately realized it was past midnight in New York. She picked up the phone.

"Is that my Weeny One?" the baritone voice inquired.

"Oh! Is that my Pappy?" She smiled at her father's pet name for her as a child and her own stock response. "How are you? How's the therapy going?"

"Really well, thank you. And you were right. I'm almost ready to graduate from the walker to a cane. My left hand wants to stay in a fist, but that's getting better. Still not a lot of tactile sense in it though. For instance, I can't feel change—quarters, dimes, nickels—in my pocket."

"Therapy will help the fist, and sensation may come back. You keep up the good work, Dad. Do everything they tell you to, even if it seems like busywork."

"Yes ma'am."

They both laughed.

"How're *you* doing?" he asked.

"I'm—okay. You knew I was back with Charles, or you wouldn't have called me here."

"Yes, I heard. How is that infidel?"

Her dad had warned her about marrying an unbeliever. What could she say? "He's in New York on business right now. Mad, because it takes time away from studying for his actuary exam."

"Of course." There was a pause. "Leslie, I've been thinking a lot about you. Do you think you could shake loose from Charles and the kids in the next few weeks to come see me, just for a couple of days? A weekend, even? I'll pop for the airfare."

She felt her stomach knot. She much preferred to keep their relationship on a long-distance basis. *I don't want to go,* she thought. *Not the least little bit.* But he was asking her in what, for him, was a specific way. Maybe he wanted reassurance about his therapy. If she could give of herself for her patients, couldn't she do that for her own father?

"I—I'd like to," she lied. "I'll have to run it by Charles. With the exam coming up . . ." She didn't finish the sentence.

"I think Zoë would help with the kids, get them out of Charles's hair, if that's what's bothering you."

"You've talked with her?"

He sounded amused. "We're not exactly enemies, you know."

"Right. Well. Let me see what I can do, Dad. I'll get back to you."

"I'd really appreciate it."

"Talk with you soon then."

"Your Pappy loves his Weeny One. 'Bye."

Pappy. Weeny One. The familiar names, his undeniably tender tone took her back thirty years. She could remember the good times. How he'd carry her upstairs at night, singing, "Upster, boost-er; up we go to bed." How he'd protest good-naturedly as she climbed up under his newspaper onto his lap and spelled out the headlines. How he took the family on vacations together at a Wisconsin lake. How a summer rainstorm drenched her when she went after "just a few more blueberries" and she found him standing under a towering pine tree, bone-dry, puffing on his pipe.

But she could also remember his harshness, his dictatorial tone, his thinly veiled disappointment in her lack of musical ability.

Maybe, she told herself, *the stroke has mellowed him. I know I ought to go.* But the very idea filled her with dread. *I feel so ambivalent about him,* she realized, *it's almost a love-hate relationship.* She took a sharp breath as she suddenly saw the parallel. "Sort of like my relationship with Charles," she whispered.

23

❦

From Zoë's Prayer Journal

October 17: Dear Lord, thank You for the closing of that escrow on the lake property. It seemed to go on forever, but Your timing is perfect. (You know how much I needed this income right now.) Timing. Oh, Father, what is Your right timing for Leslie to visit her dad? Benjamin wants her to come so much, and I think going to him could help her in ways she can't see. Please, if I take care of the kids, may Charles be agreeable. And oh, Lord, show me how I can minister to Charles, who must be in such pain to be so angry. I love You Lord, and only ask You to use me. I'm available. I pray all this in the name of Your dear Son, my Lord and Savior, amen.

IN THE TWO DAYS REMAINING BEFORE CHARLES'S RETURN, Leslie's thoughts of her father returned again and again like a recurring symphonic theme.

I despise these love-hate feelings I have toward him, she told herself. *I know I ought to be a dutiful daughter and go. He obviously wants me, maybe needs me. I feel so selfish, not wanting to go. What is it with me? What am I afraid of? That he'll light into me like he did that time when I was practicing the piano? I'm not an eight-year-old any longer.*

"Ahhhhh." She let her breath out in a long sigh as she understood: *I feel so stripped by Charles—he makes me feel like an eight-year-old. And I don't know if I can handle more criticism. Especially by another man who's close to me. She shivered. That's probably the best reason for going. I need to face him. Need to stop behaving like a cowering child, grow up and be an adult with him.*

She thought back to her conversation with Michelle. "Oh, Lord," she said aloud, "am I going to be a wimp forever with the men in my life? Maybe this is the place to start." She turned the idea over like a polished stone in her hands. And at last she could say aloud to herself, "Yes. This is where I begin. Even though my stomach is in knots and I'm scared silly, I'll go. I'll tell Charles it's been over a year since I've seen Dad, that he's ill and might not live all that much longer, that he needs my professional input, and that it will give him—Charles—time to study."

It had better be soon, she realized. *If I wait much longer, it'll be time for Charles's exam, and then we'll be into the holidays and it may be hard to get reservations.*

She thought about Charles's return and could feel her whole body begin to tense. Would he be exhausted, a basket case, leaving a path of destruction wherever he went? All the more reason, perhaps, to get herself and the kids out of his way for a few days.

The next day, looking at the children's schedules and her own, she selected a three-day weekend two weeks away so she'd get a good advance fare. No sense in her dad paying more than necessary for her ticket. At work she cleared the time with Terry and made a note to phone Zoë. But at midday, before she could call, her mother stopped by with a sack. "Hope you don't have lunch plans," she said.

Leslie shook her head.

"I just discovered this little 'epicerie.'" Zoë grinned. "That's French for deli. But wait till you taste these sandwiches: lamb with sun-dried tomatoes on walnut-wheat bread. And tuna—we're talking fresh tuna—with fresh basil on a baguette. We'll share 'em both, okay?"

Leslie smiled and gave a what-can-I-say? shrug. "Do I have a choice?"

They took the lunch into the meeting room.

"Well?" Zoë asked as Leslie bit into the tuna sandwich.

"A cut above peanut butter."

Zoë swatted her hand. "You're impossible!"

"No, you are. What a great idea. This is fabulous." Leslie paused for another bite. "I was going to call you. I guess you know Dad phoned after you left the other day. Wants me to come visit."

"Right." Zoë's eyes grew wide and earnest. "He really wants to see you, Leslie. Says he's been doing a lot of thinking."

"That sounds scary."

"Not to worry. It's good. Leslie, if you decide to go, I'll take the kids, and I hope Charles will be so ecstatic to be free to study, he'll be agreeable."

"Well, I never know what I'll get from Charles. You know that. But if it works for you, I'll try to make reservations for two weeks from Friday. Go early Friday and come back late Sunday. That'll give us the best part of three days." She looked at Zoë and grimaced. "My palms are sweating already."

"Trust me. It'll be good."

Leslie stared at her mother's soft face with the deep laugh lines around the mouth, more lines radiating from the outer corners of her eyes. "I do trust you, Mom." She could feel her heart rate accelerate as she tried to decide whether to tell her mother about . . . It was difficult even to think it, much less express the problem that troubled her so. Now, suddenly, she felt an urgency to verbalize it. She took a quick breath. "And Mom, I need to tell you something." She glanced away. "A confession."

Zoë leaned forward. "Of course."

Leslie bit her lip. "This is hard. I—I've been drinking wine with Charles."

Zoë gazed at her with compassionate, unjudgmental eyes. "But honey, you've always said you hated the taste."

"I know. And I do."

"How did it start then?" Zoë's voice was gentle.

"It was one terrible weekend when Charles had been tearing me apart. He poured, said, 'This will make you feel better,' and I just—did. And I knew right then that it wasn't good for me. But after that first time, Charles expected it, assumed it."

Zoë nodded.

"And there was always some crisis where I didn't want to refuse, make him angrier."

"Does it also—" Zoë hesitated. "—numb the pain?"

Leslie stared at her. "I guess you're right. Mom, I know this isn't right for me. I know I should be able to handle it with prayer. I should be able to say no. I should *do* something." She closed her eyes a moment. "And here's the worst part. I know God must be so disgusted with me for not resisting the temptation, for being so weak. He doesn't even seem to be there when I pray. And at church I feel like an outsider looking in the window. I don't belong."

Zoë looked at her daughter and her frightened-doe expression, feeling an overpowering sense of sadness. *Talk about sabotaging herself!* Zoë thought. *How can Leslie cope with Charles when she's numbed and depressed by alcohol? How can she know how much God loves her and hear His voice in her life if she feels separated from Him? What does she have without Him?*

Leslie looked at her mother from beneath her bangs. "Do—do you think I'm an alcoholic?"

"What do you have? *A* glass of wine?"

Leslie nodded.

"Then I hardly think so." Zoë looked at her daughter and saw tears brim in her eyes. "What about when Charles is gone?"

Leslie shook her head. "What about it?"

"Are you drinking now?"

Leslie's face registered surprise. "No-o-o. In fact, I never thought of it."

"Then it's Charles—" Zoë clenched her fists under the table and for a moment felt a flash of rage. "It's almost—almost satanic, as though he wants to hook you—or certainly to control you." She took a deep breath, hearing her own judgmental tone, and gentled her voice. "Or maybe he just wants a drinking buddy. It helps justify his own drinking."

"Oh," Leslie said. "I'm certain that's true. The irony is that he seems at his sweetest when we're both drinking. That's when we get along best."

"Sure. Because you're both blocking out the truth, avoiding the real issues." She saw Leslie nod sheepishly. "Oh, honey, I'll pray that God will help you break this pattern, that He'll give you the strength to say no, even if it makes Charles mad. And Leslie, God *is* there for you. He's promised He'll never leave nor forsake you."

❧

That afternoon David stood in the parallel bars, exulting. "I'm getting a lot stronger! Try to push me over," he challenged.

Leslie pushed against him and he stood firm. "You definitely are stronger," she agreed. "I think you're ready to try a couple of steps today."

David's turquoise eyes opened wider. "You're putting me on."

"Nope." She moved inside the parallel bars, facing him. "Now Brynne's going to kneel behind you and move your feet. Try to put your weight on your right foot now, David. Good."

Brynne moved David's left foot forward.

"Good. Now weight on your left foot," Leslie directed. "Feel steady? You sure?"

David nodded, and Brynne moved his right foot forward. "Great! Look at you! Now, one more. Terrific!"

"Yeah, look at me, I'm shakin' like a leaf." David's legs trembled, and he squinted as perspiration dripped into his eyes.

"All *right!*" Leslie gave him a thumbs-up. "That's enough for today."

David eased back into his wheelchair and closed his eyes. "Hard to believe . . . how much work that was."

"Yes. But remember how hard it was to stand at first? Look how far you've come. Faster, really, than I hoped. Keep this up, and you'll be walking to the end of the bars."

David looked up and grinned. "Yeah! That's right. And then a walker. And then—the LA marathon!"

She laughed. "It'll take time," she cautioned.

"Lady, you are such a soggy blanket."

She smiled. "I'll try not to drip on you. I know it's hard, but David, don't rush it."

"O-*kay.*" She heard his grudging tone before she saw the twinkle in his eyes.

৵

Just after Michelle went to bed the next night, Leslie heard the key in the front door. "That you, Charles?" she called from the family room.

"You expecting someone else—with a key?" Charles's tone was light as he shut the door. She walked to meet him and kissed him. Gin. The aroma was overpowering.

"How did it go?" she asked.

"Well. I think I did some good." He gave her a wide but mechanical smile. "And I was very charming."

"I'm sure you were."

He pulled off his necktie and looked at his watch. "It is midnight, New York time. A beer—and then bed. Tomorrow, I have to really knuckle down to study. Wish I could take some time off, but we are flooded at work." He went to the kitchen and found a bottle of beer, pouring it meticulously into a glass to leave just an inch of foam. "Everything go all right here?"

"Yes. Scott's enjoying swim team. He has his first meet on Saturday. It's just a little dual meet, but he's excited."

"That so? I bought myself a stopwatch while I was in New York."

"A what?" She wasn't sure she'd heard correctly.

"A stopwatch, Leslie. Surely you know what that is!"

"Yes, of course. But—"

"You're always saying I should be more involved with Scott. This way I can keep track of his times."

She sighed inwardly, sensing the pressure Charles could put on Scott. "I think he'd be very happy if you'd just come to a meet now and then. This is low-key competition, Charles. It's about having fun. Do you really think you need to—"

"Leslie! This is all really very simple," he said as though explaining it to a kindergartner. "Swimming is all about time. I am going to chart his times." Before she could respond, he changed the subject. "Now, how about Michelle while I was gone? Did she stay under control?"

Now is not the time, Leslie thought, *to get into that.* "We, uh, had some rocky moments. I'll tell you about them later. But I think we've come to an, um, understanding."

"Hmm." He stroked his moustache.

"Charles, going back to your studying. Since you want so much to really dig in, I thought I'd go see my dad in two weeks—just a three-day weekend. He's asked me to come. It's been over a year since I've seen him. You know he's had the stroke, and well, he might not live all that much longer. I get the feeling he needs my professional input too. Mom will take the kids, so you can be alone and concentrate on your studying."

Charles blinked. "Why, that will be good. Thank you." He licked the beer foam from his lips and pointed his index finger at her. "And in the meantime, Leslie, I warn you, any interruptions, any distractions or unnecessary irritations and—well, let me simply say that you and your children will regret it very much indeed."

24

*

"BOYS NINE AND TEN FIFTY-YARD FREE," THE VOICE BLARED
over the PA system by the pool. Scott wriggled out of his
sweats. His gait seemed awkward, self-conscious, as he moved
toward the end of the pool. Leslie could feel his tension.

"Swimmers to the starting blocks," came the voice again.
Scott, reed-thin in his striped Speedo, stepped up on the block
at lane two and looked straight ahead.

"M-a-a-rk!"

Scott bent and grabbed the bottom of the platform. The
gun sounded. Momentarily rooted to the block, he dove into
the water a little behind the other five boys. Rangy arms
reaching, legs churning up a plume of white water, he passed
one boy before he hit the end of the pool, then lost him on the
turn.

"G-o-o-o-o, Scott, go!" Leslie yelled. Scott touched the wall to finish second from last. "Yea, Scott! Good swim!" she shouted, proud of his first race.

A voice at her elbow said, "Did you see that? Lost a full second on the start."

She turned to see Charles, stopwatch in hand.

"Charles!" she exclaimed. "I thought you needed to study."

"Just taking an hour off. Breaststroke his next event, is it?" He started toward Scott.

"Where are you going?" she asked.

"To talk to Scott."

"Oh, Charles, David doesn't like parents talking with the kids during a meet."

"Nonsense!" Charles made his way to the area where the team sprawled on the warm concrete to watch and wait for their next events.

Leslie saw Scott's expression of surprise, quickly followed by what she could only describe as alarm. *He's afraid of his father,* she thought. Charles pointed to his stopwatch and gestured toward the blocks as he talked. Scott nodded. As Charles walked away, Scott hunkered down underneath his towel, looking smaller than ever.

Later, as Scott prepared to swim breaststroke, he grasped the platform as the PA resounded, "Swimmers, take your marks."

Scott fell forward into the water and another swimmer followed just as the gun went off.

Two reports of the gun. "False start!"

Leslie watched Scott and the other boy pull themselves out of the pool and remount the blocks. "Oh, Lord, don't let this spoil his race," she prayed softly. "And don't let him do it again and get himself disqualified."

The race began, and Scott seemed to be swimming through glue.

"Well, he certainly blew that one," Charles said even before Scott finished.

"Yea, Scott, yea!" she shouted, as he came in dead last.

"Leslie," Charles hissed. "You are making an ass of yourself. You do not cheer for the last-place finisher."

"Yes," she said. "I do."

Charles gave her a look of deep pity. "I will be leaving now. What can I say? The child is a loser."

Afterward, as she drove Scott home, he said, "Man, I didn't know Dad was coming."

"I didn't either. Make you nervous?"

He wriggled down in the car seat. "What do you think?"

"He give you a hard time about your start?"

"Yeah. In front of everybody. Embarrassing."

"Of course it was. But Scott, Dad's trying to be part of your life, trying to be involved."

"I suppose."

Some involvement, Leslie thought. *Sometimes I wonder if Charles has been reading a book on how to destroy other people's self-confidence.* She pressed her lips together. *Or maybe he wrote it.*

"Well," she said, wanting so much to reassure him, "I thought you did great for a first meet. Could you hear me cheering for you?"

His expression was glum. "I can't hear anything when I'm in the water."

"Oh." She pondered some way to distract him. "Speaking of cheering, how'd you like to come in and cheer for your buddy David next week?"

"How come? What's happening?"

"He's starting to walk in the parallel bars."

Now she had his attention. "No foolin'? Yeah, I'd like to be there. Maybe I could, like, sorta be *his* coach."

"We'll do it on Wednesday, before swim workout."

"Cool."

⌇

That night, as Charles began pouring the wine, Leslie said, as casually as she could, "I don't really feel like wine tonight. I'm just going to have a Diet Squirt." She reached for a can from the refrigerator and took it into the family room.

A moment later Charles joined her with two glasses of wine. He set one down on the coffee table beside her Squirt. Hadn't he heard her? Surely he saw the can.

"Cheers!" he said, lifting his wine glass toward her.

She held out her soda can. "Cheers."

"Come, now, *Les*-lie, soda water is not fit for cheers. That's for babies. Be a grownup, for pity's sake."

"I really don't feel like wine tonight," she said.

"All the more reason to have it. It is good for whatever ails you. Why, it's even in the Bible. 'A little wine, for your stomach's sake.'"

She stared at him, remembering that even Satan quoted Scripture—and to tempt Jesus Himself. Charles tapped his foot impatiently, and the down-turned slashes of his tobacco-brown moustache paralleled the slant of his eyebrows. Leslie tried to look at him but couldn't. He'd warned her not to distract or upset him. An innermost part of her warned, *Danger!* Slowly, she set the can down and picked up the wine glass.

Charles smiled, "To your good health."

For that moment Leslie felt an overwhelming sense of relief over escaping the threatened eruption. But even as she brought the glass to her lips, a feeling of self-disgust inundated her. Charles had won. Reduced her to scum. Again.

⤳

"Hey, Scott, whatcha doing here?" David asked, his face registering surprise when he found Scott waiting at the physical therapy center on Wednesday.

Scott grinned. It would be fun to switch places with David. "Came to root for you. Figured you do that for me at workout and meets."

"Fantastic. You can count while I warm up before I get in the parallel bars."

After David finished his warm-ups, Leslie stood between the parallel bars and motioned him toward her.

As David moved his wheelchair, he told Scott, "I was proud of you at the meet on Saturday."

"Yeah?" Scott said. "My dad wasn't."

David shot Leslie a look and pursed his lips. "Scott, I know your dad's a real smart hombre, but who knows more about swimming: him or me?"

"Well, you, I guess."

"Okay. I say you did a good job." David pulled himself up at the parallel bars.

"Ma-a-rk!" Scott called out. He stood beside the bars, trying to remember all the things David said to him. "Go, David, go!" he shouted.

David nodded. "You fire the gun, Leslie."

"Bang!" she said.

With Brynne moving his feet, David took one step, then a second, and a third.

"Good, David," Leslie encouraged.

"Yeah," Brynne said. "I don't have to move your legs as much as last time."

"Go, David, go!" Scott cheered.

David grunted and took another step—and another.

"Help him, Lord," Scott prayed softly. Then, "Move those legs! Keep it up. Keep going even when it hurts. No pain, no gain!"

At last David reached the end of the bars.

"Good effort, David! Good job," Scott exclaimed, and Leslie laughed at how well he'd picked up David's own favorite coaching words.

When David was seated in his wheelchair, Scott gave him a towel to wipe his face.

"Thanks, coach," David managed. "Couldn't have done it without you."

᙭

By the following week David could stand up by himself without hanging on to the parallel bars.

"Your balance is good now, David," Leslie encouraged. We just need to work hard to get your legs to move. The nerves seem to be functioning. It's a strength issue. You're doing well, but you're still fatiguing pretty easily."

"I'm workin' on it," he said as he walked between the bars. "When do you think I could try a solo?"

"Whoa, Nellie!" Leslie held up her hand. "Not yet. How about playing ball? You up for that?"

"You know me!"

Leslie grasped his gait belt while Brynne tossed him a medicine ball. He caught it but dropped it to grab the bars.

"I'm teetering," he said.

"That's okay," Leslie said, handing him back the ball. They completed two ball exchanges before David had to grasp the bars again.

"That's good, David," Brynne said.

"Yeah. Gettin' better."

"Okay, Brynne will work some more with you on this on Friday. I'm going to take off to go see my dad."

David kept his eye on the ball. "That good?"

"We'll see. He's had a stroke."

"Well, you know how to help him with that." David grabbed the bars again. "If you're as good for him as you are for me . . ."

"If he'll let me help him."

"Stubborn, huh?"

"Yes, and that's undoubtedly good for his recovery."

"But that can be kinda tough on you," David said.

Leslie nodded. "You've got it, you seventy-year-old in a boy's body."

"'Do not be anxious about anything, but in everything, by prayer and petition—'" David quoted from the fourth chapter of Philippians.

Leslie picked it up. "'—with thanksgiving, present your requests to God.'"

"'And the peace which transcends all understanding, will guard your hearts and your minds—'"

"'—in Christ Jesus.'" Leslie finished the verse.

"Hey, we make a good team!" David exclaimed.

"We do—and thanks for the reminder of the way to peace, David."

↝

Leslie stayed late at work to keep extra appointments Thursday, then hustled at home to leave everything in order for Charles. At midnight she stood in the kitchen and went through a mental checklist. *Let's see. Laundry done. A roast for Charles to carve for dinner Friday and Saturday, the scalloped potatoes he loves, plenty of salad fixings, munchies, beer. That should hold him. Kitchen floor and counters clean. Rest of the house in order. Kids have their stuff together to go to their grandmother's.*

She headed upstairs, wondering if she'd forgotten anything to take with her. *Won't need much for three days,* she'd decided. She'd already packed wool slacks and a sweater for Chicago's fall weather in a carry-on bag. And avocados, her dad's favorite. She'd tuck in last-minute things in the morning, be ready to leave with Charles. He'd actually offered to drop her off at the Orange County airport on his way to work.

She arrived at the airport the next morning an hour and a half early for her flight. Charles barely stopped the car in his haste to get on his way, and when she leaned over to kiss him, he didn't turn toward her, and she caught him on the cheek. She couldn't help but notice the couple standing beside a Bronco, indulging in a long, lingering kiss. Charles delivered his parting shot as she got out of the car. "Well, certainly nobody will miss you in that gaudy gold jacket. Maybe you should phone your father from the airport and tell him to get out his sunglasses."

Other people had told her the jacket was perfect with her autumn coloring. She sighed and made her way to the airline counter. The bag was heavy with an extra pair of shoes, her Bible, another book for the plane.

After she'd checked in, she walked toward the gates and saw she had time for a cup of coffee and a muffin. She'd had no time for breakfast, what with Charles's last-minute demands for celery, not carrots, in his lunch, and for regular coffee for breakfast instead of decaf. And Scott couldn't find his homework, and Michelle absolutely had to have a particular pair of socks that couldn't be found. Maybe, before she got to Chicago, her heart would stop racing from the pace of the last twenty-four hours.

It was only when she was on the plane and it began to accelerate down the runway that she started to relax. As the plane left the ground and the captain explained the sharp, nearly vertical ascent out of Orange County "to be good neighbors to our friends below," she thrilled to the lift. *Wings. Like the wings of a dove.* "Far away would I fly," she echoed the words of the psalm.

The ocean sparkled like crinkled aluminum foil beneath them, and she could see fishing boats and a lone sailboat headed out of Newport Harbor. When the plane banked and turned back over toward the southern part of the county, she searched for their house, but managed only to locate the YMCA pool.

I love flying, she thought. *It's lovely, not being either where I came from or where I'm going. Here, for a few hours, I'm suspended between problems.*

Leaning back, she thought again of the wings of a dove. Reaching in the seat pocket for the Bible she'd taken out of her flight bag, she looked for the verse. Ah, there it was—Psalm 55:6 and 7. "Oh, that I had the wings of a dove! I would fly away and be at rest—I would flee far away and stay in the desert." Well, Chicago wasn't exactly a desert.

Why, she wondered, had the psalmist wanted to flee?

She looked at verses 4 and 5: "My heart is in anguish within me; the terrors of death assail me. Fear and trembling have beset me; horror has overwhelmed me."

Well, surely it can't get *that* bad, she said to herself.

25

From Zoë's Prayer Journal

November 1: Lord, I had to hurry home and write down what You showed me while I was swimming just now. As I prayed my way through the alphabet and got to the letter H, I began to pray for Leslie's happiness. And You corrected me! You said, not audibly, but very clearly, "Zoë, My number one concern is not Leslie's happiness, but her holiness. I want to grow her up, in Me." Oh, Lord, how about maybe just a little bit happy? It's hard for me to let go. Yet I thank You for showing me Your perspective. Your picture is much, much bigger than mine! Now, Lord, bless Leslie's time with Benjamin. May there be a reconnecting in love. I praise and thank You, Father! In Jesus' name, amen.

LESLIE STARED OUT THE WINDOW AS THE PLANE BROKE through a low cloud cover, descending into Chicago. Already the glorious reds and golds of fall had fluttered down from the trees, which lifted black, forlorn arms into the sky. She glanced at her watch. Almost four o'clock Chicago time, and already, car headlights shone along the streets.

No wonder I felt depressed in Chicago in the late fall and winter, she thought. Even now, she could feel her mood darkening, dread overshadowing her anticipation of being with her father. *Only three days,* she reminded herself, *and I'll be back where the sun's still shining.*

Oh, Lord, she prayed silently, *help me be helpful and not revert to playing the eight-year-old, like I did last year when I was here—and so many times before. Give me the capacity to love Dad, even if he's not lovable, even if he's as dogmatic as he was in the past. And Father, watch over Charles while I'm gone. Draw him close to You. Give him the gift of faith.*

At her dad's Evanston apartment she knocked, and finding the door unlocked, let herself in. She could smell the sweet aroma of his pipe even though he'd abandoned it several years ago, and it was familiar and comforting.

"Dad?" she called. "It's Leslie."

"In my study," came his deep voice.

She set her carry-on bag in the entry and walked through the living room, dominated by the rich black of the Steinway grand. The mellow hues of worn oriental rugs accented the hardwood floors. A few steps down the hallway, then she paused at the door of his study. Seated at his office desk, his walker off to the side, her dad wore a wine-colored velvet leisure jacket that gave his cheeks a healthy glow. Silver goatee trimmed precisely, brown eyes bright under snowy eyebrows, he looked dapper as ever—but shockingly thin.

"There's my Weeny One!" he cried, spinning in his desk chair to face her, opening his arms to her.

"Pappy o'mine!" She ran toward him and hugged him, kissing his cheek, feeling the familiar prickle of his goatee.

He held her so long, she almost lost her balance as she leaned over him. "I'm very, very glad you're here," he murmured, and when she pulled back, she was surprised to see his eyes glistening.

"Sit thee down," he said, indicating the love seat arranged in an L with his desk.

She sat and fingered her necklace, wondering what to say.

"Flight okay?" he asked.

"Fine. Thanks for the ticket. Terrible movie. Fine flight." She examined her fingernails.

"Well, now, tell me about Scott and Michelle." He leaned forward.

"They're growing up fast, Dad. In Michelle's case maybe too fast." She reached into her purse. "Here. I brought some pictures." She handed them to him and he put on his glasses, examining the topmost snapshot.

"Oh, Leslie, she's lovely!" he exclaimed. "I see a lot of you in her." He looked up. "I'll wager the junior high boys are standing in line."

"Yes, but unfortunately, she thinks they're all dorks. She likes—shall we say, more mature men. I've had quite a time with one of them. He's sixteen, and he's led her—quite willingly, I might say—into trying pot, booze, skipping school." The minute she finished the sentence, Leslie worried she'd said too much. Would her father blame her?

He shook his head. "What's that all about? She trying to get your goat?"

"Looks that way. But we've had our moment of truth, and I pray we've turned a corner."

"Good for you. And Scott?" He turned to the next picture. "He's still a real string bean, isn't he?"

She nodded. "Some people think he looks like you, when you were ten or so."

"That right?" Her dad sounded pleased.

"Uh-huh. I've worried about Scott a lot, as you know, because he's so self-conscious about his hand. But Dad, he's on a swim team now, coached by a young man who's severely handicapped—in a wheelchair, and they are buddies. I feel very encouraged."

"That should be a big help." He gazed at the photo then looked up. "Zoë must love him swimming. She's still at it every day, isn't she?"

Leslie nodded. "She taught him to do a flip turn."

He laughed. "That's Zoë!"

She gave him a close look. "Dad, you look good. But something's missing."

He looked puzzled. "What's that?"

She smiled. "Your bay window. Without that belly you're looking very svelte."

"Yes. Well, that just sort of disappeared when I got depressed—after the stroke."

"A depression's not unusual," she offered.

"Well, I was lower than a snake's underside. Wasn't interested in anything, including food. I didn't much give a you-know-what."

My strong dad, always on top, calling the shots—how difficult this must have been for him, she thought. She reached over and touched his hand, which rested on the arm of his chair. "That was really hard, Dad. But you're one tough guy, and you obviously decided, somewhere along the line, to take control again."

He shook his head. "Nope. It was more like asking the Lord to take control."

She raised her eyebrows, surprised.

"Yup." He nodded. "Me, that stubborn old goat."

She thought back to his years of perfunctory church attendance. He'd taught her Christian values but never seemed to *know* the Lord, to have a personal relationship. "Dad, that's wonderful! No wonder you look so good. But be honest now, you must get really frustrated from time to time."

"No. Not from time to time. About every thirty seconds."

The phone rang. He reached over with his right hand and picked it up. "Lang."

Just like Charles declaring "Harper" when he answers the phone, she thought.

He listened a moment, "No, no, no, Eleanor!" His voice rose almost to a scream. "Use your head, Eleanor. That is not what I told you. Now, listen very carefully, and I will speak slowly. I—need—you—to—come—in—at—eight—thirty—in—the—morning."

He's talking like Charles, she thought, wincing for poor Eleanor.

"Eleanor, can you read?" he continued. "I wrote it all out for you! Look at the note. Yes. Yes. *Yes.*" He slammed the phone down, muttering, "The woman's an idiot. Not just dumb. Stupid. There's a difference, you know." He turned to Leslie. "Did you enjoy that?" he demanded.

She took a deep breath, determined not to kowtow to him. "No, Dad, I didn't. I don't enjoy hearing anyone torn apart."

His eyes flashed. "You don't understand," he cried.

To Leslie the tone seemed to say, "You dummy, you've never understood." Feeling the old panic rise, she waited a moment before she stood. "Dad, I'll just put my things in my room. Where would you like me?"

His tone moderated. "The guest room. Just past the bath."

She started for her room but his voice stopped her.

"Uh, Leslie . . . What I was saying just now is that it's hard for anyone to understand the frustration I feel, having to depend on others for things I always did myself. I can't even drive a car. I need this woman to come in every day or I couldn't survive—and she drives me bonkers."

She nodded, relieved at his explanation. "It's a major adjustment, Dad."

"Well," he shook his head. "Listen to *me* telling *you*. You know the problems. You probably see crips like me all the time." He smiled. "I have to say I now have new respect and admiration for your work. These young therapists have been great with me." He gave her a quizzical look. "I just hope you don't carry on conversations with other people in the room during therapy, as though your stroke patients didn't exist."

She smiled. "No, dad. I give my full attention."

He nodded. "Thought so."

✲

Eleanor had left a standing rib roast with potatoes browning in the oven and a salad in the refrigerator, ready to toss. Leslie cooked some broccoli, and dinner was ready.

When they were both seated, her father reached for her hand and bowed his head. "Thank You, Lord, for bringing my precious Weeny One all this way. Bless our time together. And bless the food You've given us. Amen."

"Amen," Leslie added. She looked at the lustrous pink slices of roast beef. "Would you be insulted if I offered to cut your meat?" she asked.

"I'd be eternally grateful," he said. "It's this left hand . . ."

"Right." She nodded.

"No, left."

"Okay, Abbott," she laughed, "who's on first?"

She watched him during dinner. "I think you're doing

really well with your left hand, Dad. It does still want to stay in a fist, doesn't it? If you take hold of a cup, can you let go?"

He grasped the cup and it was clear that it took effort to release it. "Not easy," he admitted.

"It'll come," she said.

As they finished dinner, Leslie decided to make a point. "Whether she's an idiot or not, Dad, Eleanor can definitely cook."

"She can do that," her father admitted. "I guess I'm fortunate to have her."

After dinner Leslie followed her dad into the living room.

"There will be a sonic boom at any moment—" He looked over his shoulder and gave her a wry smile. "—because of my dazzling speed."

"But Dad, you look very secure with the walker," she said. "I'll bet it won't be long till you can use a cane."

"That's what I'm working toward. And I'd like more mobility with my left arm for conducting." He eased himself down in a chair beside the stereo.

"Of course you would. Let me see how far you can lift it."

She watched him. "Pretty good elbow and shoulder control, Dad. Good! Let's see if we can help that hand, so it can be expressive again." She took his hand and gently worked on his fingers, stretching one at a time.

"In-home therapy! How about that!" He gave her a grateful smile.

"Are you still planning the Christmas concert?" she asked.

He seemed surprised by the question. "Of course!"

She gave him a hug."I like your attitude, Dad."

"I thought we'd have some music now," he said, "Thank God for CDs. I could never manage the old manual systems—arms, needles, and records. You in the mood for Brahms?"

"Fine."

He turned the system on, managed to remove the disc from its case with his right hand, and slipped it into the player. Orchestral music filled the room. He raised his finger. "The germ-motif," he whispered. "That little theme runs all through this symphony."

She had always loved hearing music with him. He never seemed compelled to "conduct" as he listened. No hand or body movements, except for an occasional bob of the head or an arching of one eyebrow at a phrase of particular beauty.

She remembered how difficult it had been for her to listen to classical music for years after he left. Even now she only rarely tuned it in or sought it out. Silly, she thought.

Without a word they shared the noble ending of the andante, the energy of the third movement, and the building tension of the closing movement. Now and then their eyes met in an unverbalized *Wasn't that wonderful?*

"How beautiful," she sighed as the final notes faded away. She stood and walked over to him, taking his hand between hers. "I feel very close to you when we listen together."

"Beauty is bonding," he said.

The thought clung to her later as she got ready for bed. "Lord," she said, "what a remarkable connecting experience that was with Dad. I know You are the One who orchestrated it, and I thank You."

The next afternoon they listened to more music, sipping tea as they savored a Beethoven string quartet, the Liebestod from "Tristan and Isolde" and several Schumann piano pieces.

"You're a good listener, Leslie," he said. "Do you remember

when I used to bring records home from the university, and you'd play 'em over and over—especially the parts you liked?" He chuckled. "You darn near wore out that one particular variation in the Rachmaninoff Rhapsody on a Theme of Paganini."

She remembered well, those wintry hours by the hi-fi. "Yes, and sometimes you'd bring me opera scores to follow while I listened to the records."

"You were in high school," he recalled.

"Yes." She looked at him, then away. "That ended—that and a lot of other things—when I was eighteen."

He nodded, watching her carefully. "You were very angry when I left."

"Angry?" She thought back. "No."

"Well, you should have been!" he exclaimed. "It was a rotten thing for me to do to you kids and your mom. You didn't deserve it. It was a selfish, irresponsible betrayal of all that was dear." He frowned. "Why weren't you mad?"

She bit her lip. "Because I was too filled with guilt. And shame." She saw his eyes asking for more. "I loved you, admired you so—idolized you, I guess. And I thought if I'd been better—smarter—more gifted—more what you wanted me to be . . ." She couldn't finish the sentence.

"Leslie, listen to me!" He pointed his index finger, as though urging musicians to respond. "Way, way off! It was nothing of the sort. The problem was that your idol had feet of clay. It was my midlife crisis, plain and simple. Went berserk. Grass greener, filly prettier, on the other side of the fence. It had nothing to do with you or your mother or anyone else at home. It had everything to do with me and that gorgeous young soprano, Frances Kern. She's famous today, but she was just starting her career at that time and looked very fresh and exciting to me. I divorced much too hastily. And when the affair died down, I knew I'd been an idiot, but it just seemed too late to come back. I thought you understood that."

"I heard what people said at the time, and hearing the gossip was hard. But you see, Dad, I knew the real reason you left. I knew I was a disappointment to you then. And to tell the truth, even now, I feel like I don't meet your expectations, don't do enough for you, don't come to see you often enough."

"Well, you don't understand!" he exclaimed, and she cringed at the familiar words. But his voice turned tender. "It's time, Weeny One, that I taught you the facts of life."

She laughed in spite of herself. "Not the birds and bees again."

"More important. First, I love you because you're you, Leslie, and because you're mine. It has nothing to do with how smart you are or what you do or don't do." He gave her the familiar, "are-you-hearing-me?" look. "I have absolutely no expectations of you. Zero. Zip. I love you just the way you are. Always have. Always will."

She stared at the tender earnestness of his face till it blurred before her eyes. Why did his words—just a few sentences strung together—affect her so deeply? *Because,* she realized, *this is what I've been wanting, wishing, longing to hear all my life. And never thought I would.* Pulling a tissue from her pocket to catch the tears, she blurted, "That's too good to be true."

He reached over and touched her arm. "It is true. And I should have told you this long ago, but I somehow thought you understood. Just recently I got to feeling there was some unfinished business between us. That's why I asked you to come. I'm so glad I got to tell you this."

"Me too." She blew her nose and reached for another tissue.

"And I want you to know something else that I was reminded of today and yesterday. Other of your siblings played or sang better than you. But nobody listened like you. You always really *heard* the music." He thought a moment. "Maybe that's what makes you so successful in your field. You listen." He considered the thought and gave a small nod. "Anyway, with the music, you had—have—a special understanding, a heart-response. And I always loved that about you."

She stared at him. "Really?"

"Really." He held out his arms, and she hurried to his embrace.

"Dad," she murmured, "that was an incredible gift—what you just said."

"I'm glad," he whispered. "Very glad." He released her gently. "Now," he said, reaching for his walker, "I'm going to lie down and get a load off my rear end."

"Good idea. While you're napping, I'll put together that apple crisp you used to like."

"You'd do that for your mean, demanding old man?"

"I would."

 ॐ

After dinner that night he showed her the program of Christmas choral music he'd planned. "A nice balance of the esoteric, the familiar, and the modern," he said, closing the manila folder.

On the front she saw the words, *"Soli Deo gloria,"* written in her father's precise hand.

"To God be the glory?" she asked.

"To God *alone* be the glory," he corrected. "I've done performances for people in the past, and they were just that—performances. This time God will be the audience, and it will be worship. I promised Him that after the stroke. Worship through beauty." He winked at her. "You see, after all these years, I finally know what that means."

She nodded. "And it will show. He'll be glorified."

"That's my prayer. Maybe you can come back. Would Charles come?"

"I doubt it." She tilted her head to one side and asked, "Dad, you were pretty plain about not wanting me to marry him. Do you remember?"

"I do. I thought it was too quick—after Tom's death. And I was worried about your different backgrounds. You were a pretty rooted Christian. Charles flat-out denied Jesus as anything more than a teacher." He studied her. "And—I thought I saw a mean streak." His eyebrows asked the question.

"You're asking me if you were right," she said. She nodded. "You probably were. But a lot of our problems are my fault."

"Just like my leaving was your fault?" he asked.

She gave a helpless shrug.

"Do me a favor. Think about it."

But when she went to bed that night, all Leslie could think about was her dad's statement that afternoon. "I love you because you're mine . . . It has nothing to do with what you do or don't do . . . I love you just the way you are . . ."

She got down on her knees by her bed. "Oh, Lord, what a gift! It is so amazing. It's like—it's like—oh, I see! My earthly father's love is like a reflection of my heavenly Father's unconditional love. A love with no strings attached. A love that doesn't keep a record of wrongs or mistakes, that hangs in there, never fails. Oh, *what* a gift! Thank You, Lord!"

The next morning she and her dad went to church together, and it was déjà vu, sitting again with her dad in this traditional church, Gothic in design, with light flooding in through stained-glass windows. *This old place is so different from my church,* she thought, *with its contemporary design and worship. Yet I feel roots here.* She noted that several couples still sat in the same pews they'd occupied fifteen, twenty years ago. *There's a solidity, a continuity that I miss.*

The processional began, and she realized how long it had been since she'd heard and physically felt the rumbling bass of a pipe organ, sung the traditional hymns. It was good, and she found herself wishing her mother could be there too—especially now that she could feel her dad participating, not just observing.

She hadn't recited the Apostle's Creed in years. Together the congregation began, "I believe in God, the Father Almighty, Maker of heaven and earth; and in Jesus Christ, His only Son our Lord."

How full of biblical truth these familiar words are, she thought.

" . . . rose from the dead; He ascended to heaven and sits at the right hand of God the Father Almighty. . . ." *And how especially fitting today to reaffirm,* she said to herself.

". . . I believe in the Holy Spirit . . ."

Oh, I do—to teach me, guide me, she reflected.

". . . and the life everlasting . . ."

Yes, she prayed silently, *and I thank You, Lord—especially for that promise for my dad.*

Even the Sunday message on God's love, taken from 1 John, seemed tailor-made for her. She'd study the passage further, she decided, after she got home.

❧

Later, as Leslie and her father lunched before she left, they chatted easily, comfortably, laughing together over times past.

"Remember how you'd take me, all by myself, shopping downtown at Field's for Mother's Christmas gift?" she asked.

"Yes, and we'd stop for a treat, and it would be twenty below, and I'd suggest hot chocolate, but you always wanted a chocolate ice cream soda."

"Darned right. And I seem to recollect that's what you had too. Oh," she recalled, "and remember the Christmas I was going to *die* if I didn't get a sled, and on that shopping day—Christmas Eve—I dragged you into the sports department to show you the Flexible Flyer I wanted. You kept a perfectly straight face—and had that sled hidden all along." She smiled. "Where *did* you hide it, Dad? I looked everywhere."

"I knew you would. You were too doggoned smart. It was in Mr. Pratt's garage across the alley. You called him Jack Spratt."

She laughed. "We had good times, Dad."

"Yes we did, and though you don't look as much like your mother as Tracy, you had your Mom's special joy in life." He gazed at her a moment. "Still have that?"

"Not always," she admitted.

"Not at home?" he asked.

"Not much."

"You know about the frog in the pot of water on the stove? The heat increases so gradually, he doesn't even feel it till he's stewed."

"You think I'm getting cooked?"

He raised his frosty eyebrows. "Is your marriage getting better, staying the same, or getting worse?"

She sighed. "Worse."

"Leslie, we men are a stubborn lot. We like to play king. We tend to get away with what we can get away with. It can escalate. We really need a woman to say, 'Stop!' when we get out of line. That's not being a bad or rebellious wife. It's being a partner and a true helper."

She smiled. "Are you and Mom in cahoots?"

"I don't have an agenda, Leslie. God's at work in your life.

But—don't sell yourself short, dearest one. You are a beautiful, capable, intelligent young woman." He winked. "I just wish—those bangs—I'd like to see more of your lovely face."

She threw up her hands. "You *are* in cahoots. Not with Mom. It's you and a young patient of mine."

⟳

Leslie was still smiling when the plane took off for California that afternoon. She looked down on the fertile fields, purple in the waning sun. "Good roots," she said. "Sustaining roots. Oh, Lord, You give so much more than we think or ask!"

26

DURING HER FLIGHT BACK, WHEN THE ATTENDANTS BEGAN
serving beverages, Leslie suddenly realized she'd never even
thought about drinking anything alcoholic at her dad's. *Mom's
right. It's only when I'm with Charles,* she thought.

"Oh, Lord," she whispered, her head turned toward the
window, "You tell us there's no temptation from which You
won't provide a way of escape. I *don't* want to be caught up in
this—I guess it must be a stronghold. I don't want to use the
wine to temper my pain or to mask the issues anymore. Please
help me. You've promised that when I'm weak, You will give me
strength. I need it, to withstand Charles."

She tilted her seat back and slipped from prayer to napping
and back to prayer most of the way home. *What a great way to
fly,* she thought as she meditated on all the implications of
unconditional love. *How gracious of You, Lord,* she prayed, *to*

give me an earthly picture of Your heavenly love. How good to know that neither my dad in Chicago nor You, my Father in heaven, require me to earn Your love. It truly is a love with no "gottas." And it's so freeing! I don't have to work and work and fret and fret over whether what I've done is enough. I think for the first time I'm beginning to understand the meaning of the word, Abba, that I know means "Papa," or "Daddy." I'm getting a glimmer of what it can be to have that intimate relationship, in which You, Abba, put Your arms around me, hold me, keep me safe and secure, listen to me, whisper in my ear. Oh, thank You, Father, for these new beginnings!

It was only as the plane landed that she wondered if Charles would be there. She'd posted a note with her dad's phone number and her return flight number and arrival time on the refrigerator. But Charles hadn't actually said he'd come. She probably should have asked her mother to come get her.

In the airport she pressed past other passengers being greeted by friends and relatives. He'd never meet her inside the airport, she knew. But would he be outside? She took the escalator downstairs, and just as she stepped through the automatic doors, she saw Charles's gray Toyota pull up to the curb.

He got out of the car, smiling, and gave her a warm kiss. Not quite like the couple she'd seen by the Bronco when she'd left, but a definite improvement over the immovable cheek she'd pecked on her way out of the car.

He'd already had a drink, she noted. He opened the car door for her, closed it, and put her bag in the trunk. He concentrated on traffic as they emerged from the darkness of the airport structure into the sunlight. When they were safely on the San Diego Freeway, he said, "Did you eat on the plane?"

"No," she said. "Dad and I had a late lunch."

"Well, then, shall we go somewhere and have a bite? Zoë will not bring the kids home for another hour or so."

Charles, taking her to a restaurant? Amazing! Even fast food would be an unexpected pleasure.

"I heard about a diner that has chocolate sodas," he said.

"What a coincidence," she said. "Dad and I were talking about chocolate sodas this noon."

"They are difficult to find these days. We could split something and have room for the sodas."

Of course. Ever the money-manager. "That would be really nice, Charles," she said.

She was relieved to see that there was no beer or wine on the menu at the diner. They shared a plate of pasta, which indeed, was ample for two.

As he meticulously twirled the strands on his fork, Charles asked, "So how did you find your father?"

"Quite well. Better than I expected."

"Aha. Would you say he is making a good recovery?"

"Yes. And, Charles, he's softened. The Lord has obviously been at work in his life." She was afraid she'd become teary again if she told him all that had happened. "He expressed a lot of love. It was a good time for me."

"I remember him as a bit of a curmudgeon. Maybe a rather accomplished curmudgeon. You always seemed to be walking on eggs with him, trying to accommodate him."

She stared at him. Charles had just described life with himself. "Maybe," she said. "But not now."

"Perhaps that will help your self-confidence."

Charles doesn't have a clue, she thought, *about what he does to my self-confidence.*

He interrupted her thoughts. "Leslie, please don't cut your pasta. Twirl it. That is the correct way."

She knew that. She'd just become preoccupied with their conversation. She considered replying, "Yes, Ms. Vanderbilt," but instead asked, "How did your studying go?"

"Quite well. But I still have the material on actuarial math to cover, and it is a bear." He looked at his watch and sighed. "Just ten more study days."

"You'll do it," she said confidently. "I'll try to keep things down to a dull roar. I heard about a fellow who studied for his bar exam in San Francisco by riding the BART from one end of the line to the other, again and again. He said he could concentrate better there than at home."

"I can understand that," Charles said. "Oh, here are our sodas." He looked at them and then held up his hand to the waitress. "Oh, miss, no, no, no! I did *not* ask for chocolate ice cream. A chocolate soda is properly made with vanilla ice cream and chocolate syrup."

The teenager gave him a puzzled look from beneath purple-lidded eyes. "Okay." Picking up the tall glasses once again, she took them away.

"Can you believe that?" Charles said to Leslie in ringing tones. "What a stupid girl!"

"I think we're seeing a little generation gap, Charles."

"I think we are seeing poor training." His face turned sullen. "I hope they use enough chocolate syrup. And enough ice cream," he said. "I should have asked."

"It'll be fine," she said.

"We shall see."

She could sense Charles tuning up for a battle. But when the sodas came, they were dark with chocolate syrup, brimming with vanilla ice cream.

"Perfect," Leslie said as she took her first sip.

Charles took a long drag on his straw and spooned ice cream

into his mouth, adeptly missing his moustache. "Quite good, I must admit."

~

"That was a treat, Charles," Leslie said as they drove into the garage.

"You are welcome." He looked into his rearview mirror. "I believe our peaceful interval is about to end."

Looking back, Leslie saw her mother's car and hurried out of the garage to hug Scott and Michelle. "Missed you!" she said as she put an arm around each of them and walked toward the door.

"Missed you too, Mom," she called over her shoulder. "Come on in. I'll put on some coffee."

"Ah, Mother Lang, thanks for putting up with the kids. Yes, do come in," Charles said, kissing her on the cheek.

Zoë hesitated. "Just for a moment. I really am eager to hear about—Chicago."

The kids were both talking at once.

". . . and Gram is coming to my next swim meet," Scott exclaimed.

And Michelle was telling about ". . . this neat girl from church that Gram knows real well. We never stopped talking the whole day."

"I want to hear all about it," Leslie told them. "Just let me talk to Gram for a minute, hmm?"

Zoë and Leslie sat down together on the sofa in the living room. "The leaves are off the trees in Chicago already, Mom. They had an early cold snap and rain with heavy wind."

Zoë smiled. "And how was the weather in Evanston?"

"Sunny." Leslie took her mother's hand. "You were right. I have such a lot to tell you. Mom, Dad was just wonderful."

Zoë looked heavenward. "Thank You, Lord." She smiled at Leslie. "That's all I need to hear right now. We'll do lunch."

"Only if it's lamb with sun-dried tomatoes."

"Listen to this spoiled daughter!" Zoë stood. "You know the standard mother's reply."

"We'll see!" Leslie answered.

They hugged. "Mom, thanks for urging me to go to Dad's. You were right. But then, what else is new?"

Zoë kissed her fingers and touched them to Leslie's lips. "I love you. I'll call you. I'll just go tell Scott and Michelle good-bye. They were great."

Leslie followed her mother to the family room and watched her hug Scott.

"Thanks, Gram," Scott said. "Neat time."

"Good. I'll see you at your meet Saturday," Zoë promised.

She turned to Michelle. "Those were excellent waffles you made, young lady. Better than mine."

"Oh, *sure*." Michelle eyed her dubiously.

Zoë held up her hand. "Scout's honor."

"Thanks for introducing me to Carrie, Gram. She thinks I should come to the junior high retreat this month."

"Well, talk to your mother and dad. Maybe that could work."

"Yeah. I will. Thanks, Gram. Love ya."

After she walked Zoë to the door, Leslie came back to the kids. "So it was a good time?"

"Really!" Scott said. "Gram really understands kids. She says it's because she never grew up." He frowned. "'Course, she did. But she hasn't forgotten how it feels to be a kid."

"Yeah," Michelle agreed. "She musta figured I'd be major bored after the first day, so she had this cool girl—Carrie—over for lunch. She doesn't go to my school, but she's just my age, and man, we never stopped talking. I mean, we just really hit it off about *everything*. And we laughed at more crazy stuff!"

"Great! You two plan to get together again, then?" Leslie asked.

"Uh-huh. Um, I explained I'm grounded. But she could ride her bike over here, y'know. And Mom, there's a junior high retreat up in the mountains in two weeks. I think I'd like to go if it doesn't cost too much."

"Sounds good. Get me some details." *Careful not to sound too excited,* Leslie exulted silently. *A new friend who'd actually created enthusiasm in Michelle over a church retreat! Hallelujah!*

As she went to bed that night, Leslie thought, *Thanks to this weekend, and the way the Lord worked, I'm not the same person anymore. I have a new relationship with my dad, a new relationship with my Abba. In Him I'm stronger. And I know our marriage can be stronger and better too.*

꒰

On Tuesday Leslie and Zoë lunched together, and her mother brought the lamb sandwiches.

"No wonder I'm spoiled," Leslie said. "I brewed some chocolate almond decaf for 'dessert.'"

"Lovely. Now, tell me about Evanston."

Leslie gave her the full rundown.

"That pleases me so much—both for you and for him," Zoë admitted. "I prayed for reconnection."

"And that's what happened. But even more, Mom, it's made me so aware of God's unconditional love."

Zoë nodded. "Agape. I just finished leading a study on agape love. You might want to look at it."

"I would. But first I'm going to get myself to the support group tomorrow night. I had to work late last Wednesday, getting ready to go to Chicago. And I promised Michelle—and myself—I'd go."

"I'm glad."

"But I was wondering something, Mom. On the way home from Dad's, I was praying and I felt like I really want to start journaling my prayers each day. You've told me how you do it, but would you run it past me again? Don't you start with a review of the previous day?"

"Right. You know I got all this from our pastor, who got it from a writer named Gordon MacDonald. So first thing I write, 'Yesterday,' and I do a little rundown of what I did, what happened. Then I rate the day on a scale of one to ten in three areas: spiritual, physical, emotional. This might sound too much like a formula, but . . ." she gave a rueful smile . . . "Sometimes looking at the previous day propels me right into confession. I see where I really got off track. But normally I begin my prayers with praise. You know the ACTS acronym?"

Leslie nodded. "Adoration. Confession. Thanksgiving. Supplication."

"Right. That's the general pattern, though if something's burdening me, I may run straight ahead with supplication or asking. But now the most important part. It's listening."

"That's it? You just listen? Don't say anything or write anything?"

Zoë shook her head. "I just wait on the Lord for—oh, I don't know—several minutes. I never hear an audible voice, but often some idea or message comes—something that clearly isn't my own thought. Sometimes it's a scripture. Sometimes it's a picture—something visual." She paused. "And sometimes there's nothing at all."

"I'm going to start tomorrow," Leslie decided. "If I get up earlier—yes, that's the only way it'll work."

That night Leslie set a timer to go off at 5:45 the following morning and put it on her nightstand. The next day she managed to catch the timer on the second beep, and Charles barely stirred.

Alone in the family room she took a loose-leaf notebook and began her first day of journaling. When she'd finished her time of asking, which included a prayer for Charles's salvation as well as his preparation for his exam, she opened her old King James Version to the fourth chapter of 1 John, the basis for the sermon she'd heard with her dad on Sunday. She began reading at verse 7. "Beloved, let us love one another, for love is of God; and everyone who loves has been born of God and knows God." It continued, "He who does not love does not know God, for God is love. In this the love of God was manifested toward us, that God sent his only begotten Son into the world that we might live through him. In this is love: not that we loved God, but that he loved us and sent his Son to be the propitiation for our sins."

She closed her eyes. "Oh, Lord, that *is* love. I learned Sunday that *propitiation* means satisfaction. Jesus paid the price for our sins, and it is finished and You are satisfied. Thank You, Father!" She sat a moment. "Now I just want to come into Your presence and listen to You."

She heard only the clock ticking, and it went on for what seemed an eternity. Yet she felt so comfortable, so content, that she stayed. And gradually, six words seeped into her consciousness. *Leslie, I am satisfied with you.*

She exhaled slowly and felt tears seep from her eyes. "Oh, Lord, just as I am, right? Thank You for that! Thank you!" she whispered. She lingered there, not wanting to move, till she heard the shower running upstairs.

When the family gathered for breakfast, Leslie wondered if her face was shining like Moses' when he came down from the mountain. Charles was silent, preoccupied, and said little as he ate. Thinking economics, finance, figures, she decided. When she mentioned that she'd need to leave the house at 6:45 for a meeting at church that evening, he simply said, "Hmm."

But after he left for work, she went to the kids. "Michelle, I promised you I'd go to the support group at church, and tonight's the night. I really need your cooperation—and yours too, Scott. Your dad's in the homestretch of studying for his exam. Can I count on you to stay out of his way and not disrupt him in any way while I'm gone?"

"I'm not *about* to get him riled up," Scott said.

"Me either," Michelle promised.

☙

Leslie went to work on such a spiritual high that day she couldn't wait to share it with David during his ten o'clock appointment.

"Man, you look great!" he said as he wheeled into the gym. "New vitamins?"

"New time with the Lord," she said. "I started journaling my prayers this morning and spending some listening time. It was—*wonderful.*"

"I can tell. Your face is shining."

She looked at him carefully. "You okay?"

"Great," he assured her, heading for the parallel bars. He took a couple of steps with Leslie and Brynne standing a few feet away. "You're doin' so well, David, pretty soon you'll put us out of business," Brynne said.

Suddenly, his knees began to shake. He tried to press up

with his arms, muscles bulging, but his knees and hips buckled. Leslie and Brynne reached out for him, trying to grab his arms, but he fell, landing on his rear end.

"What happened?" Brynne cried.

"My legs just gave way." He sat, stunned.

"Does anything hurt, David?" Leslie asked, trying to keep the panic out of her voice. *How could I let this happen?* she screamed inwardly.

He wiggled his legs. "No. But man!" he exclaimed. "What's that all about? My legs suddenly turned to noodles. What's goin' on anyway?"

"Maybe you have a bug coming on or something," she said, trying to hide her anxiety.

"Yeah, but remember Monday, my legs went weak on me for a minute, and I couldn't get my balance?"

She nodded. "Let's have you rest awhile and then do muscle testing. Can you get into your chair?"

"Yeah, I think I can at least do that."

She put the chair behind him, and he was able to lift himself in. He sat, head down, taking deep breaths.

Leslie waited a bit then said, "Okay, let's go over to the mat."

When he'd transferred to sit on the mat, Leslie knelt next to him. "Okay, straighten your knee. Hold it there." She pressed down on his knee. "Now match my pressure. Resist against it. Relax. Okay. Now lift your leg. Hold it there. Resist my pressure." She continued testing him in a variety of positions.

"Whacha think?" David asked, his voice anxious, face intense. "Level with me."

She had to be honest. "It looks as though, for some reason, your hip and knee muscles have weakened. I'll retest you tomorrow if you'll go home and stay in bed the rest of the day."

"And if it's the same?" He frowned.

"Then I'll talk with Dr. Scanlon. He may want to do an MRI. It'll show us nerves and muscles, give us an idea of what's going on."

David's head fell forward. "Man, I can't believe this!" he muttered. "I was doin' so good. On my way to skiing double-black-diamond runs." He wiped perspiration off his upper lip. "Now I'll be lucky to go down a bunny slope on a sled." He closed his eyes. "Oh, Lord, please don't let me go back to square one. You wouldn't let me improve this much and then not be able to walk, would You?"

Leslie knelt down beside him, oblivious to whoever might be in the room, and put her hand on his shoulder. "Oh, Lord, You tell us You are Jehovah Rapha, the Lord who heals, and You have been healing David so beautifully. Father, may this be only a temporary setback. May it be Your will to renew David and strengthen him. How does that Scripture go? 'Those who hope in the Lord will renew their strength. They will soar on wings like eagles . . .'"

David continued. "'They will run and not grow weary, they will walk and not be faint.'" He nodded. "Okay, Lord, I'm hopin'!"

"Me too, Father. We pray in the name of Your Son, who loved us and died for us, amen."

"Thanks," David whispered, then wheeled his chair slowly to the door.

After he left and she'd called Dr. Scanlon and faxed him the results of the muscle testing, Leslie sat at her desk and prayed once again. "Oh, Lord, I should have been more careful. Did I get caught up in the excitement of how well he was progressing and press him too soon, bring him ahead too fast? Could I have hurt him? And did he do damage when he fell? Please help us. I'm scared!"

27

⁂

LESLIE DROVE TO PICK UP THE KIDS WITH HER THROAT feeling tight and constricted from the tears that threatened to flow. Again and again, she saw David's legs trembling and failing, his collapse to the mat. *I can't bear to see him crash after progressing so well. Is it all to be taken away?* she wondered. *Was it my fault, being too much in a hurry?*

As she drove Scott to his swim workout, she said, "You may find David a little—um, unsettled this afternoon."

"How come?"

"Remember how he stood and began to walk last week? Well, he tried to stand again today, and his legs just gave way. He fell on his rear end, and we had to help him back into his chair. Evidently there's been a sudden weakening of his leg muscles."

She braked for a stop signal and glanced at Scott.

His eyes looked immense. "But he was doin' so good when I was there!"

"I know. I can't figure what happened."

"Maybe he missed me coaching him."

She smiled. "Maybe so, Scott."

"Well, we gotta pray for him!" he exclaimed. "I know that'll help."

When they arrived at the Y, she switched off the engine, then they turned to one another, and she placed her hand on Scott's.

"Oh, God," Scott prayed, "please help David. He's such an awesome guy, and he's been workin' so hard. This just doesn't seem fair. Please, make this just a little glitch—nothin' permanent. And help him not to feel all bummed out. In Jesus' name, amen."

Leslie gave his hand a squeeze. "That was really a nice prayer, Scott. I prayed with David this afternoon. You know what a great attitude he has with his strong faith. He trusts God." *And that,* she thought, *is what I need to do.*

They walked together to the pool. David gave Leslie a jaunty wave as she settled in a chair with a magazine to wait. Scott went over to him and gave him a high five, and Scott laughed at something David said.

All through the workout she found herself looking up from the magazine, marveling at David's coaching-as-usual determination.

"Hey, you water bugs," he yelled at the six- and seven-year-olds who'd stopped swimming to spit water at one another. "Cut the monkey business!"

And he never stopped encouraging. "Nice arms on the butterfly, Terry. Get that head up out of the water when you breathe on breaststroke. Jack, your kick's poopin' out. Pick it up, pick it up!"

He's going to be okay, no matter what, Leslie told herself.

❧

It was 5:35 by the time they got home, and Leslie knew she'd have to hustle to get dinner on and be out the door for church by 6:45. As she hurried with the beef and rice, she told herself, *I am* not *going to let anything keep me from this meeting.*

Charles thundered in a few minutes before six. "Nobody seems to understand the pressure I am under. My plan was to be home by five, do some studying before dinner," he complained. "No block of time now." He opened the refrigerator door. "We might as well have a drink."

"Oh, honey, I can't have a drink now. Remember, I told you this morning: I have a meeting at church at seven tonight. I'll need to serve dinner soon after six."

He slammed the door shut and turned toward her. "You told me no such thing! Meeting at seven? Ridiculous. Forget it."

She could feel her chest tighten. "No, Charles. I can't do that," she said quietly.

"Selfish bitch!" he exclaimed. "All you think of is Leslie, Leslie, Lesss-lie!" He jabbed his forefinger toward her. "You go out of town and leave me to fend for myself, get my own meals together, do everything around the house, and now you rush me to the dinner table so *you* can get to *your* precious meeting." He grabbed her shoulders. "Watch it, Leslie! You are walking on very thin ice."

She stared at his moustache and said nothing. At last he released his grip and reopened the refrigerator door. She turned back to tearing the lettuce for the salad and heard the squeak of the cork in the wine bottle. "I'll eat when I'm ready," he declared, taking his glass into the family room.

She looked at her watch. She could make it if they sat down for dinner at 6:15. She put the salads, water, and milk on the table, combed her hair, and got herself ready to leave. At 6:14, she called, "Dinner's ready!"

After Scott and Michelle appeared, Leslie went to the door of the family room. "We're sitting down now, Charles," she said.

He didn't look up, didn't respond, but she could see the sullen set of his face.

She joined the kids at the table. "Okay. Would you say grace, please Michelle?"

"Where's Dad?"

"He'll be along. Go ahead, Michelle."

"Thanks, Lord, for all Your blessings. And thank You for the food you've given us. Amen." Michelle looked up. "What's buggin' Dad?"

"He looks mad." Scott's voice held an anxious edge.

"Evidently he didn't hear me when I said I have a meeting tonight," Leslie said.

"He wanted you to drink with him," Michelle said.

She nodded.

Michelle seemed to read her mind. "Don't let him stop you from going tonight."

"I admit I'm a—a little concerned—" She couldn't finish the sentence. She was afraid Charles would take his anger at her out on the kids. Again.

"We'll be okay, Mom," Scott assured her. Then he whispered, "Kinda interesting to see the difference between David and Dad when things don't go right. I mean, it's mega-tough for David right now. And he just acted like nothin' had happened."

"Yes, he did," Leslie agreed. "Do you think part of the difference is that David has the Lord?"

"Yeah. Probably."

After Leslie cleared the salad and entrée dishes and brought in the baked apples, Charles wandered in.

"Oh!" Leslie said. "I'll just give your dinner a zap in the micro."

"Don't bother," said Charles, sounding the martyr. "I'll just eat it cold."

She ignored him and put his plate in the microwave, rinsing dishes and loading the dishwasher while she waited. In a moment she brought him his steaming dinner plate and went back to the sink. 6:45. Now perhaps she could get away.

"My wineglass is empty," Charles announced.

So fill it, she wanted to say, but she didn't want to give him an excuse to be vicious with the kids. Obediently she went to get it, filled it, brought it back to him.

"The problem with the Phillies is their management," he was telling Scott. He swept his hand to one side for emphasis and tipped over his wineglass.

"Now look what you made me do!" he cried to Leslie as the wine spread over the table. "You clean this up!"

"I'll do it, Mom." Scott started to get up.

"No, your mother made me spill it." Charles yanked Scott back into his chair. "She will clean it up."

Leslie gritted her teeth, went to the sink, grabbed a towel, and came back to mop up the wine.

"It's wet under my plate too," Charles complained.

Finishing the cleanup, she shot Michelle and Scott an anxious look. Michelle gave her a tiny nod.

She took the towel into the laundry room, grabbed her purse, and said, "See you later."

"Leslie—" Charles called.

She pretended not to hear him and hurried out the door.

"I thought Charles understood me this morning," she muttered as she drove to church. "I should have repeated myself, been sure he heard me. That was really my responsibility."

By the time she found the support group, hidden away in a windowless meeting room, they'd already begun. She looked at the circle of women of all ages, only one of whom she knew.

"I'm so sorry," she said. "I'm Leslie Harper."

"No problem," said the woman whose cheerful rounded face was framed by tight curls. "I'm Kathy. Fix yourself a nametag and join us."

Scrawling her name hastily, Leslie pulled the gummed backing off the tag and slapped it on her sweater. They waited till she was seated then went around the circle, introducing themselves.

"Now," Kathy said, "we were just starting, and I'd asked the question: How do you know that God loves you? What evidence is there that He does—or doesn't? Mary, you were saying—?"

Leslie glanced around the group. All different ages. One looked like she was only a teenager, and another could easily be a grandmother.

"He's always provided for me," offered a heavyset woman with red hair.

"Good," Kathy said. "What else?"

"He's kept me going when things got tough. Was always with me," another woman said.

"And—and—" began an anorexically thin, dark-haired woman, "He's protected me."

Kathy allowed a silence, then looked at Alice, the one woman Leslie already knew, a woman who'd always looked so put-together, took trips to Greece, Costa Rica. "Alice? I think there's something on your mind."

Alice crossed and uncrossed her legs. "Yes!" she declared.

"I know this isn't what you want to hear, but I'm not at all sure God loves me. I feel like there's been this dark shadow over me all my life. There's been one bad thing after another, starting when my mother died and I was six years old." Her voice grew high and tight, and she frowned and blinked. "I feel like I'm not good enough for Him, that I keep making bum decisions, that He's just given up on me."

"Okay, Alice. Anyone else ever feel like that?"

Two other women cautiously lifted their hands.

"What can we say to them?" Kathy asked. "What evidence is there that God loves them?"

Leslie looked around the circle. Wasn't anyone going to say it? She waited, then cleared her throat. "He sent His Son to die for us," she said, and her voice sounded small and frail.

"Bingo!" Kathy exclaimed. "Romans 5:8 tells us, 'But God demonstrates his own love for us in this. While we were still sinners, Christ died for us.' And 1 John 3:16: 'This is how we know what love is: Jesus Christ laid down his life for us.'" She smiled. "So, you see, the question of whether God loves us or not was settled once and for all on the cross. If He never did another thing for us, Calvary is sufficient proof that He loves us. 'For God so loved the world. . .' Let's personalize John 3:16: For God so loved *Alice,* He sent His only begotten Son. And that Son, Jesus, died for Alice, so that her sins would be forgiven, and she could stand before a righteous God cleansed, just as though she had never sinned." She looked around at the other women who had raised their hands. "Put your name in it, Tina. And JoAnne."

"For God so loved me, Tina, He sent His only begotten Son," the woman in the black sweater said.

"For God so loved me, JoAnne . . ." JoAnne let her voice trail away.

"Good! Let's look at some Scriptures that show us the scope of God's love for us," Kathy said.

She went on to read several Old Testament Scriptures that emphasize God's "unfailing love," noting how many Psalms focus on God's love. "Psalm 136," she pointed out, "gives us a repeated refrain at the end of each verse: 'His love endures forever.'" She looked up. "Forever is a very long time!" She glanced around the group. "You are lovable to God!"

Leslie heard the woman in black let out a soft sigh. Another began to cry softly. *This,* Leslie thought, *is just what God's been showing me ever since Chicago. Amazing, how He fits it all together!*

After a moment Kathy said, "Now, are you getting a different message from anyone in your life?" She held up a forefinger. "Remember, anything we say here stays right here. Confidentiality is essential in this group. So . . . is anyone hearing some things that make you feel unlovable?"

Several women twisted in their chairs.

"Your body language is shouting," Kathy said good-naturedly. "Okay, let's be more specific. Anyone here ever been called names?"

A chubby blonde woman raised her hand. "Tonight it was 'slut.' And 'sloppy pig.' Other times, everything from 'lesbian' to 'holy roller.'"

"'Dummy.' That's one I get a lot," said Tina.

"'I get called, 'Honey,' but you should hear the sarcasm," another woman said.

"Lowlife! . . . Pervert!" came other voices.

And finally Alice said, "I can't repeat the names my husband calls me—not in church. They are wicked, and they cut me to the quick."

There was a murmur of assent.

"Words wound!" Kathy nodded. "Verbal abuse can be more

crippling than physical abuse. The trauma just isn't visible, like a black eye is."

Right! Leslie said to herself, and she saw several others nod.

"All right, then," Kathy said. "So we all know what it is to be called demeaning, insulting, even blasphemous names, to have labels slapped on us. How about having your feelings discounted? Have you ever been told, in a very put-down, critical tone, 'You're too sensitive,'" for instance?"

Leslie nodded. "A lot. The message is, I shouldn't feel the way I do."

"Or how about 'You're always making a mountain out of a molehill'?" Alice asked.

"Or, 'I just can't imagine what you're so upset about,'" the thin woman added.

"And here's a similar one with a little different twist," Kathy suggested. "The big put-down, as in, 'What would *you* know about *that?*'"

Leslie could feel the women's guardedness melt away as they warmed to the subject.

"Yesterday," the blonde woman remembered, "when we had dinner with two other couples, someone asked me about a world news situation. George immediately said, 'My wife wouldn't know about that. She doesn't keep up with current events.' And I'm the one who always turns on the TV news!"

"Yes!" JoAnne agreed. "And my husband refuses to let me have a part in our financial planning because he says, 'You wouldn't understand. You're not good with figures.'"

"Oh, *yes!*" Alice nodded. "'This is too complicated for you, honey.'"

"And when I didn't laugh at an off-color joke the other evening," the woman in black interjected, "Harry said, 'What's the matter, Tina? Don't you *get* it?'"

I'm not the only one! Leslie thought. *I'm not weird! Oh, Lord, there is a lot of pain in this room.*

The discussion continued as Kathy helped the women identify other forms of verbal abuse.

"We'll go into this in more detail next week," she promised, "and we'll begin looking at ways to deal with these assaults. But right now, let's come back to God's love." She looked around the circle, and her face mirrored the earnestness of her voice. "God, who created you, who knows you better than any person in this world, treasures you, calls you 'beloved.' He loves you just the way you are. And—let's look at Romans 8:38 and 39."

The women thumbed through their Bibles. "I have it," one said. "For I am convinced that neither death nor life, neither angels nor demons, neither the present nor the future, nor any powers, neither height nor depth, nor anything else in all creation, will be able to separate us from the love of God that is in Christ Jesus our Lord."

"Right!" Kathy beamed. "Chapter 8 of Romans begins with the statement that there is now no condemnation from God for those who are in Christ Jesus. And it finishes by telling us there is no separation from His love." She allowed that to penetrate. Then, "Remember that this week if you're reviled or belittled or called names. God is truth. He knows you, and He says you are acceptable to Him and He loves you. Let's pray that we would all understand that. Let's pray as Paul prayed for the Ephesians in chapter 3 of the book of Ephesians. Choose a partner, and pray verses 17 to 19 for one another."

Alice gestured to Leslie and crossed the circle to sit next to her. They opened their Bibles and took turns praying the Scripture for each other.

Leslie began. "And I pray that you, Alice, being rooted and established in love, may have power, together with all the saints, to grasp how wide and long and high and deep is the love of Christ, and to know this love that surpasses knowledge—that you, Alice, may be filled to the measure of all the fullness of God."

Alice repeated the prayer, using Leslie's name.

The room was silent. Then Leslie added, "Oh, thank You, Lord, for these prayers. Thanks for this group. Thanks for the focus on You. Father, watch over each woman here. Protect her and keep her in Your love. We praise You and thank You, Father, in Jesus' name."

The women lingered for coffee, all clearly reluctant to leave.

"It's comfortable here," the blonde woman said. "And it's so good to know I'm not the only one. My problem is I just don't want to go home."

"Me either! I just never know what I'm going to get," said the one in black. "It's the uncertainty that's crazy-making. If one of the kids pulls the wrought-iron railing away from the wall, I don't know if my husband will go out and get tools and fix it, or light into me with a five-minute diatribe on what a lousy mother I am."

"Do you notice how much alike we are?" another asked.

"Sure!" Leslie laughed. "We have a common antagonist."

"Foxhole buddies," Alice agreed, hugging the two women next to her.

As she drove home, Leslie reviewed the evening. What a relief to know she wasn't alone, that other women suffered from emotional and verbal assaults. But it was more than that. "God loves me," she said aloud. "He made me. He knows me better than anyone." She gave herself an affirmative nod. "He knows—and I know: I am not a selfish bitch."

28

꒰

From Zoë's Prayer Journal

November 7: Good morning, Lord. Again, I thank You for answering my prayers for Leslie and Benjamin way better than I dreamed or asked. I'm so grateful both for Benjamin's new relationship with You and for his new relationship with his daughter. And for Leslie's new understanding both of Your love and her dad's. And now I thank You that Leslie finally made it to the support group and is strengthening her new perspective in a setting of love and understanding and shared experience. Father, I pray that these women, for whom being torn down is almost a daily experience, may continue to build up one another in love and according to Your will. Thank You for Your love, Father. In Your Son's name, amen.

THE NEXT DAY WHEN DAVID CAME IN FOR RETESTING, HE flashed his typically broad smile. But Leslie could see the tension in his arms as he gripped the wheels of his chair. "I ate six helpings of spinach," he announced. "Figured what was good for Popeye . . ." His smile faded. "Could we, ah, get to it?"

"Of course."

Oh, Lord, she prayed in her spirit, *may there be a difference!*

"Get your bod down on the mat, David," she said.

Leslie repeated the manual muscle testing she'd done the day before.

David shook his head. "No better, huh?"

"Pretty much the same." She put her hand on his shoulder. "I'm baffled, David."

"Yeah." He glanced down at his legs. "They *look* so much better than they did." He looked up at her. "So now what?"

"I'll call Dr. Scanlon. I'm sure he'll want to run some tests." She wanted so much to encourage him. "Hopefully this is a reversible problem. For sure, I'll be praying it's just temporary."

"Me too!"

That afternoon David phoned her. "Dr. S. called," he reported. "I'm scheduled for an MRI Monday morning."

"Good." She nodded. "I think this is important. It'll show us what's really happening."

"Yeah." His voice sounded tentative. "I'm not sure if I want to hear."

"Yes, you do," she assured him. "Then we'll know where to go from here."

He was silent a moment. "I hate those MRI machines."

"Think of it as the tube of a wave. You told me how you loved to look through that tube when you're in it, body-surfing."

"Yeah. Good idea." More silence. "I don't know how long it will take to get the results."

"But you'll let me know as soon as you do."

"Sure. Um . . ." He seemed to want to prolong the conversation, and she could see her next patient would be ready for her soon.

"Yes?" she asked.

"Um, I think Scott's improving already. Hope we can keep his dad off his case."

"Me too. This is the last weekend before his actuary exams, so Charles may not come to the meet tomorrow."

"That would be better for Scott."

"I agree. David, we're all praying for you. My mom, Scott, and you know I am."

"I do. I can feel it. Thanks. Have a great day in the Lord."

"I will. You too."

☙

Charles was already home when she arrived that afternoon.

"You look glum," he said as she came in the door.

"Oh," she said, surprised he'd noticed. "Guess I'm concerned about David. He wasn't any better today. Has his MRI Monday, and hopefully, that'll tell us what we need to know."

Charles's eyes narrowed. "Strikes me you have an inordinate amount of interest in this young man."

She stared at him. "What do you mean?"

"Listen to yourself, Leslie. Again and again I hear, like a broken record, 'David, this,' and 'David that.' Never have I heard such tedious detail about a single patient."

She thought a moment. "Perhaps not. But remember, I'm involved with him on two levels. Both as a PT and as the mother of a boy he coaches. So I probably know him better than I know some of my other patients."

"No," Charles persisted. "It's the way you look when you talk about him." He stroked his moustache thoughtfully. "What is going on here, Leslie? Hmmm?"

I will not put up with these innuendoes, she thought.

"Charles, what are you trying to say? David is a kid! He's almost young enough to be my son."

Charles gave a knowing smile. "Well, some women like them young." He paused. "Are paraplegics impotent?" he asked.

"Oh, Charles!" she exclaimed. "Where in the world did you get such a sick idea? I will not stand here and listen to this."

She started up the stairs, but he grabbed her arm and pulled her back.

"Charles!" she shouted. "You're hurting me!"

"Mom?"

They turned to see Scott at the top of the stairs. He looked from one parent to the other, a frown of puzzlement and concern creasing his forehead.

"Yes, Scott?" she managed.

"Your mother is busy," Charles snapped. He released her arm, and she could see the imprints of his fingers on it. "She and I are going to sit down and have a drink and talk."

"Uh, okay," Scott said.

"I need to change my clothes," Leslie said. "I'll be right back."

As she ran upstairs, she prayed softly, "Lord, I'm beginning to wonder about Charles's sanity. David and me? What could be more ridiculous? And now what am I going to do? Charles is angry already, and he wants me to have a drink with him. Oh, help me, Lord. Give me Your strength."

She changed to jeans and a turtleneck, and when she came downstairs, indeed, Charles had poured two glasses of wine. She took a soda out of the refrigerator and joined him in the living room.

"What is that?" he demanded, pointing to the soda.

"It's—let's see—" She held up the can and examined it. "It says 'caffeine-free Sprite.'"

"For pity's sake, Leslie, I can read. My point is, I have poured a glass of wine for you."

"I see that, Charles, and I appreciate your thinking of me. But I don't care for wine tonight."

"There you go again! Always, always have to do everything your way. Denying me the pleasure of companionship with my wife."

"But Charles, I'm here. We can talk. What difference does it make if I have wine or Sprite?"

"You have absolutely no comprehension, have you? You simply do not *get* it, Leslie. Lord, what I put up with!" He sat brooding, and the silence weighted the air till Leslie felt stifled.

Perhaps she could distract him with snippets of her day. "Paul, the man who spun out on his motorcycle and a truck ran over his legs . . . and a young diver with a neck problem . . . and a man who—"

"Stop it!" Charles shouted. He picked up her wineglass and set it in front of her. "You will drink this," he ordered.

A scream from the kitchen shattered the tension. "Mom! I've cut myself!" Michelle came into the living room, her hand wrapped in a towel that was staining rapidly.

"Oh, honey!" Leslie ran to her and took her upstairs to the bathroom. Michelle shut the door and shook with silent laughter. Pulling the towel off, she put her hand under the faucet. "Ketchup! Looked real, didn't it?"

"Michelle!" Leslie protested.

"Did you see Dad's face? It was white. I knew *he* wouldn't volunteer to help me. He has this thing about blood." Michelle turned toward the door. "Ow!" she bellowed and shook with laughter again.

"Michelle, I can't believe you would—"

"Well, I could hear what was goin' on, and he was gettin' so mad, y'know. I thought he was gonna start pouring wine down your throat."

Debating whether to chastise her daughter or thank her, Leslie tried not to smile. "Michelle, that was very perceptive and very creative of you. But I don't approve of decep—"

She looked at Michelle's face, red with the effort of containing her glee, and try as Leslie might, she couldn't control herself. Laughter bubbled from her throat. Suppressing it with supreme effort, she heard Michelle choke and break into another barely restrained paroxysm.

They tried desperately to keep the volume down. Tears ran down their cheeks, and they sank helplessly to the bathroom floor. Each time Leslie began to recover, Michelle started afresh, triggering a new outburst from Leslie.

Leslie's ribs ached, and she gasped for breath. At last she stood, dashed water on her face and dampened a washcloth for Michelle. She looked at her daughter, shaking her head. "You are too much!"

"Got ya off the hook, didn't I?"

"Yes." Leslie promised herself she wouldn't laugh, at least long enough to make a point. "But honey, one thing I need to say. You're going to have to trust me to take care of myself. I can't learn not to be a wimp if you keep bailing me out." *But,* Leslie immediately wondered, *would I have given in to avoid an explosion, or could I have been strong?* She wasn't sure.

"Oh, yeah. See what you mean."

"And another thing. Even though you may not agree with him, your father is to be honored. It's not just me saying so. It's God. So in the future please consider that before you decide to deceive him—no matter how good your reason."

"*O-kay.*" Michelle gave an exaggerated pout that quickly evaporated as she reached into the medicine cabinet. More laughter, Leslie knew, was just a breath away. "I'll just put a Band-Aid on. See, I really do have a cut. I didn't lie." She pointed to a small paper cut on her finger. "That's what gave me the idea."

Leslie looked at the tiny cut. "Oh, indeed. This probably requires stitches!"

And they lost it all over again.

At last Leslie said, "I'd better get back in the kitchen or your dad will come knock on the door. Honey, you do get my nomination for an Academy Award."

Michelle bowed. "I accept, and I do want to thank my producer and my psychiatrist and . . ."

Leslie grinned then put her finger to her mouth. "Shh. I'd better get back now. Maybe with this distraction . . . Hopefully, I can just go back and start getting dinner ready."

"Man, I'll be glad when his exam is over," Michelle said. "Dad's startin' to lose it. You could cut the tension with a machete. If he doesn't pass, I think I'll go be a missionary in Uganda. Couldn't be any worse than hangin' around here."

"Oh, I'm sure he'll pass, Michelle. Your father's a very bright man." But even as she said it, Leslie felt her spine prickle. What if . . . *No,* she told herself, *he will pass.*

She opened the door cautiously, grateful for the cool air, and headed for the kitchen.

She took out the stew that was thawing in the refrigerator. Still hard. It would need some time in the microwave.

"Michelle all right?" Charles asked from the living room.

"Yes." Leslie bit her lip hard to stop that recurring urge to laugh aloud. Shoving the stew into the microwave, she added, "Don't know about you, but I'm starved. I need about fifteen minutes to get dinner ready. The president's on at six-fifteen. Did you want to catch that on the tube?"

"Oh, yes. Matter of fact, I do."

Leslie smiled. *God promises to give us a way of escape from temptation,* she thought. *But who'd think it would be a scheming twelve-year-old? Oh, I suppose I should have been harder on her. But darn it, she is clever.*

꙳

Charles pushed a chair across the linoleum to the kitchen counter and climbed up on sturdy six-year-old legs. In his hand he held a leather belt, a hand-me-down from a cousin. He wanted so much to wear it, but he had a problem. It was too big for him. His grandfather had already put a new hole in it with his pocketknife, but it was still too big. *If I could just get a knife and make one more hole,* he thought . . . He reached over to the knife rack and found a small knife with a sharp point. Now he'd just push it through the leather. But it wasn't easy. He pushed and pushed. Suddenly, the knife slipped and stabbed his left thumb. Blood bubbled from it, forming an arc like the flow from a drinking fountain. It spilled from the counter onto the chair, splashing down to the floor.

He screamed, "Mother!" But his mother was gone. Gone for such a long time.

His grandmother rushed in. "Oh, Charles," she cried, "what have you done? You'll bleed to death."

"I . . . want . . . my . . . mother!" he howled, feeling his life splatter away.

"Charles. Charles! Wake up!"

He heard Leslie's voice, felt her hand shaking his shoulder.

He groaned and reached for her, hanging on with the desperation of a man sinking in deep waters.

"It's okay, Charles," she murmured.

As the panic gradually abated, he eased his desperate embrace slowly, then turned on his back. He couldn't speak. "Another bad dream? Can I do anything for you?" Leslie's voice sounded far away.

He shook his head and lay there, feeling as weak as if he'd lost copious amounts of blood. In a moment he heard Leslie's breathing grow soft and even. After a while he got out of bed and went for a drink of water. *This won't do it,* he thought, even as he turned on the faucet. He turned it off and went downstairs.

Blood, he thought. *Michelle's blood this afternoon.* He swallowed. Now the dream.

Opening the liquor cabinet, he swore softly. All out of bourbon. What else was there? Brandy, and not a very good brandy at that. It would have to do. He didn't bother with a brandy snifter, but poured the amber-brown liquid into a tumbler and took a swallow. The rawness choked him. But in a moment he took another gulp, and another. He leaned against the counter, remembering life at age six.

Of course, he hadn't really bled so profusely. But he did recall crying again and again for his mother, and then remembering she was gone. Gone for his last two birthdays. Gone like his father, whom he'd never known.

He thought back to five years of shuttling from one set of authoritative grandparents to the other, with an uncle and an aunt who were rigid and humorless somewhere in between. He could see their cold, American Gothic faces, the frowns when he laughed. And then, oh, the hope, the joy he felt when his mother wanted him. Wanted him, when he was nine years old, to live with her and her new husband.

Stupid kid. Found out soon how well off I was before, he remembered. His "new dad" was a brute. Charles could still smell the whiskey on his breath, see the veins of the powerful man's forehead standing out blue against his anger-reddened face. And he could feel and hear the slash of his belt, the shakings that made Charles feel like a rag doll, the repeated banging of his head against the wall. Why? Because Charles spilled his milk. Or forgot to shut the door. And sometimes for no reason at all that he could see.

And his mother! Charles slammed the glass down on the counter. She'd said nothing, done nothing. Simply cringed in a corner or covered her face or left the room. Selfish bitch! He drained his glass and pondered what being her son had taught him. Two things, he decided. He had learned what it is to be powerless and what it is to hate.

He emptied the brandy bottle into his glass and drank without stopping till there were only little rivulets on the sides of the glass. These he meticulously licked away. Then he sat on the couch until his tongue felt numb and his face grew slack. Now he could sleep.

29

~

SATURDAY MORNING, SCOTT SHUFFLED INTO BREAKFAST sniffling and swiping at his nose with a well-used tissue.

"Oh, honey, do you have a cold?" Leslie asked.

"Yeah," he nodded. "Started in the middle of the night."

"Bummer," Michelle said. "Now you'll hafta miss the swim meet."

Charles looked up from his newspaper. "Miss the swim meet? Here, let me feel your forehead."

Scott leaned forward, and Charles reached over to touch him.

"No," Charles declared, "you do not have a fever. You will swim."

"But Charles," Leslie protested, "do you think it's wise for him to be getting in and out of the water and sitting outside between events? It's November. It's only 55 degrees this morning."

"I assume the pool is heated to—oh, probably eighty-five degrees?"

"Seventy-nine or eighty," Scott answered.

"There!" Charles smiled triumphantly. "Warmer than this room. Scott, you will swim." He turned to Leslie. "Now, please spare me this namby-pamby carrying-on about the temperature and the wind and Lord knows what else. No more coddling, Leslie! This won't hurt him a bit. Why, I walked to school in pouring rain when the temperature was just above freezing, and I did not so much as own a raincoat. I did not catch pneumonia, and neither will Scott."

"But Charles, you know how Scott tends to get bronchitis. Remember last year? It went on for months, and . . ."

"Leslie!" Charles's voice rose. "*Shut up!*" He looked at Scott. "There is also a matter of loyalty to the team. Now eat your breakfast and get ready to go."

Leslie crumpled and uncrumpled her napkin. She could feel Michelle watching her. *I've seen Charles dig his heels in before,* she thought, *and he's not going to change his mind. Especially now. If I try to go against him on this, Charles is likely to take Scott to the meet himself—and be angry about that.* She looked at Scott, dutifully eating his cereal. *Well, he doesn't have a fever. It could be an allergy,* she told herself. *Maybe I do coddle him too much.* Scott sneezed and blew his nose.

Leslie glanced at Charles and recognized the rigid line of his mouth, the steely set of his eyes. Mulish resolve.

Michelle saw it too. "Can I come with you?" she asked.

She doesn't want to be home alone with her dad, Leslie realized. "Do you mind, Scott?" she asked.

"That's okay."

Good, she thought. *The three of us can do something together after the meet, leave Charles to his studying.*

Later, as they started for the meet, she was half-tempted to go somewhere else instead. But Scott assured her, "I'll be okay, Mom. It's just sniffles."

"I brought extra towels," she said. "And you have two sweatshirts with hoods. Just do me a favor and try to stay out of the wind, honey. We sure don't want a repeat of last year. You felt rotten for so long."

"I'll be fine." He thought a moment. "I just hope we do good for David. To cheer him up, y'know."

"He'll be happy just to have you do your best," she assured him.

While the swimmers warmed up, Leslie and Michelle took a short walk, returning to the pool just as Zoë arrived.

"Thanks for coming, Mom." Leslie hugged her. "But isn't Saturday a workday for you?"

"Well, it is," Zoë admitted, "but I can stay for part of the morning till I have an open house. I promised Scott, and I really wanted to come." She gave Michelle a hug. "I'm so glad to see you, dear heart. What did you decide about the retreat?"

"Well, I want to go, but I've gotta ask Dad, and he's not in a very good mood. If I sign up by tomorrow, I save fifteen dollars. If I wait, it costs more, and registration might be full."

"I'd really love for her to go, Mom," Leslie said. "Better start prayin'."

"I already am." Zoë stood near the pool, watching Scott warm up. "This is so good for him, isn't it?"

Leslie gave her a rueful smile. "I hope so. He has a cold, but Charles insisted he should swim anyway."

"Insisted is right," Michelle added.

"Do you think it's wise?" Zoë asked Leslie.

"No."

Zoë nodded. "Like that, eh?"

"He's gettin' weirder and weirder the closer his test comes," Michelle noted.

"Oh, Lord, protect Scott. Keep him warm and safe," Zoë murmured.

They sat down together, and Zoë looked first at Leslie, then at Michelle. "I wonder how many other swimmers have three generations of rooters. Let's do it all together when he gets on the block. We'll all say, 'Go, Scott, go!'"

The meet began, and when Scott stepped up for the freestyle, the three of them chorused their cheer. He looked straight ahead, but none of them missed the pursing of his lips as he tried not to smile. He finished fourth, and Zoë shouted, "Way to go, Scott!"

"He's also swimming backstroke today," Leslie noted. "Not his best event, but that's okay. Good experience."

"Right," Zoë said. "I think he's improved a lot in this short time. And isn't that David good with the kids? I've been watching. He is adorable."

"That guy gettin' ready to swim right now is a hunk," Michelle interrupted.

"He is," Zoë agreed as she looked toward the boy with the mature build standing at the third lane. "Maybe you should take up swimming, too, Michelle," she teased.

"Naah," Michelle said. "Too much like work."

Zoë laughed but stopped as she glanced to her left. "Don't look now, but Charles is here."

Leslie exhaled sharply. "I didn't think he'd come. But—oh, I see—he's checking up." She stole a quick look. "I hope Scott doesn't see him."

Zoë looked at her watch. "I'm going to have to leave before backstroke. Maybe I can distract Charles and keep him from going over to Scott. See you later."

Mom to the rescue, Leslie thought as her mother made her way over to Charles. Soon Leslie could see an animated conversation. Charles gestured and laughed. How charming he could be—with everyone but his immediate family. They talked until the nine- and ten-year-old boys backstroke was announced. Then Charles moved closer to the pool.

The race began, and Leslie could see Scott flagging after the turn. *He doesn't feel well,* she thought.

He finished last. She glanced anxiously toward Charles, just in time to see him turn abruptly and head toward the parking lot. Good. At least he wouldn't bug Scott now.

When the meet ended, Michelle said, "Meet you at the car," and hurried over toward the swimmers.

How nice, Leslie thought. *She's going to talk with Scott.* Leslie started toward the car then decided to talk with David. As she headed toward the team, she saw her daughter smiling, tossing her copper-colored hair back as she talked with the "hunk." She definitely had his undivided attention.

Leslie shook her head. *Is it safe to take her ANYWHERE* she wondered.

David was busy talking with two other parents, but she caught his eye and pressed her hands together, as in prayer. He nodded and mouthed, "Thank you."

↷

After the meet they went to the mall for pizza.

"I didn't know you knew Larry MacAdam," Scott said to Michelle.

"I didn't. She gave a smug smile. "But I do now. Is he really only thirteen?"

"Almost fourteen. Isn't he a great butterflier? He's been competing since he was five."

Michelle laughed. "Yeah. I was really impressed with his *swimming.*"

Scott cocked his head quizzically.

"His bod, Scott. Haven't you noticed his bod?"

"Oh, yeah," Scott murmured.

"When's your next meet?" Michelle's green eyes gleamed mischievously, and Leslie didn't miss it.

"Two weeks," Scott said.

"Hmm. Same weekend as the retreat. Maybe I'll come here instead." Michelle turned to Leslie. "Dad's not going to let me go anyway, y'know. I really need to ask him tonight, and the state he's in, fat chance! You *know* he's going to have a cow about the bucks."

I do not want her staying home just so she can flutter her eyelashes at this "hunk," Leslie thought. *But she's right. Now, with Charles's exam just days away, is not the time to approach him about something that costs.* "How much is it?" she asked.

"A hundred ten dollars if I sign up tomorrow. One twenty-five after that."

"Let me think about it, Michelle," she said.

They spent the rest of the afternoon in the mall, arriving home in time for Leslie to prepare dinner.

When Charles came downstairs at 5:30, she decided not to mention seeing him at the swim meet. "How'd your studying go?" she asked.

"Quite well, really. I believe I am beginning to feel more confident."

"Good. We're having chicken and dumplings tonight. Thought you could use some comfort food."

"Very nice. I'll pour some wine." He got out two glasses.

He never gives up, she thought. "Pour for yourself, Charles. I'll get what I want."

"I'll get what I want," Charles mimicked her in a high

falsetto. But he poured one glass, taking it into the family room to watch the end of the PGA tournament. "Incredible control," he noted as she joined him in time to see a perfect putt. "I do admire that man's composure."

She went back and forth to the kitchen, adding the dumplings to the chicken, making the gravy. Charles came into the kitchen once to refill his wine glass and gave her a kiss. "This takes some doing, doesn't it? Nice of you to fix my favorite dish," he said.

She watched him pour, surprised at his congeniality. Maybe they'd actually have a relaxed meal together.

Upstairs she could hear Scott coughing. Not a good sign. When she called him to dinner, his face looked flushed, his eyes dull.

"You don't look so hot, Scott," she said.

"Yeah." His voice sounded hoarse. "Well, I'll be okay."

As they sat down at the table, he was racked by coughing fits.

"Cover your mouth, Scott," Charles ordered. Then, "Why don't you trade places with your mother, instead of sitting right next to me? I don't want to be sick for my exam."

Nice to see such tender concern, Leslie thought. *Wonder how long it'll take him to lay into Scott about the meet.* She was surprised that he remained pleasant till she brought in the lemon pudding.

"What happened to you on the backstroke today, huh, Scott?"

Scott's head jerked back, and he winced. "You were there?" he rasped.

"Yes, I was there. So what happened?" Charles persisted.

Scott looked away from his father. "I dunno. I just felt tired. Like I was swimming through glue."

"He wasn't feeling well, you know," Leslie interjected—and immediately regretted it.

Charles pointed his index finger at her. "I am not addressing you, Leslie. Please have the common sense and good manners not to interrupt."

"I really think, Scott," Charles paused to wipe his moustache with his napkin, "that if you can't do any better than last place, you should discontinue this pathetic effort."

Leslie saw Scott's chin quiver and feared that if he broke into tears, he'd earn Charles's further contempt.

"Hey, hey, Dad!" Michelle's green eyes flashed. "Scott's only been on the team a month."

Charles turned to her and gave her a withering look. "What I said to your mother applies to you, too, Michelle. I am not speaking to you. You may be excused."

"Good idea!" Michelle muttered, leaving the table.

Scott broke into another paroxysm of coughing.

Charles gave him a disdainful glance. "Perhaps you should leave, too, Scott, and take your germs elsewhere." He turned to Leslie. "Have him sleep downstairs tonight. I don't want to listen to that trained seal act all night."

I will be so glad when this exam is over, Leslie thought as she loaded the dishwasher. Then things will be better. But in the meantime, the decision on Michelle's retreat can't wait. And I know what to do.

But first she found a thermometer and went to Scott, who was lying on the couch in the family room.

"Open up," she said, and popped the thermometer in his mouth. While she was waiting, she smoothed his hair back. "Scott, your dad is irritable because of the exam coming up. I don't think he really meant it about you quitting the swim team. You really shouldn't have been in the water today. But the point is *not* whether you come in first or last or somewhere in between. David is well pleased with you. And I am well pleased too."

Scott nodded.

In a moment she took the thermometer. "Uh-huh."

"How much?" he asked.

"Would you believe a hundred and twenty?"

"Sure," he laughed.

"It's a hundred and one. You feel achy?"

"Uh-huh."

"I'll get you something." She went to the bathroom for a Tylenol and a glass of water. "Better push the fluids. You warm enough?"

"Yup."

"Okay. Call me if you need anything." Leslie kissed his forehead and went up to Michelle.

Sprawled on her bed with a paperback, she looked up at Leslie. "Well, anyway part of dinner was almost pleasant."

Leslie nodded. "Michelle, I've been thinking about the retreat. I have a little emergency fund—money I stashed away when we were at Tracy's. It will cover the hundred and ten dollars."

"Really?" Michelle's face came alive, and Leslie thought what a pretty contrast it was to her studied sullenness.

"Really." She smiled. "Unless you'd rather go to the meet."

Michelle thought about it. "Not really."

"Okay. This, for the moment, will be between us. Can I count on you?"

"Well, sure!" She jumped up and flung her arms around Leslie. "Thanks, Mom!"

Leslie left Michelle's room feeling energized. She'd made her own decision—one she knew was good. *My training and my work make me strong physically,* she thought. *But this sense of inner strength is new. And it feels great. After the exam's over, Charles will understand. He won't be so on edge, and with what I'm learning from my support group and with my new trust in God, I'll be able to take a stand for what's good and right. We'll have more of a partnership.*

As Leslie started downstairs, Charles called out to her from his study. "Don't forget about Scott sleeping downstairs tonight. I need my rest."

She rolled her eyeballs, à la Michelle. "I know, Charles."

30

"AND THEY'LL KNOW WE ARE CHRISTIANS BY OUR LOVE, BY our love," the praise group sang. "Yes, they'll know we are Christians by our love."

The Sunday morning service over, men and women brushed past Leslie to leave as she remained seated in the pew. She listened to the words of the song, reflecting the pastor's message, "Love One Another," and wondered, *Do others know I'm a Christian by my love? At work, maybe. But at home? Does Charles?*

DO I love him? She sighed. *Yes, deep down, in spite of everything, I do. But there definitely are times—be honest, Leslie—a lot of times I don't like him. I know I need to be truthful with him, not let him walk all over me, but can I "tell the truth" and do it "in love," as the Bible says? It would have to be an agape love—that unconditional love that's not based on a person's merit or behavior.* She shook her head. *No. Never. Not in my own strength. Impossible.*

She closed her eyes. *But Lord, You tell us all things are possible through You and that if I pray in Your will, it will be done. And Your own Word says to love our neighbor as ourselves. Obviously, Charles is my nearest neighbor, isn't he? I want to be obedient, but I don't even know how to begin. Will You teach me how?*

By the time she rose to leave, the singers were putting away their mikes and gathering their music, and the church was almost empty.

She walked slowly down the aisle and out the door onto the patio, blinking at the brilliance of the sun.

"Mom! Mom!"

Leslie could hear Michelle's shout all the way from the grassy area beyond the pavement. Squinting through the throng gathered between services, Leslie saw her daughter running toward her, a willowy blonde in tow.

"Mom," Michelle repeated as they reached Leslie, "This is Carrie. She's my friend—y'know, that I met at Gram's."

"Carrie." Leslie took her hand and looked into a face that shone with a radiance that seemed to come from deep within. Even her hair glowed with golden highlights in the sun. "I'm so glad to meet you. I've met your mother and dad but not you. You're just as pretty as Michelle said."

Carrie blushed. "Thanks. I'm glad to meet you too, Mrs. Harper."

"Mom, we're both all signed up for the retreat, and it's gonna be so cool!" Michelle lifted her fist high in the air.

Leslie smiled. This was more like the exuberant Michelle she'd known before puberty struck. "I'm glad." She turned to Carrie. "I hope you'll come over to our house before that."

The two girls looked at each other and grinned.

"She's comin' over Tuesday after school," Michelle announced.

"Great." Leslie glanced at her watch. "You ready to go, Michelle? I want to pick up some more cough medicine for Scott. And maybe a movie for him. You can choose what you think he'd like." Seeing the glimmer in Michelle's eye, she added, "No severed heads or buckets of blood."

They said good-bye to Carrie, picked up the prescription and the movie *Aladdin*.

All the while, Leslie wondered how she might show love and encouragement to Charles. Do little things, she decided.

At home Scott was asleep on the couch in the family room, but he roused when they came in.

"Hey, dude, brought you *Aladdin*," Michelle said.

"Cool." Scott's voice was a hoarse whisper. "Dad's been workin' hard all morning," he volunteered.

"Right. And I was thinking it would be nice if we did something to encourage him." She pondered a moment. "What if—" Leslie kept her voice low and conspiratorial. "What if we fixed him something—you know, the day of his exam is going to be a hard day—so what if we put together a sort of survival kit for him? You know, aspirin, antacid."

"Yeah!" Scott said. "Maybe some gum. And Lifesavers."

"That's good. What else?"

"I know. A towel to wipe the blood, sweat, and tears," Michelle suggested. "Or a washcloth would be okay. Oh, and maybe some Wash 'n' Dry's."

"Sure, and how about an energy bar?" Scott frowned. "Or can they take food in?"

"I think not," Leslie said.

"Oh, I've got it." Scott's face brightened. "Some worry beads."

"Cool, Scott," Michelle said.

"Wish we could give him a cross—to remind him to pray," Scott said.

Michelle looked at the ceiling. "*I . . . don't. . . think . . . so.*"

"Okay, let me know if you come up with anything else," Leslie said. "I'll get a little box or a case to put it all in. We can give it to him Tuesday night."

～

At work on Tuesday, Leslie waited anxiously to hear the results of David's MRI. *If he doesn't phone by three, I'll give him a jingle,* she decided. But at 11:30, Terry told her, "David calling."

She ran to her office and grabbed the phone. "What's the news, David?"

"Well, they're going to give me a stronger anti-inflammatory. Dr. Scanlon talked with Dr. Steiner, the neurologist. They think the nerve roots may be swollen, and that's what caused the muscles to weaken—hopefully temporarily—and the medication with bed rest will help.

"That sounds encouraging," she said.

"Well, yeah, but I'm really bummed. I mean, did you catch the bed rest part?"

"Sometimes rest can be the best thing," she offered. "Can you—how does that psalm go? 'Rest in the Lord, wait patiently for Him'?"

"Yeah, yeah, I know!" He let out a big sigh. "Yeah, 'course I can. But somehow I don't feel satisfied. I mean, would just swollen nerve roots cause this sudden weakness? What do you think?"

"It could. You see, nerve roots exit the spinal column like

branches coming from a tree trunk. When they're swollen, they don't conduct messages properly to the muscles. If the swelling's severe, there might be no strength. But you have some strength, so that's encouraging."

"Yeah . . ." He didn't sound convinced.

"David, these things take time to respond. Why not try resting? Give it a week. It can't hurt!"

"No," he said reluctantly. "But man, a whole week! How about—four days?"

"Come on, David!" she exclaimed.

"Okay, five."

"Da-vid!" she exclaimed.

"Yeah, Leslie, but the kids. I need to get back with the kids. They have a meet comin' up in ten days."

"They will survive. I promise you. Look, I'll be praying. And remember, Jehovah Rapha is the Lord who heals."

"Right." He paused. "This is the week your husband has his actuary exam, isn't it?"

"It is."

"I'll be praying for him."

"David, you are a rare bird to remember that in the midst of your own problems. Thanks. I appreciate that." She smiled. "I told Charles I was praying for him, and you know what he said?"

"Let me guess. 'Don't waste your time?'"

She laughed. "Close. 'Suit yourself, but it will not do any good.'"

"Well, that's all *he* knows. Hey, I guess this is one good thing about being beached. I'll have a lot of time to pray for people. I'll let you know if I suddenly get radically better."

"Keep in touch, whatever happens." She hung up, marveling at David's sensitivity and maturity. She thought about the bond she felt with him because of their mutual love of Jesus. She couldn't begin to explain it to Charles. He wouldn't, couldn't understand. But it made Charles's insinuations about her relationship with David seem infinitely pathetic and sad. *Someday Charles will understand,* she told herself. *Someday he'll know the Lord.*

That noon the physical therapy staff held a lunch meeting to plan a "Help for Your Aching Back" seminar.

"It will be good for our existing patients and possibly bring in some new," Terry pointed out.

"I think it's a terrific idea. I'll put together a flier," Leslie offered.

After lunch Terry turned to Leslie. "How's life on the home front?"

"A little tense right now. Charles has his actuary exam Wednesday."

"Pressure with a capital P!" Terry said. She stared at a distant point for a moment. "Would it be helpful if you both had something to look forward to?"

Leslie gave her a tell-me-more look.

"We have a condo in Mammoth, and nobody's using it this early in the season. Would you two like to get away and maybe do some hiking in the Sierra? There isn't any snow around the lakes yet."

"What a spectacular idea!" Leslie exclaimed, remembering her prayer for a way to show love and concern to Charles. "We could use some time alone. You'd do that for us?"

Terry shrugged. "Of course. You and I are long-time friends. And I've only seen the nice side of Charles. He's always been so affable when he's stopped by, or at our center picnic."

Leslie nodded. Mr. Congeniality. "I'll suggest it tonight—no, tomorrow when we give him the survival kit. Thanks, Terry!"

As she headed for her desk, she thought, *This could be a beginning to a new relationship. Pressure off. Time to communicate. Maybe I can get Charles to talk a little about his past. It would be so good for him to stop burying it, share it with someone.*

⁓

Dinner on Tuesday evening was like a silent movie. Charles gazed into space as he chewed, obviously lost in a maze of figures and procedures. Neither Michelle nor Scott seemed to dare to break the hush, and Leslie, too, quelled every impulse to speak except for the essentials of serving the dinner. As they finished their pot pies, she saw Scott and Michelle exchange mischievous glances and worried they'd goad one another on to an explosion of laughter. Better break it up, she thought, sending Michelle to dish up the ambrosia for dessert.

It was only as Charles took his first spoonful of fruit that Scott spoke, and after the long silence, his voice sounded unnaturally loud. "Um, Dad, we got to thinking. You've really worked hard, studying and all. So—" He looked over at Michelle.

"So we put together a present for you." She brought a hinged plastic box out from beneath the table.

"What is this?" Charles inquired warily.

"It's a survival kit. For tomorrow," Scott said.

"Look inside," Michelle urged.

Charles lifted the lid. "Why, look at this. Aspirin, Tums, mints, even gum." He held up the washcloth. "And this?"

"It's to wipe your brow, Dad," Scott explained.

"Oh, of course. And um," he fingered the beads.

"Worry beads. Very calming," Michelle told him.

"Well, now, thank you very much. I shall probably need all of these tomorrow."

"And I have a surprise, too, Charles," Leslie said. "It's a sort of antidote for all the stress." She handed him an envelope.

He tore it open, pulled out a card and read, "This certificate good for one weekend in Mammoth. Preferably next weekend." He stared at it, then at Leslie, his mouth pursed in thought. "There you go again," he said.

She frowned, bewildered. "Wha—"

"Trying to control me, tell me what to do."

"But Charles, I thought you'd enjoy getting away . . ."

He gripped the edge of the table. "My, yes. Of course, I would be filled with delight to get in the car and drive five hundred miles."

"Three hundred and seventy-five," she murmured to herself. She looked across at him. "But Charles, you haven't read it all. What does it say below the words, 'weekend in Mammoth'?"

"Relax and leave the driving to me," he read. He gazed at her and gave an abrupt, joyless, "Ha-ha. *I* am going to relax while *you* drive. Very amusing."

Leslie saw him take a breath to continue, and to her surprise, she found herself standing. "Why don't we talk about it after your exam."

"We will talk about it now, since you brought it up."

"No." Though she felt her legs tremble, her voice remained firm. As she walked toward the hallway, she listened for his footsteps behind her, but she only heard him say, "Your mother always has to have her way."

"Sure," came Michelle's voice. Fortunately Charles didn't seem to hear its caustic edge.

❧

During the night, Leslie heard Charles up four times. "Oh,

Lord," she whispered under the covers, "calm him and give him rest."

The next morning he rose at five, and at breakfast, the only sounds were the clank of spoons on bowls, the crunch of Grape-Nuts. When Leslie kissed Charles good-bye and she and the kids chorused a "Good luck!" he merely nodded and was gone.

During the day, she thought of Charles repeatedly.

Between patients she prayed, *Lord, may it be going well. Give him a clear mind and complete recall of all he's studied.*

That evening, she planned dinner so she could leave by 6:45 to go to the support group at the church. But Charles was not there at six.

Traffic, probably, she told herself. *But if he's really late, do I dare leave? He'll want to talk about the exam, I'm sure.*

At 6:15, she pondered whether to serve the three of them or to wait for Charles. *I'll wait another few minutes,* she decided.

At 6:20, she heard the front door open, and she ran to meet him. "Charles! How did it go?"

He tossed his jacket over the stair railing, and Leslie could see sweat stains on his shirt. He stared at her, his face drawn and pale, etched with lines she'd never seen before. "Terrible," he snapped.

She tried to reassure him. "I always felt that way after exams."

"No, this is different." He shook his head vigorously. "It went very badly." His mouth twitched and he rubbed his hands together. "Just—I don't know—did not study the right things. Could not think straight. Found myself in deep distress on the actuarial math portion."

"Oh, but Charles, it always seems that way when you—"

"Listen to me, Leslie!" he shouted. "It does not just *seem* this way. I am giving you facts. I do not lie or exaggerate. You don't know what you're talking about. I do." He ran his fingers through his hair. "Now, the question is, how did this happen? I thought a great deal about this as I drove home, and it is very clear. One . . ." He began counting on his fingers. "The constant distractions and irritations within the family. Your silly Mammoth idea, for instance, the very night before the exam, broke my concentration. Two, who could possibly concentrate with a wife who constantly overspends, creating a negative cash flow and saddling me with financial burdens? Three, your mother is forever intruding and trying to influence you and the children, as well as me—as if she could!"

The children, she thought. *Oh, I don't want them to hear.* "Charles," she ventured, "let's sit down."

Charles seemed not to hear her. "Four, you, Leslie—" He pointed an indicting finger. "You gave your father higher priority than your husband. You went rushing off to be with him in Chicago, and your husband be damned. Five, my *wife*—" He buttered the word with sarcasm. "My wife is carrying on with a younger man. Six, your stuffy Puritanism won't allow me to unwind in the evenings with a shared glass of wine."

He took a breath, and Leslie could only listen, steeling herself for more. "Seven, you threw a major disruption into my life when you left and took my children with you. Eight, you've insisted I come to 'support' Scott's abysmal swimming performances. Nine, Michelle is a silly, conniving troublemaker. And ten, your prayers are an ineffectual sham."

The heightened color of his face had deepened with each grievance he listed. Now he turned abruptly away from her, grabbed his jacket, and reached for the doorknob. "I am going out, and I will come back when I am quite ready."

She put her hand on his. "Please, Charles. Let me—" She

tried desperately to think of something to keep him from leaving. "Let me pour you a drink."

He shoved her aside, yanked the door open, and stepped out, slamming it shut.

She looked behind her to see Michelle and Scott, eyes like quarters. *Oh, no, they'd heard it all!*

"Poor dad." Scott stared at the door. "We better pray for him!"

"Whoo-boy!" Michelle breathed.

31

*

LESLIE AND THE KIDS STOOD IN THE ENTRYWAY, STARING AT each other. They heard the car door slam and the engine start.

Was there anything she could do? Chase after him and stop him? Hardly. She felt a chill of premonition of some yet-undefined disaster as she looked down and realized she had a death grip on the stair railing.

At last Scott spoke. "Think he really flunked?"

Leslie shook her head. "I gather a pretty high percentage don't pass. He seems very certain."

"What d'ya think he's gonna do?" Scott wondered.

"Get drunk. What else?" Michelle said.

What else, is right, Leslie thought. *If he's going to drink, I wish he'd do it at home. He could be a menace on the streets. How awful if he'd be involved in an accident.* "Look, kids," she said, as much for herself as for them, "Dad sounds really upset right now. But it'll all work out. He'll cool down." She took a deep breath. "Let's see now," she stalled, trying to decide what to do.

"Dinner," Michelle prompted.

"Right." She hesitated. "I'm just not sure what to do about my support group."

"What's to wonder? Go," Michelle said.

If only it was that easy, she thought. *But what if Charles comes back in a rage and takes it out on Michelle and Scott? I can't take that risk.*

She heard Scott clear his throat. "Aren't we forgetting something?"

She gave him a quizzical look.

"We need to pray for dad."

"Oh, Scott." She hugged him, knowing he surely had heard Charles's remark about his abysmal swimming and marveling that her son would still insist upon praying. "You're the only one who's thinking straight."

Michelle made a face as they joined hands in the kitchen, and Leslie shot her a warning look.

"Dear God," Scott began, "Dad's hurtin' and we ask You to help him feel better and also to keep him from any trouble or accident, wherever he's goin'."

"Yes, Lord," Leslie added. "Protect him and comfort him, and use this setback to draw him near to You."

There was a long silence before Michelle finally spoke. "Yeah, heavenly Father, You say You love sinners. Help us to love them, too. Amen."

Leslie squeezed each child's hand and said, "Thanks, gang." Then she served their plates and called Zoë. *Darn, the answering machine.* Leslie waited for the beep. Then, "Mom, it's Leslie. If you get in before, um, seven, give me a call. I wondered if I could possibly drop Scott and Michelle off just while I go to my support group. Thanks."

"Y'think Dad might come back and get ugly?" Michelle asked.

"Probably not. He may not even get home while I'm gone. But I think it will be better this way," Leslie said.

She had just dished up her own plate when the phone rang.

"Hi, darlin'. Mom. What's up?"

"Charles showed up just long enough to say he'd blown the exam."

"Oh, surely not," Zoë said.

"He seemed very sure. Went out again, didn't say when he'd be back."

"You don't want to leave the kids there alone. Very wise. Of course, bring them over. They can help me make white chocolate fudge for a thank-you gift."

"Think that's safe? Think there'll be any left?"

Zoë laughed. "I have enough fixin's for two batches."

"Thanks, Mom. I love you."

She replaced the phone and turned to Scott and Michelle. "You're going to go help your grandmother make white chocolate fudge."

Scott rubbed his hands together. "I think I can handle that."

"Zits. That's what'll happen," Michelle grumbled.

"You don't have to *eat* it, just help make it," Leslie reminded her.

"Yeah, sure," Michelle groaned.

※

When Leslie walked into the support group, she did a double take. "Sandra!" she exclaimed. She'd seen the woman at church but hadn't talked with her since that condemning night with the prayer group two months ago. She could still hear Sandra's dogmatic advice to her: "Be the submissive wife to Charles that God called you to be."

Sandra gave an embarrassed grin. "Fancy meeting you here."

Leslie went over to sit beside her. "You sure you're in the right place?" she whispered.

Sandra nodded.

"But I had no idea, the way you talked to me the last time we met with Norma."

Sandra looked straight ahead, avoiding Leslie's eyes. "Well, now you know it was just talk. I was talking to myself, actually, trying to tell myself everything would be all right with Marvin."

Leslie put her hand on top of Sandra's. "I'm so sorry. But I think you're in the right place."

It seemed an effort for Sandra to look at Leslie. "I hope so."

Kathy settled her ample body in a chair. "All right, let's get started now. Someone feel like praying?"

A woman in a baggy taupe sweater raised her hand. After a moment she began, "Oh, Lord, thank You for the bond we have in Your love and in our circumstances. Please be our guide tonight and help us keep our eyes on You. In Jesus' name, amen."

"Thanks," Kathy said. "We have a newcomer tonight, and her name is Sandra." She smiled at her. "Welcome! I'm Kathy. And on my left is—"

"Alice. Hi."

As each woman introduced herself, Kathy's glance moved around the circle, and the tenderness of her eyes carried an unspoken benediction. "Okay, last week we talked about how much God loves us—so much that while we were still sinners, He sent His Son to die for us. Let's examine the nature of that love a little.

"Remember, we saw in Romans 8:38 and 39 that it is forever, that nothing can 'separate us from the love of God that is in Christ Jesus our Lord.'" She smiled. "Now what else can we say about God's love?"

"We don't have to earn it. It's unconditional," Leslie said, smiling to herself as she remembered her time with her dad.

"Right! We see that in Ephesians 2:4 and 5. 'But because of his great love for us, God, who is rich in mercy, made us alive with Christ even when we were dead in transgressions—it is by grace you have been saved.'"

Kathy looked around the group, a serene little smile on her round face. "But not only that, God's love is adoptive. By that I mean it establishes a relationship in which we are His children and can call Him that most tender of names, 'Abba,' which is like 'Papa,' or 'Daddy.'"

Yes! Leslie said to herself.

Kathy continued, "Ephesians 1:5 tells us God 'predestined us to be adopted as his sons—'" She looked up. "Or daughters, if you prefer." She looked back at her Bible. "—'through Jesus Christ, in accordance with his pleasure and will—'"

A blonde lifted her hand. "I just love that, 'in accordance with his pleasure.' God's actually *pleased* to adopt us!"

Kathy nodded. "Right! Now, how durable is that love?" She turned back in her Bible. "Isaiah 54:10 explains, 'Though the mountains be shaken and the hills be removed, yet my unfailing love for you will not be shaken nor my covenant of peace be removed . . .'"

Kathy grinned. "So don't fret—even if the ground shakes as it does from time to time here in California, His love will not be shaken or removed." She looked around the circle. "What else can we know about God's love?"

"It doesn't let us go?" The responding voice was tentative, unsure.

"Exactly! Listen to what Isaiah tells us in the forty-third chapter. Let's look at it."

In a moment Alice read, "'When you pass through the waters, I will be with you; and when you pass through the rivers, they will not sweep over you. When you walk through the fire, you will not be burned; the flames will not set you ablaze.'"

Kathy waited a moment before she asked, "Anyone feel as though you're passing through deep waters, walking through fire?"

The group exploded in whoops, "yes's" and "You better believe it!"

Throwing up her hands in mock surprise, Kathy laughed, "Imagine that!" Then, sobering quickly, she asked, "So how do we walk through those waters? Tonight I'd like to look at some of our responses to verbal and emotional abuse. But first, why does this abuse tend to paralyze us?"

"Because it so often catches us off guard," the red-haired woman said.

Another agreed, "It comes when I least expect it."

"Because he's so forceful, sometimes so angry, it's impossible to get a word in edgewise," Alice said.

"Because I think it must be my fault. I must have in some way caused it," someone added.

Kathy made notes as the women related a dozen reasons for feeling intimidated and immobilized. When they had finished, she said, "All right, let's address these answers one by one. First, let's consider 'It must be my fault.' Anyone want to comment on this?"

The woman in taupe raised her hand. "When I'm told so often that my husband's anger is my fault, that I'm wrong, I start to believe it."

"Of course you do. It's the same as telling a child again and again, 'You're a bad boy.' After a while he believes it—and acts it! Another thing to remember: We live in a cause-and-effect world. We tend to think, *Oh, my, look at this effect: Harry is angry with me. Then the cause must be me.* Is this always true?"

The woman shook her head. "It might be a fight with his boss."

"Or something that happened on the freeway," offered another.

"Or what his mother said on the phone."

"Right," Kathy nodded. "Or the onions at lunch that didn't agree with him. *Or* something from way back in his childhood. So, please! Ladies! Don't be so quick to take the blame. You don't have to be a scapegoat. Scapegoats, remember, were a part of Old Testament worship. On the Day of Atonement the high priest laid his hands on the head of the goat and confessed the people's sins. Then the goat was led away into the wilderness to die." She looked around the group. "Jesus changed all that. Jesus is our once-and-for-all scapegoat. Think about it. He died for our sins. You don't have to play that role. God doesn't ask you to!"

Leslie exhaled slowly. She'd never seen it that way. Certainly Charles had made her—and the kids—his scapegoat just an hour or so ago. But now—Jesus as our final scapegoat. She'd have to think about it.

Kathy continued, "Now another thing about this idea of our being the cause of the abuse . . . Is whether you're right or wrong the point? Let me ask you, If you made a mistake—say, forgot to take your husband's clothes to the cleaners, would he be justified in beating you up? No. He might be angry, but he has no right to vent his anger in violence. Isn't the same thing true with verbal abuse—that there is no justification for lashing out with angry, demeaning words?" She paused and let the women think about it. "The Bible tells us that adulterers, thieves, drunkards, and *revilers*—that's another name for verbal abusers—will not inherit the kingdom of God. So if you ever might possibly be wrong—" She winked. "—which, of course, you never are—but if you should happen to be at fault, are there other ways for your mate to get his point across? Certainly! Could he simply say, 'I'm upset because I depended on you to get my suit, and I need it'? Believe it or not, some men might actually say, 'No big deal. Could you get it tomorrow?' Or maybe even, 'I'll stop for it tomorrow.'" Kathy glanced around the circle. "Ladies, don't buy into taking the blame. That is a lie. There is *no* excuse for abusive treatment!"

Kathy looked back at her notes. "Now, how about when a man is so forceful, sometimes so angry, it's impossible for you to get a word in, and maybe he goes on and on? What are your alternatives?"

"You have to let him get it off his chest," the blonde murmured.

Kathy let the group think about it. "That's one way," she said carefully. "Is there a better way?"

"Yell back at him?" Alice's voice was so timid, everyone in the room knew she'd never dare. She laughed nervously.

"Do you think that would be fruitful?" Kathy asked.

The women all shook their heads.

Thinking back to the previous evening, Leslie looked up at Kathy.

"Leslie? An idea?" Kathy asked.

She took a deep breath. "Well, yesterday I tried to do something nice for my husband, and it backfired and he shouted about how I always want my own way."

"Excuse me for interrupting," Kathy said. "But is that a familiar phrase? 'You always want your own way'?"

The women nodded and murmured, "Uh-huh!"

"I'm sorry, Leslie," Kathy said. "But I wanted you all to recognize that tactic. Go ahead."

"Well, he was under pressure with a professional exam coming up, and when he lit into me, I said, 'Let's talk about this after your exam.' He wouldn't let go of it, said we *would* talk about it now. And—I don't know where I got the strength. I was really surprised. I said, 'No,' and walked out of the room."

Alice and Sandra both gasped.

"Hooray for you!" Kathy exclaimed. "So you simply removed yourself from the situation." She looked closely at Leslie. "That was hard."

Leslie nodded. "It really was!"

"But it took you out of the so-called discussion and allowed him to cool off. Good. Any comments?"

"I'd be afraid my husband would come after me, madder than ever," the woman in taupe said.

"Or maybe yank me back in the room," the one with red hair said.

"He might," Kathy agreed. "What could we do ahead of time to help forestall that kind of reaction to us when we take a stand?"

There was a long silence. Then Alice timidly offered, "Maybe talk to him beforehand, sometime when he's not mad. Tell him that his angry words hurt a lot, and next time he does it, you will ask him to stop." She shook her head, an expression of incredulity on her face. "Listen to me! That'll be the day."

"Yes," Kathy said, "that *will* be the day. I tell you what. Let's role-play this. Alice, I'll be—what's your husband's name?"

"Harry."

"Okay." Kathy moved her chair close to Alice's, facing her, and sat with her arms crossed. She deepened the pitch of her voice. "Well, now, Alice, you wanted to talk to me?" She stared at Alice.

Alice swallowed. "Yes, Harry. Um . . ." She started to cry and dropped her chin. "I don't think I can . . ."

"Yes you can!" Kathy urged.

Alice looked up and bit her lip. "Harry, when you're angry at me, when you shout and call me names—"

"Names?" Kathy demanded. "What do you mean by names?"

"Well, you know—" Alice looked across the circle, her eyes pleading for help.

"Yes, yes?" Kathy pressured.

"Names like *slut* and *pig* and *whore,* Harry. When you call me names like that and tell me you wish you'd never married me, that hurts me. Terribly."

"Yes!" another woman whispered.

"When did I ever do that?" Kathy demanded in a low, gruff voice.

Alice shrugged helplessly and looked toward the exit. "I can't . . ."

"When did I ever do that?" Kathy repeated.

"This morning, Harry," Alice managed. "And so, Harry," her voice grew stronger, "if you do that again, I am going to point it out to you and ask you to stop."

"That is the silliest thing I have ever heard. Are you crazy?"

Alice stood. "No, Harry, I am not crazy, and if you can't stop talking to me like this, I'm going out for a walk."

The group broke into applause.

"Good, Alice. Good!" Kathy said. "Did you see how she drew some lines, set some limits? Practice it! Role-play with each other. It works!"

The women paired off and practiced together till Kathy called out, "Okay, ladies. Doesn't time fly when we're having fun? Next week, we'll address some of the other problems you brought up tonight, but I thought it was important to work on this one first. We need to close now, so let's finish with prayer. Does anyone have a pressing prayer need? Remember, all that is said here is confidential. It's not to go outside this room."

Leslie swallowed. "I do. My husband took that exam today, and he came home long enough to say he was sure he failed. He went out again—drinking, I'm sure."

Kathy nodded. "Anyone else?" She waited awhile, then said, "All right, join in as the Spirit leads."

As the women prayed for safety for Leslie and the children, for Charles's healing and his salvation, she felt tears coursing down her cheeks. Tears of concern, she realized, but also tears of gratitude to be enveloped in this blanket of prayer. At the end she cleared her throat and added, "Thank You, Lord, for these loving prayers and that You do hear them. Watch over each woman in this room during the week. Help each of us to walk through those waters and that fire and to keep our eyes on You and know that Your love will never fail."

After coffee Leslie walked outside with Sandra. "How was this for you?" she asked.

"Hard. But good," Sandra said. She stopped and turned toward Leslie. "Leslie, I want to ask you to forgive me for my simplistic counsel at our prayer group. And for not being honest with you about myself. I realize now I was really in denial."

Leslie put her arms around Sandra. "Of course, I forgive you. And now we can pray honest prayers for each other, can't we?"

"Yes, we can," Sandra murmured.

As they parted, Leslie said, "I'm going to remember what Kathy said about being a scapegoat. That was a really unique viewpoint to me."

"Me too. Thanks, Leslie." Sandra waved and got in her car.

Leslie walked to her car, got in, and sat for a moment. *Jesus is the final scapegoat,* she repeated in her mind. *He said, "It is finished." God doesn't ask me to be a scapegoat. Amazing!*

She turned the key in the ignition and headed for her mother's.

There she found the fudge finished, including a plate for them to take home.

"I'd better taste it. To be sure it's okay," Leslie said.

"You used to say, 'to be sure it's not poison,'" her mother recalled.

"Well, that too." Leslie bit into a piece of fudge as the kids waited for her verdict. "That is fabulous!" she said, taking another bite. "Can anything this good be really bad for me?"

Scott nodded. "It starts with lots of butter."

"Don't tell me the rest. Ignorance is best." She hugged Zoë. "Thank you so, so much, Mom. The group was really worthwhile. I'd hate to have missed it. And I feel fortified for—whatever."

Zoë nodded. "The kids and I prayed for Charles. Now I'll pray for all of you." She hesitated. "Sure you don't want to stay here tonight? There's room."

He'd be really *upset if he thought we deserted him,* she thought. "Thanks, Mom. We'll be fine."

Scott and Michelle hugged Zoë.

"Thanks for teaching us bad eating habits, Gram," Michelle said.

"That's what grandmothers are for," Zoë laughed, opening the door for them.

⌥

At home Charles's car was not in the driveway or the garage. Leslie urged the children on to bed and suddenly realized how exhausted she felt. She had just finished brushing her teeth when she heard a car door slam in front of the house. She went to the window and, in the illumination of the streetlight, saw Charles lurching toward the door. She stood listening, praying, as he labored over opening the door. At last he came in, and she heard him crashing about downstairs. She could feel her heart thudding. Pictures of slashed wives, children slain in their beds flashed through her mind. She waited. No sense in panicking prematurely. But what if she needed to call 911? Would she be able to get to the phone in time? Maybe they should have stayed with Zoë.

She listened. Not a sound. She counted to one hundred. Still nothing. She remembered the portable phone in the bedroom, grabbed it, and carefully made her way out into the hallway. As she started down the stairs, she stopped at a small sound behind her. Scott. "It's okay, honey," she whispered, determined not to lean on him. "Go back to bed."

After she reached the landing of the stairs, by the light in the hall, she could see into the family room. A floor lamp was overturned, a jacket on the floor. She looked closely at the couch, positioned with its back toward her, and saw a foot extended past one arm. She stole down the last flight of stairs and into the family room. Charles lay sprawled on the couch, mouth open, snoring. She touched his arm. "Charles."

No response. She shook him gently. Nothing.

She remembered the struggle of hauling a one-hundred-and-five-pound Michelle upstairs the night Jason brought her home. No, she'd go upstairs for a blanket.

Scott sat on the topmost step. "It's okay, honey," she repeated. "Dad's asleep."

"Okay," Scott whispered.

She watched him head for his room, took a blanket from the linen closet, and went back to the family room.

When she tugged off his shoes, Charles muttered a stream of profanity. Then he was quiet. She spread the blanket over him and wearily dragged herself up the stairs, stopping in Scott's room to tuck him in. "Thanks for wanting to help, Scott. Don't worry, Dad'll be fine there."

Fine for now, she thought. *But what about when he wakens?*

Please God, she prayed, *no matter what happens tomorrow help me—and the kids—not to be scapegoats.*

32

⁓

From Zoë's Prayer Journal

November 11: Time to level, Lord. Judging from Charles's track record, I'm worried he may take out his failure and embarrassment on Leslie. Oh, Lord, put Your guardian angels around her and the kids. Deliver them from evil. And Father, please use this low point in Charles's life to help him see his need for You. May he cry out to You in his distress. Thank You that You are there for us, faithful and true. I love You, Lord! Amen.

THE NEXT MORNING LESLIE WAKENED WITH A SENSE OF dread resting square in the middle of her chest, heavy as a rhinocerus. *I'd love to pull the covers over my head and stay here,* she thought. She sighed. *Nope, not with a schedule like I have today.*

She listened. Not a sound from below. She got up, showered and dressed, and went downstairs. Charles lay sprawled on the couch in virtually the same position as the night before. Did he intend to go to work? Should she waken him? He could be furious if she didn't, she decided.

She put her hand on his shoulder. "Charles. Charles, it's six-thirty. Are you planning to go to work this morning?"

Charles snorted, belched, and seemed to struggle to open his eyes. All he could manage were tiny slits. He winced and closed them again. "Huh?"

"It's six-thirty, Charles. Thursday morning."

He groaned and, in the jerky motion of a crude animated film, managed to sit up and swing his feet off the couch. He hunched over, held his head in his hands, and moaned softly.

Sin is costly, she thought. "Do you want to go to bed upstairs?" she asked.

He shook his head carefully.

"Going to try to go to work?"

He didn't answer. Then, finally, "If I can. Strong coffee, Leslie. Not decaf." He stood on shaky legs, steadying himself against the couch. For a moment she thought he'd fall. But at last he wobbled his way to the stairs. He stood at the bottom for a moment as though contemplating a mountain ascent. Finally he grasped the railing and hauled himself upstairs. After a while Leslie heard the shower. It ran for a very long time.

While she was measuring the coffee, Scott appeared. "How's Dad?" His voice sounded anxious.

"A little unsteady and not feeling exactly terrific, I'd say. But I guess he's thinking of going to work."

"D'ya think they'll fire him?"

She turned toward him. "For failing the exam? Are you worried about that? No, honey. They won't do that. He just might not get the promotion he was hoping for. But we'll be fine."

⌇

When Charles finally appeared at the breakfast table, Leslie's righteous "serves him right" feelings dissipated with her first good look at him. His eyes were rimmed with red, lids swollen. His face looked ashen, puffy, and he'd cut himself shaving. Obviously he was in pain.

"What else would you like?" she asked, bringing him his coffee.

"I don't know," he muttered. The mug shook in his hand, but he managed a sip, grimacing as he swallowed.

"Aspirin?"

He nodded.

She went to the medicine cabinet and brought the container to him. "Juice?"

He didn't say no, so she poured a small glass.

He used it to swallow two aspirin.

"Sure you want to go to work, Charles?"

"Sure that I do not. Rather resign and go to the Galapagos," he muttered.

Michelle clattered in, sat down, saw her dad and barely disguised a gasp. "Dad, what happened—" She stopped as she saw him flinch.

"What happened to what?" he growled.

"Nothing. Never mind."

They ate in silence till Charles left the table.

"Man, he looks wasted," Michelle whispered. "If he was that drunk last night and tryin' to drive, lucky he didn't get busted." She thought a moment. "Did I look that bad after—y'know?"

"You were not a thing of beauty," Leslie said.

"Yuck. I'm not gonna do that again."

"Me either," Scott chimed in. "Not even the first time."

"Good. Glad to hear it," Leslie said.

༃

Midmorning at work Leslie called David at his apartment. "This is your bed check," she announced when he answered.

He groaned. "Big Therapy Mama looking over me. Yeah, I'm here, lying in bed, right where I'm supposed to be. Did you know there are 365 'fear not's' in the Bible?"

"Really? What'd you do? Count them? Isn't that a little like counting the angels on a head of a pin?"

"No, I didn't personally count 'em. But I just read that. Isn't it great? A 'fear not' for every day of the year. Anyway, the message is pretty clear. I'm not to be afraid of what's happening or what's going to happen. Fear isn't from the Lord. Also, I've decided to stay put tomorrow—not try to coach at the pool."

"Now you're getting smart. Give the bod a chance to heal itself. You have enough help there to lie low a few more days then?"

"Yeah, except for this weekend. Clyde, my roommate, is gonna be gone, and I've made a bunch of calls but haven't found anyone."

"Maybe from the church. Or—" She stopped. "Could Scott stay with you, bring your meals to you, do what you need?"

"Sure. I mean, it's basically keeping me fed and watered. Sure, he could. But he wouldn't want to spend his whole weekend that way. I mean, it'd be best if he could sleep over."

"I don't think that's a problem. I'll talk to him and get back to you."

"Thanks. And hey—have a great day in the Lord!"

"You too, David. 'Bye." She hung up thinking how pleased Scott would be to help his idol and how much David always helped Scott.

She had solid appointments with only a half-hour for lunch, moving smoothly from a patient with a "frozen" shoulder to another with neck strain, two stroke rehabs, and a postsurgery knee replacement. There was little time to think of Charles till Terry called her to the phone midafternoon.

"Leslie." Charles's voice sounded almost normal.

"How *are* you?" she asked.

"Better. I took a long walk at noon. The cool air helped."

"Good."

He hesitated. "I was thinking. About your 'certificate' for Mammoth." He sighed. "You were right. I could really stand to get away."

Had she heard him correctly? "You were right"? Quite a different tune than his derision over the idea on Tuesday.

"Tomorrow?" she exclaimed, wondering how she could manage it, yet realizing Charles had to do it *his* way. "I—I'll try to figure it out," she muttered.

"You do that," he said.

She hung up the phone and found Terry. "Charles agreed to go to Mammoth."

"Great!" Terry grinned.

"Yeah, but he wants to go tomorrow morning."

Terry raised an eyebrow. "Like that, huh?" She frowned, looking at the schedule. "Light day. We can juggle."

"Oh, thanks, Terry!" Leslie gave her a hug. "Let's see," she pondered. "God's already provided a place for Scott. (Thanks, Lord!) He'll stay and help David this weekend. I'll think of something for Michelle.

"She could come with us," Terry offered. "We're going to the high school football game Saturday, probably have Mexican food afterwards. She could stay the two nights. Be company for my eleven-year-old."

"Oh, but that's such an imposition," Leslie protested.

"I wouldn't offer if it was. Think about it."

"I will. Thanks. Thanks a lot."

3~

When she picked up the kids at school, she told Scott, "I have a job for you this weekend."

He made a face. "Take out the trash. Clean out the gutters. Or have you thought of some other gross-out thing?"

"This is worse. Much worse."

He waited. "Well?"

"Go take care of David."

"Say what?" Scott's face came alive.

"He needs someone to help him so he can stay in bed and get well. You'd sleep over."

"No foolin'!" He slapped his thigh. "Yeah. Sure."

"Good. He really needs you, and it works out great, because Dad and I are going to Mammoth this weekend."

Scott wiggled his finger in his ear. "I sure thought I heard a 'no' from Dad the other night."

"Well, he changed his mind."

Scott shrugged. "Whatever." He thought a moment. "What'll I need to do? I won't have to lift David, will I?"

Leslie laughed. "No. It's mostly bringing him food, liquids. You can call him tonight, and he'll explain what he needs."

Michelle leaned over from the backseat. "You guys actually going to Mammoth?"

Leslie nodded.

"Well, now I believe in miracles."

"I think this will be good. Put some miles between all Dad's hard work—and his disappointment. He deserves a break."

"Yeah. I suppose."

Leslie stopped for a traffic signal, looked back, and saw Michelle purse her lips. "Good thing I'm not grounded anymore, as of this weekend." Michelle flashed a wicked grin. "Now who can I call?"

"Call the wrong person, and you could find yourself grounded again, young lady."

Michelle rolled her eyes. "Don't wor-ry."

"Terry—at work, you know—invited you to come with their family to the high school football game, then sleep over."

"Oh, swell. Perfect strangers."

"No, they're not. You've met Terry lots of times, and you had a good time with their kids at the center's picnic last summer."

"Yeah. I suppose." The martyred tone.

⁕

The phone was ringing as they came in the door at home. "I'll get it." Michelle ran for the phone. "Ground control."

Leslie shook her head, smiling.

"Oh, hi, Carrie!" Michelle listened a moment. "Oh, yeah, that sounds great. But my folks are goin' out of town, and Mom wants me to stay with her office manager's family."

Even from across the room, Leslie could hear the enthusiasm in Carrie's voice bubbling over the phone.

"Oh, neat," Michelle said. "Just a minute." She held the phone against her chest, her eyes pleading. "Carrie's inviting me to go with her family to the San Diego Wild Animal Park, says I can sleep over Friday and Saturday at her house. This way we could go to church together Sunday."

"Sounds good to me. I know her folks from church." She looked at her watch. "I'll check in with her mother tonight and see what you can bring."

"It's a yes!" Michelle shrieked, and Leslie could hear an echoing exultation from Carrie.

They talked for another half-hour while Leslie prepared dinner. When Michelle at last said good-bye, she turned to her mother. "Mom, this is perfect!"

"It is indeed," said Leslie, grateful to have both kids happy and settled during her absence.

~

As soon as the kids left for school Friday, without discussion, Charles slipped behind the wheel of the car. At 7:30 they pulled out of the driveway, with Charles grumbling only a little over Leslie's plan to have breakfast at Kramer Junction.

Traffic was light as they headed up the Santa Ana Freeway and onto the 55. Charles said nothing, and Leslie decided to take advantage of the time to pray. She pulled out her note-book and journaled her prayers as Charles connected with the 91. Then she leaned back against the headrest for her listening time as they drove up and over the San Bernardino Mountains. The drone of the engine and the hum of the tires, interrupted by rhythmic little thumps as they passed over pavement joints, helped her relax. Then a scripture surfaced in her mind as though spelled out in neon. "Be still and know that I am God."

Oh, yes, Lord, she responded silently. *I do want to be still before You. What a joy, just to be in Your presence.*

"Stupid idiot! Imbecile!" Charles exploded as he stamped on the brakes.

Leslie opened her eyes to see a car squeeze in front of Charles just in time to avoid a head-on collision with an oncoming truck. Close! It was a moment before her heart stopped racing. "Good driving, Charles."

"Half the people on the road are menaces," Charles

grouched. "I'd be doing the world a favor if I carried a gun and shot them."

Wonderful solution, she thought, but instead she gestured out the window at the high desert vegetation. "I love Joshua trees. I think I read they're named after Joshua because they look like they're lifting their arms to praise God. They do have a lot of personality."

"Ugly, if you ask me," Charles replied.

Leslie shrugged and tried not to think of the times she had traveled highway 395 when she was married to Tom. He'd actually given names to some of the trees and loved to do his tour-guide shtick, pointing out all the scenic highlights. She could hear his voice: "And on your right, ladies and gentlemen, the Outpost Cafe, soiree salon for semi drivers and home of the much copied but never equalled date shake . . . And on your left, the Al-a-bam-a Hills, setting for countless Westerns and the famous 'Gunga Din.'" *I miss that playfulness,* she thought. *Did I make the right decision after Tom died—to marry a—well, comparatively speaking, a stuffed shirt? Oh, but there was a flip side to Tom's fun and games. Irresponsibility. Look how good Charles is at taking care of us. We're secure. I need to count my blessings.*

"Nine-twenty-nine," Charles interrupted as they pulled into the parking lot of a restaurant at Kramer Junction. "Early. We are making excellent time. I do hope they have proper pancakes."

In the eleven years they'd been married, she had not yet figured out Charles's definition of a "proper" pancake. She suspected that *any* pancake would be too thin or too thick, too light or too doughy. She braced herself when Charles ordered pancakes, eggs over easy, and bacon. *If I order waffles, I can always trade him if he doesn't like. . . Wait a minute,* she told herself. *If he doesn't like them, it's his problem. I don't have to fix it. Codependent No More*—isn't that the name of a book?

Their order came quickly. Charles lavished the pancakes with butter and syrup and cut a precise little triangle of a bite. She tried not to look, instead watching the butter melt into little shining puddles in each square of her waffle.

Charles's "Hmm!" held a tone of surprise. "Not too bad," he said.

She relaxed. Maybe he was loosening up, even changing, not being so picky. Maybe they could have a good time together this weekend.

Fifteen minutes later Charles stared at his plate, clean except for the sprig of parsley. "It was gluttony," he admitted. "Really quite acceptable, I must say."

As they left the restaurant, she said, "I'll drive. You can sleep it off."

"I accept," Charles said.

Charles tilted the seat back and snoozed as she drove on through Red Mountain and over the crest where she caught her breath at the first glimpse of the jagged Sierras. She glanced at Charles. *The poor guy must be exhausted,* she thought.

When he wakened, she said, "I was thinking about your birthday as I was driving. It's only two weeks away. What would you like?"

"Oh, Leslie, do we have to go through that again?" Charles pleaded.

She glanced at him. "I suppose we don't *have* to. It's just that birthdays were always very big in my family. More important than Christmas, in many ways, because they're your own special day."

"All right, they were big in *your* family. Charming."

"I can understand that they weren't in yours, Charles, but you really seem to hate birthdays. Do you have any idea why that is?"

"Certainly."

She waited, and when Charles didn't volunteer any more, she asked, "Yes?"

She could see the muscles in his jaw tense. "All right, I will tell you," he said at last. "After I finally went to live with my mother—and that monster she married . . . Well, it was quite a few months before my birthday rolled around. And I looked forward to it. I thought, finally I would have a proper birthday. And that morning at breakfast my stepfather handed me a rather important-looking package, all wrapped and tied with ribbon. And when I opened it and lifted the lid on the box, there was nothing but a note." He swallowed. "It said, 'You are a nothing, so your gift is nothing.'"

Tears stung her eyes, and pain pierced her chest. "Charles!" she cried. "That is unspeakably cruel!" She braked and pulled over to the shoulder of the road, bringing the car to a stop. Tears flowing down her face, she turned, reaching out to embrace him.

But he sat, staring straight ahead, his face an expressionless mask. "Well, I was right," he said. "You are too frail and sensitive to handle my past. It was a very long time ago, you know. It is of no consequence now."

33

OF NO CONSEQUENCE, LESLIE THOUGHT, UNABLE TO STOP HER tears. *But it is.* It's devastating! Her heart ached for Charles as she saw him as a vulnerable, wounded eight-year-old. She longed to console him but knew he would not, could not accept her comfort. Perhaps he felt he'd already revealed too much or that he would show weakness if he embraced her love and concern.

Oh, Charles, she wanted to say, *don't keep stuffing the past away. Be real, be honest. Stop fighting to always be in control. Talk! Talk about what happened, how you felt.*

"Look at you!" Charles exclaimed. "Have you put yourself into such a state you are unable to drive?" His face was a stoic mask. "Come, come! Pull yourself together, woman!"

"I can drive," she said quietly. She pulled a tissue from her pocket and wiped her eyes and nose. Checking her rearview mirrors, she waited for a truck to pass.

After she pulled back on the highway, they said little to each other as they continued north. At one point she ventured, "I love the Owens River Valley. There's always something different in bloom." She looked out at the clusters of gold flowers along the road. "I tend to forget it's a valley because the Sierras are so awesome, they diminish the Inyo Mountains on the east side."

She drove on toward Lone Pine, adding, "But look how the valley narrows here. That's Mount Whitney over there. Highest in the continental US."

Charles leaned toward her to look out. "Which one is it?"

"See the one that looks highest from here? That's because it's closer. Whitney's behind it." She stole another quick look out her window. "Oh, look at those lenticular clouds above the mountains today. Stunning!"

Charles merely grunted. Then, "Are you watching the gas?"

She nodded. "Yes. We can make it to Bishop. Look, there's snow on the mountaintops and down the gullies. Bet it'll be a good ski season."

"Oh, hooray," Charles said without enthusiasm. "What a silly sport. Strap boards on your feet, ride conveyances up the mountain, slide down the mountain, then do it all over again."

Leslie smiled. "And baseball? Hit the ball and run around a diamond?" she teased.

"Not a parallel!" Charles exclaimed defensively. "Baseball is a game of skill and strategy."

Oh, and skiing's not, she thought. But instead she said, "Aren't the colors in Owens Lake amazing? It always looks like a pastel painting with big sweeps of pink and green."

"Dust from the lake is a problem," Charles said. Later he pointed to a sign, "Elk."

Leslie nodded. "You see them sometimes."

A moment later Charles laughed. "Ah, yes. Some are black and some are brown and white."

She looked out at the grazing cattle and chuckled. "Right!"

After they filled the gas tank, Charles drove on from Bishop. As the road curved to the left and the mountains lay straight ahead, Leslie felt a growing sense of excitement. She remembered when she was little and her family drove to a Wisconsin lake every summer. As soon as the pine trees began, she would feel all aquiver, as though injected with some wonderful stimulant. Now she savored that same sense of anticipation.

They reached the town of Mammoth Lakes in the early afternoon. The mountain looked barren and just a little formidable without its winter dressing of snow. Leslie stared at its brown volcanic rock, interspersed with the deep green of pines and firs. *You're stunning, but I like you best softened and draped with white,* she thought.

After they had settled in their condo, they decided to head for Devil's Postpile and take a short hike from there. Past the ski area's main lodge, the road curved up an incline to a panoramic vista across a broad valley to a craggy range of mountains. "Let's stop for a minute," Leslie suggested. "This is such a pretty view, especially of the Minarets. I once snow-shoed up here under a full moon, and I could see rabbits hopping through the—"

Charles didn't stop. "*Must* we keep dwelling on your past history, Leslie?"

She shrugged inwardly. Perhaps she was talking too much. After all that was another life, and yes, another marriage.

The parking lot and picnic area at Devil's Postpile National Monument looked desolate with only five other cars there, and the ranger's station was closed. They crossed the meadow and hiked to the pile of elongated gray-black rocks. Taller than a five-story building, it indeed resembled an askew pile of posts.

Devil's Postpile may be a picturesque name, Leslie thought, *but to me it's a mighty testimony to* God's *power.*

Charles, walking away from her as he commented on the geology, took out his camera, complaining that the rocks' contours were in shadow.

After they'd walked around and to the top of the pile, Charles said, "As I read the map, we have at least two options, considering the time of day. We could hike to Rainbow Falls or we could go to Minaret Falls."

"Either would be fine," Leslie said, suspecting that if she chose one, he'd want the other.

"Mmm," Charles pondered, consulting his watch. "I think Minaret Falls. I believe we cross the river. Where is that bridge?" He looked toward the parking lot. "Oh, yes, back there; I see it."

Leslie let Charles lead the way. After they crossed the bridge, the trail backtracked along the river, thin and shallow after the summer dryness, thirsty for the melting of winter snows that were still to come.

The way to the base of the falls was quick, and, Leslie thought, easy. But Charles paused to catch his breath before they made their way to the top of the falls. "Altitude," he huffed.

"Mmm," she agreed. "I can feel my heart pound. Even down in this valley, it's probably seven thousand feet."

Charles looked up. "You go first."

"All right." She climbed easily up the steep path, listening to the crescendo of the rushing water.

When she reached a vantage point near the top where the main cascade of the waterfall sparkled in the sun, she sat and waited for Charles to catch up with her.

Panting, he sat on the rock beside her and gazed at the falls. "Well, this isn't much," he said.

"It's almost winter," she reminded him. "All the streams are low."

"Well, it was your idea to come now."

She let it go.

Charles busied himself taking pictures, while she felt the warmth of the sun, both from above and in the rock beneath her. *Sometimes,* she thought, *people get so busy trying to capture the beauty, they miss it all.*

She followed Charles as he made his way back down. To her the most beautiful part of the falls was at a lower point. While he snapped pictures she sat on a fallen tree. Below the grand cascade another fall streamed, high to her right. But as she looked across the craggy expanse of rock nearby, water seemed to spring from everywhere. It bubbled from beneath rocks, foaming white, gleaming silver, flowing like liquid emeralds. She counted more than a dozen sources amid the gleaming rocks.

Living water, she thought. *El Shaddai, the pourer-forth of blessings.* She blinked and leaned forward. Was it possible? Yes, flowers, blooming, growing from the very rocks.

"Thank You, Lord," she breathed. "What a picture of Your bountifulness—if that's a word, and if it isn't, it should be! Oh, Father, give Charles eyes to see all that You have for him."

That evening Leslie cooked a simple pasta dinner at the condo, and Charles drank most of a bottle of wine. When she didn't touch what he'd poured for her, he reached over and drank it as well. They started to watch a movie and found themselves falling asleep.

"It's the altitude," Charles said, rubbing his eyes as he headed for bed.

❧

The next morning Leslie awoke a little after seven. Slipping into her robe and slippers, she stepped out on the balcony of the condo. She shivered in the mountain air and looked up at the Sherwin Mountains. They stood stark and pale against the deep blue of the sky. A jet vapor trail stretched overhead, a soft, white ribbon, already diffusing, like a barely remembered dream.

Dreams. Charles had wakened, thrashing and swearing, from another nightmare during the night. For the zillionth time she wondered what manner of ghost or demon had persisted in haunting him through all their years together. If only he would talk about the dreams. If only he would explore their roots. Did she dare ask? Yesterday he'd grown agitated when she wept over his revelation about his cruel birthday package. *But,* she told herself, *it was my response that upset him, not his talking about it. If I steel myself not to be so reactive, maybe he'd be willing to talk.*

Would there ever be a better time than now, while they were away, while there were no interruptions? As she stood listening to the contentious cacophony of the Steller's jays in the trees, she prayed aloud, "Oh, Lord, set Charles free from the demons that dog him. Help him to look at the truth, and may that truth set him free."

She heard Charles slide open the door behind her. Joining her at the railing, he said, "I am tired, and I need a good breakfast. Do we have eggs?"

She shook her head.

"I need protein. That means we will have to go out for breakfast."

Two meals out yesterday, and now breakfast as well? She was astonished. "Why not? We're on vacation."

"That is true," he said.

"They used to have spectacular cinnamon buns at a little place by the main mall," she remembered.

"Well, then." His smile was amiable. "Shall we?"

She nodded and started toward the door. "Do you want to dress for hiking, maybe go straight to a trailhead from breakfast?"

He shrugged. "Might as well." He frowned. "But let us not do another of those tedious climbs."

She turned back toward him. It seemed to her that by definition, hiking in the mountains involved climbing uphill. And there were so many scenic trails, breathtaking destinations. "Oh," she said, disappointed. "I was thinking maybe of going to Mammoth Crest." She remembered how, at each turn of that trail, a new vista unfolded, how first you could look down on one lake, then, from a little higher, two lakes, then three.

"From the very top you can look over into Yosemite and see Half Dome. It looks very tiny," she said softly.

He shook his head, and she half-expected him to say, "There you go again, trying to run things." But he simply stated, "That does not interest me."

"I see. Then what do you have in mind?"

"Hot Creek. I saw the sign on Highway 395, before the turnoff for Mammoth. I have never been there."

"Oh. Well, it's interesting, of course. In my college days kids liked to go there for midnight skinny dipping. But it's not really a hike. You park the car and walk down a short way." She started to suggest hiking to Rainbow Falls after Hot Creek. After all the path wasn't too steep. Instead she said, "Guess we can decide later where to go from there."

He didn't reply. "Shall we leave in fifteen minutes?"

"Fine."

At breakfast the cinnamon buns came promptly, and Charles broke one apart to lavish it with butter. His eyes responded while the first bite was still in his mouth. "Mm-hm." He nodded.

They ordered more buns and shared a huge omelet. Afterward Charles leaned back, looking relaxed as they finished their coffee.

"Charles," Leslie ventured, "you had another nightmare last night."

"I am aware of that, Leslie."

"They've been more frequent recently, it seems."

"Oh, I don't think so." He took a sip of coffee.

"You've never told me what they're about. Is there a common theme?"

Charles's pupils dilated. "Yes. And that is all I am going to say."

She put her hand on his, feeling a flood of compassion. "Honey, I hate to see you so—so bedeviled. Would you consider talking about the dreams with a professional who deals with this sort of thing?"

Charles grasped the edge of the table. "A shrink? Is that what you're suggesting?" he demanded.

"A counselor. Maybe a psychologist. I can get references at the church."

"Oh, yes, lovely! By all means! A holier-than-thou. A 'let-God-heal-you' crackpot! Leeches, that is what they are. Keep you coming and coming till you are so dependent, you cannot detach. Parasites, sucking your blood—and your bank account." He was shouting now, and she saw a waitress stop and look across the room at them. "Leslie, once and for all, *lay off!*" He stood, and the chair grated against the wood floor. Slapping a ten-dollar bill on the table, he strode for the door.

She started to follow him then realized the ten didn't cover a tip. Fishing a couple of bills from her wallet, she went back to the table and put them down.

He was already at the car when she caught up with him. He didn't speak as they drove to Highway 395 and headed south.

Not a good idea, trying to get him to talk, she chided herself. She slid down in the car seat, overwhelmed with despair for him. *He is never going to look back at his ghosts. Never.* She sighed. *The only way not to anger him is to stay with surface talk—or not to talk at all,* she thought. *Here I am again, walking on eggs, afraid to open my mouth.*

They turned off the highway, and the car jostled over the washboard ridges in the gravel road. Then, "Is that it?" Charles asked as they came over the crest of a hill and saw a plume of vapor beyond the trees. "Ah, yes." He sniffed the air. "I smell the sulfur."

They pulled into a parking area. Only one other car was there. As they got out and Charles locked the car, he tossed the keys to her. "You carry these. You have bigger pockets."

They walked toward a sign and paused to read it. "Hot Creek—evidence of a fiery past. You are standing at the bottom of a large volcanic basin." The smaller text explained that the ten-by-eighteen-mile depression in the earth's crust had been created by an eruption 700,000 years ago and that the still-hot magma heated the water from the Sierra Nevada Mountains that filtered through cracks.

"Ancient history," Charles murmured.

"Shall we walk down?" she asked.

"Les-lie, please. All in good time. Will you stop trying to manage me, direct me, manipulate me? I am a patient man, but you truly test the tolerance of a saint!"

She could go on ahead, but what was the point? She waited. *He won't budge,* she realized, *till he feels in control.* She looked around at the pine trees, which seemed to spring forth from solid rock. A bizarre area, it had always been disquieting for her with its record of casualties. For a moment she considered not walking down at all.

Finally Charles started down the path, and she followed. Pausing at another sign, he read, "'Dangerous area. Scalding water. Unpredictable eruptions. Unstable ground. Sporadic high pollution. Sudden temperature changes. Broken glass. Arsenic in water. We recommend that you remain on paved and wood paths and do not enter the water.'"

He looked toward her. "Are they trying to tell us this could be hazardous to our health?"

"Something like that," Leslie said, shivering. They continued walking. In the water upstream, above the hazardous thermal activity, she could see two people swimming.

They came to another sign that informed them that twelve people had lost their lives here since 1968 and many others had been injured.

Hazardous is right, she thought.

Now they were close to the stream, where steam vents released their vapor, springs of boiling water bubbled, and occasional small geysers spewed into the air. They paused by a light wooden fence and looked down a steep cliff to the cauldron below. "Danger! Scalding water. Keep out," warned the sign.

"I guess so!" Leslie murmured.

What a contrast this was to the "living water" at Minaret Falls the day before. *This is more like the lake of fire in the book of Revelation,* she suddenly realized, and she quickly prayed in her heart, *Oh, Lord, save Charles. Deliver him, please.*

They walked upstream, where the water was comparatively still. The couple she'd seen before now lounged in the stream, passing a brown bottle back and forth, laughing.

"We will go in the water," Charles said.

Caught off guard, she looked at him to see if he was serious.

"Why not?" he asked.

"I don't have a suit."

"Do you think they will care?" Charles gestured toward the couple. "They will not even notice. They are quite stoned." He unzipped his jacket.

"You go ahead," she said.

"No. With you."

"No, thank you, Charles. I'll just wait in the car." She started back, but he followed so closely he stepped on her heels.

"Here is the problem," he bellowed at her back. "This is a microcosm of our entire marriage. The trouble with you, Leslie, is that you *will not* knuckle under! You must always have your way. You must always do it your way. You make the decisions. You tell me what to do. And when you are not able to do that, you manipulate. Thwart my every dream. Sabotage my every desire. Hinder my goals. Why? Because you are preoccupied with yourself. Because you are cold, unfeeling, incapable of love. You are disgusting! You are loathsome! I would be far, far better off without you."

As Charles's voice modulated from a shout to a scream, she walked faster, wanting only to get out of there, praying silently, *Oh, Lord, give me the wings of a dove.*

Then an echo of her dad's advice years ago surfaced: Never turn your back on a dog that comes after you.

She stopped and turned to face him, but the moment she looked into his eyes, dark and glistening as coal, she knew it was a mistake, like trying to face off an enraged dog.

Charles's sweaty cheeks bloomed with bright red patches. His breath came in short gasps. His lips, peeling from the mountain dryness, stuck to his teeth near the gums, exposing a mirthless grin. He grabbed her by the shoulders and pushed her toward the edge of the path, close to the sign that read, "Danger! Scalding water."

34

CAUGHT OFF-BALANCE BY THE FORCE OF CHARLES'S SHOVE, Leslie staggered back.

"Damn you, woman!" he screamed, grabbing for her throat. She clutched at his hands but couldn't break his angry grip, and the pressure made her head begin to throb. To her side she could see the fragile wood fence, and she remembered the cliff just beyond it, the vast bubbling stew of water below.

Fight! Fight for your life! her instincts shouted as she felt the edge of the "Danger!" sign stab her hip. Bracing herself against it, she closed her eyes, summoned all her strength, and thrust her knee into Charles's groin.

He screamed, doubling over, and she was free. She fled up the path, never looking back.

Might only have a minute or so lead, she told herself. *Maybe only seconds. Mustn't stumble. Keep going. Run!*

Up the hill she sprinted, heart pounding.

Is he behind me? Got to look. No. Not yet. Quickly now, Leslie—cross the parking lot, she coached herself. *Find the car keys in your pocket. Oh, no! They're caught. Okay, got 'em. Steady, now. Key into lock. Wrong key. Oh, God! Where is it? Here—this one.*

"Yes!" she exclaimed as she turned the key in the lock. Scrambling into the car, she locked the door and exulted when the engine started immediately. Putting the car in gear, churning dust behind her, she raced out the gravel road.

Only when she reached the highway and saw no other vehicle behind her could she say, "Thank You, Lord!"

She looked up the road toward Mammoth Lakes. *No,* she thought. *Can't go there. What if I'm there getting my clothes and he comes back? Leave 'em, forget it. Run!* Quickly she turned left on Highway 395. Heading past Crowley Lake, she wondered if the highway patrol still waited for speeders in this area. *I could use a good ol' CHP right now,* she thought. *Charles could report this car stolen. Or could he? It's registered in both our names. Should I stop and phone the police? No, don't dare. He could steal that other couple's car and come after me.*

Come on, now, Leslie, he couldn't just steal their car, she assured herself. *He doesn't know how to hot-wire a car to start it without keys. But what if they left the keys in the car? They might have. They didn't look quite all there. What color was the car? White? I'm not sure. Yes, I think it was white.*

Be calm, Leslie. Just keep going.

From far behind she could see a car overtaking her. Panic engulfed her. "It's Charles!" She knew it. "He'll run me off the road," she muttered. She accelerated. *If I can just get to Bishop,* she thought, *I'll report what happened. There's no place to stop to call now till Bishop.* She tried to sort out what happened. It

seemed so unreal. Like a dream. Or like one of Charles's terri-
fying nightmares. But no, she could still feel him stepping on
her heels. Hear him ranting behind her. See his mouth, his
teeth bared like a rabid animal. Feel the grip of his hands on
her arms, around her throat.

She wiped her forehead with her jacket sleeve. She was
much too warm, but she didn't dare stop to take off the jacket.

A truck loomed in her rearview mirror. No, there hadn't
been time for Charles to get to the highway and hitchhike. But
it was huge—a semi. She pulled far to the right and let it pass,
holding her breath till it continued down the road.

Going down the Sherwin grade, she glanced at the
speedometer. *Eighty-five. Better cool it. Stop trying to second-
guess, just concentrate on getting there.*

When at last she reached Bishop, she pulled into the first
filling station and asked directions to the police station.

"Go on down the road to Line," said the woman with henna
hair. "Turn right. You can't miss it."

"Uh—Line is a street?" she asked.

The woman smirked, obviously disgusted at her stupidity.
"Yeah." She started to walk away then turned and added,
"You'll see it, from this street, on your right."

"Thank you."

A few moments later Leslie parked in front of the beige
brick-and-stucco building. She had difficulty getting out of
the car. Her legs felt stiff but weak, and she had to will them
to move, to take her through the door.

Inside a lanky man in a navy-blue police uniform bent over
a filing cabinet, and a radio squawked intermittently in the
background. He turned as she shut the door. "Yes?"

"I, uh . . ." She gripped the top of a chair, suddenly afraid
she might faint.

"You okay, lady?"

"I—yes—no." She took a deep breath. "I've just fled from my husband. He tried to push me into the hot springs—you know, at Hot Creek, south of Mammoth." Now the words tumbled out. "I know this is a different county, but I was afraid to stop, afraid he'd catch up with me, run me off the road, finish what he started to do."

The officer sat down at the desk and motioned her to a chair beside it. "I can have a deputy come down from Mammoth and take the information," he offered.

"Oh, no, no! I don't want to wait. That would take an hour or more."

"Well, then, I'll be glad to take a courtesy report and fax it up."

"Courtesy report!" she shouted. "He tried to kill me!"

"Well, ma'am, if you want to file charges, you'll need to go to the district attorney up in Mono County. You live up there?"

"No, no. I'm from Lake Forest." She saw his quizzical look. "Southern California. Orange County."

"And that's where you're headin'?"

"Yes. Oh, yes! I want to get home."

"Then I'd suggest you get in touch with your local authorities, get a restraining order when you get home."

"Then—then I have no protection till then?"

"Like I say, I'll be glad to take a report."

She swallowed hard, on the verge of tears. Would no one help her? Was she at the mercy of a crazy man?

"Do you need to counsel with someone?" His voice softened. "I can refer you to Wild Iris. They deal with abuse here."

"No!" she shouted. "I just want to get home safely!" She slumped in her chair. "I'm sorry. Yes, please take a report."

He pulled out a form and a pen. "Okay, let's take it from the top. Name?"

"Leslie Patterson Harper."

"Address?"

"24032 Melody Lane, Lake Forest."

"Husband's name?"

"Charles A. Harper."

"Now. When did all this happen, Miz Harper?"

She looked at her watch. "About ten."

He looked up, eyebrows questioning.

"This morning," she added.

"And you were at Hot Creek, you say?"

"Right."

"Exactly what happened?"

"My husband wanted to go in the water, and I said I'd wait in the car. He followed me, shouting about how he'd be better off without me. Kept stepping on my heels, and I finally turned to face him. He grabbed my arms, then my throat. Began pushing me toward the edge of the cliff." She stopped, swallowed convulsively as the appalling truth registered. *He wanted to kill me.*

"Yes?" His milky-blue eyes studied her.

It was a moment before she trusted herself to speak, and she heard the quaver in her voice. "I kneed him in the groin. He doubled over, let go of me, and I ran to the car."

"You just had one car there?"

She nodded. "It, uh, it's registered in both our names. He can't come after me for stealing it, can he?"

"No, ma'am. That's not a problem."

She released her grip on the edge of the chair.

"But I have no protection, now, driving home? I mean, what if he finds me?"

"Well," the officer droned, "'pears to me he'll have to find a car first. Where's he gonna get one, and how long you think it'll take him? Did he have credit cards with him?"

"I think so."

"He could fly home, too, from the airport, y'know."

She gasped. "That's right. The airport's very near Hot Creek. He could get that couple that was in the water to drive him there. He could be waiting for me when I get home. Worse yet, he could get to the kids before I do."

"Lemme check the flights." He consulted a list of numbers and punched the phone keypad. "Yeah, Maddie. You got any flights south today? One gone to LA already, huh? Nothin' to Orange County? You get a guy named Harper on that flight?" He waited. "No? Okay, thanks, Maddie."

She stared at him. "Could he have gotten there in time, maybe used another name, be on that flight? If he did, he could get into LA very soon. Take the shuttle home. Be there mid-afternoon." She looked at her watch. "I can't get back till between five and six. I'd better call my mom."

"Pay phone over there." He nodded toward the doorway.

"Thanks."

She made a credit-card call to Zoë's office. "She's with a client right now," the receptionist said.

"Please page her," Leslie pleaded. "It's an emergency."

She waited. And waited.

"Want a cup o'coffee, Miz Harper?"

She shook her head. "Better not. I'm vibrating already."

At last her mother answered.

"Mom!"

"Leslie." Zoë's voice mixed surprise and concern. "You all right?"

The moment she heard her mother's voice, Leslie began to cry. She took a shuddering breath, and it was a moment before she could manage, "Yes. But I've got a peck of trouble."

"Oh, honey, what happened? Charles?"

"Yes. He lost it, went berserk, blew his stack. Tried to push

342

me into the hot springs near Mammoth. I kneed him and got to the car and got away."

"But you're all right, thank God. Honey, you handled that well. Where are you now?"

"Bishop. Police station."

"Good. Tell me what I can do."

"What I'm worried about is that the officer here suggested Charles might get to the Mammoth airport—it's near Hot Springs—and fly home. He could get to our house before I do, and he is very, very angry. I don't want him near the kids."

"But isn't Scott at David's?"

"Oh, of course!" She slumped against the wall, relieved. "And I'm sure Charles doesn't know where he lives. And Michelle's at Carrie's. Charles doesn't even know her last name."

"Excellent. Now, Leslie, please, when you get here, don't you dare go near your house."

"I won't. I'll come to your place."

"Not at home," Zoë cautioned. "It'll be safer at the office. No, wait. I'll meet you at my company's Laguna Hills location. I don't think Charles would think of that."

"Okay," Leslie said, grateful for her mother's wariness.

"Oh, Lord, keep Leslie safe as she travels home, in Jesus' name!" Zoë prayed.

"Thanks, Mom. I hope to be there before six."

"Fine. But be sure you stop for something to eat, won't you, dear? Keep up your strength."

"Ye-e-e-s, Moth-er," Leslie laughed for the first time. She hung up and walked over to the officer. "Thank you so much, officer . . ."

"Denton," he supplied.

"Officer Denton. I feel a world better." She held out her hand, and he shook it vigorously.

"You take care now. And try not to worry. Get yourself a restraining order, first thing you get home, hear?"

"I will. Thanks again."

She opened the door and looked up and down the street before she stepped outside. Just as she reached her car, a white vehicle rounded the corner. She ducked behind her car, waiting till it was past and she could see a lone woman driver. She let her breath out slowly. *I don't think I'd make a very good fugitive—or spy,* she thought. *I'm getting positively paranoid.*

She drove around the block, stopped for traffic at the highway, and headed south, checking frequently in the rearview mirror. "Lord, just get me back to my kids. Just get me back safely," she prayed. As she passed the sign indicating a 55 m.p.h. speed limit, she turned on the cruise control, fished a tape of praise music from the storage box beside her, and shoved it into the tape deck. *Glad I'm not in Charles's car,* she thought. *He thinks the very presence of Christian tapes might contaminate him.*

"We exalt You . . . We exalt You," the chorus sang out.

"Right," she said aloud. "I do exalt You, Lord. Surely You provided a way of escape, just as Your Word promises. Oh, Lord, I feel like You've literally helped me overcome a demon. Thank You!"

***

The pain was so intense, Charles could not stand upright or even shout at Leslie. "Bitch . . . bitch . . . ," he moaned. He tried to straighten up, took two steps, doubled over again, groaning. Once, as a teenager, he'd suffered a blow to his testicles, and he'd thought the pain was acute then, but it was nothing like now.

Leslie knows her anatomy too well, he thought bitterly.

He could walk only a few steps at a time. By now Leslie obviously could have run far ahead. But she couldn't get—He remembered the car keys and screamed out a curse. He'd just handed them off to her. Made it simple for her to take the car. What had possessed him? He glanced at his watch. It had been a little after ten when he suggested swimming. A full ten minutes had elapsed. It took him eleven minutes, with frequent stops, to walk up the path. And when he reached the parking lot, indeed, he saw that Leslie's Chevy was gone.

He swore and sat down carefully on a rock. *My God!* he thought suddenly. *I almost did a terrible thing! What was I . . .* Then his anger reignited. *Crazy woman, prying, prodding, probing! Why couldn't she just knuckle under?*

He tried to think. What were his options? Walk back down and try to get that couple in the water to drive him somewhere? Where? Surely there was no car rental in Mammoth. Could he hitchhike? Not until he got out to the highway, and he wasn't at all sure he could walk that far. Wait till he caught up with that slut! By God, he'd pay her back if it was the last thing he ever did.

As he sat recuperating, he heard a plane low overhead and looked up to see its wheels down for landing. Ah, of course! The airport was very close. He felt in his pocket for his wallet. He could fly home. If he could just get to the airport. *Surely someone else will come,* he thought. *Surely,* he told himself. *Patience, Charles.*

He'd just checked his watch—10:31:30—when he saw the pickup truck approaching. A forest ranger. Perfect. He walked slowly toward the truck when it stopped by a trash bin and gave his best smile. "Am I glad to see you! I seem to be stranded here. My wife—she went berserk on me and took off in my car."

"So what can I do for you?" the ranger asked.

"You headed into Mammoth? I really should file a complaint."

"Nope. Due at Crowley Lake in fifteen minutes."

Charles thought about his gear at the condominium, and especially the wine he'd brought. A shame to lose that.

"Well, could you possibly take me to the airport?"

"Yup. When I finish here."

"Thanks. Thanks very much. Take your time."

It was ten minutes before the ranger signaled Charles that he was ready to leave.

"I really appreciate this," Charles said. He groaned as he sat gingerly in the pickup.

"You okay?"

"Yes. Fine."

The ranger accelerated. Charles hadn't noticed how rough the road was, coming in. He braced himself with his two hands on the seat, trying to lift his body and avoid the painful impacts.

"Thanks! Appreciate it," he said as he got out of the truck at the airport. Then he saw the plane on the tarmac and moved as quickly as he could into the building.

"Yes?" The woman at the desk asked,

"Ah, yes. Have you got a plane to Orange County today?"

She shook her head. "LA. Leaves in five minutes."

"Ah. How much?"

"Ninety-nine dollars."

Charles flinched. "Is there a bus?"

She shook her head. "Bus south's gone a'ready."

"All right." He reached for his billfold.

"Cash or credit?"

He thought a moment. There was $150 in his wallet. Maybe it would be better if she didn't have his name, in case Leslie went to the police. "Cash," he said, counting out five twenties.

"Name?"

"Henry Johnson."

"Okay, Mr. Johnson." She handed him a dollar. "Luggage?"
He shook his head.

"Better get on out there." She pointed to the door.

Charles heard the plane's engine rev and hurried outside.
As he climbed into the twelve-seat plane, he wondered if he'd
lost his mind. Flying jumbo jets was bad enough, but he was
going over the Sierras in *this?*

He looked down the aisle, with one seat on either side. Well,
at least he wouldn't have to sit next to anyone.

As he fastened his seat belt he focused on all the painful
ways he might get even with Leslie. *Should have called the highway patrol, asked them to stop her,* he brooded. *On what basis?
Stolen car? No, her name is on the registration. Damn that
woman! Damn her to hell!* He'd make her pay for this soon
enough. And if she wanted a divorce, she might have to pay
him. After all she had a good job. One thing was sure: he'd get
those kids from her. In fact, the kids—yes, a very good way to
get back at her. He gnawed at a fingernail. What he needed
right now was a good, stiff drink.

After the plane landed at LAX, Charles walked to the clos-
est airport bar and ordered a double. Then, taking the airport
bus from Los Angeles, he reached home at three that afternoon.
Would Leslie drive straight home or go back to the condo in
Mammoth? No, she'd never risk going to Mammoth and having
him catch up with her there. She was afraid of him, and that
suited him just fine. *Let's see* . . . If she drove straight home,
she'd arrive sometime between five and six. And she probably
wouldn't come to their house. She'd definitely get in touch
with her meddlesome mother though. Maybe the best defense
with Zoë was a good offense. He'd call and give her his version
of what happened before she could talk to Leslie.

Between four and seven he called three times, but reached only Zoë's answering machine. He tried her work number but was told she wasn't available; would he care to leave a message?

Yes, he would. And it would not be pretty. But he hung up instead. He poured himself a glass of whiskey and sat, trying to decide what to do next.

35

⁊

THANK GOD IT'S TOO EARLY IN THE SEASON FOR SKIERS and too late for fishermen, Leslie thought as she noted the light traffic heading south on highway 395. "I will trust You, Lord," she said again and again as the odometer clicked off the miles.

She didn't stop till Kramer Junction. How cramped her legs were! She did some stretching exercises against the car before she went in and sat at the counter. Maybe some soup. She opened the menu. Ah, chicken with rice was the soup of the day. She visualized a clear, easy-to-swallow, soothing broth. But the waitress brought a pasty-looking bowlful, so thick that the spoon rested on top. *Wallpaper paste,* she thought. She took a taste. The flavor wasn't bad. Better eat a little, keep up her strength. She smiled at the echo of her mother's words. She managed only a small amount, ate the crackers, and headed back to the car.

On the homestretch now, she told herself as she slipped back behind the wheel. Till then the trip had been a blur, with her mind, her body, her emotions still in shock. Now she began considering what to do. Yes, she and the children needed a safe place to stay, but how should she cope with Charles? No contact, except by phone. That was a given. Separation. Definitely. But forever? She'd seen her friends go through such ugly divorces. And Charles would be mean.

And what should she tell the children? That their dad had tried to kill her? She sighed. Was it necessary for them to know all the details? No. After all, he was, and would always be, their father.

She connected with Highway 15, and as she headed down the grade from Cajon Pass, the guilt began to surface, and she felt herself begin to sweat. *If I'd kept my mouth shut, I wouldn't be in this mess. Right now, Charles is saying it's my fault. As always, there's some truth there.*

After she turned onto the Santa Ana Freeway, she drove straight to the real estate office. *Charles would never think to come there,* she told herself. Nevertheless, she scanned the parking lot carefully before she pulled in.

She found Zoë working at a computer. "Darling!" she exclaimed, jumping up to hug Leslie.

"Oh, Mom . . ." The tears she'd held back for almost six hours began to flow.

Her mother gathered Leslie into her arms, stroking her hair, whispering the same little soothing "shh, shh" sounds Leslie remembered from infancy.

When at last Leslie stopped weeping, Zoë passed her a box of tissues and motioned to a chair. "I'm so glad you're all right, honey." She gazed at her with immense tenderness. Then her tone turned practical. "Now. I have a safe place for you and the children. I was concerned about your safety this weekend because you can't file for a restraining order till Monday. At first I thought of a shelter. Then I realized that I have a furnished condominium on the market. I know the owners well, and they're in New York till January. I talked with Harriet, and you and the kids are welcome to stay there. She'd be happy to have you water the plants, and so would I, so I don't have to do it. It's in Laguna Hills. I'll give you the keys."

"You're terrific, Mom."

Zoë waved the praise away. "Will you be okay alone tonight?"

"You think I should pick up the kids?"

"Definitely not. Don't spoil their weekend. Besides, David needs Scott. Oh!" She looked at Leslie. "What if they should go back to the house for something? Hadn't you better call Carrie's parents and David, just to be safe?"

Leslie nodded, looked for the phone numbers in the phone book, and called David first. "David, I'm back. I'll explain later, but under no circumstances is Scott to go to our house. I'll pick him up tomorrow and explain then."

"Got it," he said quietly.

She left a similar message with Carrie's mother and looked up to see her mother frowning.

"I don't like the idea of you being alone in that condo tonight," Zoë said. She thought a moment. "I'll come stay there. We'll have a slumber party."

"Thanks, Mom. I'm just—this is so weird—so beyond my wildest nightmares. And I . . ."

"You what?" Zoë's voice was gentle.

"I really precipitated it. I was trying to get Charles to talk about his past. If only I—"

"Leslie, dear one," Zoë interrupted. "I want you to edit 'if only' from your vocabulary. If it hadn't been this, it would have been something else. Charles has been a ticking time bomb for years, and his failing the actuary exam set it off. If this hadn't happened, sooner or later he'd have blown up over something else. *Please,* my darling. You are not to blame. If you feel you were at all out of line, confess it to the Lord. Then let it go. You cannot be responsible for Charles's behavior. He has choices. And he made a very bad one this time."

Zoë saw the tears gathering in Leslie's eyes once again. "No guilt, Leslie," Zoë repeated. As she gave time for the words to register, she looked at Leslie, wishing she could take the pain and shock for her, give her an injection of courage. With no makeup, her auburn hair tucked behind her ears, Leslie looked so young, so vulnerable.

Leslie caught her mother studying her, and Zoë quickly said, "Now, let's go get a little something to eat. I haven't had dinner, and surely you haven't. There's a Coco's on the way to Harriet's condominium, and you can get as much or as little as you want there." She reached for her purse. "Bet you'd like to freshen up first. It's across the hall. You need some lipstick?"

Leslie stood and nodded. "All I had in my pocket was my wallet and keys—and thank God I had them." She paused. "You know, I wouldn't even have had the keys if Charles hadn't made me carry them because my pockets were bigger!" She looked up. "Thank You, Lord." Then she added, "Mom, I was so scared I didn't even go back to the condo, just headed for home."

"Good decision." Zoë gave Leslie the makeup bag from her purse. "You can get your other things from Mammoth later."

She watched as Leslie crossed the room. *Oh, Lord,* she prayed quickly, *You know I've expected a blowup, and I thank You that she wasn't harmed. Help her to take all the necessary steps for her safety, and Father, please calm Charles. Defuse his anger and keep him from any retribution, any further abuse. Help him trust in You.*

She finished her computer entries, exited the program, and checked for messages at home. Someone had called three times but left no message. Charles? she wondered.

At dinner Leslie spilled out the story of the entire weekend, beginning with Charles's recounting of his cruel birthday present, culminating with the look on his face as he shoved her toward the edge of the cliff.

Zoë shook her head. "The poor, miserable man! What a terrible thing to happen to a young child. I am very sorry for him, and I can see the sources of his anger. And I'll continue to pray for him." She put her hand on Leslie's. "But Leslie, clearly, he intended to, as they say, 'do you great bodily harm.' Thank God you're fit and strong. Please, dear, don't go soft and don't be hard on yourself. At that moment by Hot Creek, Charles was as dangerous as a rabid dog." She looked into her daughter's green eyes, trying with all her might to reassure and encourage her. "You did the right thing, and now it's important to take care of yourself—and the children. I pray that you will follow through on this restraining order first thing Monday." She picked up the dinner check. "And don't worry about how to go about it. I can tell you exactly where to go."

"You've been very thorough, Mom. Please don't think I'm not grateful. Did you research all this after I called?"

Zoë shook her head. "I had a battered wife in a Bible study I taught. She went to an agency called Domestic Violence Assistance, and they walked her through all the steps, filling out the forms, going to court—the whole bit. But they're only open on weekdays."

Leslie's eyes widened and she took a sharp breath. "I have to go to court?"

"Don't worry. They'll help you with everything."

Leslie put her elbows on the table and covered her face with both hands. "This is overwhelming."

It is, Zoë thought. "Of course it is, love. But you're not alone. You have family to stand by, to help. Yes, there's a lot to think about. But try to take it like eating an elephant: one bite at a time."

❧

Leslie fell into bed that night so exhausted she went to sleep promptly. But later she wakened again and again, the day's events replaying in her mind. Sometime around five she fell into a deep sleep, rousing to an aching awareness when she heard Zoë in the kitchen a little after seven. Her dusty hiking clothes lay on a chair beside the bed. Wrapping herself in a blanket, she went to the door of the kitchen. "Mom, I just realized I don't have any clothes."

Zoë looked up from the coffee maker. "Poor little waif! I thought of that too. I wondered about my going to your house, but I'm afraid Charles would be there and try to follow me back to you."

"No, don't go. I can wash these things. I see there's a washer and dryer. But I was wondering about church. Today's Sunday."

"Oh, I don't think going back—"

"No, not to our regular church. But there must be something nearby."

"Ah. Good idea. There's a community church that meets in that mall where Coco's is. Now, something to wear. . ." Zoë brightened. "I know. We'll look in Harriet's closet."

"Mom!" Leslie protested.

"Oh, she wouldn't mind. I mean, for church." She winked. "Her clothes would be blessed. I'll go look."

In a moment, Zoë was back with a silk jogging suit. "Tah-dah! Casual but plenty dressy for California. The teal will be perfect on you." She blew a kiss into the air. "Thanks, Harriet!"

"You sure, Mom?"

"Positive." She held the outfit out for Leslie.

"Okay." Leslie took it to the bedroom, put it on, and came back to the kitchen.

"Pants a little roomy," she reported, "but the jacket covers that. Sleeves a tad short, but I'll just push 'em up. I thank you, too, Harriet."

"Now," Zoë said. "Coffee's ready, and I found some whole wheat English muffins in the freezer." She saw Leslie's look. "Don't worry, I'll replace them. We'll have to do shopping for you and the kids."

Leslie managed half a muffin and some coffee, but it only added to the ponderous weight of unease in her stomach. Zoë watched as Leslie twisted her wedding ring on her finger and said softly, "I'm not sure if I can do it—tomorrow."

"Why is that?"

Leslie mumbled something undiscernible.

"Pardon me?

"I don't know if I can do this to my husband," Leslie whispered.

Zoë restrained the sigh she felt and remembered all the battered women she'd read about who refused to file charges. She kept her voice low, reasonable. "Leslie, did your husband or did your husband *not* try to kill you yesterday morning?"

There was a long silence. "I don't think he really knew we were in such a dangerous spot. I don't think he'd actually have done it."

"You must have thought so at the time. You told me he was raving, furious, saying he'd be better off without you."

Silence.

"Was that accurate, Leslie?"

Finally Leslie nodded.

"Dear heart, you're such a warm, loving person. I know it's difficult to face all this. But Leslie, you must protect yourself—and your children. You're safe for today, but what about Monday? Will Charles be waiting for you when you go to work? Might he try to get the children at school? He must be extremely angry that you hurt him, left him stranded, Leslie."

"I—I just feel I'd be signing a death warrant for our marriage."

"Maybe. At least for the marriage you've had. But it could result in a new, better marriage. Think about it. Pray about it."

And now, say no more, Zoë added to herself, *or she'll dig her heels in.* She stood. "I'll call and see what time services are."

～

They went to the ten o'clock service. As they came through the door into the simple auditorium, Leslie saw the loaf of bread and wooden chalice on the table at the front. *Communion. Good.* She needed to focus. This would help.

Loaves of bread were passed along the rows, and each worshiper broke off a piece, waiting to partake together. When everyone was served, the pastor said, "And Jesus said, 'This is my body, given for you. Do this in remembrance of me.' Let us eat and remember."

Leslie placed the bread in her mouth and murmured, "Oh, Jesus, thank You for Your overwhelming love—that You loved enough to die for me."

Later she received her tiny individual cup of grape juice. As she looked down at it, she saw the ceiling lights reflected in the liquid, moving ever so slightly, pulsing like a living thing, she realized, from the pulse in her own thumb. From somewhere in Scripture she remembered, "The blood is the life." Yes, she thought. It is. Eternal life. And life for today, tomorrow.

The choir led a song that was new to her, called "Arms of Love."

> *"I sing a simple song of love*
> *To my Savior, to my Jesus . . .*
> *In Your arms of love,*
> *Holding me still, holding me near*
> *In Your arms of love."*

She looked at Zoë and saw the tears in her eyes. They clasped hands, and Leslie wished this lovely shared moment would never end.

⌘

Later that day Zoë urged Leslie to lie down for an hour. "You have to be exhausted, both emotionally and physically," her mother pointed out.

After a long time in the quiet of the bedroom, Leslie felt herself relaxing, drifting off. Suddenly her entire body jerked as a thought pierced her consciousness. "My husband hates me," she said aloud. *Yes,* she thought, *the man who promised always to love me hates me.* Tears seeped from the corners of her eyes into her hair. There was no mistaking the hatred in his eyes at Hot Creek. He had to hate her to push her toward the cliff.

I've failed in the most intimate relationship two people can have, she thought. *Marriage is a covenant, and the covenant is* broken. *This is the second marriage that's gone wrong. I always make wrong choices. Is there some terrible dark cloud hovering over me?*

To her surprise, little by little, her body began to relax again as though a balm had been spread over her. And the song that had touched her in the morning repeated in her mind. *In Your arms of love, holding me still, holding me near in Your arms of love.*

"I want to receive that love," she breathed. "Receive it as all I really need. Oh, Lord, help me to release the *need* to be pleasing to Charles, to be loved by him.

36

❧

From Zoë's Prayer Journal

November 14: Oh, Lord, I'm late having my time with You today because of staying here in the condo with Leslie. Thank You, Father, for making a way of escape for her from Hot Creek. Father, I confess now I've been very directive with her because I'm so worried she'll weaken and go back. But Lord, You've told me that You're more concerned with her holiness than her happiness. So help me to let go and let You show her Your way. I will trust her to You. And Father God, please make this a wakeup call for Charles. I claim Your Word: "Heal him, and he will be healed; save him, and he will be saved." In Jesus' name, amen.

AS LESLIE GOT UP FROM HER REST THAT AFTERNOON, SHE stared at the wall. *Is this really happening to me?* she wondered. *Maybe I'll wake up and find it's all a dream.* "Don't I wish!" she said aloud.

She sighed and forced herself to review her game plan for the rest of the day. She'd pick up Michelle at 4:30 at Carrie's, but Scott would stay over one more night with David.

I don't want to break the news when I pick Scott up for school tomorrow, she thought. *Better to stop by on the way to get Michelle at Carrie's.*

She found David's number and called.

"Yo!" David answered.

"You two fellas staying out of mischief?" Leslie asked.

"Of course not!"

"Seriously, is Scott doing okay for you?"

"Better than okay. But how about you?"

"I've been better." She hesitated. "Uh, David, I think I'd better run by and talk to Scott for a minute. I don't want to take him by surprise tomorrow."

David's voice sounded guarded. "What's up?"

"I assume Scott's right there, so I'll just clue you in, and you don't have to respond. My husband got really angry at me yesterday at Hot Creek. You've been there. Remember the boiling water? Well, he tried to push me over an embankment. I ran to the car and took off."

"Uh-huh." David's kept his voice matter-of-fact.

"I got away and drove straight home. My mom has me in a condo in Laguna Hills, and that's where I'll stay with the kids for a while. I'm going for a restraining order tomorrow to protect us. Don't know if Charles is even back yet, but wherever he is, he's *really* angry now."

"Right."

"I'm not going to give Scott all the details."

"Right."

"But tell him I'll swing by for a few minutes. Can I bring you anything?"

"Sure. Beer." He chortled. "Us guys have been drinking up a storm, and we're runnin' out of beer."

Leslie gave him a Bronx cheer. "Good-*bye*, David."

When she reached David's apartment, Scott came to the door. "Hi, Mom. What's up?"

She hugged him. "Hi, honey. Missed you." She stepped into

the living room and looked at him closely. "Bet you didn't miss me. What've you been up to?"

"Well, chess. Card games. Taking turns reading to each other. Some videos. Talkin'. David has some great swim videos, done with underwater cameras. You can really see the strokes. He thinks I could be good at butterfly."

"I bet you could." She pulled him down beside her on the couch. "Honey, I want to talk to you a second. Then I'll go in to see David."

"Yeah?"

"Scott, you know your dad and I have had some problems. I thought our going to Mammoth would help. But it didn't. In fact, he got very, very angry at me up there. I had to run away, take the car, so he's undoubtedly madder than ever."

His eyes looked serious, intent, as he listened, but she couldn't begin to discern what he was thinking. At last he said, "What'd he do?"

She hesitated. "He was, as I said, very angry. He grabbed me and tried to hurt me."

"Bet you were scared," he said.

She nodded, grateful for his understanding. "Right now it seems safest for us not to go home. So Gram arranged for you and Michelle and me to stay in a condo in Laguna Hills. Till things calm down, you know? I just didn't want to spring this on you on the way to school tomorrow."

He nodded.

She put her hand on his. "I know this is tough for you to hear, Scott. Are you okay to stay here tonight? Do you want to come with me?"

He shook his head. "Nah. Gotta take care of David."

She smiled. "Atta boy." She hugged him again, feeling the tension in his body, hating how hard this was for him as well as her. "Don't worry. It'll work out." She stood and called out to David, "Ready or not, here I come."

"Always checkin' up on me," David complained as she reached the doorway to the bedroom.

She went over to the bed. "Glad to see you're behaving."

"Well, that Scott—he's tough—and strong. Leslie, I sure appreciate having him here."

"And I was glad to know he was—here."

David nodded. "I'll be sure he's presentable in the morning. You'll be by about seven forty-five?"

"Right." She turned to Scott and put her arm around him. "See you in the morning, honey."

She let herself out of David's apartment and drove to Carrie's house. Carrie's mother Jackie, an adult version of the willowy Carrie, greeted Leslie with enthusiasm. "Hi. Hope you had a good time. We certainly did with Michelle. You have one honey of a daughter."

Leslie smiled at Michelle, across the room. "She really is!" She turned back to Jackie. "This was so good of you."

Jackie swept her hand in an it-was-nothing gesture. "She was no trouble at all. We'll do it again."

"No, our turn next. We'll plan a time after the retreat," Leslie promised. "Thank you so, so much."

As they drove away, Michelle launched into a complete account of the weekend. "Wild animal park was hot . . . This cool show with the birds . . . We rented this far-out movie about these three dudes from New York who get stuck in a little town . . . And then he goes . . . And then the other guy goes . . . And then the horse . . ."

By the time she'd finished, Leslie knew more about the movie than if she herself had seen it. When at last she could get a word in, she asked, "You hungry? How are you on meals today?"

"We had brunch after church. I'm kinda hungry."

"Okay, let's stop and get something. What are you in the mood for?"

"Rhubarb pie."

"Pie? After the stuff you probably ate this weekend?"

Michelle held her fingers up in a scout's honor. "They eat real healthy. Lots of fruits and veggies. Well-l-l, we did have cookies-and-cream frozen yogurt. But that was the absolute worst we did. Honest, I didn't pork out."

"Okay." Leslie headed for Polly's Pies in Laguna Hills. Not likely Charles would cross the freeway to eat.

"Where's Dad?" Michelle finally asked as they walked into the restaurant.

"That's what I want to tell you about."

When they were seated, Michelle said, "So?"

Leslie folded her paper napkin again and again, pressing the creases in with her forefinger. "Well, to get right to the point, the weekend blew up on Saturday morning. Your dad became very angry, and I took off. Drove home."

Michelle's eyes grew larger. "Left him there without a car?"

Leslie nodded.

"Hey-hey, way to go, Mom! Whoo-boy! I bet he was really p—"

Leslie interrupted. "He undoubtedly is very angry."

"You haven't talked to him?"

"No, and I won't—for a while."

Michelle leaned forward. "What d'ya think he'll do?"

"I don't know. And that brings us to my next point. Gram has a listing in Laguna Hills—a condo, and the owners have agreed for us—you, Scott, me—to stay there. It's best your dad not know where we are for a while."

"Really!" Michelle stared at her mother. Then she smiled.

"Heh, heh, just left ol' Mr. Charlie in the dust, huh? So what'd he do? Try to—"

"You ready to order?" came a young voice.

"Burger with fries. Milk." Michelle said.

"And you, ma'am?"

"Um. Vegetable soup. A bowl." She looked at Michelle. "Probably pie later."

"So?" Michelle gave Leslie a questioning look. "Did he try to beat you up?"

"Michelle, no matter what happened between your father and me, he *is* your father, and you are to honor him. I don't care for this 'Charlie' stuff."

"Sheeshe!" Michelle muttered.

"Now, about what happened. No, he didn't try to beat me up. But he did grab me and try to hurt me."

"And you're not gonna tell me any more. O-*kay*." She sulked. "Man, nobody tells me anything."

Leslie smiled at her long-suffering daughter. Then, "Honey, the details aren't important. But I will tell you this. Tomorrow I'm going to get a restraining order that says your dad can't come near any of us."

"Like that, huh?"

Leslie nodded.

"Does Scott know?"

"Yes, I stopped by David's to tell him. Didn't want to hit him with this when I pick him up tomorrow."

"He shook up?"

"I suspect so." She looked up as the server brought her soup.

"Hamburger coming right up," he said.

"So tell me more about your weekend," Leslie said. "Carrie's mother is really nice, isn't she?"

"Oh, yeah. And her dad too. He's a real sweetie. Man, he can't do enough for Carrie's mom, and he jokes and laughs a lot with the kids. He's kinda like a kid on steroids himself."

Leslie laughed and thought, *This is good. Michelle gets a chance to see that all dads aren't like Charles.*

"Carrie and I are definitely best friends. We even know what the other one's thinkin'."

Leslie nodded. "I had a friend like that when I was your age. I'm so glad *you* do."

"You know somethin' kinda weird?"

"No, what?"

"Carrie and her folks have agreed that she won't start dating—one-on-one dating—till she's sixteen."

Terrific! Leslie thought. "And what do you think of that?"

"Seems kinda radical. But maybe it's a good idea. It doesn't mean she can't go to parties and stuff. Actually . . ." She smiled. "Carrie's mom gave her a choice of either waiting till she's sixteen or till she's the same age as her mom was when she started dating."

"Oh?"

"'Cept her mom won't tell her what age that was!"

Leslie laughed. "I knew I liked that woman. So Carrie decided on sixteen."

"Yeah." Michelle thought a moment. "Maybe it's smart to wait till you're more mature." She gave her mother a quizzical look. "How old were you when you started dating?"

"Nineteen," Leslie deadpanned.

"Gimme a break, Mom!"

She smiled at her daughter and reached over to touch her hand. "Tell you what. I'll make you the same deal as Carrie if you like."

Michelle grinned and tossed her head. "I'll think about it."

⌘

The next morning, before she took the kids to school, Leslie called the office.

"Sorry to bother you so early," Leslie apologized to Terry, "but that wonderful weekend you gave me kinda backfired, and I won't be able to come into work first thing."

"What's wrong?"

"Charles lost it up in Mammoth—at Hot Creek, to be exact. I had to run from him. Haven't talked with him since then, but I'm sure he's still angry and probably vindictive. I need to get a restraining order right away. I'm not at all sure he won't try to catch me at work today, and I don't want any unpleasantness there."

"I hear you. But Leslie, are you sure you want to get the restraining order? A friend of mine was in a similar situation, and she was counseled not to get one—that it can tick a husband off so much he can become more violent."

Leslie felt her stomach begin to burn. "Oh, swell. Uh. Well, thanks for telling me, Terry. I'll think about that. I'll be in for sure tomorrow. And today if I can work it out." She paused, feeling guilty for the time she'd missed at work. "I'm sorry, Terry."

"Hey, you gotta do what you gotta do."

As she drove the kids to school, Leslie mulled over Terry's statement. She could well imagine that the restraining order would enrage Charles even more, maybe drive him to . . . Images flipped through her mind of spurned lovers and husbands who ignored restraining orders and appeared suddenly to knife or shoot their wives—and children. Was this a good idea after all?

After she'd dropped off both of the kids, she drove to a

wooded park and sat in the car praying. "Oh, Lord, I'm afraid not to get a restraining order, and now I'm afraid *to* get one. Show me what to do." Then she sat and waited. After what seemed a long time, a Scripture she didn't even realize she knew came into her mind. *For God has not given us a spirit of fear, but of power and of love and of a sound mind.*

She blinked and looked up, seeing the sun's early rays filtering through the trees and turning droplets of dew to sparkles of crystal. "Thanks, Lord," she breathed, feeling an infusion of strength. Raising her fist, she cried out, "I will not live a life ruled by fear of Charles anymore. No—more—scapegoat!"

⤝

A few minutes after nine that morning, Leslie stepped off the elevator and into the Victim-Witness Center in Santa Ana. Ten women sat waiting, some with small children crawling and whining around them. Some of the women looked up apprehensively as she opened the door to come in. *They're afraid their husbands will come after them, even here,* she realized. She swallowed, gave her name to the receptionist, and sat down. Looking around at the women, she saw the fear and, in some cases, anger in their eyes. The room, though cold and institutional with its linoleum floor and gray walls, felt charged with emotion.

She let her gaze move from one to another. What a cross section—everything from a woman in a designer suit to a teenager in torn, filthy jeans. Hispanics, Vietnamese, Anglos, and a handsome black woman nursing her infant. One had her arm in a sling. Another's eye was black.

It could be worse, Leslie thought. *So much heartbreak so much trauma, so much pain.*

Now and then the door by the receptionist opened and someone called a name. While she sat, five other women arrived, one with four preschool children. Leslie sighed and waited. And waited some more, staring at the squares on the floor.

At last she was called into a much larger room and assigned to one of several desks where women sat, ready to give assistance.

As Leslie sat down, the woman said, "Hi, I'm Sherry. How may I help you?" Her tone was pleasant, but Leslie could see in her eyes that she'd seen it all, heard it all, and worked on overload.

"I—" Leslie cleared her throat. "I want a restraining order. For my husband. I'm afraid he'll, um, hurt me. Or my children."

"Then there have been incidences of abuse?"

"Yes, and threats."

"All right. Here's your paperwork. Be sure to tell everything you can think of. Especially physical. Exactly what he said. You take it over to one of those tables." She indicated the long, cafeteria-style tables. "Do you have any questions?"

Leslie stared at the forms, and the print swam before her eyes. "Uh . . ." She could sense Sherry watching her.

"Do you need some help?"

"I'm just feeling a little overwhelmed."

Sherry's no-nonsense voice softened. "Come back to me if you have any questions."

"Thanks." Leslie took the papers to a table and sat down.

Just like the DMV, she thought. *Eleven years of marriage reduced to filling out a form, like applying for a driver's license.*

She took a deep breath and concentrated on answering the questions, filling in the blanks, putting down everything she could think of, including Charles's slapping of Michelle.

When at last she'd finished, she went back to Sherry, who

inspected the forms. "You did a much more thorough job than most. So you basically want a stay-away order."

Leslie nodded. "Right. I do not want him to come where we are living, where the kids go to school, or to the pool where my son swims, or where I work."

Sherry scribbled on the paperwork. "Okay, the next step is going to court. It'll be some time this afternoon. A commissioner will review your application, and if he okays it, a hearing date will be set."

"What's the time lapse here?"

"Two weeks, usually, till the hearing."

Leslie caught her breath. "Am I protected during that time?"

"Yes. You get a temporary restraining order. And you have to have papers served to your husband during that time."

Leslie sighed. "Thanks."

Sherry smiled and held out her hand. "Good luck."

Leslie left the office and looked for a phone. She called the office.

"Hi, Terry. Leslie. I'm in Santa Ana, and—"

"Oh, Leslie, Charles was here."

Leslie felt her heart accelerate. "No fooling!"

"Yes, sweet as could be. Admired my sweater. No mention of the weekend. Of course, he wanted to know where you are. I played dumb, just said you'd called in and said you wouldn't be in today."

"Thanks, Terry. I—I'm sorry, but it looks like I'll be here well into the afternoon. I'll come in, though, if I can get there before four."

"No, don't. You have enough going on. We'll be okay."

"Sure?"

"Sure. And good luck."

As Leslie waited, listening to the footsteps, watching the sheriff's deputies with their guns, she looked up to see a woman who might well have been in a traffic accident. Two front teeth were missing. Green-and-purple bruises surrounded both eyes and spread down one side of her face. A bandage covered her upper lip.

"May I?" she asked, looking at the chair beside Leslie.

"Of course."

"I'm Betty," the woman said.

"Leslie." She couldn't stop herself. "Oh, Betty, you poor thing!"

"Not a thing of beauty, am I?" Betty gave a crooked smile. "But one helpful friend pointed out that these colors are in my color palette."

Leslie laughed, then quickly sobered. "Are you in a lot of pain?"

"I'm okay. At least I'm doing what I should have done nine years ago."

"You mean this has been going on all this time?"

Betty nodded. "I've left three times. And gone back. It always got worse. Abuse escalates, you know. The more they get away with, the more they do." She pulled a picture from her purse. "Next time I think about going back, I'm gonna look at this."

Leslie glanced at the Polaroid print. The woman's face was so swollen, her features were unrecognizable.

"That was five days ago," Betty said.

Leslie felt faint. *There but for God's grace . . ."* Betty looked at her with concern. "You okay?"

Leslie swallowed. "I think maybe my blood sugar is down. What would you say to some lunch?"

"Great!"

The two women went to the cafeteria for a sandwich, sitting outside even though the November day was cool. By the time Leslie was called into court, she knew Betty's entire history. And her words, "Abuse escalates, you know," had strengthened Leslie's resolve.

At 4:30, Leslie walked out of the county building with her temporary restraining order and the papers for Charles, which she would ask someone from work to deliver for her.

That evening she asked God for His strength, went into the bedroom of the condo, closed the door, and called Charles.

"Charles, it's Leslie."

"Where the hell *are* you? Where the hell is my car?" he shouted, but he didn't wait for an answer. "I am not at all certain I want to speak with you after what you did to me. I am not sure if I can forgive you, Leslie."

She shook her head in disbelief. "Forgive *me*, Charles?"

"Well, yes. For injuring me grievously and painfully. For literally stealing my car. Leaving me stranded. You are fortunate I did not charge you. This is extremely serious, Leslie."

Leslie's anger flared, and it was an effort not to shout back. But she asked quietly, "And trying to push me into Hot Creek is not serious?"

"Oh, come now, Leslie! You always did have a vivid imagination, and you are completely devoid of a sense of humor. Surely you did not take me seriously."

Oh, right, Charles, it was just a joke, Leslie said to herself. Then, "Yes, Charles, I did. And I'm calling to tell you that I now have a temporary restraining order that says you are not to come near me or the children. Not where we are staying. Not at my work. Not at their school or at the pool. Stay away, period. The hearing is in two weeks, and I want you to know that papers will be served to you in a day or so."

Charles snarled, "You call yourself a Christian?" His voice was so loud she held the phone away from her ear. "You had better start reading your Bible, lady!" There was a brief silence. "Well, I guess I should not be surprised," he almost whispered. "This is certainly typical of you, Leslie. Overreaction. Oversensitivity. You are truly pathetic!"

She was sweating now, but she kept her voice firm. "Call it what you will, Charles." And then, to her surprise, she heard herself say, "But I will not be your scapegoat any longer. Good night."

37
꒱

CHARLES SLAMMED THE RECEIVER SO HARD IT BOUNCED OFF
the base. He banged it into place, muttering, "Silly bitch!"
Heading for the bar, he refilled his glass with bourbon.

He gulped the drink, sat down, and searched his memory.
Did he know an attorney? If Leslie was going to play dirty, he
could play dirtier. She thought she could have the court tell
him what he could do and where he could go, did she? He'd
give her a mighty fight at the hearing.

She brought it all on herself, he brooded. Always digging,
probing, constantly asking questions. Curiosity killed the
wife!

He laughed at his clever twist on an adage. Finishing the
bottle of bourbon, he laid it on its side so the last few drops
would accumulate. Meantime he'd switch to wine. But he
found only half a glass left in the bottle in the refrigerator. He'd

have to go out for more. And while he was out—maybe—yes, it was a good idea—he would stop by that pushy, holier-than-thou mother-in-law's and tell her just what he thought of her. Maybe, it suddenly occurred to him, Leslie was there.

The room seemed to tilt a little when he went to grab his car keys, but getting out to the garage proved no problem. He backed the car out and turned into the street, thinking vaguely how dark it seemed. Driving out of the tract and onto Toledo Way, he heard a car honk long and hard at him, and he swore back at the driver. He crossed Bake Street, hearing a screech of brakes to his right, and had traveled only a short distance when he saw the flashing lights behind him. He swore and accelerated. But before he reached Alton, the black-and-white car forced him to the right, and he stopped. In a moment he heard a knock on his window. He rolled it down and muttered a stream of invectives.

"Sir," the deep, calm voice interrupted, "California Highway Patrol. Your headlights are not on. May I see your driver's license, please?"

Charles fumbled in a pocket and found no billfold. He patted his other pockets. Nothing. "No," he said.

"All right, would you get out of your car, please?"

"Not only no, but hell no!" Charles replied, glaring at the officer.

"I will ask you one more time, sir. Please get out of the car."

Charles stared straight ahead and didn't move.

In one quick motion the officer reached in the window, unlatched the door, and pulled Charles out of the car before he could brace himself. The uniformed man was huge. Charles swung at him but missed. The officer grabbed his arm and twisted it behind him. Charles swore at him. "You're hurting me!" But he couldn't fight the hold.

"You're coming with me," the officer said, handcuffing him quickly and forcing Charles toward the car with the flashing lights.

"Damned if I will." Charles struggled to break the officer's hold but quickly found himself thrust into the backseat. "Surely, officer, y'r—you are not going to inciner—incar—incarcerate me."

"Yes, sir, that's exactly what I am going to do."

❧

Leslie returned to work Tuesday, finding a day so full of makeup appointments from the previous day, she had little time to think about anything but her patients.

Midafternoon David called. "Got the results from the second MRI. Dr. Scanlon finally admitted he was concerned about a fracture in the vertebrae."

"Me too, David."

"But the MRI didn't show anything. Bone scan was normal. Blood work okay. So the diagnosis is that the nerves were irritated by the stress of standing. I have a prescription for a new anti-inflammatory, and I'm s'posed to ease back into activity slowly."

"Good!" Leslie felt a surge of hope. If there were no fractures, no severe nerve damage, David had a chance of walking. "What did Dr. Scanlon say about therapy?"

"Wants me to start tomorrow. He'll be in touch with you."

"Fine. You know, David, I'll actually be glad to see your ugly face here again."

"Gee, that really warms my heart!" His tone grew serious. "Did you get that restraining order?"

"I did. Charles was not exactly—cordial—when I told him."

"Figures. Hang in there. I'm prayin' for you."

"Thanks, David. I'll transfer you to Terry, and she can give you an appointment for tomorrow. See you."

The rest of the day sped by, and she hurried to pick up Scott and Michelle. When they reached the condominium, Leslie changed into her freshly washed hiking jeans and turtle-neck, wondering when Michelle would start complaining about needing clothes from home. She switched on the TV in the family room to catch the news as she prepared dinner.

"A late-breaking story in Orange County after this," the news anchor promised. During the commercial, Leslie turned away to put the french fries Scott had requested into the oven and to adjust the flame under the porkchops. Then she heard, "A twelve-year-old mystery may be heading for resolution in Orange County."

Leslie turned toward the TV and saw an orange prison jumpsuit. "Charles!" she gasped.

She ran to the TV and switched it off, impulsively wanting to shield the children, who were both watching from the couch.

"Hey!" Scott sprang up and ran to turn the television back on again.

". . . under arrest as a suspect in the Sally Jameson murder, twelve years ago in Garden Grove," the news anchor contin-ued. "We take you now to Orange County Jail and reporter Nate Matthews."

"Call it luck, call it fate," said a reporter standing outside the jail, "but a drunk-driving arrest may have uncovered a killer. Charles Harper was arrested in Irvine last night and taken to Orange County jail—'"

"No!" Scott screamed.

"Sh-h-h!" Michelle warned.

"—was fingerprinted," the newscaster continued. "Harper's prints, fed into the computer system, matched those found at the scene of an unsolved murder that took place more than a decade ago. Harper is an insurance actuary, married for eleven years, with two children. He has no previous police record, not even traffic tickets."

"*Dad?!*" Michelle shrieked.

"No way!" Scott insisted.

Leslie sank down on the couch and put her arms around the kids, drawing them close to her.

The newscast cut to a photo of a woman with tightly curled blonde hair. "Twenty-two-year-old Sally Jameson was found dead in her apartment from a blow to her head on January 5, 1983. No witnesses ever came forward, and although an itinerant worker confessed to the crime, it was subsequently found that he had been in jail in Mexico at the time of the murder. Jameson had last been seen at a Garden Grove bar around nine or ten the night of January fifth, and time of death was determined to be about eleven that evening."

The voice droned on with other news, and for a moment Leslie thought she might be ill. She swallowed against the gag reflex and closed her eyes. "T-turn it off, Scott," she managed.

Then the room was silent, except for the sizzle of the chops in the kitchen. At last Michelle said, "Well, for sure he can get really *ug*-ly, but Dad *killing* someone?"

"We don't know he *did* it!" Scott shouted, standing in front of the couch. "Police can be wrong, Michelle!"

"But the fingerprints, Scott!"

Scott grabbed Michelle's arm and tried to twist it. "Stop it! *Stop* it!"

Michelle stood up. "Okay . . . Okay, Scott. Cool it, man."

Leslie stared into space. The children's voices sounded very far away. "Yes," she echoed, "police can be wrong." She felt as though she had entered another dimension, as unreal as a *Star Trek* voyage. Somewhere she could hear something cooking, but she didn't care. And slowly an eerie sense of relief filtered into her consciousness as she realized she didn't need the restraining order. She was safe from Charles now.

"Mom?"

She realized Michelle had spoken to her several times. "You want to lie down, Mom? You don't look so hot."

She shook her head. "Just give me a minute. This is so unreal. I—" She looked up at the children and reached out for them, tears rising. "Oh, my darlings."

Scott and Michelle knelt by her, and they huddled together in a long hug.

At last Scott said softly, "Think we oughta call Gram?"

Their whispers drifted away, but Leslie could hear them, somewhere as in a dream. An occasional word, "shock . . . dangerous . . . safe . . ." filtered through.

Yes, they're safe now too, she thought. *Were we always in danger, all those years? Were we living with a murderer?* She shook her head, trying to focus her thoughts. The ring of the phone jarred her back.

"I'll get it," Michelle said. Then, "Hi, Gram. Oh, Gram, you been watching TV? Gram, I—we feel like we've been hit by a mega-bomb. Yup. Yup. Kinda zoned out. Mom?" she called. "Wanna talk to Gram?"

Leslie nodded and forced herself to walk to the phone.

She leaned against the counter. "Hi, Mom," Leslie heard herself say.

"Leslie, dear heart. I guess we both saw the same thing. Channel five? How are . . . are you? . . . Oh, honey, you must be in complete shock."

"Right."

"A reporter just called me. Amazing how they track you down. I didn't reveal where you are."

"Good. I—I don't want to say anything, Mom. I—I suppose I ought to go see Charles. I don't—don't know if I can."

"I gather there will be plenty of time. You needn't be in a rush." Zoë was quiet a minute. "Leslie, do you suppose this could have something to do with Charles's recurrent night-mares?"

Leslie jerked upright. "I hadn't thought of that. I hadn't thought of anything, to tell the truth, except how *extreme* this is. I mean, am I suppose to believe I've been living with a mur-derer for eleven years?"

"I know, I know. Of course, there may well be some mis-take," Zoë said.

"Yes."

Silence.

"Do you want me to come over, Leslie?"

"No, Mom, I—I just want to be with the kids."

"Of course, dear. I understand." Her quiet tone changed. "Oh, Lord," she pleaded, "sort this out. Show us the truth, and give Leslie, Michelle, Scott—and me too—the grace to handle it. In Jesus' name."

"Amen. Thanks, Mom. Bye."

"Man, is this a bombshell?" Michelle took the phone from Leslie. "I turned off the porkchops. Can I fix a plate for you?"

"No, thanks, honey." *I need a moment,* she thought, *just a moment by myself. Got to regroup.* "I'll be back in just a sec," she told them and went into the bedroom.

Without turning on the light, she knelt by the bed.

"Oh, Lord," she whispered, "I don't even know what to say. You promise that Your Holy Spirit will be our intercessor when we don't know how to pray, and I ask that right now. Oh, Father, did Charles do it? Have I been living with an impostor all these years—a man claiming to be honest and upright? Is that the reason he wouldn't go to counseling, wouldn't allow me to ask questions about his past? Have we all been living a lie? My plea is just one word: Help!"

Then she thought of the kids and the shock they had to feel. "Please, Lord," she added, "give me strength to be there for them when they need me. Is there something I could say, right now, that might help them?"

She waited and in a moment remembered a Bible verse about God and the fatherless. Turning on the light, she looked at the concordance in the back of her Bible. She turned to Psalm 68:5. Good, she'd read this passage to them. And then wasn't there something about God's faithfulness to all generations? She found it in Psalm 100. "Oh, Lord, You are so good!" she murmured as she left the bedroom, her fingers keeping the places in her Bible.

In the living room, she found the kids using the remote to flip channels on the TV. "We thought there might be something else," Michelle explained. "But all the early-evening newscasts are over."

Nodding, Leslie switched off the TV, sat down with them, and opened the Bible. "I—I think God showed me some verses that might help us all. You must feel like the bottom's dropped out of your lives, and so do I. But listen to this." She opened the Bible to Psalm 68. "It's talking about God here. 'A father to the fatherless, a defender of widows, is God in his holy dwelling.'"

"Yeah. Good. I feel kinda fatherless," Scott said.

"And I feel a little like a widow," Leslie nodded. She looked down at her Bible and turned to the other verse she'd found.

"And this is in Psalm 100, verse 5. 'For the LORD is good and his love endures forever; his faithfulness continues through all generations.'" She looked from Michelle to Scott. "That includes your generation. And mine. Let's try to hang on to that."

She closed her Bible and stared at the stove. Food held no appeal, but she said, "Guess we ought to have dinner." She jumped up as she remembered the french fries. "Uh-oh." Grabbing a hot pad, she opened the oven door and pulled out the pan. Not quite burned but definitely crisp. "Get the salads out of the fridge, will you, Michelle?" she asked as she served the plates.

As they sat down at the table, Michelle said, "Those were good verses, Mom. Now we better pray."

"Yeah," Scott said.

"Well, you're the man of the family," Michelle pointed out.

Scott seemed to grow a little taller. He bowed his head. "Father, we, ah, don't know what to think. But we do believe You're in charge of this whole mess. We ask You to watch over Dad, who's gotta feel grossed out if this is true and grossed out, too, if it's not. Be faithful to all generations, like You promised. Oh, and Lord, please bless our food, in Jesus' name."

"That was perfect, Scott," Leslie said.

She looked at her plate, wondering if she had the energy to lift her fork. Michelle took her knife and fork to cut a bite of porkchop, and the minute she pressed down with the knife, the overdone porkchop shot off her plate across the table.

Scott began to laugh, "Pork's—supposed—to—be—well—done," he managed.

Then they were all laughing uncontrollably, tears coursing down their cheeks.

When they recovered, Leslie said, "The french fries are losers too. Just eat your salads, and I'll think of something."

Who, she wondered, *could possibly swallow porkchops and french fries at a time like this, anyway?* What the kids needed was comfort food. Something soft and creamy and soothing. She looked in the refrigerator. Only two eggs.

"I'm looking for something that doesn't stick in our throats."

"Something that slides down real easy," Scott agreed.

"I know," Michelle said. "If we have the fixings . . ."

She got up and went to the refrigerator. Opening the freezer door, she noted, "There's frozen yogurt." She opened the refrigerator. "And chocolate syrup. And milk. Everything we need." Glancing over at the counter, she saw the blender. "Aha!"

Why not? Leslie thought, and started to get up. But Scott was already on his feet. "I know how to do this," he said.

Good, Leslie thought. Give them something to do, keep their minds off Charles a moment longer. She watched as the kids plopped ingredients into the blender, gave it a whir. Her mind began to whir. *I need to call the jail,* she thought. *Need to find out everything they'll tell me.*

The thud of a glass placed in front of her made her jump. The kids had produced decent-looking shakes.

She'd have to at least taste hers. "This really *is* comfort food," she said and then surprised herself by drinking most of it.

When they'd finished, she told them, "I need to make a phone call. Will you two clean up?"

In the bedroom she looked up the number for the Orange County Jail and dialed. A recorded message gave the location, told her she needed the inmate's booking number to obtain information. It also said that if an inmate was returning from court, to call after 3 in the morning to allow time for processing. Then there was information on posting bail and signing up to visit, and saying that she could remain on the line for further information.

She waited, examining her cuticle, winding the cord around her finger, receiving repeated messages that someone would be with her in a moment. At last she heard the line ringing. But no one answered. She began counting: twenty-one, twenty-two, twenty-three . . . On the thirty-sixth ring, an operator asked if she could help her.

"Yes, my husband has been booked, and I don't know the booking number, but I want to know when I can see him."

"Visiting hours are Thursday, Friday, Saturday, and Sunday from eight A.M. to six P.M.," the operator recited.

"But today is Tuesday. Does that mean I can't see him till Thursday? Are there no visiting hours on Wednesday."

"Only by special arrangement."

"But how do I do that?"

"Just a moment please."

A click. Another click. *Buzz. Static. Dial tone.*

She threw the receiver on the bed in exasperation, wanting to scream. "My husband's in jail on suspicion of *murder*—of *killing* someone," she muttered, "and I can't talk to a single human being who will give me a clue about what's going on. This is infuriating! I'm going to write letters. I'm going to send a telegram to my congressman. I'm going to call TV stations! I'm going to . . ."

She sighed, picked up the phone, and started over again.

38

LESLIE TRIED AGAIN AND AGAIN THAT NIGHT TO CALL THE
Orange County Jail for information on how to see Charles
before Thursday. By eleven she had learned only his booking
number and that no bail had been set for him.

At last, exhausted, she gave in to the system. She wasn't
sure she was ready to see Charles the next day anyway. She
needed first to get used to the idea of—she could barely verbalize it, even in her mind—Charles in jail, Charles linked to a
murder. A part of her wanted to postpone forever her facing
him, hearing and seeing his reaction, knowing the truth. Or
would Charles tell her the truth? He'd lied before—maybe even
lived a lie throughout their marriage. Could she trust him now?

It was very late before her mind stopped racing and she fell
asleep. But she awakened in time to journal her prayers. That
morning she ended with a plea for Scott and Michelle: "Please,

make them strong enough to withstand any mean responses from the other kids, because, Lord, You and I know well how deeply words can wound."

Later, at work, Terry met her at the door and gave her a long, warm hug. "My God, I never imagined . . . Oh, I don't know what to say. I'm just so glad you're okay—that—" She drew back, still stammering.

"It's okay," Leslie said. "I don't know what to say—or think—either. I can't see Charles till tomorrow, so I just want to put in a normal day—whatever that is."

"I appreciate it," Terry said. "Let me know if there's anything—anything at all I can do."

"I will."

The other personnel of the center came to hug her.

"Hey, I'm so sorry." Kelly said.

"Oh, Leslie. This is unreal," said Brynne, shaking her head.

"Is it—is it all over the paper this morning?" Leslie asked.

Terry nodded. "First page of the Orange County section in the *Times*."

"It was in the *Register*. Front page," Kelly added. "Told how all the neighbors said Charles was a quiet man, kept to himself."

"Isn't that what they always say about killers? Quiet; a loner?" Leslie sighed. "I was afraid of a lot of press." She headed for her desk, praying, "Lord, help me through this," and forced herself to look at her appointment schedule. Ah, David at ten. A bright spot.

At five before ten, David rolled in with the gusto of a famished man ready to dig into a feast after days of fasting. Eying the equipment in the exercise room with open-mouthed eagerness, he rubbed his hands together, and his eyes crinkled as he grinned. "Man, am I ready! Where do we start?"

He doesn't know what's happened, she thought and smiled at his enthusiasm. "Carefully. Very carefully. We'll start with some biceps curls."

David groaned. "Back to square one." As he took the weights, he looked at her carefully. "You look beat. What's up?"

"You must not have had the TV on—or read the newspaper."

"Guilty," he said. "Some guys stopped by last night. And I just caught the front page and sports section of the *Times* this morning."

"Charles is in jail," she said quietly.

"Hey! You get him on assault?"

"No, he got a DUI. They ran a fingerprint check. Seems Charles's prints match prints from an unsolved murder twelve years ago."

David stopped his curls and whistled. "Think there's something to it?"

She shrugged. "I have no idea. But you know, I've felt for a long time there was some—some demon—maybe not possessing Charles but certainly pursuing him."

"So maybe it's his past."

She shrugged. "Maybe."

"And if it is, no wonder he was so edgy, so needing to always be in control." He thought a moment. "Man, I'd better pray for him."

"He definitely needs it. Thanks." She motioned to the mat. "Okay, David, let's get to work."

As he transferred from his wheelchair, David asked, "How'd you find out? He call?"

She shook her head. "On TV last night. Okay, David. Arm lifts."

"Good God!" he exclaimed, as he pressed with his arms to lift his buttocks off the mat, lowering himself slowly. "You and the kids must be in total shock." He concentrated on his lifts a moment. "How's m'bud Scott doing?"

"In denial, basically. His stance is that we don't *know* his father did anything wrong."

David nodded. "That's Scott. And I bet Michelle's gone into orbit."

"Uh-huh. Oh, David, pray the kids at school won't be too vicious."

"I know what you mean." He thought a moment. "I think I'll try to head the swim team off at the pass—say something to them first, before they start jabbering. I'll tell 'em Scott's a separate person from his father. He's still Scott, and we treat him exactly the same as before."

Leslie felt her eyes mist over. "I'd be grateful. Now, let's get the medicine ball."

༄

That afternoon Leslie picked Scott up from school first. "How'd it go?" she asked, trying to hide her anxiety.

"Well," he hesitated. "There was some whispering. But nobody really said anything to me." He was quiet a moment. "Miss Atkins called me aside a minute and said she was really sorry, and we have to remember that in this country we're innocent till found guilty." He looked Leslie in the eyes as though making a point specifically to her. "And she said she was available for me to talk to anytime."

"That was nice."

He nodded. "Course, when we find out it's all a mistake, there won't be any problem."

Leslie winced inwardly. "Oh, Scott . . ." she began, then stopped.

"Well, there won't!" Scott insisted.

"Right," she breathed.

At the junior high Michelle stood waiting, and for a

moment Leslie thought she could literally see the storm cloud surrounding her daughter. Michelle yanked the rear door open, threw herself into the seat, and slammed the door so hard the windows rattled. "Well!" she fumed. "It's like there's a big skull-and-crossbones sign on my back, or like I have leprosy or something. All the kids are like totally freaked out. And that zit-face Travis who used to call me all the time? I heard him say, 'Stay away from that chick. Her dad's a killer.'"

Leslie shifted into park and turned back, reaching for Michelle's hand, but she folded her hands under her arms and stared defiantly at Leslie.

"I'm so sorry, Michelle."

"Not as sorry as I am!" Michelle snapped. "My life is basically ruined. That's all. I'm going to have to move to—to Zimbabwe or somewhere no one knows me."

"It'll be okay when we find out it's all a mistake about Dad," Scott offered.

"You stupid or something?" Michelle shouted, leaning toward Scott. "You know he did it. He's mean enough to."

"No, he's not!" Scott screamed.

"Ha! Well, at least I'm not related to him. He's not *my* dad. You're the one who has his wicked genes, Scott!"

"Stop that, please, both of you!" Leslie intervened. "It's hard enough for all of us without lashing out at each other. We must be civilized and remember to treat each other the way we'd like to be treated. Is that clear?" She waited and saw Scott nod. Michelle sat motionless.

"Now," Leslie continued. "Tomorrow I'm going to go see your dad, and we're all going to have to support each other till we find out exactly what is going on." She turned to Scott. "Scott, I need your cooperation very much. May I count on it?"

He sat, chin quivering, taking shallow breaths for several seconds. Finally, "Yes."

She twisted in the seat to look at Michelle. "Michelle, I need and want your cooperation. May I count on it?"

Michelle sat, her mouth set in an angry inverted U. No response.

"All right. Let me know when you make a decision." Leslie turned, shifted into drive, and headed for the condominium.

Thursday morning Leslie spotted a headline on the second page of the Orange County section: SUSPECT IN 12-YEAR-OLD MURDER PLEADS NOT GUILTY. She studied the article about Charles's arraignment, held the previous day. His attorney had requested a time-waiver for the preliminary hearing, with the date set for December 12.

Surely he's allowed phone calls, she thought. *Wonder why he hasn't called. Wonder what I'll find when I go to the jail today.*

She used her lunch time to drive to Santa Ana, eating half a sandwich in the car as she fought the traffic on the freeways.

I hate this Civic Center—never know where to park, she fretted as she exited the freeway and found Flower Street. At last she pulled into a parking lot, crossed the street, and walked into the jail building.

A deputy sat at an information desk just inside the door.

"I'd like to see Charles Harper. I'm his wife." She gave his booking number.

"Right. You have a photo ID?"

"My driver's license."

"Fine. Fill out this form, please."

Of course. Another form. Leslie filled it out, then the deputy checked her ID and said, "We'll send a slip up to him that you're here. Have a chair over there."

She joined five people who sat waiting, including two

women with small children. This time she'd brought a newspaper, but she was too nervous to concentrate. Suddenly she wondered if Charles might refuse to see her. She had no idea what his mood, his attitude, would be. His words on Monday still resounded in her head: "overreacting . . . pathetic!"

Again she sat listening to resounding footsteps, babies crying.

It was almost two o'clock when her name was called and she took the elevator to the second floor. Stepping into the visiting area, she saw a series of booths with telephones. A thick glass partition separated visitors and prisoners. Tears stung her eyes as she passed one fragile visitor, hand pressed against the glass partition to "touch" the hand of a burly, bearded man on the other side.

At last Charles shuffled into the room, head down, seemingly pounds thinner than a few days earlier. When he sat down and lifted his head, Leslie could see deep shadows beneath his eyes, which were veined with red. The orange of the jumpsuit drained the color from his face, rendering it the pasty color of bread dough.

He looked so Godforsaken, Leslie could feel no anger. Just pity.

He lifted both hands in a what-can-I-say gesture and looked away. The sudden pain that gripped Leslie's chest surprised her, and she realized how much she had expected—no, hoped—he'd say it was all a mistake, thump on the table, call all authorities idiots. Instead, before her sat a beaten, resigned shell of a man, a stranger.

At last they both picked up their phones. "Hello, Charles," she said.

"Hello, Leslie. Thank you for coming."

There was a long silence. Then Leslie said, her voice shaking a little, "Charles, I have to hear it from you. Is it true?"

She couldn't hear his reply.

"I'm sorry?" she asked.

His voice was husky. "Yes, it's true."

She sighed and started to ask what had happened but stopped herself. He didn't like her to probe; she'd certainly learned that. So she waited, smelling the disinfectant used to clean the area, trying to breathe through her mouth to minimize it.

Finally he looked at her, then quickly away again. "I'm so ashamed," he said. He waited a moment before continuing. "You deserve to hear the whole story, Leslie. We did not even meet—that woman and I—in the bar, but we were both there. I just saw her. And she—you know—sent potent come-on signals across the room. She was attractive in a common sort of way, wearing a very short skirt and a very tight V-neck top that showed all of her, ah, attributes. When she left, I was not altogether sure if she wanted me to follow or not. But I was alone. And I thought, Charles, you are always so cautious. Maybe this could be an adventure." He gave a bitter laugh.

"So I finished my drink. And then I went out. There was no one else in the parking lot but us. We talked for a minute, and then she smiled a seductive little smile and said, 'Why don't we have a little drink at my place?'"

Charles swallowed and rubbed the back of his hand over his forehead. "So, she, um, gave me her address. She left first, and I followed a minute later. Her apartment was not very distant, and I went and rang her bell and she let me in. She fixed us drinks, and we, you know, laughed and joked. And she was moving in close to me. So I started kissing her, and she seemed more than a little responsive, and I went a little further."

I don't want to hear this, Leslie thought. *I do not! But she let him go on.*

391

"And then, suddenly, she turned all 'back-off-buster.' I thought she was teasing, that it was part of her way, that she wanted me to be assertive. So I decided, well, I will ease her down on the rug here. She—" He closed his eyes. "She lost her balance, and I fell with her, and her head hit the corner of a glass-topped coffee table."

Leslie closed her eyes, wanting to cry out, "Stop!"

But Charles continued, "Suddenly there was blood every-where—I mean *everywhere,* and her mouth was open and she wasn't breathing and I couldn't get a pulse." He pressed his lips together and looked down. "I panicked and grabbed a towel to get the blood off my own hands. And with it still in my hands, I ran, and I never saw a single soul all the way out to my car. I always thought that was so very strange." He sat, his face con-torted, his breathing labored, like the times he'd wakened from the nightmares.

"The next day it was in the papers," Charles continued. "She was a waitress in a coffee shop, I learned, but she had a record for drugs and prostitution." He gave a rueful smile. "Picked a dandy, didn't I?" He swallowed with difficulty. "The police had no suspects. Then a guy confessed, but he was a loony. I kept waiting for the police to come ring my doorbell. But it never happened. By the time I met you, the memories had begun to fade, and I felt pretty safe."

"But you weren't safe from the nightmares. That's what they were all about, wasn't it?" Leslie said.

He nodded.

"And that's why you didn't want me prying."

"Yes." He looked up at her and his chin began to quiver; she could hear him breathing even harder. He set the phone down and buried his head in his hands, and huge convulsive sobs took possession of his entire body.

She reached toward him, stopped by the glass, once again wanting to comfort him, knowing she couldn't and that, in fact, there had always been an invisible emotional wall between them.

He took a shuddering breath, picked up the phone, and muttered, "I made sport of you for crying on the way to Mammoth. Now look at me." He wiped his nose with his fist.

"Charles, I am so sorry you've had to live with this all this time. Is there some—well, some sense of relief now?"

He nodded. "Yes. But look what I've done to you."

Had she heard correctly? Was he actually thinking about her?

"And now there is no way I can make it up to you," he continued. "I am going to jail. The only question is, to jail for what? If there is a trial, it will be to determine what I am guilty of. And it will be costly. Then Scott and Michelle will have an inmate for a father."

"But isn't it clear it was an accident? You didn't go there with the intent of . . . you didn't mean to . . ."

"And there are no witnesses. Well, we shall see, shall we not?" Charles managed a grim smile.

"I see in the paper that you have an attorney, Charles."

He nodded. "I called him Monday night. He was there for the arraignment and is coming again this afternoon."

"Good. Do you feel he's—"

A deputy approached Charles and said something to him.

"What's that about, Charles?"

He shrugged. "He says I have an appointment in medical. The intake procedure is very thorough. Mental screening, medical triage."

She blew him a kiss, and he gave her a faint smile. She watched him stand, turn, and walk toward the door.

She heard a woman visitor crying and hurried to the elevator and out the door, across the street to the parking lot, knowing her own emotional floodgates were near to breaking. She unlocked the car and climbed in. There, safe in her own glass-and-steel isolation cell, warm from the sun, she wept. Wept for Charles, the abused child. Wept for Charles, the fugitive, for though he hadn't been running physically these twelve years, he definitely had been fleeing emotionally.

She wept for the wasted years with him—but no, they weren't wasted, for they had given her Scott. She wept for her own deception, for all the emotional battering she'd suffered. And she wept for the kids' future as the children of a criminal, for the additional humiliation and ridicule they would undoubtedly suffer at school.

When she could cry no more, she realized, *There is one thing. I won't have to walk on eggs anymore. I won't have to try to second-guess what will come next, or try to sidetrack it, ward it off. The kids and I can safely move back home tonight.*

Maybe God has given me the wings of a dove!

The thought made her shake her head. *But oh, Lord, we need to be careful what we pray for. Getting what we ask—it may not be what we expect!*

39

WHEN THE DOOR CLANGED SHUT ON HIS EIGHT-MAN CELL,
Charles hurried past the five men watching TV, feeling half-
sick from his meeting with Leslie. *I've blown one thing after
another,* he thought as he stumbled into the bunk area where
two others lay with unfocused, aimless eyes.

"Wife takin' it hard?" The one with the scraggly beard
looked up at Charles.

"Could be worse," Charles mumbled, climbing up onto his
upper bunk and stretching out on his side, head toward the
wall. He needed to think, and he definitely did not want any
further questions.

Talk and more talk. That was just one of the problems of
being cooped up with seven other human beings—if you could
call them that. He half-wished he'd been arrested for something worse so he'd be separated from the others, perhaps in

his own cell, no matter how small. At least there would be some privacy. He tried not to think of where he might be once he was sentenced.

What an abysmal disaster he'd made of his life! If only he hadn't gone out in the car last Monday when he was drinking, the past might never have been uncovered. Yes, and if only on that night twelve years ago he'd called the police right then and there. He could have saved himself and his family the ghastly nightmare they were living right now. But no, if he'd called that night, he might never have met Leslie or had Scott. And now, what if, having hidden the truth away all these years, he was convicted of murder? What if he got life in prison, even death? His heart raced and his face burned.

He turned on his back and tried to take slow, deliberate breaths. When he'd calmed a little, he reviewed Leslie's visit, seeing again the dark circles under her eyes, her impulsive gesture of reaching out to him only to be blocked by the glass. She'd reached out to him many times—like on the trip to Mammoth—and he'd never been able to receive from her.

He replayed their conversation. She hadn't cried or shouted or hurled accusations. In fact, she'd been astonishingly calm—even compassionate. Was she in shock? Probably. Carefully he went over his account to her of the—the catastrophe twelve years ago. It was basically what he'd told his attorney. Why, then, did he have this sense of unrest, of heaviness at the bottom of his abdomen? It was like—he hesitated, trying to understand. Ah, it was like when he was a child and had lied to his mother so she wouldn't tattle to his brutal stepfather. But where was the lie today? He didn't know.

In the TV room he could hear Eddie, one of his cellmates, telling for the umpteenth time how he and two other men had tried to rob a bank and bungled it in a manner worthy of a

Keystone Cops comedy. Each time Eddie told the story, he embellished it a little more.

People tend to do that, Charles realized, to make the past more interesting, funnier, more dramatic. Or, he suddenly saw, sometimes they "pretty up" the incident, to make it more palatable.

Is that what he'd done through the years—edited the events so they were more comfortable for him—and were now more palatable to tell to others?

No, he thought, surely not. *It was just as I told Leslie. Wasn't it?* He rolled from one side to the other before he could admit, *I need to really think about what happened. I need to—no, I don't want to do that. But yes, I need to think back to that night, in the woman's apartment, and to go over, step by step, exactly the way it happened.*

He clenched his teeth and forced himself to travel back in his memory twelve years, beginning at the bar. How many drinks had he had there? More than two, he guessed. Then he moved on to the rendezvous with the girl in the parking lot, the drive to the apartment, all the details of the conversation, of the woman coming on to him. It was as though she was holding out a tantalizing package, saying come and get it, then saying no, there's nothing here for you.

Suddenly he felt the emotions rise all over again: the disappointment, the frustration, the anger. And all the lies he had told himself through the years slid away as he saw himself as he was that night: consumed with rage, determined to get that present she seemed to offer so enticingly, fixed on having her.

He heard himself cry out and sat up, sweating profusely. *I lost it that night,* he admitted. *That is the reality. It was as though all the anger I felt all my life exploded and by heaven, I would, for once, have what I wanted.*

His body shook as though he had a chill, and he saw once again the fear in the girl's eyes. It was like—oh, God, it was like Leslie's eyes at Hot Creek! He fell back on the bunk, trembling uncontrollably. What if he had killed his own wife? Her strength and decisiveness, infuriating at the time, had actually saved him from a brutal act.

He pulled the rough blanket up over him and huddled beneath it, trying to stop shaking, trying to warm the icy flow that seemed to course through every vein and artery.

"Oh, God, what I did to that poor little blonde!" he muttered under his breath. "What I've done to my own wife—and to my children!"

❧

That night, when Leslie met the children at school, she proclaimed. "Good news! We're going home now."

Neither of them responded.

"It'll feel good to be back with your things, won't it?"

"Yeah, sure," Michelle grumbled.

"Did you see Dad?" Scott asked, rubbing his hand back and forth on the edge of the car seat.

"Yes, I did. I'll tell you about it when we get home. Did your day go better, Michelle?"

"No."

"I'm sorry. Well, it will be good for you to get away on the retreat tomorrow."

"I'm not going." Michelle's tone was emphatic.

"Oh, I'm sorry to hear that," Leslie said carefully. "What changed your mind?"

"That's a dumb question! What changed my mind? Everything! How can I face a new bunch of kids who know about me and think I'm a carrier of some deadly disease?"

"Oh, Michelle, I'd be nervous too. But I don't think it'll be like that at all. I think they'll be focusing on God, not you. I wouldn't write it off so quickly."

Michelle said nothing.

A few moments later, as they came into the house, the kids made a beeline for their rooms. Walking slowly through the house, Leslie found the bourbon bottle on its side in the family room, the empty wine bottle on the counter of the kitchen, assorted dishes in the sink.

And as she walked upstairs and into their room, her knees suddenly felt rubbery as an overwhelming sense of déjà vu washed over her. *This is just like when I went home after Tom died,* she realized. *No, not quite, because Charles doesn't drop his socks on the floor or pile ski stuff on chairs and in corners. But to see the things Charles has worn, touched, used—it's so eerie.*

She remembered, after Tom died, catching the scent of his sweaty clothes in the hamper and half-expecting him to appear again. Now, at the door of the bathroom, the aroma of Charles's aftershave startled her. Yes, it was exactly as though someone had died. And certainly the Charles she knew—or thought she knew—had.

She stared at their wedding picture on the dresser and wondered if her marriage was dead too. Sitting heavily on the bed, she pondered what to do next.

"Mom?" Scott stood in the doorway.

"Yes, honey."

"Tell me what Dad said when you saw him." His face was so full of hope she thought her own heart might shatter. How to break the news?

"Sit down, honey." She pulled him down beside her and put

her arm around him. She felt him tense, perhaps knowing already she hadn't the answer he wanted.

"Scott, your dad told me exactly what happened that evening. The woman invited him into her apartment. He didn't break in or anything of that sort. And your dad did not go in with any intention of harming her. I'm not an attorney, but I'd say it was basically an accident. He, um—" She searched for the right words. "He pushed her, and she lost her balance and fell and hit her head on the corner of a glass table."

Scott stiffened. "And he just left her there?" His voice rose. "I don't believe it!" He broke away from her and ran from the room, sobbing. She heard his bedroom door slam.

Leslie covered her face with her hands and wept.

"Mom?" Michelle sat on the bed beside her.

Leslie nodded but kept her hands over her face. Michelle stood and came back with a tissue.

"Thanks, honey." Leslie wiped her eyes.

"Is it true, then? Did Dad say he did it?"

Leslie repeated her summary for Michelle.

Michelle nodded. "So even if he didn't mean to, he killed her and he ran away and lived as if it had never happened." Michelle's eyes hardened with a loathing so bitter Leslie gasped. Then her daughter's voice came in a low, almost guttural tone. "I hate him," she said. "I *hate* him. I hate him for what he did to that woman and for what he's done to us. I don't ever, ever want to see him again, y'know—not as long as I live."

Leslie stared at Michelle as she flew out of the room and new tears formed. She couldn't remember ever feeling so bereft, so totally alone.

She looked once again at their wedding picture. "Look what you've done, Charles!" she muttered.

⌇

Charles was surprised, the next day, when the guard passed him a visitor's slip. He felt sure Leslie wouldn't be back so soon, and he'd seen his attorney the day before as well. He groaned as he looked at the slip. Zoë Lang. *Oh, God, that meddlesome woman again. I don't need this!* It was bad enough seeing Leslie, without facing the embarrassment of dealing with her mother. He started to write "refuse" on the slip. Then he thought, *The day's dragging on forever. What else do I have to do? At least it would take up some time, take me out of this abominable cell.*

As he started into the visiting area, it suddenly struck him. She had come to try to "save him." He knew it. And he might have to be rude. Well, and why not? After all what did he have to lose now? He had surely lost Leslie and the children. So what did he need now with Zoë?

Seated in her booth on the other side of the glass, Zoë looked younger than he remembered. A new hair style, perhaps. Smoother, not so curly.

She smiled at Charles and picked up the phone. "Hello, Charles," she said.

"Hello, Mother Lang." Might as well say it. "Look. I am going to be blunt. If you have come here to save me, I am not interested." He looked into her eyes, tender, compassionate, and hastily looked away. "I have quite enough problems already, thank you." He sighed. "And quite frankly, I am in no mood for God. I'd appreciate it if you would refrain from using the G word."

Zoë laughed, and the corners of her eyes crinkled. "Okay, Charles, I hear you." She held up her hand. "Spiritual truce?"

"Spiritual truce." He felt relieved, more in control.

"What I really came for is much more mundane. Leslie felt badly after her visit yesterday. She forgot to ask what you might need." Zoë pulled a pad of paper and a pen from her purse.

He was surprised, but then the woman did have a practical bent. Very well, since she asked, he would tell her. "Yes, as a matter of fact, this place is not equipped like the Hilton. A pad of yellow, lined paper. I understand they will provide something to write with here. Maybe some paperbacks. Nothing too profound."

"Can I bring food? Do you know?"

"Negative. But you might try a bottle of bourbon."

Zoë's pen poised over the pad. "Right." She played it straight. "Bourbon." She wrote it down.

They looked at each other and both laughed.

"Look," he relaxed a little. "It is thoughtful of you to come. You must think I am—what is Michelle's favorite word? Ah, yes. Scum."

"That's not the point, Charles. It's what G—" She clapped her hand over her mouth. "Whew! That was close."

"You really can't help it, can you?" He shook his head. "You live and eat and breathe your God."

"Guilty," Zoë nodded. "Charles, what I do want to say is that I am so sorry for all that's happened in your life."

His shoulders sagged. How could he be angry with her when she seemed so caring? He needed all the kindness he could get. And she deserved more than sarcasm from him. "Mother Lang, I want to say that—" He struggled with the words. "I am very sorry for the grief I am causing Leslie and the kids. And I'm sure you too." He felt his hand shake as he reached up to stroke his moustache. "I've created one devil of a mess."

"I appreciate that, Charles. But I want you to know that I'm convinced that despite all that's happened, your life is *not* over."

He cocked his head. "Yes, well, it is looking like an excellent imitation of that right now."

"I don't think so." She raised both eyebrows. "And I am old and wise."

"Old, maybe," he muttered.

"All right, Charles. You get the last word. For now." She stood, still holding the phone. "See you."

He looked up at her and shook his head. "I was afraid of that," he teased.

Zoë smiled, hung up the phone, and waved as she left.

40

∾

From Zoë's Prayer Journal

November 19: Dear Lord, thanks for my visit with Charles yesterday. Oh, please help me to be patient with my son-in-law and to show him Your love. And Father, Leslie tells me how angry Michelle is. Help her, and please don't let it keep her from going on the retreat tonight. If there's anything I can do or say, please show me. And Lord, wrap Your arms around this whole family. Be their High Tower, their hiding place. Thank You that You are in control, that You know both the beginning and the end of all this. In Jesus' name, amen.

LESLIE DIDN'T BOTHER TO CHECK HER ANSWERING machine till Friday morning, then found it full of calls. Friends offering prayers and support; her dad's sweet voice, expressing his love and urging his "Weeny One" to be strong in the Lord; Tracy saying she'd bring dinner; and the press. She'd get back to them when she could, but the most urgent was the last message: Carrie urging Michelle to call. Leslie hurried to tell Michelle.

Michelle's face lit up, then darkened. "Bet she's not my friend anymore."

"Would she call if she wasn't your friend?" Leslie asked. She looked at her watch. 7:15. "She'd be up now. Why don't you call her?"

"I—don't—think—so."

But a few minutes later she heard Michelle on the phone. Snatches of the conversation drifted from the family room. "Nah—I don't see how . . . so hard at school . . . be an outcast."

"Oh, Lord," Leslie prayed. "Give her the courage to go."

Later Michelle came into breakfast, her eyes red and swollen. "I really wanna go on the retreat, but I'm scared, Mom."

The phone rang, and Michelle started to reach for it.

Leslie held up her hand. "Let's let the answering machine screen callers for us, Michelle. I don't want to talk to a reporter."

In a moment Zoë's voice warmed the room. "Hi, darlin's. Anyone around?"

Still sniffling, Michelle picked up the phone. "Hi, Gram. Oh, okay. Yeah." She listened a moment. "Well, see, Carrie thinks I should go, but I—I dunno."

Hearing the anxiety in her granddaughter's voice, Zoë made a quick decision. "Darlin', it would take guts to go. But haven't I always called you my gutsy granddaughter? You are good at doing hard things. And you know something? Every time you've done a hard thing, it's turned out really well. Remember how afraid you were of the high dive? Now it's a piece of cake. Remember how your heart went pitty-pat when you had a role in that school play? The audience clapped and clapped."

"Well, yeah."

"Okay, then, Michelle. Are you going to sit around with your thumb in your mouth this weekend while everyone goes and has a great time?"

She heard Michelle giggle. A long pause. "Guess that sounds kinda dumb."

"Ah, that's my gutsy granddaughter! But listen, dear heart, I love you, gutsy or un-gutsy!"

"Thanks, Gram. Love you too. Wanna talk to Mom?"

"Who? No, I wanted to talk to you. But now that you mention it, is Mom doing okay?"

"Yeah. Thanks again, Gram." And as Michelle hung up, Zoë heard her say, "Decided to go, Mom."

Zoë gave an exultant thumbs-up. "Thanks, Lord. May she meet *You* in the mountains."

⁂

As Leslie drove Scott to his swim meet the next morning, she wondered how Michelle's first night at the retreat had gone.

Speak to her, Lord; be real to her, she prayed silently.

Scott's voice interrupted her. "I want to go see Dad."

She'd been expecting it. "Well, sure, Scott. We can do that. How about tomorrow?"

"Yeah. Sunday's good. Right after church."

After they arrived at the pool, Leslie settled into the stand as other parents gathered around her. They were starting to become bleacher buddies, and she smiled and greeted them. Then, as the meet began, she heard a woman behind her ask, "Which one is the son of that man they arrested for murder?"

Oh, no! Leslie thought. *It's here too.* Taking a breath, she turned to face the woman. "He's the one in the red sweatshirt, talking to David right now. He's my son."

406

The woman flushed. "Oh. Thank you. Um—excuse me. Sorry . . ."

Leslie reached back and touched her hand. "Don't be embarrassed. I understand."

When the call came for nine- and ten-year-old freestyle, Leslie thought she saw a new determination in Scott's stance on the block. He started well, churned to the end of the pool, hitting the wall almost simultaneously with two of the other five swimmers. Losing a little on the turn, he swam a strong return, out-touched by seconds by the two other boys.

"Way to go, Scott!" she screamed, watching him pull himself from the water, tears blurring the scene as David pounded him on the back. A third place meant a ribbon. His first. He needed that; timing couldn't be better.

"Thanks, Lord," she whispered.

The woman behind patted her shoulder and said, "Your son did well!"

Leslie looked back and smiled. "That's going to be so encouraging."

She turned back to watch the next event. Now that she was beginning to know some of the team members, she felt an interest and concern in their performances. Michelle's "hunk," she noted, took blue ribbons in all his events.

"Nine-ten boys butterfly," the announcer echoed. Leslie leaned forward to watch Scott compete for the first time in the "fly."

The gun went off, and Scott splashed into the water. *He looks good,* she thought. *By golly, he really seems to have that undulating motion of the dolphin kick, and he's getting his arms well up out of the water.*

She could see him tiring as he returned to the finish, but a fourth—why, that was close to placing. "Great swim, Scott!" she shouted.

As they walked to the car after the meet, she started to put her arm around him, but his warning look told her that wasn't "guy stuff." *End of an era,* she thought.

In the car, she said, "You really looked great, Scott. Congratulations on your third! And your form in the 'fly' looked terrific."

"Yeah, thanks. Now I can take the ribbon to show Dad tomorrow."

And would Charles say, *Just a third? Come on, now, Scott!* She sighed. *I can't protect this kid from real life. Better face it.*

⌒

On Sunday Leslie and Scott went straight from church to the Orange County Jail. The traffic and the parking were less congested than on a weekday, but there were many more visitors. The deputy told them they would wait at least an hour, so they went out for a snack. Scott developed an acute case of jitters as they ordered and had difficulty sitting still. Finally he paced as he devoured a crusty buttermilk doughnut.

They walked back slowly to the jail, and at last their name was called and they went up the now-familiar elevator into the visiting room. Although she'd described the arrangement to Scott and told him what Charles would be wearing, he still flinched as Charles approached the booth. Charles gave his son a smile that struck Leslie as genuine—for once. He put his palm against the glass, inviting a high five, and Scott grinned and slapped his palm against the glass.

Leslie waved and said nothing. Charles picked up the phone and pointed to Scott, who grabbed his phone and listened.

"I'm okay. You okay?"

Sitting beside Scott, Leslie could hear Charles say, "As well as can be expected."

She saw Charles smile as he raised his eyebrows, evidently asking a question.

Scott pulled the ribbon from his pocket and held it up. Leslie held her breath.

Charles looked surprised.

"Got a third in the freestyle at the meet yesterday."

"No!" she could see Charles exclaim.

"Yup."

She couldn't help leaning over to listen.

"Why, Scott," Charles said. "I am very proud of you."

Leslie began to relax.

"Thanks, Dad." Scott looked down at his shoes and bit his lip. The silence seemed to go on and on.

At last Scott asked a question.

"Uh, yeah. I just kept thinkin' there was some mistake, that you didn't really do—" He bobbed his head. "—you know."

Charles nodded and his mouth twitched, but he spoke clearly enough for Leslie to hear. "This must be really difficult for you, Scott. Yes, as I told your mother, I really did. I did not intend to. But it happened."

Scott was crying now, and Leslie saw Charles's chin tremble.

"But Dad, you ran away and never told."

"That is correct." Leslie could hear fragments from Charles: ". . . not proud of that . . . not what I would tell you to do . . . panicked . . . ran . . . no one ever called . . . could not bring that young woman back to life . . . wrong . . . go on with my life . . . met your mother and fell in love . . . thought I could close the book on the past . . ." He shook his head. ". . . Should have known . . . Someday maybe you'll understand."

Scott's slender frame shook with sobs, and Leslie saw the tears on Charles's cheeks. She put her arm around Scott, but he wouldn't allow her to hold him. She gave Charles a helpless, what-shall-I-do-now? look. He formed his forefingers into a time-out signal. She waited. At last Scott's tears subsided, and he accepted a tissue from her.

"What's going to happen to you, Dad? And what's going to happen to us?" Scott asked.

She leaned close to Scott, needing to know what Charles said so she could deal with Scott's reactions. "We do not know yet about me, Scott," Charles explained. "It depends on the district attorney's office and whether we go to trial. We may not have to. There is the possibility of what they call a plea bargain, and that would be good because there would not be the expense of a trial." He looked at the ceiling. "It is painful to think what my attorney is costing already." He glanced back at Scott. "It all remains to be seen. Still, at the very least, I will be going to jail for several years. I think we can be certain of that. But Scott, it is not the end of the world for me, as—" He cleared his throat. "—as it was for that poor woman I pushed. In jail I can try to improve myself, even study for my next actuary exam. It is not forever."

Oh, Charles, Leslie thought. *Still thinking of yourself. Maybe now you'll have peace and quiet while you study!*

Scott nodded, and Charles continued. "And as far as you are concerned, my hope is that you three will be able to remain in the house if you want to. And that you will continue to learn and grow and not let this stop you. And you know, Scott, people will begin to forget all this and focus on the next headline. It will get better than it is right now. I assure you it will."

"I s'pose," Scott murmured. He looked up. "Dad, we're all prayin' for you. Me, Gram, Mom, my Sunday school class. I guess you think that's dumb, and maybe it even makes you mad, but we are."

". . . all the help I can get," came Charles's voice.

Scott managed a crooked smile. "Ya got it then."

"Thanks," Charles said, motioning to Leslie, who took the phone from Scott.

"Thanks, Leslie, for bringing him. It means a lot to me."

"Of course. I'll bring him again. And I'll be back next week, Charles."

"You don't have to. It's a long way."

"I know. But I'll be back."

⌇

Later that afternoon Leslie tried not to drum her fingers on the steering wheel as she waited at the church for Michelle and Carrie to get back from the retreat. If it hadn't been a good experience, Michelle would be a pistol to live with. It was hard enough keeping her own head above water and trying to keep Scott from going under.

"Oh, Lord," she breathed, "give me the strength to cope with however she's feeling, and give me patience and understanding."

Another car pulled in beside her, and she recognized the parents of one of the junior high boys. The man rolled down his window. "Rev up your washing machine," he counseled. "Heard it rained up there."

Wonderful! That must have really put Michelle in a jolly mood. Slumping down in the car, Leslie tried to steel herself for the worst.

She looked up as two buses pulled into the parking lot, and a rumpled assortment of jabbering preteens poured out. They stood waiting for their gear to be unloaded as Leslie stepped out of the car and looked anxiously for Michelle. At last she spotted her in the second busload, loosening her ponytail, letting her red hair blow free and glisten in the sun. She was talking so intently with one of the youth pastors she didn't even turn toward Leslie.

Then one of the junior high boys brought her sleeping bag. A phrase from her own high school physics teacher popped into her mind: "Who will be a willing slave for a beautiful woman?" Obviously Michelle had a willing slave. And probably she would consider that a positive development—unless she thought he was a dweeb.

Michelle turned and gave her slave a hug. Then she seemed inundated with hugs from girls and boys alike. She stood chattering, laughing with a group until at last she looked over and saw Leslie. Leslie smiled and pointed at the car to indicate where it was. Michelle waved, mouthed, "Gotta find Carrie," and disappeared behind the bus.

Leslie waited in the car for fifteen minutes before the two girls approached, babbling as though they hadn't seen one another for a month.

Leslie popped the trunk open, and they threw their gear in, slamming the lid. Piling into the backseat, they said in duet, "We're exhausted."

"You look reasonably dry," Leslie said as she started the car. "I heard it rained."

They exploded into laughter. "Wait'll you see what's in our bags," Carrie said.

"We had a race in the mud. It was freezing, but it was hilarious," Michelle explained. "Most of us fell—"

"—sometimes with a little help from our friends," interjected Carrie.

"And," Michelle continued, "we looked like those pictures of marines in training—"

"—or your basic mud fight," Carrie added.

"Sounds like a jolly time was had by all," Leslie said, steering the car out of the parking lot.

"Yeah, it was," Carrie said. "But that wasn't all. We had a great prayer and sharing time, and ten kids accepted the Lord."

In the rearview mirror Leslie could see the two girls grinning at one another. She waited to hear more, but the girls began whispering, and Leslie knew it was time to butt out. Obviously, it had been a positive time for them both, and she breathed a quiet, "Thank You!"

She drove to Carrie's house and waited for her to take her bags from the trunk.

"Call me!" Michelle said as Carrie waved and walked up her front steps.

All the way home Leslie heard Michelle singing in the backseat, and gradually she became aware that these were not pop hits but songs of praise.

Amazing.

When they pulled into the garage, Michelle sprang out of the car and waited for Leslie to get out. There in the garage, with its blended scent of car exhaust and stored fertilizer, Michelle moved a radiant face close to Leslie's.

"Guess what?" she cried.

"I don't know. What?" Leslie's tone reflected the excitement in Michelle's voice.

"Jesus really came into my life!"

"You? You—Michelle Louise Harper?" Leslie leaned against the car, realizing this was more than she'd even thought of praying for.

"Yup!" Michelle beamed in the light of the overhead garage light.

"Well, darling, how perfectly wonderful!"

"Yeah, that's the way it was, Mom. I mean, y'know, I've

always believed in God and that Jesus is His Son and all that stuff. And I know people like Gram have a personal relationship with Jesus. But I thought that was for other people, not me. But something happened in the mountains. Maybe I was physically closer to heaven, huh? Anyway, I just really felt Jesus speaking to me. It wasn't—" She deepened her voice. "'Michelle, this is Jesus. Listen to me.' But I sorta heard Him in my head—or maybe my heart. And He was definitely saying He loves me and wants me to be close to Him: like, me 'n' Him and Him 'n' me."

Leslie saw her daughter's face blur before her. "He does. He does love you, Michelle. He does!"

"I *know!* And I mean, it absolutely blew me away! I absolutely cried buckets. And now I feel like a whole new person, y'know?"

"And you are."

"Mike—he's in charge of junior high ministries—says I oughta get involved so I don't lose it. And I want to. I mean, get active in the junior high group, do Bible studies, help with the outreach program. Man, this high's better'n drugs'r booze!"

"It is indeed." Leslie gathered her daughter into her arms, tears of gratitude spilling from the corners of her eyes. "I think I hear angels singing, Michelle."

"Yeah," Michelle wept. "Me too."

I could stay here forever, hugging this girl, Leslie thought.

At last, they started into the house. "And another thing," Michelle continued, "in our small group, they just let me talk and talk about how I feel about Dad. And nobody told me to shut up. And then—" She stopped and turned back to Leslie, her eyes filling again with tears. "I mean, they just sorta wrapped me in this big quilt of love. I dunno when I've ever felt so much—um—acceptance. It was like they were in some weird way sorta carrying part of the garbage for me. I mean, it was nothin' like what I got at school."

Leslie nodded. "That's what fellowship is all about, it seems to me. And it *is* different from the world's attitude."

"You better believe it."

They went into the house. "Laundry room first stop?" Leslie asked. Then, as Michelle pulled the mud-laden clothes from her bag, Leslie added, "I guess!"

"Oh!" Michelle exclaimed, carefully unwrapping a T-shirt to reveal a slender pine-cone carving. "I made this for Scott for a Christmas ornament—or whatever."

Michelle actually thought of Scott? Miracles had indeed taken place on the retreat, Leslie decided.

Michelle held up the crude form of a person wearing goggles and very brief shorts. "See the Speedo?"

Leslie laughed. "He's going to love it." She stuffed clothes in the washer. "I think we'd better have a rinse first." She turned the dial to start the machine. "Your carving should help cheer Scott up, Michelle. I think he could use that right now."

"How come?"

"We went to see Dad today. I guess Scott needed to hear the story straight from his father. It wasn't easy."

Michelle nodded wisely. "Yeah. Scott was kinda in denial, wasn't he?"

Leslie smiled at her daughter's insight. "Or certainly hoping it wasn't so. Oh," she smiled, "but Scott took a third place ribbon in his meet yesterday, so he got to show it to his dad."

"So did Charles make fun of it?"

Charles, not Dad, Leslie noticed. She let it go.

"No, he said he was proud of him."

"Amazing!" Michelle thought a moment, then sighed. "I

know I need to work on my attitude about him. But . . ." Her
voice trailed off.

"I understand."

"Well, I'm gonna take Scott his present." Michelle started
toward the stairs, calling out, "Hey, Dolphin-Breath, where
y'hidin' your ugly face?"

As soon as she'd rinsed the muddy clothes and started the
wash, Leslie went to call Zoë. She'd be so pleased about
Michelle! But before she could pick up the phone, the doorbell
rang. She went to the door, checked the peephole, and saw her
mother.

Swinging the door open, she hugged her. "Mom! I was just
starting to call you."

"Well," Zoë said, "I was on my way home, and I couldn't
bear waiting to hear. Was the retreat a boom or a bust?"

"Definitely not a bust. I think she'd want to tell you herself." Leslie called up the stairway. "Michelle? Gram's here."

She could hear Michelle's feet thud to the floor, and in a
moment, she slid down the banister. "Hi, Gram! Hey, thanks
bunches for pushin' me about the retreat."

"So it was okay?"

"Wait'll I tell you!"

They went together into the family room, and while Leslie
started dinner she could hear the enthusiastic lilt of Michelle's
voice, the joy in Zoë's responses.

Later, as Leslie went in to see if Zoë would stay for dinner,
she heard her mother say, "It's important not to forgive prematurely, Michelle, or to try to tell yourself it doesn't matter. It
does. So don't force it. Be honest with yourself. And with
God."

She looked up at Leslie. "Maybe that goes for you, too,
honey. Anger and bitterness are real poisons, and we need to

grow beyond them. But in my experience forgiveness doesn't happen right away. It's a process."

Leslie thought of her mother's experience, her father's betrayal, and for the first time really, *really* understood some of the anguish Zoë must have felt in being sinned against. And her mother had not only survived but thrived and grown as a single woman. Of course, the children had been older than Scott and Michelle when Leslie's father left. Still, her mother's life showed that healing is possible.

Leslie looked wistfully at Zoë and wondered how long, how complex, and how painful her own recovery would be.

41

ॐ

DAVID PROPELLED HIS WHEELCHAIR INTO THERAPY MONDAY morning wearing the turquoise shirt that matched his eyes and a face-wide smile that deepened the cleft in his chin. "Got stronger just over the weekend!" he announced. "I can feel it." He looked up at Leslie. "And how about Scott? Didn't he do great at the swim meet?"

"He did. He was so pleased with his ribbon. Took it when he went to visit his dad yesterday."

"How'd his dad react?"

"Actually he was great," Leslie said. "But it was a hard visit for Scott. He clung to the hope that this was all some huge mistake. Reality can be tough."

"Tell me!" David cocked his head. "But we all have hope, right?"

She smiled. "Right. And listen to this." She told David about Michelle and the retreat.

He nodded. "Michelle walking closer to the Lord. Cool! Charles will be next."

"Dream on, David!"

David wagged one forefinger at her. "Oh ye of little faith! Okay now, let's work."

"Right. We'll start with some crunches."

David transferred to the mat and began. "Y'know," he said, "I was thinking about Charles. If you could erase about two minutes from his life, everything else would have been totally different." He stopped a moment. "It just occurred to me that if you could erase two seconds from *my* life—when I got caught in that wave—everything would be different."

He resumed his exercise. "What I started to say—I see people pointing fingers, but how do they know what they might have done in a situation like Charles's? None of us really has any idea what we might do, given the right—or wrong—circumstances. What does Jeremiah say? 'The heart is desperately wicked'?"

"I used to know that verse." She thought a moment. "Oh, yes, I remember. I learned the King James Version: 'The heart is deceitful above all things, and desperately wicked: who can know it?' Oh, I agree, David. None of us has any idea what we could be capable of. I once had a Bible study teacher who kept talking about 'the depravity of man.' I hated that then. Thought people were all basically good. I look around me today, and I don't think so! It's only through God's grace that we have any goodness at all."

"And thank God for that!"

She nodded and motioned to him to stop. "Okay, let's try kneeling on the mat. Let's see if those hip muscles are kicking in better.'" She watched him a few minutes. "Good! You're holding your position well, not even bending at the hips, and your balance looks good. Frankly I thought you might fall from the kneeling position. I'm almost ready to call you 'the come-back kid.'"

"I know," he said with mock modesty.

"Okay, but we still can't rush it, David. Remember what happened last time."

"Yeah, yeah. I know, I know."

He rolled his eyes, and Leslie laughed. "You remind me of Michelle," she said. "Must be generational."

꒰꒱

On Thursday Leslie went to see Charles. He looked still thinner and very tired.

"Have you seen your attorney?"

"Yes. He is trying to build a case on my upright life after the—crime. Yes, I am ready to call it a crime. But he wants to show that since then, I have never been in trouble with the law. I've held a job, provided for my family, did not fool around."

Upright? Leslie thought. *Huh? Well, I guess in some ways he was. And he did keep us comfortably housed, warm, fed, clothed.* "I see," she said.

There was an uncomfortable pause. Then she remembered the restraining order. "Oh, Charles, what about the restraining order? Will that go against you?"

He nodded. "I thought about that. But there was never a court hearing, so the prosecution couldn't dig that up."

So we just conveniently forget about that, she thought. *As though the abuse never existed.* She sighed, and there was a long silence. Finally she looked at the bags under his eyes. "You getting enough sleep?"

"It's hard—with seven other men, three of whom snore and one of whom rants and raves in his sleep."

She shook her head. "And you used to complain when I ground my teeth."

"I'd go back to that any day."

"Would they let you have earplugs? I could ask. Anything else you need?"

He closed his eyes, and it seemed to Leslie a long time before he replied. "You," he said.

"Excuse me?"

"I need you beside me. Especially till the sentencing." His eyes were soft, almost imploring.

Did he mean for her to testify on his behalf? She felt her heartbeat accelerate. Could she, under oath, declare him upright? *Never!*

"I know I do not deserve it," he continued. "And I would not blame you if you never even came to see me. But, Leslie, you are all I have. I have no idea where my mother is, and I do not care. My father is dead. I have no siblings. It would help me immeasurably if I knew you were—well, there for me. Because there is no one but you. I love you, and I need you."

She looked at him, feeling a wave of intense sadness. "Charles," she said at last, "you have never needed me before."

"What do you mean?" He seemed genuinely puzzled. "I have always needed you."

She stared at him. "That's really interesting, Charles. Why, then, did you tell me again and again what a problem I was for you, what an albatross I was around your neck?"

"I never said that!" Charles protested indignantly.

She gave him a cheerless smile. "There you go again, Charles. It used to make me feel like I was crazy when you denied ever saying certain things that I knew I'd heard. I think what happens is that you blow off steam and it's over, gone, forgotten. But you see, those kinds of cutting remarks are never over, or gone, or ever forgotten for me. They make me feel stripped. They hurt, not just when I hear them, but as I rehear them afterward again and again. I feel like a nothing. No, less than nothing."

She swallowed. "Let me refresh your memory. One day when you told me what an albatross I was, how I hindered your every dream and desire, you gave me a sort of 'report card.' You graded me as a wife, a mother, a mistress, a house-keeper. Failing grades, each and every one. By the time you were finished, any shred of belief I might have had in myself had been systematically and meticulously chopped away."

"Did I really do that?" Charles frowned. "Uh, I vaguely remember. In my study, was it? After we had gone over finances. Oh, now, Leslie, surely—"

At his condescending tone a wave of despair washed over her. She set the phone down and put her hands over her ears and closed her eyes. After a moment she picked it up again and looked at Charles, staring at her, astonished. "If you say you were joking and can't I take a joke, Charles, I shall scream. What you said that night left deep, gaping wounds!"

His shoulders slumped. "I had no idea . . . I never realized how I was coming across. Oh, Leslie—" He looked at her, his eyes glistening. "I am very sorry, Leslie."

She sighed. "Charles, are you asking me to testify what a supportive, loving, affirming husband you have been?"

"N-no," he stuttered. "Just to—you know—be personally supportive. If—if you could perhaps be there for the prelimi-nary hearing on December eleventh . . ."

She wanted to tell him she'd think about it. But he looked so pathetic. "Charles, I want to be honest. At this moment I feel no love or affection for you. But I do feel pity." She sighed. "Nobody should have to go through this alone. I'll come."

He looked as relieved as Scott when he'd learned he wouldn't be punished for breaking a window. "I am very grateful, Leslie," he said.

⌐

The following weekend, as Leslie walked with Scott and Michelle to the car after church, Michelle announced, "I think I'm ready to go see Dad."

Surprised, Leslie asked, "This soon? You sure, Michelle?"

"Hey!" Michelle held up a cautionary hand. "Not to tell him I've forgiven him or anything."

"I understand. But he's been asking about you, and I know he'd like to see you."

"Okay," she said.

"You prob'ly should see him alone, like I did," Scott said.

"That's wise—and generous of you, Scott," Leslie said. "Thanks."

That afternoon while Scott helped Zoë at an open house, Leslie and Michelle went to the jail.

"Man, this is creepy, Mom," Michelle said as they rode the elevator to the second floor. I forgot to ask you, does he have chains on his legs?"

Leslie laughed. "No, he doesn't have a ball and chains on his ankles. You've been seeing too many movies. And he doesn't have his hands bound either.

The elevator door opened,and Michelle stood as though glued to the floor. "I don't think I can do this."

"All right, Michelle," Leslie said, her voice quiet and calm.

The door clanged shut and the elevator descended again. On the first floor Leslie started to get out, but Michelle remained in the back of the elevator, her face pale. Others crowded in, and Leslie got back in. She couldn't move close enough to Michelle to speak to her. The door opened once again at the second floor, and Leslie stepped aside to let the others out. She put her finger on the OPEN button to keep the elevator door from closing . . . and waited.

"I know I need to," Michelle whispered. "Oh, God, please help me."

She moved slowly out of the elevator and leaned against the wall. Leslie waited, wondering if her daughter might faint. Then, to her surprise, the color gradually returned to Michelle's face. She took a deep breath. "I'm okay, Mom."

As Charles approached the visiting area, he looked genuinely pleased to see them. He waved, sat down, picked up the phone. Leslie took the phone on their side of the glass and handed it to Michelle, who held it so Leslie could listen as well.

"Michelle, it is very good to see you." He looked at her carefully. "What is different about you? You do not look the same. New hair style?"

She shook her head.

"Makeup?" He shook his head. "No."

She laughed. "Nope. It's more of an inside job, you could say."

He raised one eyebrow. "And pray tell, what does that mean?"

"I'm just feelin' good since the retreat I went on with the junior high kids. I felt real close to God—and to the other kids."

Charles looked past Michelle, to the right and left, and he didn't seem to know how to respond. Finally he said, "Ah, well, I suppose that is basically good."

"I always thought you thought being a Christian was dumb."

"Oh, not necessarily. I think it is a good thing for, shall we say, women and children." He thought a moment. "And especially if it keeps you out of trouble, Michelle, I think it is good. Will you, then, be spending more time at church?"

"Yup. They have some good activities and an outreach program to a special project in Santa Ana that I'm signing up for."

"That is admirable, Michelle."

They were both quiet. Then Charles said, "I guess you must be pretty angry with me, eh? Because of all this. Your mother says the boys and girls at school have not been very, uh, kind."

Michelle nodded. "Yeah, but the novelty's starting to wear off, y'know. It's gruesome, but there was a car crash that killed a kid who goes to my school. That kinda took the attention off me." She thought a moment. "About me being mad—yeah, I was, for sure. I really hated you for what you'd done to us, y'know?" She sighed. "I guess maybe I'm still mad. But I'm trying, . . . well, I'm asking God to help me forgive you."

Leslie was surprised to see tears in Charles's eyes. "Thank you, Michelle. I hope in time you can," he said.

Michelle leaned forward, her face close to the glass, and Charles, startled, moved back just a little.

"Dad," she said, "I know you don't want to hear it. But Jesus is the way to go. Especially for you right now. Without Him, you're history. Why don't you get your act together?"

Charles stared at her a moment, his mouth slightly open, eyes incredulous. Then he broke into a hearty laugh. "Michelle, my prodigal daughter! You always were the bold and blunt one. That was apparent when I first met you, and you were . . . what? Not even a year old. You are always— full of surprises." He shook his head and laughed again.

Later, on the way down in the elevator, Leslie said, "Honey, your grandmother is right. You are gutsy."

"Well," Michelle said, "I didn't plan to say that. But I suddenly realized he's kind of a captive audience, if you'll pardon the expression. At least I knew he couldn't hit me. But," she shook her head as they got out of the elevator, "I really think he's impossible."

"Mmm," said Leslie as they left the building. "Seems to me I heard you kids singing a song, with words something like, 'Nothing is too difficult, nothing is too difficult, nothing is too difficult for God.'"

"Yeah," Michelle agreed. "But, see, this is *major*. Maybe it's not too difficult for God, but wanna bet I have gray hair before I see Dad on his knees?"

42

⁂

From Zoë's Prayer Journal

December 9: Lord, lots of thanks to You this morning. For Scott's adjusting a little better to the circumstances and swimming his first individual medley tomorrow. For Leslie hanging in there. And especially that Charles actually seems to look forward to my visits now. I confess it's been hard, but I've kept my word not to talk about You. I've just cared for him these three weeks. But now, Father, tomorrow's his birthday, and You know I have this Bible ready to take to him. He may very well throw it on the floor, stamp on it, or, at the very least, say, "No thanks." Would you please prepare his heart to receive it? And then, oh, Lord, may Your Word bring him to the point one day of receiving You. I promise—I'll give You all the praise! In Jesus' name, amen.

SINCE CHARLES LIKED TO DISCUSS CURRENT EVENTS, Zoë began her visit by asking him what he thought of the latest developments in the Middle East.

"Those Israelis are a stubborn lot," he said. "But you know, I can't help but admire them. They have really hung tough over all these centuries."

Zoë resisted the temptation to talk about God's promise to Abraham and His faithfulness to preserve a remnant throughout all those centuries. Instead she switched to baseball. "What do you think about the Angels signing that new pitcher? They're saying this makes them pennant contenders."

"Hmm, well, we shall see. I'd say he's past his prime, but he did have thirty-three saves last year. Certainly the salary they are paying him is an obscene amount," he snorted.

Then Charles turned his focus on Zoë. "So," he said, leaning back in the chair, "how's real estate these days?"

"Slow. But that's not unusual for the holidays." She hesitated. "Ah, Charles, speaking of holidays, it's your birthday tomorrow, and I've brought you a gift that they'll be giving to you."

"Let me guess." Charles eyed her thoughtfully. "I know it's not a cake. Because *they* know you're just the sweet-looking sort who would bake a saw in it."

"They're right."

"And it can't be a necktie. A bit superfluous in my life right now. Nor a wood-carving kit—too dangerous. Well, I give up."

"It's a—a Bible that's set up so you can read the whole thing in a year."

Charles gave a rueful smile. "Well, I certainly will have time for that." He looked at her, the old defiance burning in his dark eyes. "Whether I will actually do it or not . . ."

"You don't have to make a commitment. No strings attached, Charles. But—" She hesitated. "You're not angry I brought it?"

He shrugged. "Actually, no. It grieves me to confess it, but

I have a modicum of curiosity. I mean, I consider myself a reasonably educated, well-read man, and this is a book I have never read."

She nodded. "Consider it part of your continuing education then. There's a lot of wisdom in there."

"*And* fairy tales, I would venture to say."

She lifted one eyebrow but didn't answer.

"If I do pick it up, do you recommend starting at the beginning?" Charles asked.

"Not really. I believe I'd start in the New Testament." She started to suggest the gospel of John, but felt suddenly that she shouldn't be too directive.

You show him, Lord, she prayed in her heart.

"Very well, I may begin there. That would be toward the back of the Bible, I believe. Actually, this could be very useful. Maybe if I read it in my bunk at night it will—" He yawned. "Put me to sleep."

"Maybe so, Charles. Maybe so."

She started to say good-bye, but something in his eyes stopped her. So she waited.

"I hate asking you this," Charles finally said. "But how do you think Leslie is feeling about me right now?" His eyes pleaded for an answer. "Do you think she hates me?"

Oh, dear, Zoë thought. *How can I be honest without betraying Leslie's confidence?* "I think she's having a tough time, Charles, and is still sorting this all out."

Charles nodded. "I—I am so filled with regret and sorrow. I wonder if she could ever, ever forgive me."

Oh, Charles, she thought. *God's forgiveness is what you need.* But she said, "I sense your tender heart, Charles."

He shook his head, and her own heart filled with compassion for his misery and guilt.

Thanksgiving had come off well for Leslie and the children, for they'd gone for a family dinner at Tracy's, together with Peter, Leslie's brother from Malibu, and his family, and Zoë. With Tracy and Greg's sons home from college, twelve gathered around the table. Charles had always been so quiet at family gatherings, the day seemed little different from other Thanksgivings, and it had been good to focus on all their blessings.

But now Christmas was coming, and Leslie worried that it might be particularly difficult for Scott.

"You haven't given me your Christmas list yet," she told him, "and it's only sixteen days till the big day."

"I don't care." Scott's voice was dull.

"Come on, honey, your dad wouldn't want you to mope around at this festive time of year."

"Well, 'Jesus is the reason for the season,' anyway," Scott pointed out.

"You're right." So why was she trying to get him to focus on gifts for himself? She decided to switch tactics. "How about we celebrate by going shopping for the kids at the shelter in Santa Ana? The church has a list of things they need. And you know better than I would what a ten-year-old boy would like."

"Yeah. I could do that." He thought a moment. "Y'know, swim team's going to stop for Christmas vacation. I'll miss that. Miss seeing David."

"Ah! I was going to talk with you about that. I really would like you to come in to therapy and help coach him."

Scott's eyes brightened. "Yeah, I'd like to do that."

He gave her a wistful look. "Wouldn't it be great if God gave him the gift of walking for Christmas?"

"Hmm, well, that might be a little soon, Scott. But," She tried to give him an encouraging smile, "He—God, I mean—knows the timing, doesn't He?"

⌁

Leslie wakened early on the morning of December twelfth, hearing the whine of a truck in low gear, the thuds of newspapers landing in driveways along the street. She put the pillow over her head. How she dreaded the preliminary hearing, going into the courtroom, seeing her husband as the accused. Even now, she could feel the conflict of seeing the man she'd married in love and trust, the man who had abused her and her children, quite possibly fighting for his life. Part of her said, *Serves him right!* Part of her said, *Poor, miserable man.* She pushed the pillow aside and said, "Lord, show me how to pray. I don't know, except to ask that Your will be done. Father, You know what is best for everyone in the whole big picture. I do ask that You would give Charles Your peace on this pivotal day of his life."

At ten that morning she exited the elevator in the court building to a blinding assault of photographers' strobes. When clear vision returned, she made her way into the municipal courtroom.

When Charles was escorted into the room, he looked almost like his dapper old self in his suit, white shirt, and necktie he'd had Leslie bring. However, the suit hung a bit loose from his shoulders. She saw his eyes search the courtroom till he found her, but his expression didn't change. Beside him sat a man who looked as though he might have been a linebacker on a pro football team. Must be Bill Wells, his attorney, she decided. She'd talked with him on the phone but hadn't envisioned such an imposing physical presence.

She listened as the deputy district attorney reviewed the police findings at the time of the crime and pointed to the "match" of Charles's fingerprints with those found at the scene. "There is probable cause," he concluded, "for committing the defendant to superior court." She waited impatiently for Wells to speak in Charles's defense, but there seemed to be no opportunity.

The judge called the deputy district attorney and Wells forward, and their discussion, though inaudible, appeared animated.

Then the judge declared, "Charles Harper will be held to answer for murder in superior court on December 27."

She watched Charles's shoulders sag while his face remained impassive. What had happened to the plea bargain? Would Charles actually be tried for murder?

Grabbing her purse, she rushed for the door, and as she exited the courtroom she was met with a barrage of questions: "Mrs. Harper, Mrs. Harper, what is it like to live eleven years with a man who's hidden a crime?" . . . "Ms. Harper, did you have any indication of your husband's past?" . . . "Ms. Harper? Over here! Over here!"

"No, nothing to say," she insisted, tucking her head down, fighting her way through the reporters, angry at the intrusion, wanting only to get out.

Then Bill Wells caught up with her, taking her arm, running interference, repeating, "Ms. Harper does not wish to comment at this time."

"Thanks!" she said when they were past the crush. "I needed that."

"Welcome," he said, and she liked his steady blue eyes. "Don't be discouraged. This hearing is simply to demonstrate what's called probable cause—sufficient evidence to bring your husband to trial. But it's also for me to see what the DA's office has. The fact that they have no witnesses gives us some strength. I still believe we can effect a plea bargain—especially when the district attorney sees the weakness of his case after all these years."

"Oh, I pray you're right," Leslie said.

"Another fortunate thing," Wells added. "The deceased doesn't have family putting a lot of pressure on the DA."

Did she have no family? Leslie wondered, unable to shake from her mind the picture of the woman she'd seen on TV. *A record of drugs, prostitution—no one around now to care. What a tragic life! What a waste!*

ॐ

The following week Zoë went to see Charles, wondering if he'd bothered to open the Bible. Surely he was depressed by the preliminary hearing.

She blinked in disbelief as she saw him come in carrying the Bible. He set it on the table and picked up the phone. "'Morning, Mother Lang."

"Hello, Charles. How goes it?"

He stared at her with one eyebrow raised, then tapped his Bible. "I began with John," he announced. "And I have been going through the other Gospels—" He opened the Bible and pointed to the beginning of the book of Matthew. "See, I learned which books are Gospels. And I have been reading all the red passages."

"Jesus's own words! Good idea. So," she asked cautiously, "what do you think of Jesus?"

"Why," Charles exclaimed, "he is radical, a revolutionary! I always thought he sat with folded hands, halo-over-the-head.

He certainly laid it on the line to those—what were they called? Pharisees. Imagine how outrageous, how audacious He must have seemed to them when He said He was God!"

"Of course. They called it blasphemy."

"But He is so clever, the way He talks with them. I have enjoyed looking at His strategy. And his methodology in teaching. Interesting." He thought a moment.

"By the way one of my cellmates is rather knowledgeable about the Bible. He spends a great deal of time reading it. It was he who recommended starting with John."

Thank You, Lord, Zoë prayed silently.

"He even looks up Greek words, tenses of verbs. I never knew the Greek language has a continuing-action present tense that basically says you do something repeatedly. A very rich language."

"Yes, it is. When you understand the root of the word and the tense, it can make a lot of difference in your perception of a passage. For instance, when Jesus says, 'Ask and it will be given to you; seek and you will find; knock and the door will be opened to you,' those Greek verbs are in the present tense. So He's really saying, *keep* on asking, *keep* on seeking . . ."

"Ah!" Charles nodded. "Very interesting. Very expressive, indeed." He pursed his lips. "I must be candid, however. Quite a bit of what I read seems foolish."

"I know. It did to me at first, too, Charles."

He looked at her thoughtfully. "I do relate, however, to Jesus talking about sinners. I am that."

"Charles," she said, "you have no idea how many people have trouble admitting it."

"Well, with me it's pretty blatant." He hesitated a moment. "In fact, I think I need to make a confession to . . . to someone." He flushed and looked away.

"What is that, Charles?" Zoë's voice was gentle.

It seemed an effort for him to look at her. "The account I gave my attorney and Leslie about the woman's death—I came to realize later it was a—a sanitized version. No, I didn't intend to kill her, not ever. But she seemed to be offering me something then refusing to give it. That made me very, very angry, and I was determined to *have* her. I was aggressive. Maybe even brutal." He hung his head as though dreading Zoë's reaction.

At last Zoë said, "That was very hard for you to remember—to admit."

He looked up at her and nodded.

"And important for you to confess." She waited a moment. "You know, Charles, the same John who wrote the gospel of John also wrote a letter, first John, and in it he says, 'If we claim to be without sin, we deceive ourselves and the truth is not in us.' We've *all* sinned. Each of us tries to live our own way, do our own thing, be independent from God. But Charles, have you seen? There's forgiveness of sin."

He raised one eyebrow.

"John continues in the very next verse, 'If we confess our sins, He is faithful and just and will forgive us our sins and purify us from all unrighteousness.'"

Charles thought a moment. "That sounds too easy, too pat."

Should I press this? Zoë thought. *Oh, I long so for him to have peace.* "You've confessed to me, Charles," she said. "Why not to God? Or is it that you don't believe God is there for you?"

"I've never believed He was," Charles said slowly. "But now—well, maybe."

"There's nothing wrong with praying a prayer like, 'God, if You're there, I want to confess my sins.'"

He pursed his lips and nodded thoughtfully. "I'll think about it."

Zoë took a breath, wanting to urge him on, then stopped. *Okay, Lord,* she prayed silently. *I sense You telling me to button my lip, that Charles needs to do this on his own, in Your timing.*

At last Charles said, "You have been studying a long time."

She smiled. "I am old—as you love to remind me. Although, actually, I am really not *very* old. I mean nowadays, sixty-nine and a half is not exactly ancient."

He sobered. "*I* will be old by the time I get out of here."

"Pooh!" she said. "You'll barely be dry behind the ears. And," she added, "you can use this time to learn a lot."

Charles nodded. "I think I need to learn a lot about myself—so I don't ever again become so angry." He closed his eyes. "I tell you the truth, Mother Lang, I used to have these vivid bloody nightmares. Now they are gone. Instead I have nightmares that I am attacking Leslie again." He shuddered.

She felt her stomach muscles tighten. "I pray that you will be able to have some counseling, Charles. And I am very grateful that you would be willing." She smiled. "I see a lot of growth in you."

"Learning the hard way."

"That's the way we all learn best."

⌇

Scott rubbed his hands as David zoomed into the therapy gym, burning rubber when he braked his wheelchair. "Aha! Here is my—victim! Are you ready to work? Are you ready to move those arms, move those legs? No pain, no gain! Mom, where's my whip?"

David groaned. "A fate worse than Leslie. Okay, where do we begin, coach?"

Scott consulted the list his mother had given him. "On the

436

WINGS OF A DOVE

recumbent bike. Get your bod over here, and I'll strap your feet in."

Leslie smiled as she watched them. How comfortable they are together now. What a blessing!

David transferred to the bike, and Scott fastened the straps. As David cycled, periodically Scott shouted, "Faster. They're gaining on you."

Later, as they tossed the medicine ball, David said, "Don't know about you, but I miss workout."

"Me, too. Wish I could swim during this vacation."

"You want to?" David asked. "I could pick you up, take you to the Y. Pool's open, and hardly anybody's there."

"Kinda like to work on my breaststroke. That's where I lose time in the individual medley."

"Sure. We could do that." David's eyes twinkled. "And I could get even with you for today."

"Uh-oh. I was afraid of that."

Leslie came in and watched, smiling. "Much better balance, David. I'm going to measure your muscle strength today, but I think we know already it's improved."

As Leslie tested his strength in various positions, she asked, "You going home for Christmas?"

David shook his head. "Thought of it. Logistics are too complicated. Decided to hang here."

"Well, why don't you join us? We're all going to work at the mission, serving dinner. Then go to my mom's for dinner, late afternoon. Can we adopt you?"

"You serious?"

"Very."

"You got yourself a new family member, lady."

As Leslie completed her manual measurements, she smiled. "Just as I thought, David. We're really seeing improvement in your strength from a month ago. After the fall, your hip extensions were a little less than two on a zero-to-five scale. Now they're halfway between a two and three. That's 50 percent of normal."

"Okay, so when can I get in the parallel bars? Time's a-wastin'."

We could try it, she thought. *I'm the one who's afraid.* She looked at the two expectant faces turned toward her. "Okay," she relented. "Just standing in the bars."

As she went to get David's leg braces, David motioned to Scott to come near. "Don't you dare tell her, but I'm already pulling myself up to stand at the kitchen counter." When Leslie returned, she and Scott helped David fasten the braces, and he wheeled up to the bars, grasped them and lifted himself to stand. "I can move. I know I can!" he said.

Oh, Lord, may he be ready, Leslie prayed. Then, "All right, David. When you're ready."

Waiting a moment for balance, David moved his left foot forward cautiously, then his right. After two more steps Leslie and Scott applauded.

"Your chair's behind you," Leslie said, and David sat down.

"I'm impressed," Leslie admitted. "You're so much stronger than when you took your very first steps back in October, before you fell!"

David winked at Scott. "I know," he said quietly.

Leslie didn't miss it. When David was back in his wheelchair, she demanded, "You been cheating, young man?"

"Moi?" David pointed to himself, eyes all innocence.

"Oui. Vous."

"You know I do everything my physical therapist tells me," he stalled.

"Yes. And maybe more?" She saw Scott struggle not to

smile. He'd never been good at subterfuge. Okay, she wouldn't intrude on their private joke. As she leaned over to unfasten David's braces, she heard them high five.

"Way to go, man!" Scott exclaimed, and she could hear his struggle not to laugh.

43

WHAT A PLACE TO SPEND CHRISTMAS, ZOË THOUGHT AS SHE
stepped into the bleakness of the visitors' area of the jail on
Christmas Eve. *You'd think they'd at least put up some fake pine
branches or red-and-green crepe paper. And a little pine spray
wouldn't hurt, to cover the eau de Lysol.* Praying Charles wouldn't
be too depressed, she waited for him to appear. She was surprised to see him looking more—*More what?* she asked herself.
Rested, perhaps.

"Well," he said, "ready for Christmas?"

"Almost." She couldn't think what to say. "Will they have a
Christmas dinner here tomorrow?"

"I assume so. They served turkey and the usual trimmings
for Thanksgiving. The pie was definitely not in a class with
yours, however."

"Of course not!" She winked. "But just think, Charles,

you'll be spared my Christmas pudding tomorrow. I know you've never been too fond of it."

"Believe me, I would be very, very glad to have Christmas pudding with you tomorrow." Charles gave a rueful smile.

Zoë's own smile faded. "I know you would. And we'll miss you. Leslie wanted to do Christmas a little different this year so the kids wouldn't miss you too much. They'll have presents after church tonight. And in the morning we'll go to the Rescue Mission to help serve dinner. The kids want to come see you after that. Then it's my place for dinner. David is coming."

"Good idea. I have, um, written cards for Leslie to attach to the gifts she got for the children from me."

She nodded. "Thoughtful of you." She waited for him to lead the conversation.

"I did not have anything else to do," he said, smoothing his moustache, "so thought I might as well read about the birth of Christ in my Bible since that is what this holiday is supposedly about." He shook his head. "One good thing about being here is that I have been spared Santa Clauses who laugh without ceasing despite their obvious high-cholesterol diets. And I do not have to deal with Rudolph. Or elves and reindeer, or all the other trappings that I always found so depressing." He paused. "But about the Bible. I was wondering something. The gospels of Matthew and Luke both have detailed accounts of Christ's birth. Why is it that Mark and John do not?"

"I suspect it's because each of the gospels has a different emphasis," Zoë replied. "Matthew wanted to show that Jesus was the fulfillment of prophecy, and it was important for him to give the specifics of Christ's birth. Luke's focus was Christ as the Son of Man—the perfect man, and of course detailing His birth shows His human-ness.

"Yes, I notice he starts by saying he's investigated everything and wants to write an orderly account."

Zoë nodded. "So Luke starts at the beginning. Mark, however, wanted to show Jesus as a servant, so he began with Jesus' ministry instead of His birth."

"I see. And John?"

"His main point was the deity of Christ. As you pointed out last week, He blew the Pharisees away when He said 'I am,' meaning, 'I am God.'" She thought a moment. "But Charles, take another look at the beginning of John. It really is, in its own way, the Christmas story." She put on her half-glasses and pulled her pocket Bible from her purse. "Notice how it says, 'The Word became flesh.'"

"Read it to me," Charles said.

She looked up to be certain he was serious and saw him nod. So she began reading the first chapter to him. "'In the beginning was the Word, and the Word was with God, and the Word was God." She glanced at his attentive face and continued. ". . . Through him all things were made . . . The true light that gives light to every man was coming into the world . . . The Word became flesh and made his dwelling among us . . . the glory of the One and Only, who came from the Father, full of grace and truth.'"

This passage always moved her so, she couldn't keep the emotion from her voice as she read, and she hoped it wouldn't put Charles off. She stopped at verse 18: "'No one has ever seen God, but God the One and Only, who is at the Father's side, has made him known.'" She closed her eyes. "Some translations say Jesus 'explained Him.' That is, showed us who God is."

Closing the Bible, she looked up and saw Charles's eyes shining with tears. "It's algebraic," he said softly. "Cumulative."

"Yes!" she breathed.

Oh, Lord, she prayed, *I do believe he's getting it! Thank You for the Holy Spirit at work in his life.*

"Thanks, Mother," he said.

It was the first time he had ever called her 'Mother,' not 'Mother Lang,' and she felt tears gather in her own eyes.

꙳

Volunteers were already bustling about the Men's Rescue Mission when Leslie, Zoë, the kids, and David arrived at nine on Christmas morning.

"Ah, this is more like it!" Zoë exclaimed, surveying the Christmas banners on the walls, the two glittering trees.

While some volunteers spread holiday cloths on the long tables, others added centerpieces, each uniquely crafted by a child's hands.

"The air feels lighter in here," David said. "You can feel the love, can't you?"

Yes, Leslie thought, you can. Love and a sense of excitement not unlike the energy and anticipation backstage, before the curtain of a play rises.

David and Scott were assigned pie duty while Leslie and Zoë would serve the vegetables and Michelle would pour beverages.

When the doors swung open, they heard an uproar near the door. "Hey, man!" came a loud voice. "No buttin' in. You get yerself to the end of the line."

The first 144 guests filed in—all ages, all colors, all sizes. A man with a white, matted beard and grimy tailored suit jacket that had once known fashion-plate days looked at Zoë through bloodshot eyes and murmured, "Bless ya, pretty lady."

Another was still muttering about "that jerk who muscled in ahead of me."

Michelle flinched when she saw and smelled the younger man with dried vomit on his sweatshirt, but she gamely served him. "God didn't promise you a rose garden here," another volunteer whispered.

"More!" a man on crutches demanded, and the helper next to Leslie said quietly, "You can come through as many times as you like. But this is your serving for now."

"Yeah, sure! The blippin' lines two blocks long," the man complained.

Then Leslie felt tears gather in her eyes as she dished up vegetables to a man who looked so much like her dad— except for his slack, expressionless face, his watery, hopeless eyes.

Others looked embarrassed to be there, but many expressed thanks.

David sang out, "Merry Christmas. The Lord bless you," to each man who stopped for pie. And as Scott added, "Have a happy Jesus' birthday," he realized how many looked at him with wistful expressions. *They're thinking, maybe, of better Christmases with sons of their own,* he decided.

By the time Leslie and her family left, shortly after two, almost fifteen hundred guests had savored turkey with all the trimmings, pie, and their choice of a beverage.

"My feet hurt," Michelle complained as they walked into the parking lot.

"Mine don't," said David, staring down at his feet on the footrests.

"My back," Zoë added, "is weary. That was a lot of time standing. But wasn't it wonderful?"

"It might have been our best Christmas yet," Leslie said.

"You know, compared to the men we served today, none of us has major problems at all."

"Amen!" said David. "Okay, now I'm going to go help Mrs. Lang fix our Christmas dinner—"

"Oh-oh!" Scott said.

"Don't worry," Zoë soothed. "We'll make a great team."

"And we'll go see Charles," Leslie said. "Probably get to your house around four, Mom."

"Fine!" Zoë waved as she headed for David's van.

As they drove to Santa Ana, Michelle said, "It was neat to see how pleased most of those old geezers were. Some were pretty demanding. But others actually had tears in their eyes."

"And you knew the way a lot of 'em scarfed that food down, they hadn't had a real meal in days, maybe weeks," said Scott. "I think we should do this every year," he added.

"A new tradition. Why not?" Leslie smiled, thinking she really should have paid for the privilege of being there. "I'm embarrassed, to tell the truth, that it took a catastrophe in our own family to bring us here. I really don't know why we haven't made giving—our time, ourselves—the main event on Christmas before."

She'd wakened that morning dreading the visit to Charles, knowing she had to take the kids but resenting its intrusion on their holiday. Now she saw it as a part of the day's fabric. It's little enough to do, she realized, for another man who would otherwise have virtually no cheer on this special day.

When they entered the visiting area of the jail, Michelle whispered, "Couldn't they at least have a string of Christmas lights?"

As they walked toward their assigned booth, they couldn't help but hear a woman shouting over the phone to the man on the other side of the glass, "I hope you rot in hell!"

"And a Merry Christmas to you too," Leslie murmured. Charles smiled as he approached them and made an obvious effort to be cheerful as they exchanged Christmas greetings. "So," he said to Leslie, "you opened your gifts last night?"

"Right. Thought it would be best to break with tradition a little." She felt Scott's hand on her arm and handed the phone to him.

"Thanks for the sweats, Dad," Scott said.

Leslie caught the words, "Swim meets," from Charles.

"Yeah. They sure will," Scott said. "Especially the winter meets. Thanks. Merry Christmas, Dad." He handed the phone to Michelle.

"Hey, Charles, cool sweater. See, I'm wearin' it." She stood up to give him a full view. "What? No, it's supposed to be this long. Yeah, thanks. And hey, it seems dumb to say Merry Christmas, but . . ." She shrugged. "Anyway, thanks."

Leslie took the phone. "Charles, I don't want to spoil Christmas, but—"

"*You* can't spoil Christmas," he interjected.

She sighed. "I know. It already is spoiled, isn't it?"

He shook his head. "Actually no. All of you being here—it's great!"

"I'm glad. But Charles, about your arraignment in superior court day after tomorrow. Do you want me there?"

"No, I know you are busy, and I feel pretty much okay about it. Wells will try again for reduced bail but thinks the DA will balk. Says they'll either set a pretrial date or a trial date. So I can't see the necessity of your coming."

"You sure?"

He nodded.

"What about the plea bargain? I felt so frustrated at the preliminary hearing."

"Wells says not to worry. He says it's typical for the DA not to back down yet." He smiled. "Seems that in this county all homicides are submitted to what they call a 'turkey shoot,' where a group of senior lawyers in the DA's office determine how to file a case in superior court. They may have already decided it's a lesser-class crime, but they still file for murder for leverage purposes."

She nodded, wondering suddenly if he could get probation and no jail time. She felt her heart thud. No, surely not.

He crossed his fingers. "Keep your fingers crossed."

"I'll do more than that. I'll pray—for fairness, Charles."

"Yes. Well, prayer couldn't hurt either."

ॐ

As she sat down for Christmas dinner at her mother's, Leslie thought, *I've been in three different worlds today. The mission. Prison. Now this gorgeous table Mom's prepared.* Her eyes feasted on the turquoise-and-wine color scheme, the flickering tapers, the angel centerpiece.

She looked around the table at her children; at Tracy, Greg, and their boys home from college; David, charming all the family; her grandmother, bent with age at ninety-two, her walker parked off to the side.

Zoë sat at the head of the table. "Now before I bring in Mr. Turkey, David's going to read the Christmas story from—" She paused and looked around the table. "—Philippians." She grinned. "Thought you were going to get Luke and 'shepherds abiding,' didn't you?"

David opened his Bible and cleared his throat. "This is Philippians chapter 2, starting at verse 5. 'Your attitude should be the same as that of Christ Jesus: Who, being in very nature

God, did not consider equality with God something to be grasped, but made himself nothing, taking the very nature of a servant, being made in human likeness. And being found in appearance as a man, he humbled himself and became obedient to death—even death on a cross! Therefore God exalted him to the highest place and gave him the name that is above every name, that at the name of Jesus every knee should bow, in heaven and on earth and under the earth, and every tongue confess that Jesus Christ is Lord, to the glory of God the Father.'" His eyes shut, David closed the Bible.

"'God with man now abiding,'" Tracy's husky voice quoted the Christmas carol.

"Oh, Father," Greg prayed, "thank You for the gift of Yourself to us—for sending Your Son, Jesus. And especially, thank You, Jesus, for Your willingness to come, to lay aside Your glory and to come to a terrifically difficult walk on earth. Father, bless each one who is gathered 'round this table. And we ask your special blessing on family members who can't be with us, especially Benjamin (Heal him, oh Lord!) and Charles (Heal *him!*) Thanks for David's presence, and especially for Yours, Lord. Bless our time, our conversation, and the food You've given us. In Jesus' name, amen."

"And a happy birthday, Jesus!" Scott added. Suddenly he looked stricken. "Oh, Gram, we didn't put Jesus in the manger like we always do on Christmas day!"

Zoë clapped her hands together. "You're right. You're the youngest here today, Scott. Better get him, poor little babe!"

Scott hurried to the fireplace, found the little box on the hearth, and placed the carved figure of Jesus in the creche of the olive wood nativity scene on the mantle.

"That's better!" he said.

After the turkey, the wild-rice stuffing, the broccoli, the

mandarin orange salad, relishes, cranberry sauce, and hot rolls, and before the Christmas pudding, Zoë said, "Let's remember special Christmases past." She turned to her mother.

Her mother smiled, looking around the table through the thick cataract glasses that gave her a wide-eyed, wondrous look. "I *know* that one night I heard the reindeer on the roof." Her voice was tremulous and sweet. "I think I was about five— yes, I was five, and my cousins and I were sleeping in the same bed, and it wasn't just me. We *all* heard the hooves and the sleigh bells."

Tracy raised her hand. "I remember the time you guys," she pointed to her sons, "were two of the wise men in the Sunday school Christmas pageant. And—how did it happen? You, Greg, tripped on your robe . . ."

"Right, and then Matt tripped over me. And we totally lost it—just lay there laughing like idiots."

"But you got it back together again, as I recall," Zoë said.

"Sort of," Matt laughed.

David smiled. "Well, this isn't very spiritual. But when I was eleven, I had a Staffordshire terrier, and he had jaws like a steel trap. On Christmas morning my mom went outside and came in screaming. The dog had eaten the lights on the outdoor Christmas tree. The sockets were all crimped together, and there were little pieces of glass on the patio."

"Oh, wow! What happened?" Scott asked.

"Of course the vet wasn't in on Christmas day—it was a Friday—so he was out for the next two days too. The dog seemed all right. So my mom said I'd better keep an eye on him and also watch when I cleaned up after him, to be sure he wasn't bleeding. Well, he seemed to thrive on his diet. The only evidence was that when I cleaned up, some were blue, some green, some red."

"Oooh—gross!" Michelle wrinkled her nose.

"*I* think it's very funny!" Zoë's mother wiped tears of laughter from her eyes.

"One of my fondest memories is when Leslie played the Christ child in our church's pageant," Zoë said. "There weren't any other newborns in our fellowship, so a girl had to do."

"I remember that," Tracy said. "You were Mary, Mom."

"Because I could keep Leslie quiet."

"No, because your face shone." She looked fondly at her mother. "It still does."

Zoë blew Tracy a kiss and went for the Christmas pudding. Just as they were finishing, the phone rang. Zoë answered, and her face lit up. "Merry Christmas to you, Benjamin!" she exclaimed.

"Merry Christmas!" the whole table chorused. Then they each took turns speaking to Benjamin.

When Leslie came to the phone, she said, "Dad, I want to hear about your Christmas program."

"Well, from a physical standpoint, I used a cane, and I sat on a tall stool."

"Good. With your tails properly draped over it, I trust."

"Of course!" He laughed, then cleared his throat. "I would like to tell you I was splendid. But Leslie, it was strictly the Holy Spirit. People said it was our best concert ever. But it wasn't a concert."

"It was worship," she said softly. "With God as the audience."

"It really was. I truly believe it glorified Him."

She felt the tears rise. "That was my prayer, Dad. I knew it would."

"Now, my Weeny One, I need to hear how your heart is."

"Well, I have to be honest. It's been aching. But today, I think, gave me a better perspective. I'm going to be okay."

"I know you are, and you are in my prayers every single day. I love you very much."

"Thanks, Pappy o'mine. I love you too."

Later, as the family dispersed and David started for his van, Leslie stopped him and knelt to whisper, "David, you saved the day. I think Scott would have felt so desolate and missed his dad so much. But you were great—at the rescue mission, reading the Christmas story before dinner, injecting your own special humor. Thanks."

"It was the Lord. You know that, Leslie. Hey, I sure thank you for inviting me. I felt kinda sorry for myself, to tell the truth, being away from my family, but I sure got over that at the rescue mission. And I couldn't have felt more at home with all of you. The Lord bless you."

"And you! 'Night."

The kids were already in the car when Leslie reached it.

"Cool time," Michelle said sleepily.

"Yeah," Scott agreed. "I'm real glad David came. He's kinda like a cross between a buddy and a dad."

Leslie smiled. "I'm glad he came too."

A few minutes later as they trooped into their house, Leslie realized that beneath the joy of what her mother always termed 'Jesus' birthday party,' the underlying emotional strain had exhausted her. It was always a tense time, visiting Charles, trying to be supportive without getting hooked into emotional dependence again. But it was especially difficult with the kids on Christmas.

Then, too, she'd had such concern about them, and how the day would be for them. Yet it really had been a beautiful day, with the focus on the gift of Jesus, not the problems of the family.

She poured herself a glass of water, kicked off her shoes, and flopped on the couch. It would be good to have tomorrow off. She'd let so many things go these past weeks, and she could use a catch-up day to pay bills, organize their business affairs—maybe even think about the future. *I'm free now,* she thought. *I can think for myself instead of having someone tell me what to think, how to feel, how to act—how to wear my hair, for heaven's sake! I've just begun to see the range of possibilities for me. I don't even have to stay here. I could fly far, far away, once Charles is sentenced. Maybe—* The thought came from nowhere. *Why, maybe Scott and Michelle and I should move to Mammoth. No gangs, no pollution. With all the athletes there—biking, climbing, hiking in summer and skiing in winter, there'd surely be work for me. And maybe the small-town closeness would be good for the kids. Great place for them to have a dog too. It's pleasant in the spring, summer, and fall. And the skiing easily makes up for any problems of cold weather and snow. The local kids even learn to ski as part of their school curriculum.*

Perhaps she should make some phone calls, explore the feasibility of working there, check out living costs and housing.

Or . . . They didn't have to stay in California. They could move to Vail—or Aspen. Or even back to Chicago. Her dad had suggested it in a recent call, and it would be good for the kids to know their grandfather better.

But that would be so far away from the rest of the family. She'd miss her mother. A lot. But was she perhaps still too tied to her? Even Mammoth would isolate them a little. Still, maybe that wasn't all bad. Starting afresh somehow looked very appealing. Oh, but what would they do about the house?

She rubbed her head. *Can't figure it all out tonight. I'll be like Scarlett,* she decided, *and think about it tomorrow.*

44

THE DAY AFTER NEW YEAR'S, SCOTT SAW THE BROAD GRIN on David's face as he wheeled into the physical therapy care center.

"Hey," Scott greeted him, "You look like you're in a good mood. It's because I'm here to coach you. Right?"

Leslie came over and took a close look at David. "Hmm. Something more than anticipation of therapy, it seems to me. In fact, I would almost say . . ." She saw David flush slightly. "Aha! I'm right. It's a *girl*."

"Oh, no! Gimme a break," Scott said in mock horror.

David held up his hand. "I cannot tell a lie. Met her at a church singles' party on New Year's Eve."

"Okay, okay," Leslie gave him a charades "more" gesture. "Vital statistics?"

"Um, course I couldn't stand beside her, but tallish, slender, athletic build, but curvy too. Blonde, green eyes. Likes to ski and wind-surf. But the big thing is, we think alike. In fact, she almost knows what I'm thinking. And I think—I think I can be my real self with her. No pretending."

"That is *so* important, David," she said, remembering all the pretending she had done with Charles, trying to be what he wanted her to be. "This is very exciting."

"Yeah. So let's get to work so I can ski and wind-surf with her and walk her to church!"

"Well-l-l," said Scott, "if that's what it takes to motivate you." He shook his head and looked at his list. "Let's warm up with the hand bike then move on to the stationary bike."

When they'd finished, Leslie pointed to the parallel bars. "What would you say to trying 'em without your braces?"

"You serious?" David cocked his head.

"I thought you were in a hurry," Leslie teased.

"I am, I am!"

When David had positioned his wheelchair at the end of the bars, Leslie cautioned, "Just a few steps. Stop when you're tired."

David stood up, and Leslie watched his legs for any sign of trembling or wobbling.

"Good!" she said. "Does it feel strange, insecure?"

"No. Kinda naked, light. But good." David took a step. Then another.

Scott stood at the end of the parallel bars. "Good, David! You look strong! Can you do another?"

David took two more steps. *He's planning to go the full length of the bars,* Leslie realized. She sent up a quick prayer.

"Good—good—good," Scott exclaimed with each step.

Leslie met him with the wheelchair.

"That was excellent!"

"I think I could do it again."

"We'll see. When you've rested, we might have another go," Leslie said.

David nodded. "Y'know, Leslie, Scott's improved his breast-stroke in our private sessions. That left leg's bendin' the way it's s'posed to now, and he's getting a lot of thrust with his arm strokes."

"And something else I've noticed." Leslie put one hand on Scott's arm, the other on his back. "You're getting muscles! Feel those triceps and lats, will you?"

"Yeah, Scott's gettin' to be an animal."

Scott ducked his head modestly, but not before Leslie saw his grin.

⁂

"I'm so sorry I didn't get here last week, Charles," Zoë apologized when she next visited him. "I never have escrows opening at the first of the year. It's unheard-of, but I've had three."

"But I know you're glad business is picking up," Charles said.

"Indeed. But what about you, Charles? I understand your arraignment in superior court went okay on the twenty-seventh."

"Yes, it was pretty much routine, I gather. Bill Wells, my attorney, entered a not-guilty plea, asked for trial setting. The date's February 12. Seems a lifetime away. But Wells still hopes it won't come to a trial."

"I hope not too."

Charles nodded and stared over her head for a moment. It was then that she noticed he'd brought his Bible. He focused back on her. "I've been reading the Book quite a bit."

"I'm delighted to hear that, Charles."

He nodded. "On New Year's Day—well, it wasn't a very good day for me. All the guys in my cell were watching the bowl games on TV, and I never really got into football."

"Not like baseball, eh?"

Charles nodded. "So there was all this hullabaloo going on in the TV room—boos, cheers, 'Git 'im,' et cetera. I tried to read one of the books Leslie brought me for Christmas but realized I'd read the same page three times. My mind was too full of myself—the mess I've made, the damage I've caused other people, the utter failure I am. But I didn't know what to *do* with it."

Zoë nodded.

"So I picked up the Bible you gave me and began thumbing through the gospel of John again, trying to concentrate and filter out all the stuff from the adjoining room. I stopped at chapter 14." He opened the Bible and read, "'Do not let your hearts be troubled. Trust in God; trust also in me.'"

"Jesus speaking," Zoë noted.

"Right. So I read on, seeing how Jesus told how He'd go ahead to prepare a place in His Father's house. Then I came to Thomas's question to Jesus: 'Lord, we don't know where you are going, so how can we know the way?'" He smiled. "That Thomas—a lot like me."

"Perhaps."

"Then I read Jesus' answer." Charles looked up at her, his eyes filled with wonder. "'I am the way and the truth and the life. No one comes to the Father except through me.' And it was as though it wasn't just in red letters; it was highlighted, just for me." He shook his head slowly. "And I can't tell you what or how, but I looked at those words and said to myself, 'This is true. I believe it.'" He shrugged. "No angelic voices, no light streaming into the cell. More like a light bulb over my head, maybe. And a 'Yes.' Not a yes-maybe, but a yes, that's true."

"Oh, Charles. That's won-der-ful!" Zoë exclaimed.

"Yes. But there's more. I knew right away there was something I needed to do—some response. And I remembered you talking about 1 John and God's forgiveness. So I found that verse." He thumbed over to it. "First John, chapter 1, verse 9. 'If we confess our sins, He is faithful and just to forgive our sins and cleanse us of all unrighteousness.' He looked up. "That word *all* seemed to be highlighted. And I realized it meant every single one—the whole long list. All the thoughtless, selfish, brutal, inconsiderate things I have done in my life."

He pressed his lips together. "So I got down on my knees and prayed what I fear was a rather crude prayer. I just spilled out all the things I know I've done and asked God to fill in the blanks of the things I didn't think of. And I told Him I was sorry and that I don't want to be that way anymore. And I also said something like, 'Oh, God, I want to be Yours, and I want You to be mine.'" He paused a moment, and a smile began to form. At last he laughed. "Right at that very moment this huge cheer arose from the TV room. For a split second I thought it was a heavenly response."

"I'm sure there was great rejoicing in heaven, Charles!"

"Think so?"

"Know so." They were silent a moment, and Zoë breathed a silent *Thank You, Lord*. Then she added, "You know something, Charles, it's still Christmas, in a way. This is Twelfth Night. The twelfth day of Christmas. And this is absolutely the best Christmas present I could ever have! I love you, and I have wanted so much and prayed so much for you to know Jesus."

"I am aware of that. You have never given up."

"Stubborn old lady," she said.

"*You* said that." He smiled, and when he looked at her, his eyes shone softer than she'd ever seen them. "You know I'm a cautious man. I thought at first I had dreamed or hallucinated. But now I think not."

"Why is that, Charles?"

"Because I feel different. It's difficult to explain. I feel—safe. No matter what happens. More relaxed than I think I have ever felt in my life."

"It's God's peace, Charles," she said softly.

"Must be. It is certainly not my own doing."

"Oh, Charles, I rejoice for you—and with you!"

"I rather thought you would. I know I have work to do. Need to re-evaluate my life, change some of my automatic responses, try to make up for the past with Leslie and the kids."

"That will come, Charles."

He held up his forefinger. "Oh, but, uh, please, do not say anything to Leslie."

"Of course not. You must tell her yourself." She beamed at him. "Someday, Charles, you may look back on this as the best Christmas of your life."

Charles lifted his eyebrows. "What did Dickens say? 'The best of times and the worst of times?'"

"Yes, and I think he also talks about the season of light, the season of darkness. This is the season of light, Charles."

"'Light of the world,' Jesus said."

"Light of the world!"

45

❧

From Zoë's Prayer Journal

*January 6: Dear heavenly Father, how gra-
cious You are, how faithful to Your promises,
and how I rejoice that Charles has said yes to
You. I pray You will continue the work You've
begun in Him and that He'll be nourished and
comforted by Your presence. Thank You for the
hope You've given him. Now I confess I can't
help but wonder how this will impact Leslie. But
I remember You've told me You are more interested in her holiness than her happiness, and I
yield to Your perfect will. Be glorified, Lord! In
the name of Your Son, amen.*

LATE ON WEDNESDAY, WEARY FROM A BUSY DAY AND FROM
fighting bumper-to-bumper traffic, Leslie dragged into the jail.
Charles greeted her with such a genuine smile—such a softened expression, her reflex reaction was that he'd been
drinking. But of course, that couldn't be.

"I'm glad you came alone," he said.

"Why is that, Charles?"

"Because I have something to tell you. Something you may
find quite surprising."

"Oh?"

He stroked his moustache with one finger. "Leslie, I—well, to put it concisely—I believe."

"Believe what, Charles?"

He tilted his head. "Why, believe in God. In Jesus as my personal Lord and Savior."

It was all she could do not to fall back in her chair. "I—I find that hard to believe," she managed.

"That's quite understandable." He looked at her with an expression of wonder. "I have been thinking a lot about how it all fits into life. And I came to the conclusion that for most people there are basically three stages of life. First, there's being a victim. I certainly experienced that. Then, the victim says, 'Huh-uh, I'm not going to take it anymore. *I* am going to be in charge of my life.' That's where I have been for a long, long time. And the third stage is—surrender."

She studied his face. *Is it possible?* she wondered. *He can be so smooth, especially when he wants something. Is he manipulating?* Immediately she felt guilty for questioning his sincerity. Still . . .

She saw the relaxation of the rigid lines of his mouth, the tenderness in his eyes—so different from the glittering hardness when he was angry at her. His profession of faith seemed genuine, but immediately she wondered, *Even if it is, will it last?*

"Leslie," he said, "I want to ask you to forgive me for all the pain I've caused you through the years. I know you probably are not ready to do that now. But I hope in time that you will. I would do anything to make it up to you." He sat for a moment, his lips pursed thoughtfully. "I have been reading various Bible passages about marriage, and I see my failures. I see my *sins*. I don't think I even knew how to love you, much less to love you as Christ loved the church." He let out a long sigh. "I was thinking about what I could do to show you how much I want now to really cherish you and care for you. But what I would like to do is not possible—here." He nodded at the glass partition.

Feeling as stunned as when she first saw Charles on television, Leslie managed, "What?"

"I would like to wash your feet." He was weeping now, and she felt tears rise in her own eyes.

"Charles—I don't know what to—" Her voice caught in her throat and she coughed. "I don't know what to do with this. It's so contrary to all that I've lived with for all the eleven years I've been married to you. I've just had a bellyful of all of that. But now—am I to believe this sudden about-face?"

He nodded. "I don't expect you to. But I hope as time goes by, you'll see it's genuine. Ask God to show you." He grinned sheepishly. "Imagine me saying that!" He gave her a tender look. "Pray about it. I hope someday we'll be able to pray together."

She closed her eyes. Hadn't that been her prayer throughout their marriage? That Charles would believe. That they could be a couple who prayed together, a family who prayed together.

Oh, Lord, she cried out silently. *The timing's all wrong! Why now? Why, just when I was convinced I could never love him again? Why when I'm feeling so free?*

After she left Charles, she sat for a long time in her car, reviewing all that he'd said. "I think I must have dreamed it all," she said to herself as she turned the key in the ignition.

She'd just entered the freeway when traffic came to a dead stop. She sat, tapping her fingers on the steering wheel, and switched on the car radio. Finally the traffic alert came: three-car collision, Santa Ana Freeway, three lanes southbound blocked. The right lane began to move slowly, and at last she exited the freeway and took surface streets. Stopped for a red light, she glanced at her watch and realized it was the night her support group met. They'd be almost finished by the time she could get there, but—

She stopped at a phone booth to see if Zoë, who'd come in to fix dinner for the kids, could stay a little longer.

"We're all fine," she assured Leslie. "Take your time."

The support group welcomed her with hugs and merciful restraint from questioning. Leslie sat down with them and said, "I'm sorry to pop in so late, but Kathy, when you finish, I'd like to say a couple of things, if it would be all right."

"Of course. We're so glad you're here. I think what you have to say is much more important than what we were just discussing."

The women murmured agreement and looked at Leslie expectantly.

"You all know that my husband had something pretty dark and awful in his past that seemed to compel him to always be in control. But I want to caution you. Please, I don't want you to start on witch hunts, thinking there's necessarily some terrible thing in *your* husbands' pasts."

"I'm so glad you brought that up," Kathy said. "Ladies, your husbands certainly have pain in their backgrounds, roots that have left them easily angered, controlling. But it may simply have been a highly directive mother or another sibling being favored—or any of a number of difficult but not unusual family dynamics. There isn't necessarily something horrendous back there. You don't have to play therapist to them."

"Right." Leslie nodded. "In fact, even if you suspect there's something difficult in the past, my advice is, don't *you* try to uncover it. That was a big mistake I made." She swallowed and tried to think how to continue. "And the other thing is—I've just come from the jail, and I'm feeling right now as though the rug's been pulled out from under me. Charles says—he says basically he's been born again."

The women gasped and Tina shouted, "Yea!" thrusting her fist in the air.

Leslie smiled. "I know. It is exciting, and I rejoice for him. If it's genuine."

"Do you doubt it?" Sandra asked.

"I know, you're thinking, 'Oh ye of little faith.' And you wonder why I'm not ecstatic. But Charles has always been manipulative. And look at the circumstances. His back is to the wall. He knows he's lost me, his family, his job, his freedom, and control of his life and of others. Now how could he change that? Think about it."

"I have read," said JoAnne thoughtfully, "that a large percentage of prison conversions don't last."

"That's just what I was wondering about," Leslie said. "And—I have to confess before you, I have so many conflicting feelings and ideas right now. This is going to sound really selfish, but I was ready to start a new life. I felt God had given me the wings of a dove, that I was free. And, though a part of me felt scared of what it might be like on my own, most of me was looking forward to it very much. Now . . ."

"Wow," breathed Mary. "Just when I was envying you for being rid of him! Nothin's simple."

"You've got it," Leslie said.

"Mercy me," said a newcomer in a soft southern drawl. "We better pray, y'all."

The group drew together and held hands while each woman prayed for Leslie to know God's way for her, for Charles's salvation to be true and real, and for Michelle and Scott to adjust.

"Thanks, guys," Leslie said, wiping the tears from her face. "I—I'll definitely be back. I may not live with day-to-day harassment anymore, but it isn't over. I need you, and I hope I can help each of you in some way, though right now I can't imagine how."

"I think you already have—tonight," Kathy said.

They all hugged, and when Kathy embraced her, Leslie said, "Your scapegoat message was a real breakthrough for me. I appreciate your ministry so much!"

Kathy released her gently. "It's why I'm here."

As she drove home, Leslie thought, *I'll have to tell the kids. Maybe this will be a comfort for them—at least for Scott. Lord, I pray it will.*

At home her mother greeted her with such a questioning expression that Leslie realized she must already know about Charles.

"Charles told you, Mom?"

Zoë nodded. "Yesterday. He wouldn't let me tell you."

Leslie sighed and tried to keep her voice light. "It's all your fault. If you hadn't given him that Bible . . ."

Zoë smiled. "My fault? I'd love to take the credit. But if you're going to blame anyone—"

"Blame God? *Blame* isn't the right word, is it? But I admit I'm questioning His timing." She looked wearily at Zoë. "You haven't said anything to the kids?"

"Of course not!"

Leslie sighed. "Guess I'd better."

"Honey, you look so tired," Zoë said, her voice concerned. "Can't you—"

"Oh, Mom—" Leslie began to cry. "How can I can trust Charles? He can be so clever. Especially when he doesn't have to be with a person all the time. Then he can be on his best behavior."

"Oh, but honey, what I saw was a lot more than 'best behavior.'"

"You think it's genuine?"

Zoë put her hand on Leslie's. "Only God knows for sure, Leslie. But you're asking my opinion? This appeared to me to be a broken man, seeing his sin, seeing the only answer to that sin."

"He—he said he wanted to wash my feet," Leslie wept.

"Did he say that?" Zoë's eyes filled. "I don't think I know any husband who has done that for his wife."

"I don't either." Leslie took a deep breath and let it out slowly. "Mom, I was just feeling so free, and now—"

"You *are* free, honey. What do you really want to do now?"

"I've thought of all sorts of things—even moving away. I guess most of all, I want to help the kids grow up well. I want to help other people in my work. And always, I want a closer walk with the Lord."

"So has anything that happened today changed any of that or threatened to stop you from pursuing your goals?" Zoë asked gently.

"No. I guess not." She sighed. "I guess I'm in shock. I think maybe I've been in shock ever since I saw Charles on TV. But it keeps escalating."

"I know," Zoë said, patting her hand.

Leslie looked up at her mother. "I wonder what Dad will think? He seemed to have kind of an instinct about Charles. And oh, what will the kids think—especially Scott? Maybe I'd better wait till tomorrow to tell them."

"I doubt they're asleep."

"So, why wait? Knowing might be helpful to Scott."

She went to the stairway. "Scott? Michelle? You asleep? I need to talk to you just a minute."

"I'll just slip out," Zoë whispered.

"You can stay," Leslie said.

"No, this will be better." She put her fingertips to her lips then to Leslie's and let herself out.

When they were settled in the family room, Michelle said, "Wha'sup?"

"I've been to see your dad, as you know. And something—well, quite unexpected happened. I think you know Gram gave him a Bible, and they've been talking about Jesus. Well, your father told me today he's accepted the Lord."

"Su-u-u-re!" Michelle rolled her eyes.

"I knew it!" Scott exclaimed. "I've been praying for that almost as long as I've known how to pray. Oh, man! *Thanks, God!*"

"Oh, Scott, you're so gulli—"

"Please, Michelle!" Leslie interjected.

"Well!" Michelle said, as though she'd simply stated the obvious.

"As your grandmother so wisely pointed out, only God knows what's in Charles's heart. I think we should pray that this *is* genuine and that during his time in prison your dad will grow in the Lord Jesus Christ. You know that Scripture says he is now a new creation."

"I'll believe it when I really see that," Michelle muttered.

Leslie reached for Michelle's hand. "Maybe you should believe that what you said to him about needing Jesus may have had some impact," Leslie said gently.

Michelle was quiet. "I hadn't thought of that."

"Man!" said Scott. "Dad and I have a whole new thing we can talk about besides baseball."

"*May*-be," said Michelle.

46

LESLIE AWAKENED THE NEXT MORNING HEARING AGAIN HER
mother's gentle chiding about blaming God for Charles's—she
hesitated, not yet ready to call it a conversion. *But Mom's right,*
she thought. *I'm not only blaming God, I'm mad at Him too. I
thought He'd freed me so I could begin a new life, and now the
plot thickens. How am I to respond? No, wait. More important,
how does God want me to respond?* She slipped on a robe, sat in
the chair by the window, and opened her prayer journal. "Oh,
Lord," she wrote. "I confess I'm angry at You, and it doesn't
feel good, and I definitely need your help. Please show me Your
way and show me the truth about Charles." She paused and
thought. "Help me to see him as You see him, because I admit
I'm skeptical, wary. And I also admit I'm selfish, wanting to
'get a life,' for a change."

She continued pouring out her heart, and when she finished
she realized how different this communication with God was

from her prayers of a year ago. She felt free now to be honest before Him, knowing not only that nothing she could say would surprise Him, but also that He would not reject her for being real and forthright.

During her listening time, a scripture drifted into her mind: "There is now therefore no condemnation to those who are in Christ Jesus."

"Ahh," she sighed. "I think You're saying no condemnation even for angry skeptics like me. Thanks, Lord. I can face this day now!"

At breakfast Scott was still beaming. "I'm so glad about Dad," he said.

"I'm glad you're glad," she said.

"And I'm glad that you're glad that Scott's glad," Michelle teased.

Leslie laughed. "Okay, okay."

"I guess I'm not fair to be so suspicious of Charles." Michelle's voice sounded reluctant.

"It's all right, Michelle. I have to admit I feel some of that too." *Truth is,* she thought, *I wonder a little if it's like a deathbed conversion.* But she only said, "God knows what's in his heart."

"*I* think it's for real," Scott insisted.

"Time will tell, won't it?" Michelle said.

Leslie stared at her. Trite, maybe, but right on. "Michelle," she said, "that's really insightful."

As they finished breakfast, Scott asked, "David doin' okay without me?"

She smiled. "He does better when you're there."

"Yeah. I miss not coaching him, now that vacation's over."

"He's looking very strong, Scott. Doing well in the parallel bars without braces. I think we might try crutches—" She thought a moment. "—late next week."

468

"If he can do that, bet he's gonna walk on his own."

"It's looking quite good." She didn't want Scott to be overly optimistic, but at the same time, she admired his confident spirit.

"Crutches," Scott mused. "That'll be a biggie. Could I come?"

She studied his eager face. "I'll see what we can arrange."

At work she found that David had the last appointment on her schedule all through the following week, so she phoned Zoë.

"Mom, I hate to impose again, and please tell me if this doesn't work. Could you possibly bring Scott to physical therapy next Thursday at four? He wants to be here when we try David on crutches for the first time."

"That sounds like a big moment," Zoë said.

"Yes, if he can handle it, it'll be a breakthrough."

"Let's see." Zoë paused. Then she said, "I have a client, but I don't know why I couldn't swing by and get Scott while she's with me."

"Oh, thanks, Mom."

"How're you feeling—the morning after?"

"About Charles? Better. Michelle said a simple but profound thing: Time will tell."

Zoë laughed. "I do love that granddaughter!"

"I know you do. And I cherish that. Thanks, Mom. Have a blessed day."

"You, too, darlin'."

❧

The following week, when Leslie visited Charles, he seemed in an upbeat mood. "Hi, Leslie," he said. "You're looking pretty today. I think I'm getting used to your hair brushed back from your forehead."

Surprised, she smiled. "Why, thanks, Charles." She hesitated. "Any news from your attorney?"

He nodded and held up his hand to display crossed fingers. "Things may be starting to break. Wells is talking with the DA's office. They're getting pretty loaded with cases, and Wells feels they're going to look more favorably on a plea bargain."

"Good, Charles." She waited a moment. "What does he say about possible sentences?"

"The possibilities are three, six, or eleven years."

"That's quite a range. What does he think?"

"Not a chance on three. Six evidently is the more typical sentence. But because of the time that's lapsed since the crime—he's not placing any bets."

"Six or eleven." Leslie thought a moment. "Those are both a long time, but—"

"But not like what I'd get for murder."

"Right. Oh, Charles, I pray for everyone's sake that this will be resolved, soon. The not knowing . . ."

He nodded. "That is the difficult part." He looked at her, his eyes tender. "I appreciate your prayers."

The next day at work Leslie and Scott watched, smiling, as David walked the length of the parallel bars without his braces. "Good!" she said. "You are doing so well! Good knee control. What do you think? You ready to try crutches?"

"Ready!" David grinned, and the light glinted from his crooked tooth. "Thought you'd never ask!"

"The trouble with you, David," she said, "is that I have to

keep pushing you. I wish you had more gumption, more drive." She smiled. "Not!"

"Okay, okay," Scott said impatiently, "let's not just stand here."

"And you, Scott," Leslie pointed at her son. "You are as impossible as David!" Looking back at David, she said, "Okay, you ever used crutches before?"

David shook his head.

"I'll give you a little demo." Leslie brought a pair of crutches from a cabinet and put them under her arms. "A little long for me, but you'll get the idea. Okay, now, watch. You advance your left leg and the right crutch. Then the right leg and the left crutch."

"Makes sense."

"Okay. Brynne?" she called. "You ready to help us?"

Brynne came into the gym with a gait belt and fastened it around David.

"Okay. On your feet. Here are the crutches. We'll be on either side of you."

David found his balance, then moved his right leg and left crutch forward.

"Good!" Leslie exclaimed. "You look pretty steady. Another?"

David nodded. "This side's a little harder."

"Take your time," said Brynne.

He took another, less steady step.

"Good, David!" Scott whispered.

"One more?" Leslie asked.

"Two more," David insisted.

When he'd taken the two additional steps, Leslie said, "Scott, bring his chair up behind him, will you, please?"

After David was seated, she asked, "How did it feel?"

"Like work." David wiped his forehead. "But great!"

"Okay, rest a little bit. You and Scott see what nefarious plots you can come up with for a few minutes."

They grinned at each other as Leslie went to take a phone call.

After a few minutes Leslie came back into the gym. "Want to try again?"

"You kiddin'?" David asked.

This time, as David took six more steps, he looked stronger, more secure. Leslie made a quick decision. With Brynne holding the gait belt, Leslie stepped in front of him and held out her hands. "Take my hands, David."

He looked at her, blue-green eyes enormous. She nodded and heard Scott at her side whisper, *"Yes!"*

"Scott, you take his crutches when he's ready," Leslie said. "Then move his wheelchair behind him."

With Brynne still holding the gait belt, David started to release the crutches, clamped his hands on them again, then let go and reached out to grasp Leslie's hands. She moved backward as he took his first step. Then another.

"Wheelchair's behind you," she whispered. As he sat down, Scott, Leslie, and Brynne applauded.

"Bravo, David!" Leslie said.

"Yea! Great walk, buddy!" Scott slapped him on the back.

Then, with David seated, they gathered into a four-fold hug. "Oh, man, that felt so good! Thank You, Father!" came David's choked voice.

"Yeah, thanks, God!" Scott echoed.

As they separated and each saw the others' tears, they broke simultaneously into laughter.

"Thanks, Lord. I needed this!" Leslie said, hugging Scott and David once again.

❧

Five days later Leslie picked up the phone to hear the operator say, "Collect call from Charles Harper. Will you accept the charges?"

"Yes," she said, feeling her gut tighten.

"Leslie," came Charles's voice. "Good news. Wells and the prosecuting attorney have asked to advance the trial date for a pretrial hearing. It's set for January 23."

"Oh, good, Charles. Does this mean they've reached an agreement?"

"It does."

"Oh, thank You, Lord!" she cried, and relief flooded over her.

"Indeed," Charles said.

"I'll be there, Charles."

"I would appreciate it. Love you. Good night, Leslie." He hung up before she could reply, and she said aloud, "Closure! Soon all these weeks of waiting will be over, and life can go on!"

❧

The days till the hearing date passed at a pace that reminded Leslie of a stroke patient's slow shuffle. But at last, on a chill, foggy morning, Leslie sat in superior court, trying to read the newspaper she'd brought but failing to focus on words. She knew that Wells and the deputy district attorney were to meet in the judge's chambers. But what if the judge said, "No way"?

She stared at the back of the man in front of her. The label of his sweater hung out over his neckline. *Charles would never do that,* she thought.

At last a marshal brought Charles in. He looked like the old, well-turned-out Charles in his suit. Then Wells and the deputy DA came through the door. When they were seated, Leslie saw Wells lean over and whisper to Charles, who nodded.

Finally the judge appeared. Papers were signed, and the judge announced, "The court accepts the record."

Leslie realized then she'd been holding her breath. She exhaled slowly. Would the sentencing take place now or later? She wasn't sure.

Then the judge said, "Mr. Harper, will you approach the bench?"

Charles stood, his body so rigid, she thought it might crack. He walked slowly forward.

"Mr. Harper," the judge said, "the court accepts your plea of guilty of voluntary manslaughter, and it sentences you to eleven years in state prison. Further, the court recommends counseling with the goal of learning to cope with your anger."

"Thank you, Your Honor." Charles voice was firm and clear.

After court was dismissed, she caught Charles's eye and gave him a thumbs-up. He and Wells shook hands before the marshal took Charles away.

Wells finished his conversation with the prosecuting attorney and came over to Leslie, putting his hand on her shoulder. "I know you're glad this is over."

She sighed. "Of course. Is there—is there a standard time for possible parole?"

Wells nodded. "It's two-thirds of the sentence. So he could well be out in about seven years. Sometimes, depending upon an inmate's work in prison and other factors, he could be eligible in half the sentence time."

"So he could even be out in five and a half years."

Wells smiled. "It's always possible."

"Thank you *so* much." She clasped his hand.

"Welcome."

It's over! It's over! she exulted. She glanced at her watch. *Two months of waiting, and it's over in five minutes.* Turning, she made her way out of the courtroom.

Outside, the media thronged around her. "Comment, Mrs. Harper?" . . . "Do you think the sentence is fair?" . . . "What are your plans?"

She recognized TV newswoman Nancy Jefferson. "Mrs. Harper! Would you be willing to talk with us now?"

She started to give her reflex "no" reaction and then thought, *Why not? It's over.* She nodded and felt herself thrust down to the end of the hallway.

"Mrs. Harper," Jefferson began, "it must have been an overwhelming shock to learn you had lived eleven years with a man involved in a homicide. Did you ever suspect?"

Leslie shook her head. "Never. I knew he had nightmares, I knew he didn't talk about parts of his past, but no, I never suspected."

Another reporter called out, "Do you feel your husband's sentencing is just?"

She nodded. "My husband didn't enter that woman's apartment with the intent of killing her. That, um, wasn't ever his purpose."

Two reporters spoke at once, but she caught the words, "An accident?"

"Yes," she said, "in my mind it was far closer to an accident than to murder." She thought a moment. "But yes, he did push her, and her fall did result in her death. So yes, I believe the sentence is fair."

"Mrs. Harper," Jefferson asked, "Judge Parsons recommended counseling to help your husband deal with his anger.

Does this mean he was abusive to you?"

Leslie swallowed and gathered her thoughts. "I don't want to comment on that personally. But—"

Several reporters spoke at once, and she held up her hand, realizing this was her chance to speak out. "I do think in today's society, we hear more about—about physical abuse, because the results are there for all to see. But verbal, emotional abuse can be as devastating as physical. The wounds just aren't visible. It's—ah, my observation that all abusive men are angry men, and, well, there's a root to that anger. With counseling there's hope that they can learn to—to understand the anger and, well, to respond in more appropriate—and safer ways."

"So," another woman reporter asked, "you have hope for your husband?"

Leslie smiled. "Of course. I have hope because of the counseling, and also because he's recently told us he's become a Christian."

"You mean he's 'born again'?" a male voice asked.

Leslie could almost see the quotation marks around the term. "That is what he tells us." She nodded, adding, "And he seems in many ways to be a gentler, more caring person."

"So what do you plan—" Jefferson began.

Leslie interrupted, "I don't know what the future holds. But with God all things are possible."

She heard the other questions but waved them off with a "Thanks very much." As she walked down the hallway, she could scarcely believe she'd been so bold. *Too much on a soapbox?* she wondered. *No, I had to say it, and I pray it may help someone.*

47

⁓

From Zoë's Prayer Journal

January 24: Lord, You have been just and merciful to my son-in-law, exactly as I prayed. Five and a half to seven years till possible parole—that's not forever. Perhaps it's just long enough to heal the hurts of Charles's past, for him to grow in You and to be equipped to live productively in the real world. I pray You will continue the work You've begun in Him and that You'll put Your shield of protection over him in prison. And I pray that You will show Leslie Your way. Thanks for giving her the courage to speak out on TV yesterday. May her message be a wakeup call for many. Also, Lord, I think there's going to be a big whammy of reality for Scott and Michelle, a sense that they really are fatherless now. Thank You that they are not Fatherless! I love You, Lord. In Jesus' name, amen.

THE DAY AFTER THE SENTENCING, IN HER OWN PRAYER journal, Leslie thanked God for resolution. "We've been on hold for almost two months, wondering what the future would be," she wrote. "Now we know, and we can get on with life."

She was grateful that Charles, too, was thinking about their future. He'd asked her to come that afternoon and go over finances, so she moved her appointments at work to allow a long lunch break.

As they met, she could see the relief in Charles's face.

"I am so glad to have this resolved!" he said.

"Me, too, Charles."

"Yes, now we can carry on, so to speak. I don't feel depressed. Just grateful to know what we're dealing with. Chino is not so far away."

"Oh," she exclaimed. "It's the prison in Chino? Why, that's only an hour or so from us."

"Right. Now, about the finances." He held up his account books, which she'd brought on an earlier visit, to make his points. "I've drawn up a budget—not that you couldn't do it yourself or that you will necessarily stick to it." He said this without sarcasm, she noted. Quite a contrast to the "review" they'd had some months ago when he'd criticized every dollar she spent.

"I did this more for myself," Charles continued, "to be sure you could handle staying in the house. Though that, of course, is up to you. Fortunately, we refinanced when interest rates were low. So I think it is feasible on your salary if you are care- ful. You can still run any questions past me if you want to." He smiled a crooked smile. "You can communicate. I ain't daid, you know!"

This expression, so unlike Charles, made Leslie laugh out loud.

"What?" he said, puzzled.

"'Ain't daid'?"

He smiled. "Be glad I haven't picked up worse here! Some of these chaps are—colorful, to say the least." Closing the book, he added, "I've also made a checklist of monthly bills and when the property tax is due. Oh, and I think we'd better halve my contributions to Raoul, but do keep them up. I'll continue to write him."

Leslie nodded. "Of course."

"I'll be sure this is given back to you." He leaned back. "Now there is something much more important to discuss about the future."

She waited.

He searched her face as though memorizing her features, and it seemed minutes before he said, "I think we should divorce, to free you to get on with your life."

She gasped. Surely she had not heard him correctly. She felt her lips part, but she was too stunned to reply. "Did you hear me all right?" Charles pointed to the phone.

"I think so." Leslie blinked. "I'm just—Charles, you are full of major surprises!"

"Hear me out, Leslie. I am no use to you for at least five and a half years, maybe seven or more. After I'm out, how long will it take me to get back in the mainstream again? Yes, I can study to advance professionally during this time. But how easy is it going to be for a convicted felon to find a job? There are no guarantees. You are a capable woman, and you will do well. I don't deserve a wife like you, and certainly you don't deserve a husband like me."

She started to speak, but he stopped her. "I believe the Bible says that if an unbelieving spouse wants to leave, you should let him go."

"But—but you told me you believe, Charles."

"Yes, but I didn't during all the years of our marriage."

"So you think God might have a—a retroactive clause?"

He laughed. "That is very well put. But that is the principle."

Thoughts tumbled in her mind like clothes tossed in a

dryer. But one stood out: *Charles is, perhaps for the first time, trying to think what would be best for me. And the children. The children!*

Charles seemed to read her mind. "And it might be best for Michelle and Scott if they didn't have to say they have an inmate for a father."

"But Charles, you will always be their father. You can't just cut yourself off. It isn't fair to them."

"I thought it might be more merciful."

Mercy, she thought. A new word in his vocabulary.

"Charles, I—I don't know what to say." She stared past him, almost numb with shock, knowing that, even after all that had happened, there was still a modicum of love left in that love-hate dance she'd always done with him.

"I know. It is a rather startling idea. But I believe when you think it through, it will make more sense to you."

"I—" She stopped, took a deep breath, began again. "I feel—touched—that you would be this concerned about us, Charles, that you would want to do what seems to you to be best for us."

"Pffft!" he exclaimed. "It is simple logic." Then his mouth began to quiver, and he bit his lip. At last he said, "But there is one thing I would like to ask."

"Yes?"

"Would you pray for me?"

"You know I will, Charles."

"No, I mean now."

She looked at him in amazement. He gazed at her, his eyes pleading.

"Of course," she said. She closed her eyes and tried to gather her thoughts. "Oh, Lord, thank You that the sentencing is done and that we all know what at least a part of the future holds for us. I ask—" She hesitated. "—that You walk each step with Charles during these coming days. Ease the adjustment, comfort him when he's lonely, give him peace when he longs to be alone and can't." She paused for a breath. "May he stay in Your Word and grow in it and in You. I ask right now that You bring some special Christian into his life in prison to disciple him and be his friend. Lord, bless him and keep him. In Jesus' name, amen."

She looked up and saw Charles's head still bowed. "I'm not very practiced at this," he mumbled, "but Lord, I give my wife and children to You and ask You to watch over them and protect them and love them." His voice grew tight. "Thanks for them, Lord. I never knew till now what a blessing they are. Amen."

They looked up at one another.

"Thanks, Leslie," Charles said.

"Thank you, Charles."

"I—" He seemed to be fumbling for what to say next, and Leslie expected a comment relative to their prayers. Instead he said, "I thought I might shave my moustache."

It was so unexpected, she couldn't help but laugh. "I'm sorry, Charles, but that isn't what—"

"I know it sounds inane. But in a cornball way it seemed symbolic. A sort of coming clean. A new man."

"I've always wondered what you'd look like without it," she admitted. "Remember? Once I asked you to shave it."

"Yes. And I wouldn't. Well, I think I will."

"I think you'll look handsome, Charles."

He seemed pleased. "We'll see."

He placed his palm against the glass. "We'll talk."

She laid her palm against his, feeling only cold, lifeless glass. "Yes."

As he hung up the phone his mouth formed the words, "I love you."

Leslie walked away slowly, trying to digest all that Charles had told her. A deputy brought her the account books, and she took the elevator down, grateful she was alone.

He wanted to pray together! she thought. *I prayed for that for years, but—sorry, Lord, I doubted it would ever happen.*

When she reached her car she sat, alternately thinking and praying.

What had he called her? "A capable woman, and you will do well."

"Well, he's right," she said aloud. "I will do well."

Then, "Oh, Lord, You've given me the freedom I asked for. But . . ."

I'll see an attorney, find out what is entailed in getting a divorce—or maybe a legal separation. I mean, let's face it, Charles is a loner. He'll be all right without me. What was it Tracy said? "Charles should have been a hermit." Look what a life Mom made for herself after her divorce. I can have a life too! I deserve it after these eleven years of—come to think of it, I've been the one in prison!

But, "Lord, sometimes You give us more than we ask for. It's the 'more' that's throwing me now."

Does a man who is just pretending to be saved say he wants to wash his wife's feet and wants her to be free to go on with her life? Yes, but what if it's one of those high-of-the-moment, experiential things that doesn't last? What about when the initial excitement wears off? Should I have a pastor from the church go to see Charles, see what he thinks?

"Lord, Your Word says you hate divorce." She said the words aloud.

Even if he has counseling, even if he tries to walk with the

Lord, could Charles revert to old habits when he's out of prison, back in the stresses of daily living? He's never handled stress well.

She forced herself to look at the clock. Twenty minutes till her next appointment. She'd have to fly.

She smiled at the word *fly.*

Now I have the wings, she thought. And as she drove down the Santa Ana Freeway, with a bright sun sparkling off the chrome and glass on the cars around her, she felt a surge of strength and freedom.

Back at work her afternoon was full, but when her last appointment of the day canceled, she phoned her mother. Good, she was in her office. *I can hardly wait to see the expression on her face when I tell her,* she thought.

"Mom? Could I stop by and talk with you a minute?"

"Of course. Come on over."

When she was seated by her mother's desk, she leaned forward. "We both were surprised by Charles's profession of faith. But today he said something else—" She stopped and reached for her mother's hand.

"Does he—" Zoë hesitated. "—want to give you freedom from your marriage?"

Leslie stared at her mother. "Why, yes. So I could be free to get on with my life. How did you—did he tell you?"

Zoë shook her head. "I just had a feeling. What did you say?"

"Told him I was completely caught off guard, couldn't answer."

Zoë nodded. "And how do you feel?"

"Mom, after I left, I felt the most incredible surge of freedom! I thought my car might lift right off the Santa Ana Freeway."

"And now?"

"It occurred to me maybe this is his chance to be rid of me."

"Leslie, why would you think such a thing?"

"He told me often enough he wanted to."

"But that was another Charles. Not today's Charles. It sounds to me like he really is thinking of your best interest."

"So then—I'm free."

Zoë looked at her closely. "I hear the words, but I don't exactly hear that freedom ringing, Leslie."

Leslie slumped in the chair. "You're right. Something's bugging me, way down deep."

"Maybe you can talk it out," Zoë suggested.

"After Mammoth I hated him. Now, when I talk to him, he does sound like a new person. And I see there's a thread of love still there. But I wanted for so long, prayed for so long to be free!"

"Do you suppose God could be calling you to something else?"

Leslie gave a joyless smile. "I guess that's what I'm afraid of."

They didn't speak for a while. Leslie could hear phones ringing, snatches of conversation in the other offices.

Finally Zoë said, "Honey, I never told you this, but maybe it will help. One morning when I was praying through the alphabet as I swam my laps, I got to H, and I said, 'Lord, isn't there any happiness for Leslie?' And He very clearly indicated to me that He was more concerned with your holiness than your happiness." She smiled. "I admit I said to Him, 'How about a *little bit* happy?'"

Leslie stared at her. "Heav-y!" She took a deep breath. "I think I need to—to think about that."

48

THE SUN STRUGGLED TO PIERCE THE GATHERING DARK
clouds over Saddleback Mountain on Saturday morning.

No wonder we all slept so late, Leslie thought as she yawned
and made her way downstairs. A glum day.

A little later Scott echoed her feelings. "Not exactly wonderful out. Wish we had a swim meet or something."

"You feeling down about Dad, honey?"

"Well, yeah. I'll be a teenager with zits and hair on my face
by the time he gets out."

"We'll still go see him, Scott. It isn't that far to Chino."

"Will we? Honest?"

"Of course."

"But us guys can't watch baseball games together."

"That's true. But you can write him and talk to him about
the players and the teams."

"Yeah." He stirred his cereal with his left hand, his chin resting on his right.

Michelle came into the eating area. "Depressing day. Feel like goin' back to bed and staying the rest of the day."

"I thought of that too," Leslie admitted.

"It's gonna be strange without Charles," Michelle said. "Hey, here I am, living in a single-parent home."

"Surely that's not unusual among your friends."

"Nope. About half of 'em are. But this is gonna be weird. It's not like Charles died or you guys divorced."

Leslie felt her gut tighten at the word. "No," she agreed, "it's not."

"Let's do something today," Scott suggested.

"Like what?" Michelle demanded.

Scott shrugged. "Dunno. Think of something."

Michelle mimicked his shrug.

"Tell you what," Leslie said. "I'm going to take a walk before it rains. You two come up with some ideas while I'm gone, why don't you? Take a look at the Calendar section of the *Times*. See what strikes your fancy."

Examining the sky, she decided it wouldn't rain for a while, so she put on shorts and a sweatshirt and headed for Serrano Park.

As she entered the dense grove of eucalyptus trees, the damp air hung still, pungent with the leaves' fragrance. The tree trunks stretched upward in multi hues of gray, green, and tan while fallen leaves transformed the ground to a textured carpet of a hundred shades of pink.

"Lord, your handiwork is wonderful," she said. "What a Master of color You are! I do praise You, Creator of the entire universe and Creator of such exquisite detail." She thanked Him for Charles's sentencing, and, yes, even for his suggestion of divorce. Then, taking a shortcut between two walkways, she shuffled through the leaves.

"Lord, what am I to do about my marriage to Charles? Is it really a question of holiness versus happiness? Holiness: that means becoming more like Christ. I think I see a mighty gap here, Father! I'm still hurt and angry and stunned and suspicious. I think I need to get outside of that and try to get a glimmer of your perspective. Would You help me?"

She stopped to stretch her hamstrings. "Okay, let's start at the beginning. Why am I here?"

She headed toward the stream. "You tell us to glorify You. And to love others. So how can I glorify You? Or, to put it another way, what is Your will for me?" She let the question hang there for perhaps a mile of walking.

"No, wait. I see something new. The bigger question is what is Your will? Period."

She felt a raindrop splatter on the top of her head. Maybe she'd be wise to head for home. Cutting through the evenly planted rows of trees, she took the path back.

"That, Lord, is a scary question: what is Your will—period? And yet—I know Your plan is perfect."

The rain was falling harder now, dancing off the water in the creek beside her, pelting down through the trees. She walked faster. "And I know You're at work everywhere, even though I may not see it. Help me see how I fit in."

She felt her soaked hair plaster to her neck and forehead. Her shoes began to squish with each step. "The thing is, You seem to have given me the wings of a dove, the freedom I longed for. But I sense maybe there's a larger dimension to this freedom."

She began to run, water splaying out around her with each step. Out of the park, down the hill to the crosswalk she splashed. The signal flashed, "WAIT . . . WAIT . . . WAIT."

"I don't want to wait," she muttered. "I'm wet and cold."

The signal changed, and she ran across the street, but the signal continued to flash in her mind. *WAIT*. "Is that the message, Lord? Wait? Wait for what? Wait to act on Charles's suggestion of divorcing?"

She took a shortcut beside the tennis court. "Wait to see if Charles's faith is genuine, if he will be healed?" She passed two children, twirling their umbrellas as they walked.

WAIT. The sign flashed again in her mind, and she slowed, overwhelmed with a sense of something big happening in—yes, in her very soul. "Ah, the bigger picture! Wait on *the Lord*. Stand still, and see what You, Father, will do? *I* don't have to do anything right now. Yes, I'm free, but I don't have to fly away."

Now the rain blew straight toward her. She could barely see where she was going. "It's starting to make sense, Lord."

A car sped past, spraying water on her. What did it matter? She laughed, and her waterlogged shoes suddenly felt lighter.

"Maybe Michelle got it right in the first place. 'Time will tell.' Oh, Father, You are good! You truly do direct our paths, just as You promised."

Licking the rainwater from her lips, she turned down their street. "Now, Lord, if it's not asking too much, help me cope with the kids today. Show us something positive to—"

She stopped midsentence, an idea forming, and she laughed again. "Father, I'm not sure if this is from You, but if it is, You truly *are* a God of details."

Just as she turned into their sidewalk, the rain stopped as if a shower lever had been turned off. What a crazy day! What a wonderful day! She hurried through the gate to the door and rang the bell.

Scott answered the door.

"Hey, Mom, what happened? You fall in or somethin'?"

"Grab me a couple of big towels, will you, honey?"

She took her shoes off and left them outside. When Scott returned, she walked across one towel to the laundry room, disrobed, and wrapped the other towel around her.

"Did you have an idea what to do while I was gone?" she asked as she came out.

"Not really." Scott still sounded glum.

"I have one."

"Yeah?"

"I'll get dressed, and let's go to the animal shelter in Laguna and see if we can find a dog."

"*Really?*" Scott exclaimed, his face so transformed it reminded Leslie of a switch from a Greek tragedy mask to a comedy mask. "Hey, Michelle!" he shouted. "We're gonna go pick out a dog!"

"S-u-u-ure!" Michelle peered at her mother over the banister from upstairs, and Leslie looked up and nodded.

"Aw-*right!*" she shouted. "I've been dyin' for a dog. Hey, how about one for—"

Leslie interrupted her daughter. "—one for each of you— right?" She laughed. "Anything's possible, Michelle!"